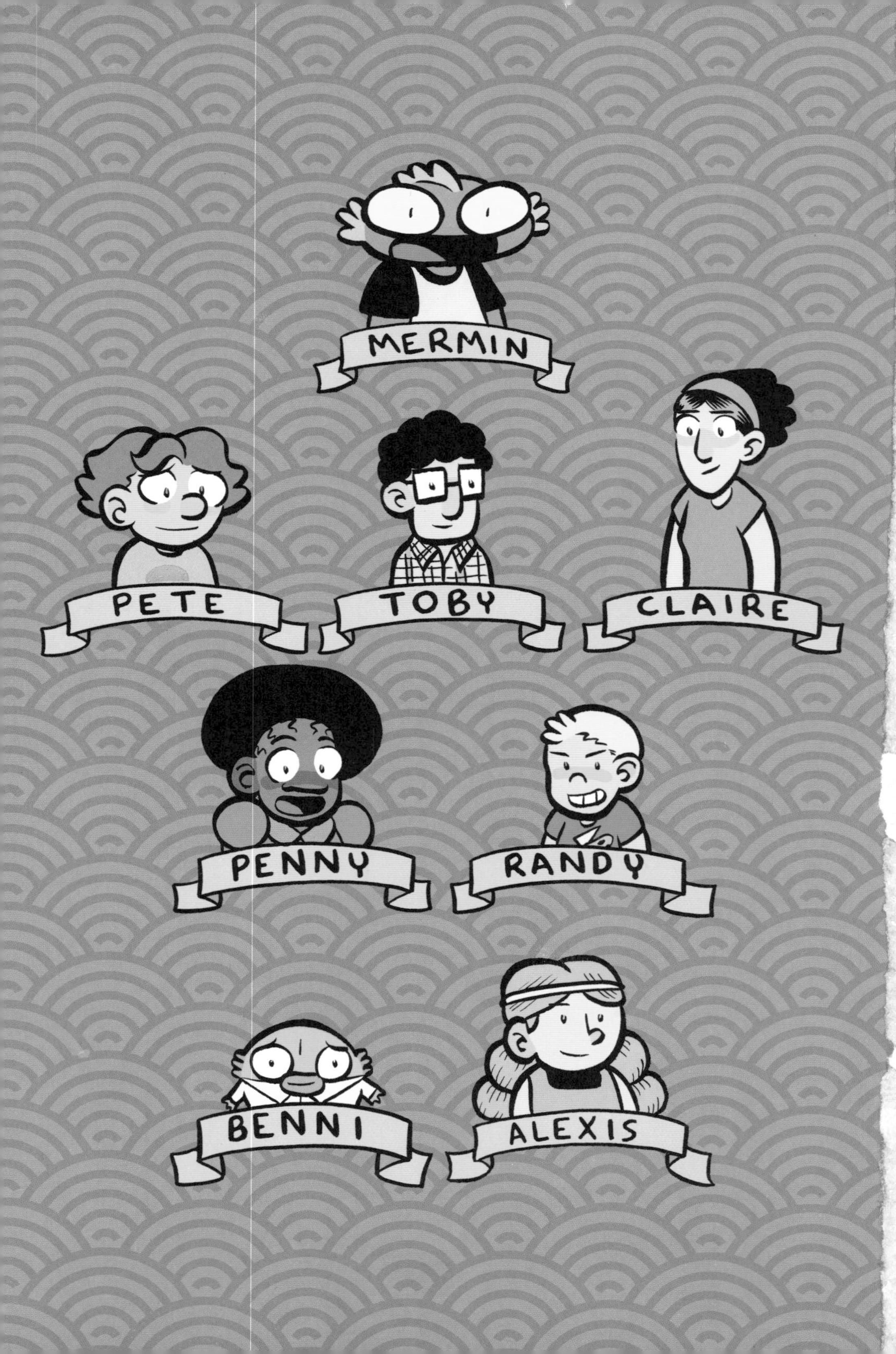
MERMIN
PETE
TOBY
CLAIRE
PENNY
RANDY
BENNI
ALEXIS

MERMIN

BOOK FIVE: MAKING WAVES

KING MERUS

QUEEN BLU

MERMA

OMER

MAK

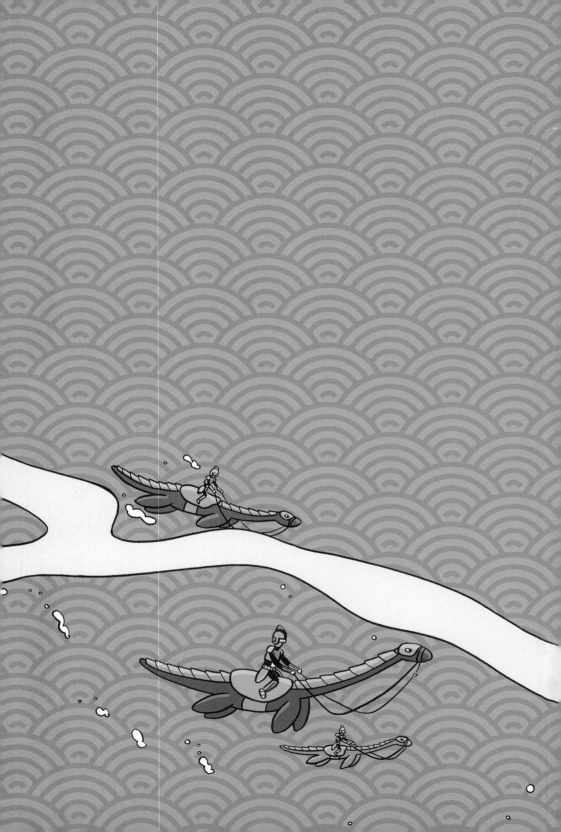

MERMIN

BOOK FIVE: MAKING WAVES

Written and illustrated by
Joey Weiser

Colored by
Joey Weiser and **Michele Chidester**

Edited by
Robin Herrera

Designed by
Keith Wood
with
Angie Dobson

Oni Press, Inc.

publisher, **Joe Nozemack**

editor in chief, **James Lucas Jones**

v.p. of marketing & sales, **Andrew McIntire**

sales manager, **David Dissanayake**

publicity coordinator, **Rachel Reed**

director of design & production, **Troy Look**

graphic designer, **Hilary Thompson**

digital prepress technician, **Angie Dobson**

managing editor, **Ari Yarwood**

senior editor, **Charlie Chu**

editor, **Robin Herrera**

editorial assistant, **Bess Pallares**

director of logistics, **Brad Rooks**

logistics associate, **Jung Lee**

onipress.com
facebook.com/onipress
twitter.com/onipress
onipress.tumblr.com
instagram.com/onipress

First Edition: April 2017
ISBN 978-1-62010-394-4
eISBN 978-1-62010-395-1

Library of Congress Control Number: 2016917152

1 2 3 4 5 6 7 8 9 10

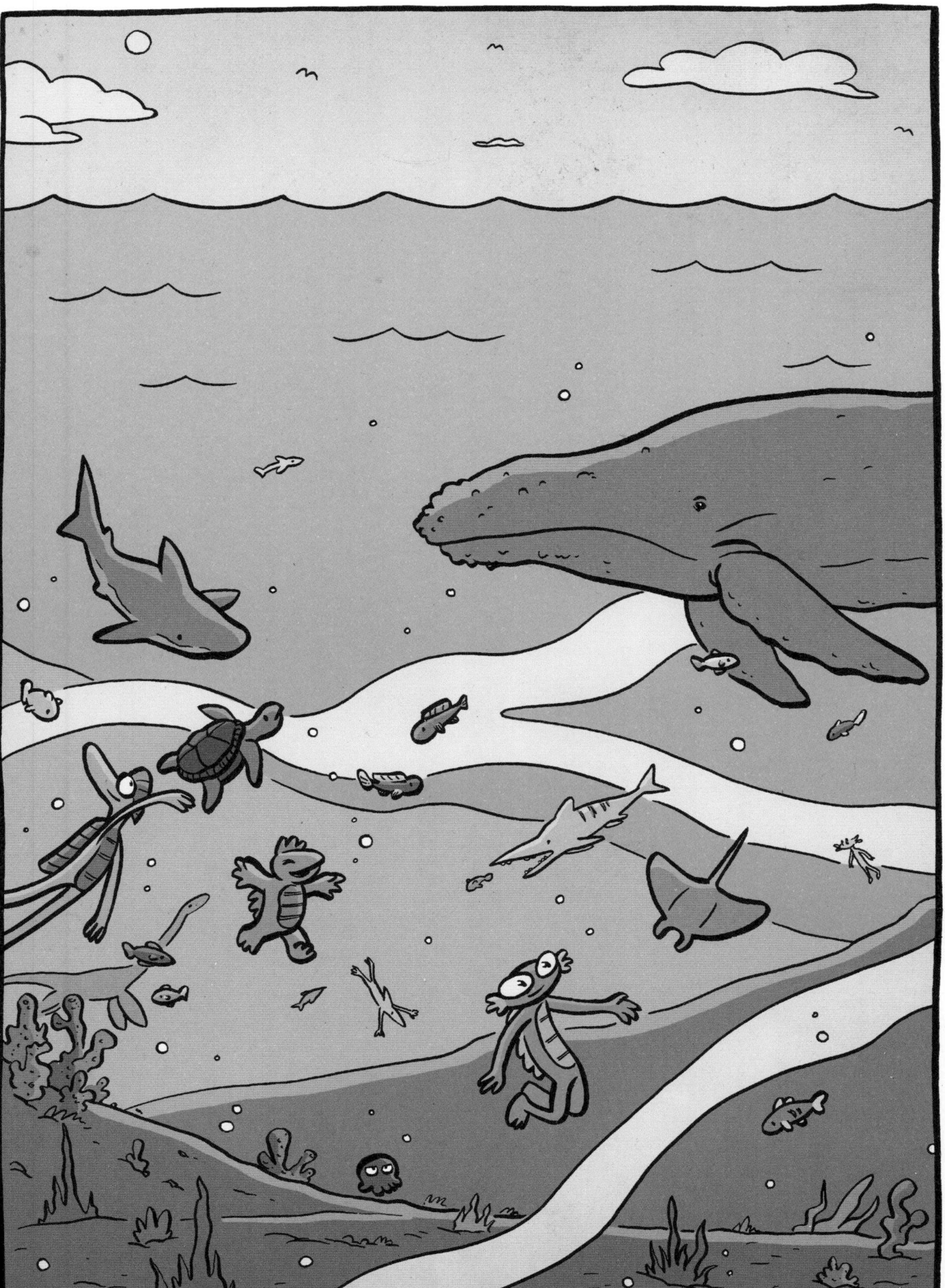

MANY TIDES AGO, THE PEOPLE OF THE SEA LIVED AMONGST THE OTHER CREATURES AT THE OCEAN'S FLOOR.

THE SEA GRANTED ONE OF THE ANCIENT SEA PEOPLE POWER OVER HER, AND HE BECAME THE FIRST KING.

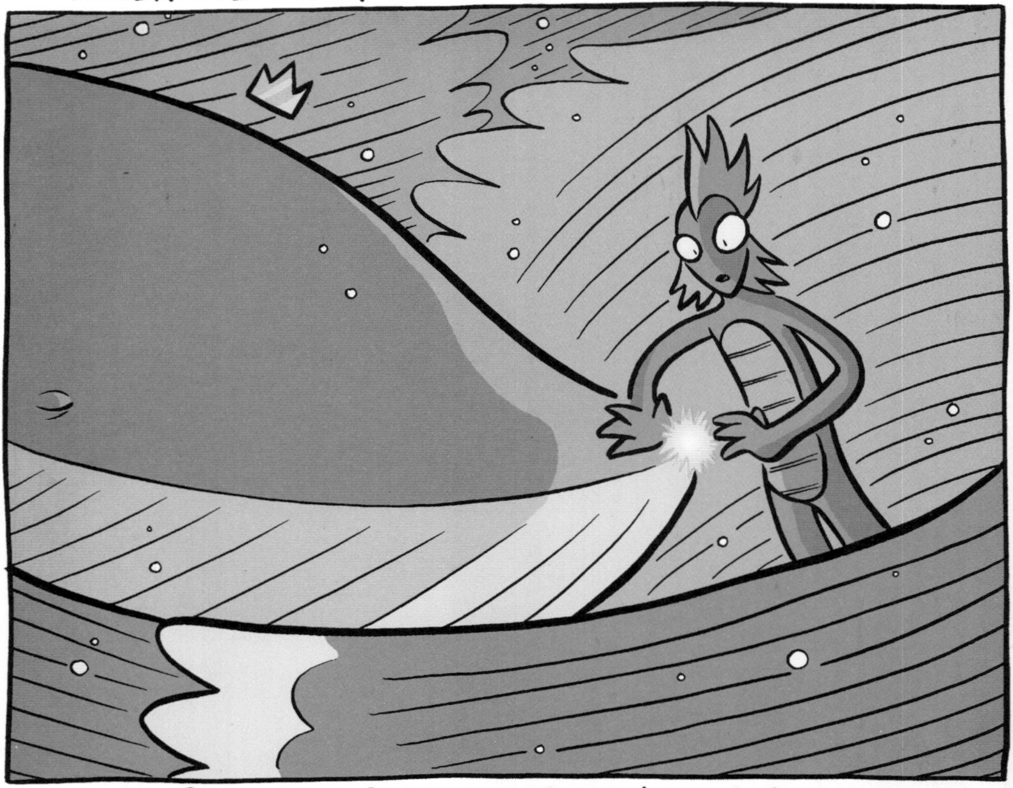

THIS POWER IS PASSED THROUGH GENERATIONS OF THE ROYAL FAMILY, AND WITH IT THEY RULE OVER THE UNDERSEA REALM.

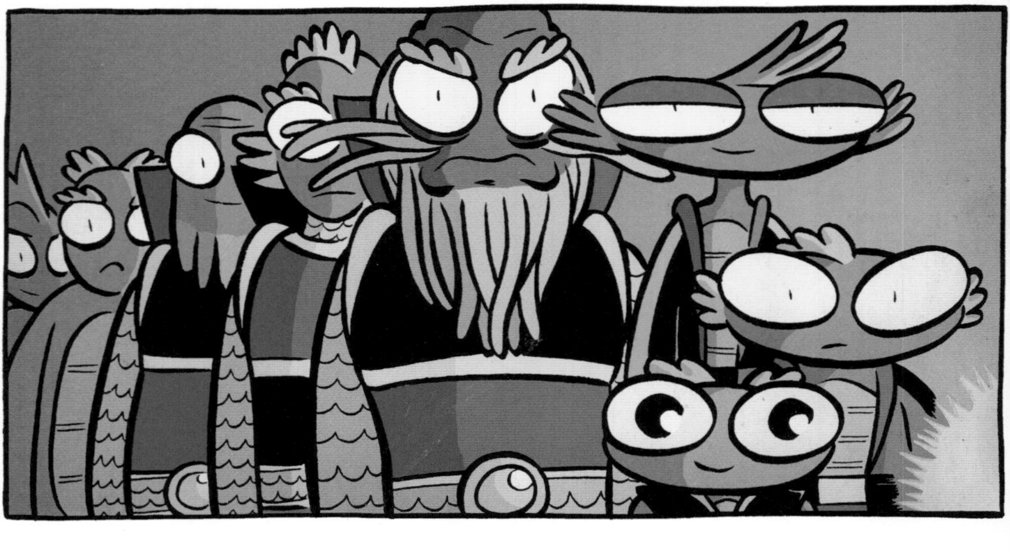

THIS WAS THE WAY FOR AGES, WHEN NEW PEOPLE FROM THE SURFACE ARRIVED.

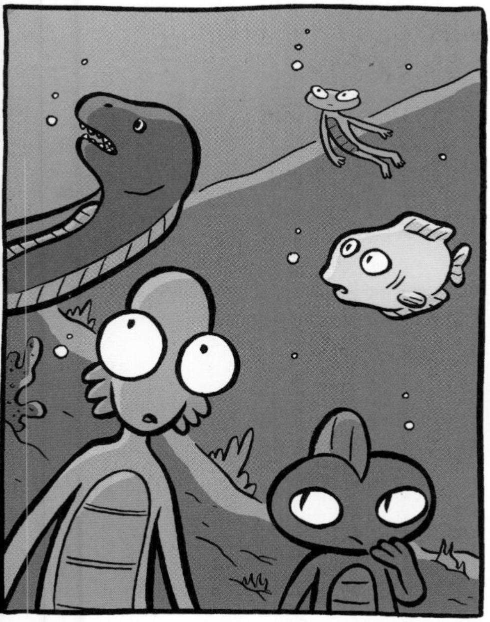

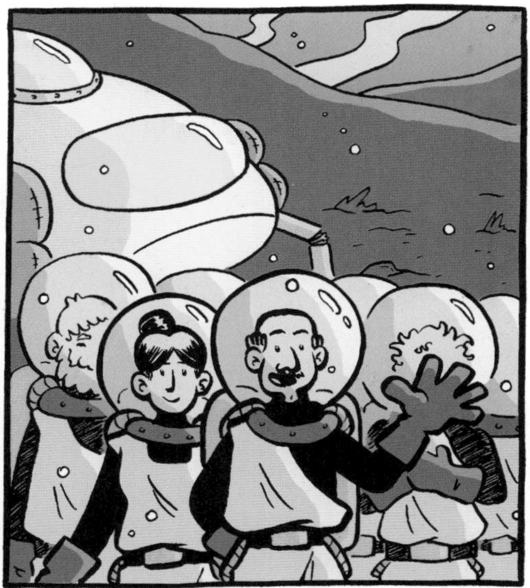

THESE "HUMANS" WERE MORE SCIENTIFICALLY ADVANCED THAN THEIR FELLOW SURFACE-DWELLERS AND CAME TO THE SEA FOR ESCAPE FROM THE BARBARISM ABOVE.

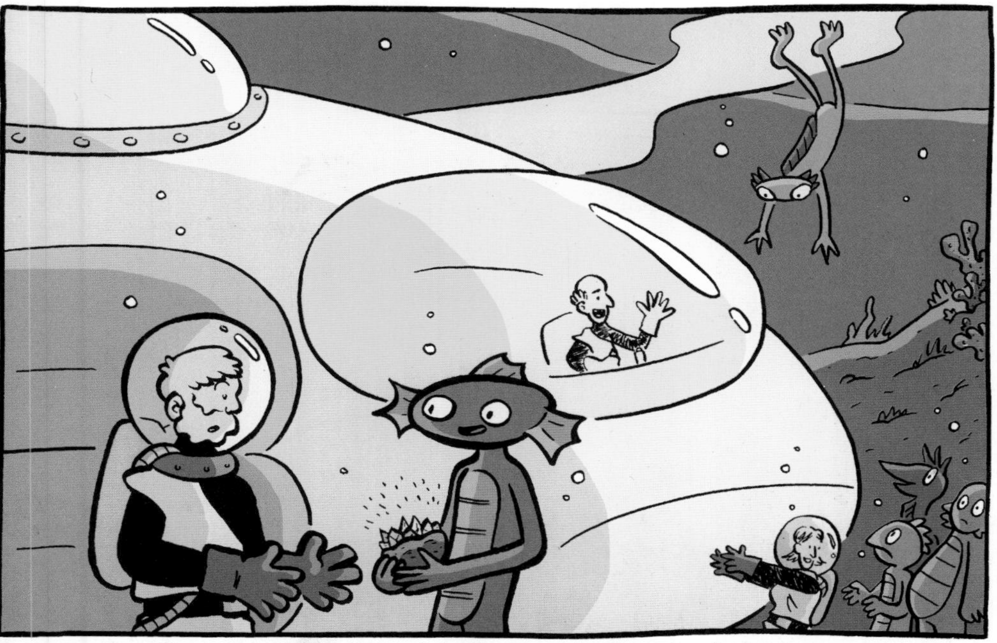

THE PEOPLE OF THE SEA SHARED THEIR KNOWLEDGE OF THE DEPTHS, LIKE THE MYSTERIOUSLY POWERFUL ENERGEODES, AND THE SURFACE HUMANS SHARED THEIR TECHNOLOGY.

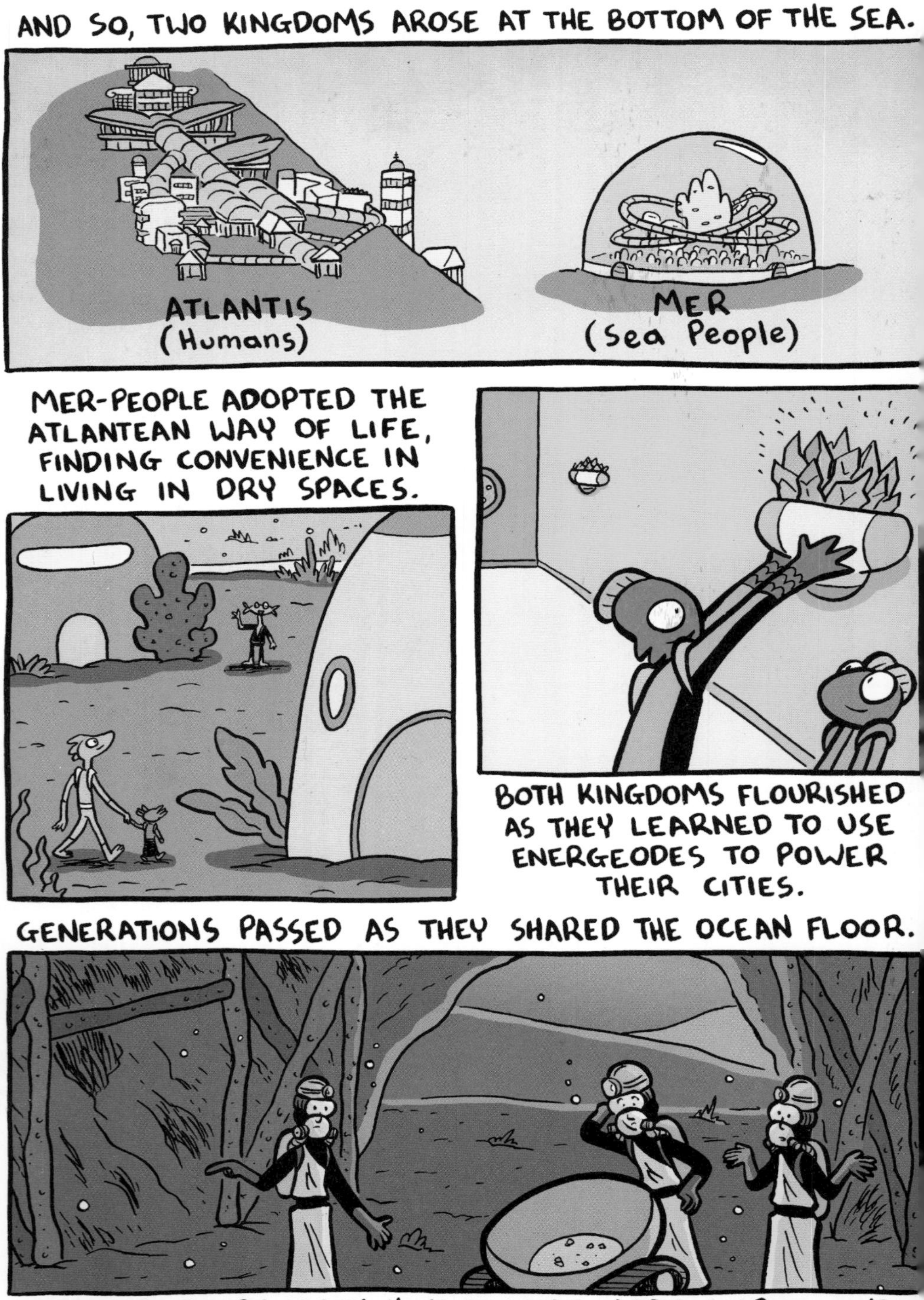
AND SO, TWO KINGDOMS AROSE AT THE BOTTOM OF THE SEA.
ATLANTIS
(Humans)
MER
(Sea People)
MER-PEOPLE ADOPTED THE ATLANTEAN WAY OF LIFE, FINDING CONVENIENCE IN LIVING IN DRY SPACES.
BOTH KINGDOMS FLOURISHED AS THEY LEARNED TO USE ENERGEODES TO POWER THEIR CITIES.
GENERATIONS PASSED AS THEY SHARED THE OCEAN FLOOR.
HOWEVER, ENERGEODES HAVE BECOME MORE SCARCE, AND TENSION OVER MINING TERRITORIES HAS RISEN.

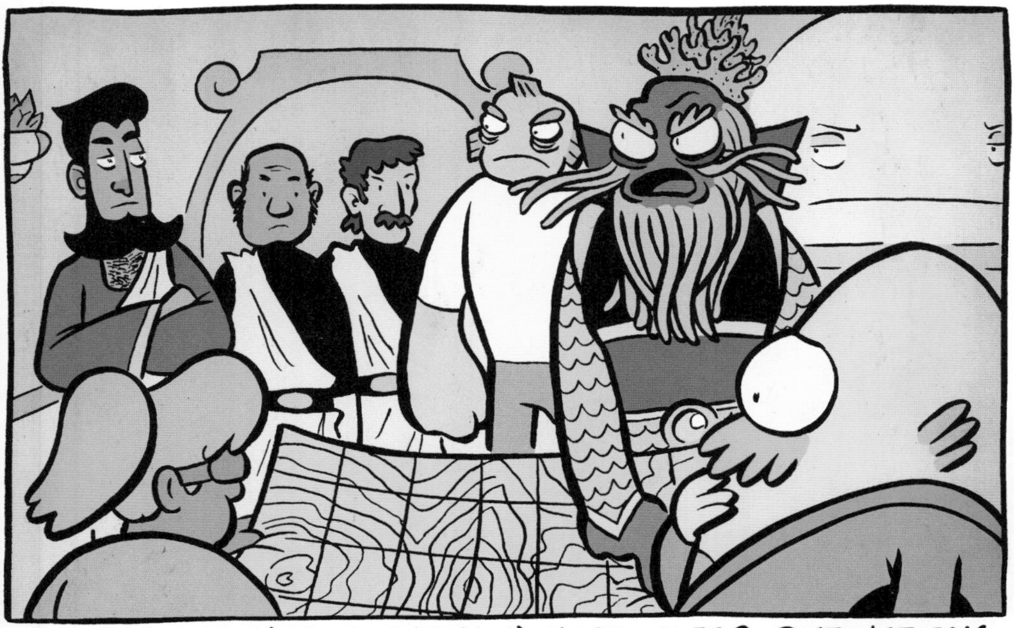

ATLANTIS AND MER EVENTUALLY MADE CLEAR DISTINCTIONS OF WHICH AREAS WITH KNOWN ENERGEODE MINES BELONGED TO EACH KINGDOM. BUT THERE IS STILL MUCH OF THE SEA FLOOR LEFT UNCLEAR WHO HAS CLAIM TO IT!

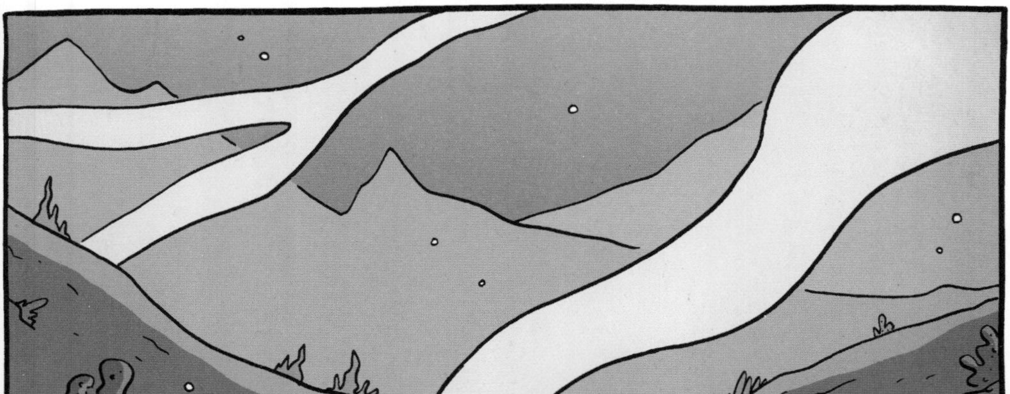

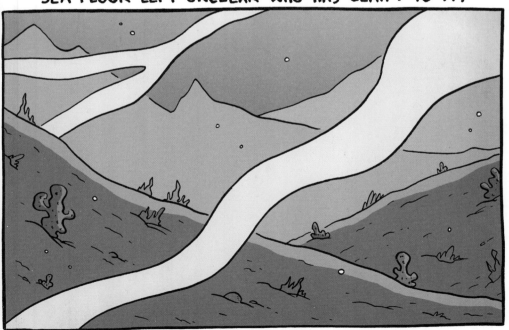

DESPITE LIVING IN RELATIVE PEACE FOR AGES, IT SEEMS THAT THE WAVE OF WAR IS ABOUT TO CRASH...

CHAPTER ONE

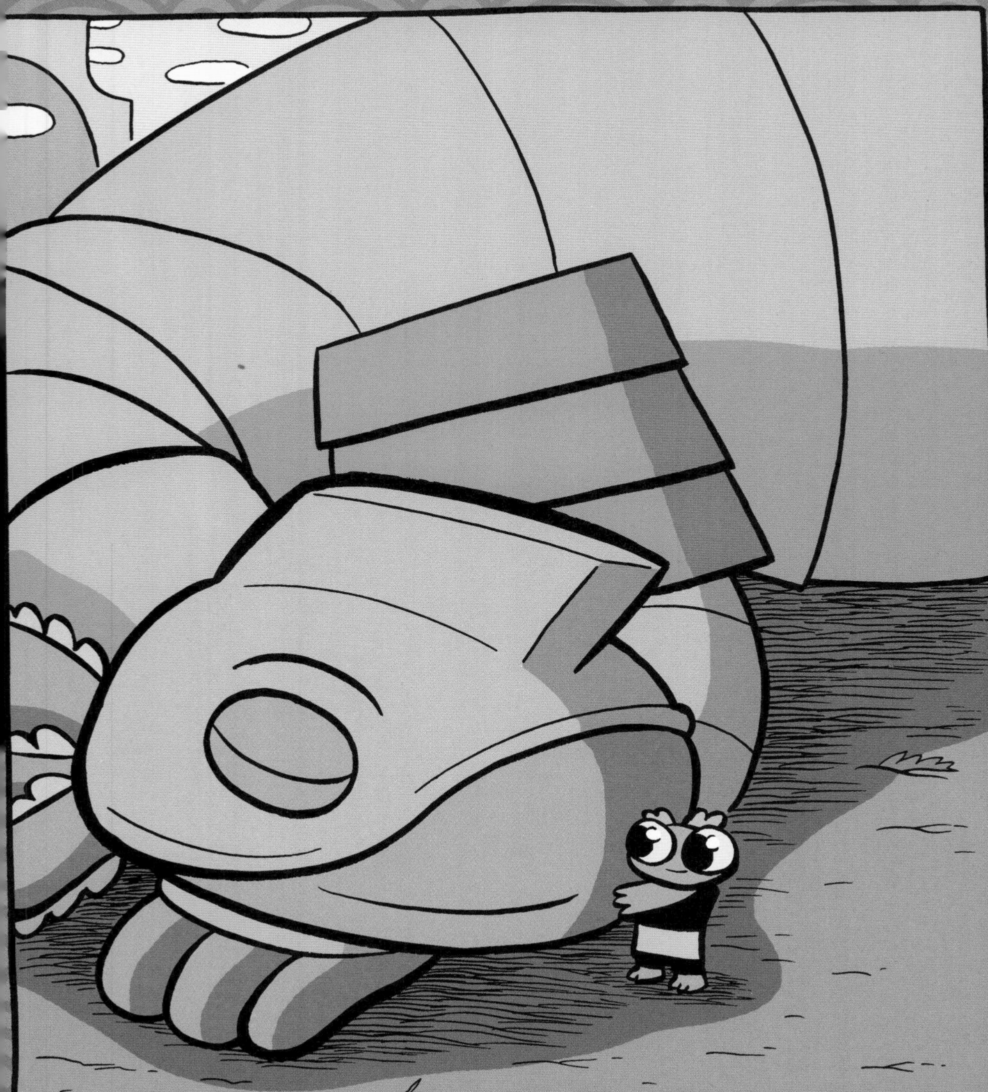

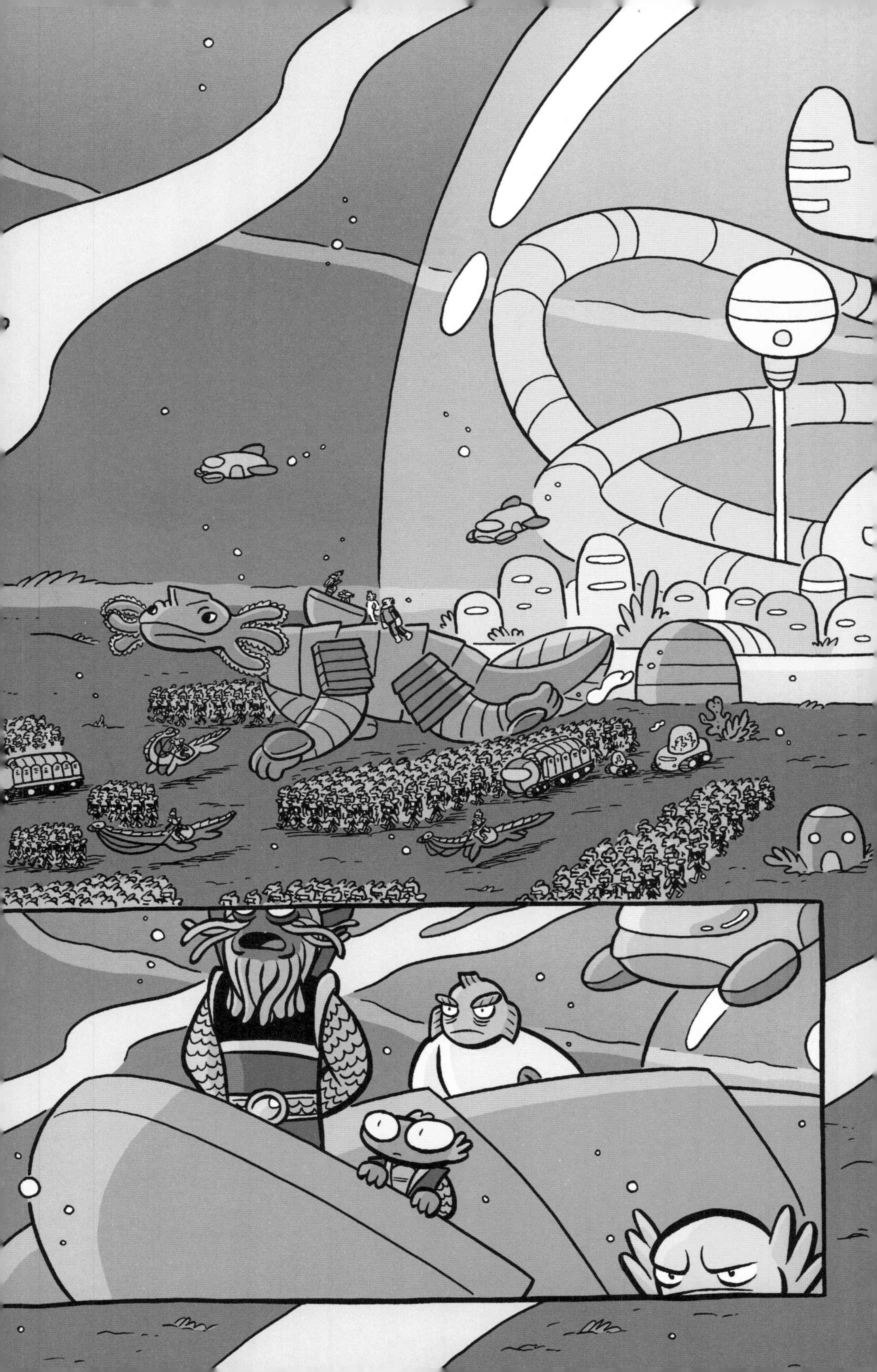

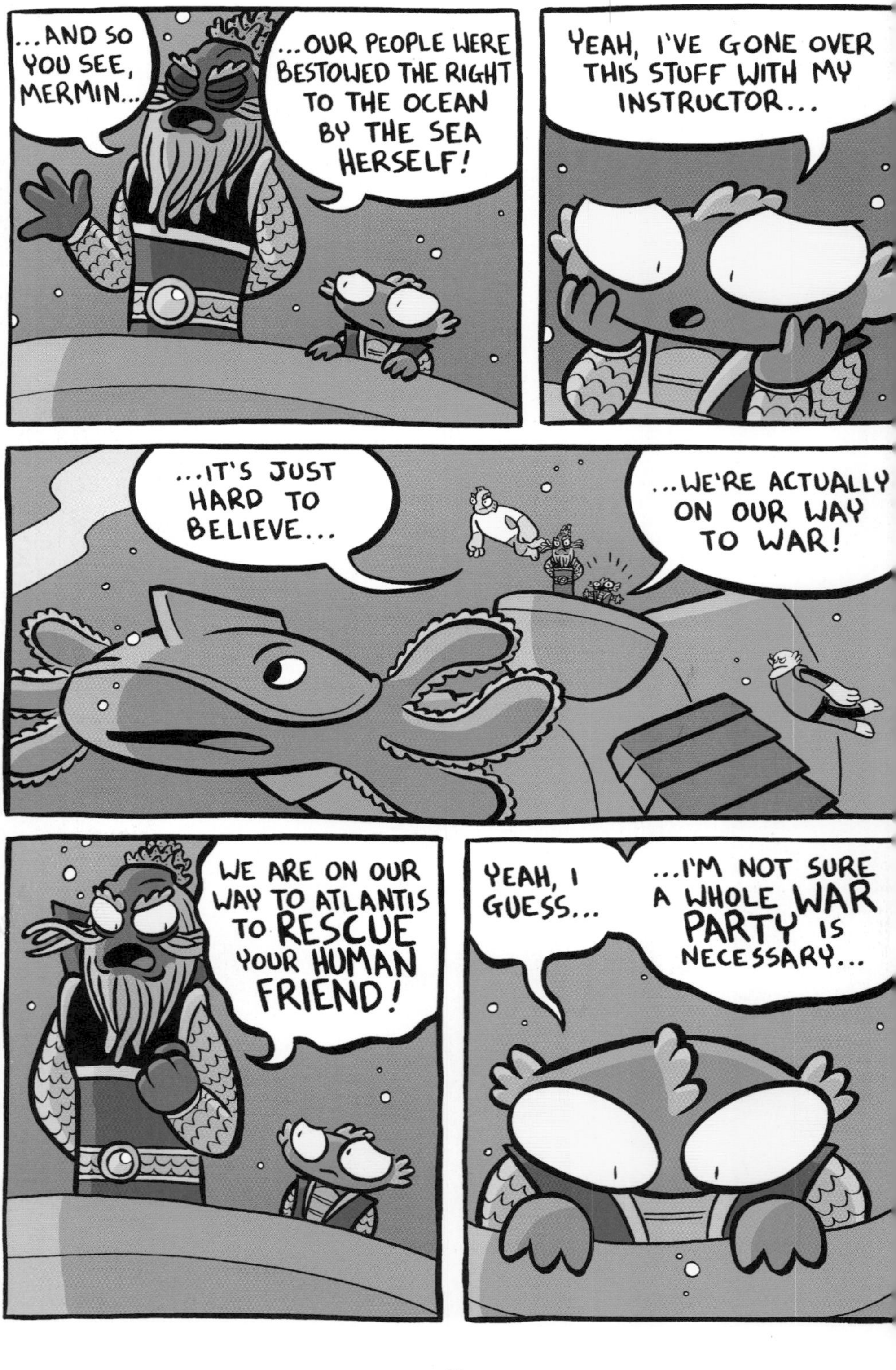
...AND SO YOU SEE, MERMIN...
...OUR PEOPLE WERE BESTOWED THE RIGHT TO THE OCEAN BY THE SEA HERSELF!
YEAH, I'VE GONE OVER THIS STUFF WITH MY INSTRUCTOR...
...IT'S JUST HARD TO BELIEVE...
...WE'RE ACTUALLY ON OUR WAY TO WAR!
WE ARE ON OUR WAY TO ATLANTIS TO RESCUE YOUR HUMAN FRIEND!
YEAH, I GUESS...
...I'M NOT SURE A WHOLE WAR PARTY IS NECESSARY...

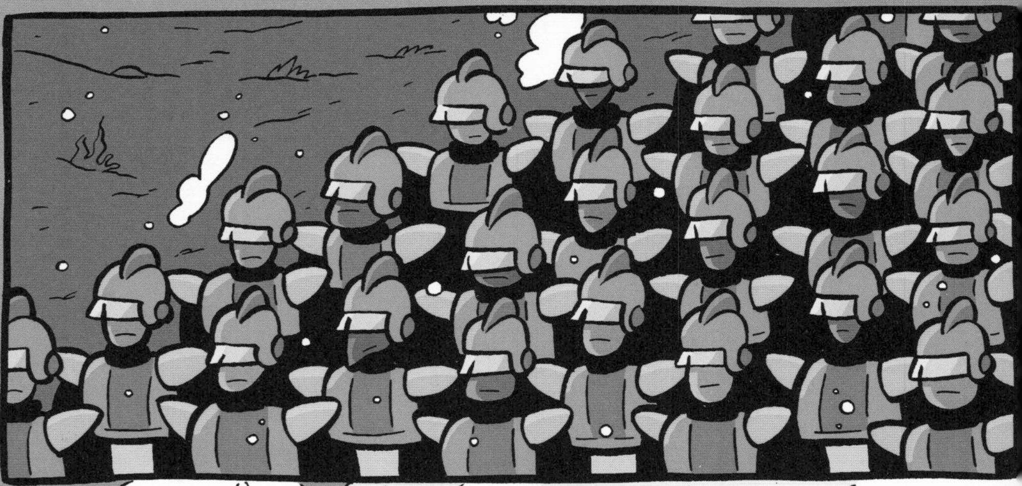

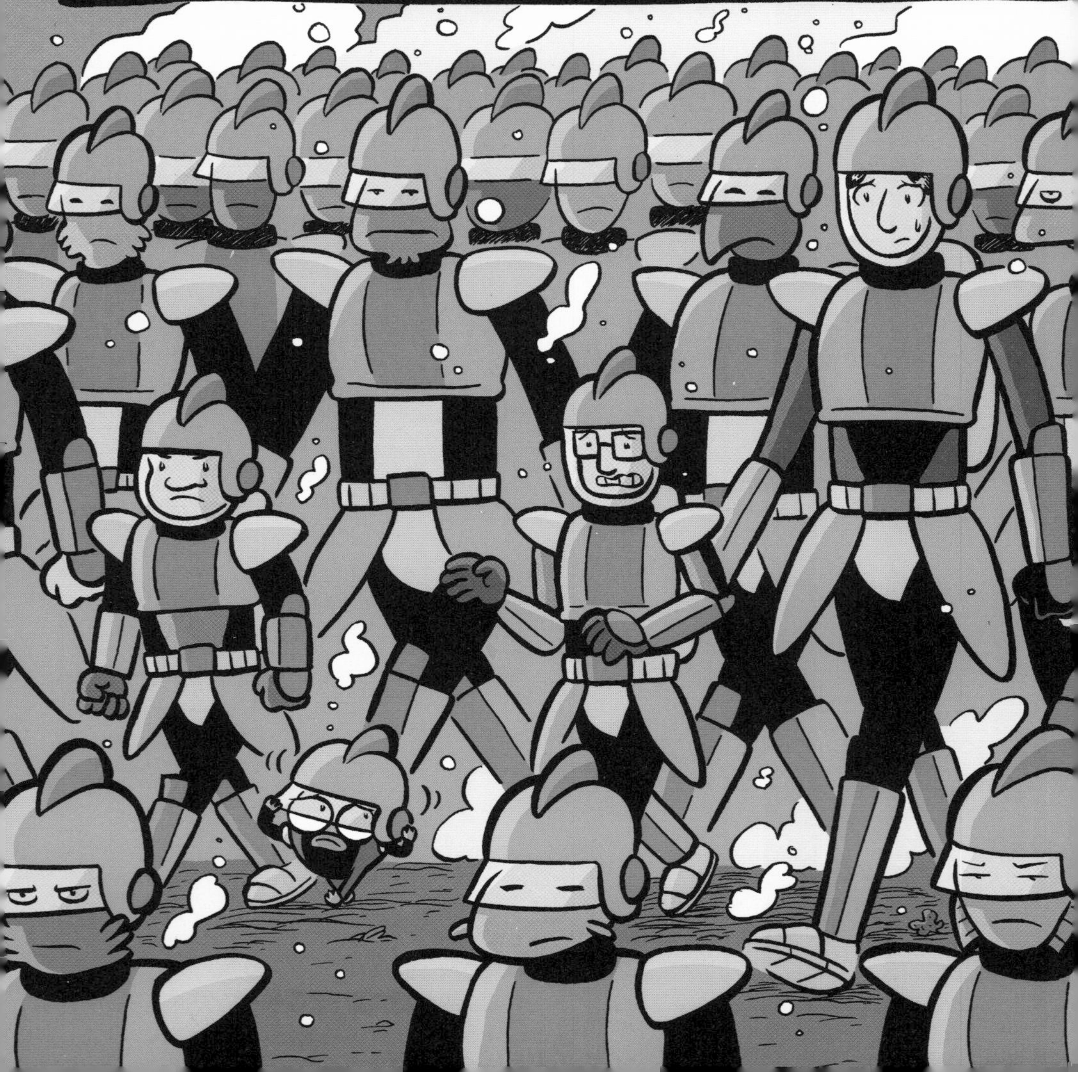

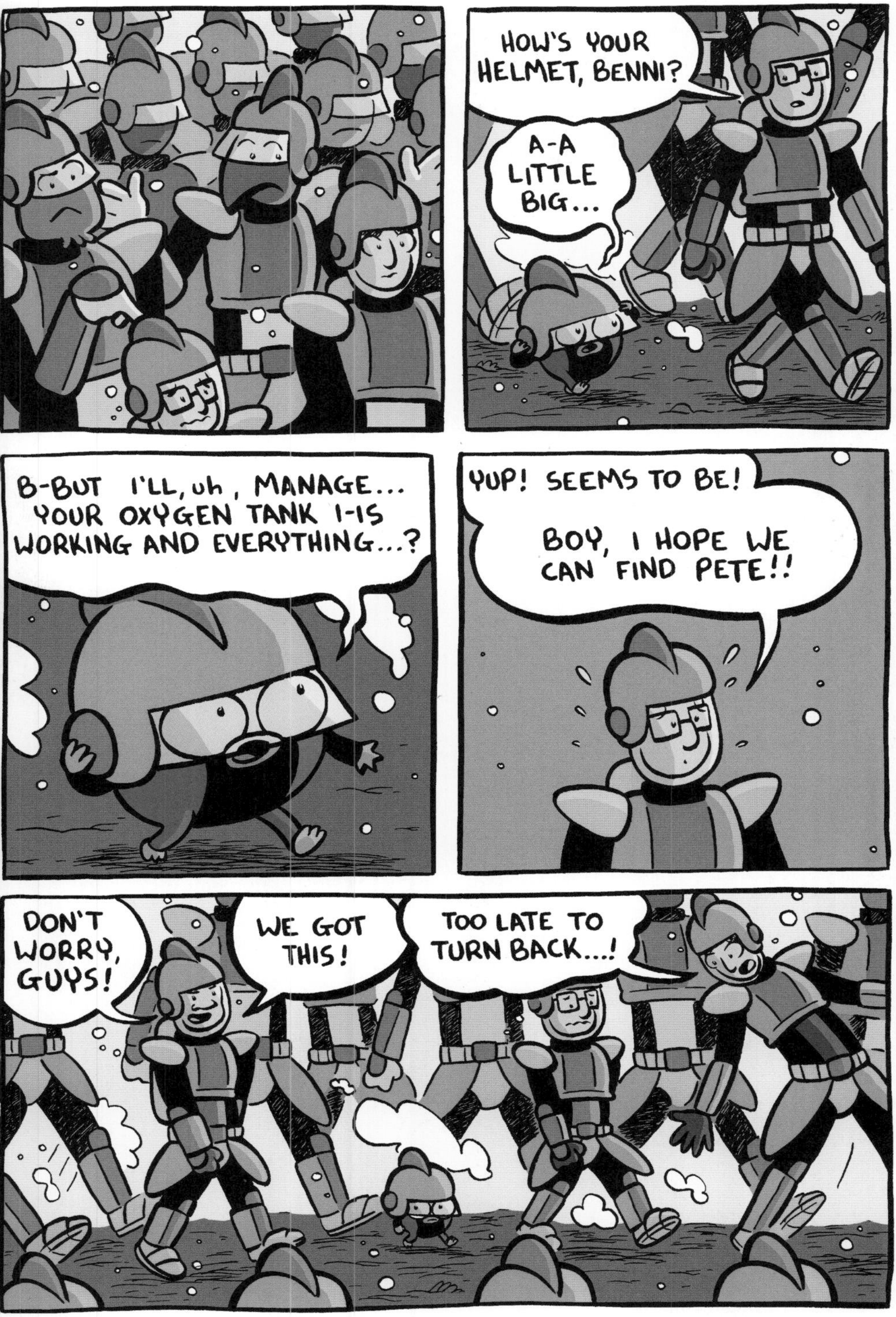
HOW'S YOUR HELMET, BENNI?
A-A LITTLE BIG...
B-BUT I'LL, uh, MANAGE... YOUR OXYGEN TANK I-IS WORKING AND EVERYTHING...?
YUP! SEEMS TO BE!
BOY, I HOPE WE CAN FIND PETE!!
DON'T WORRY, GUYS!
WE GOT THIS!
TOO LATE TO TURN BACK....!

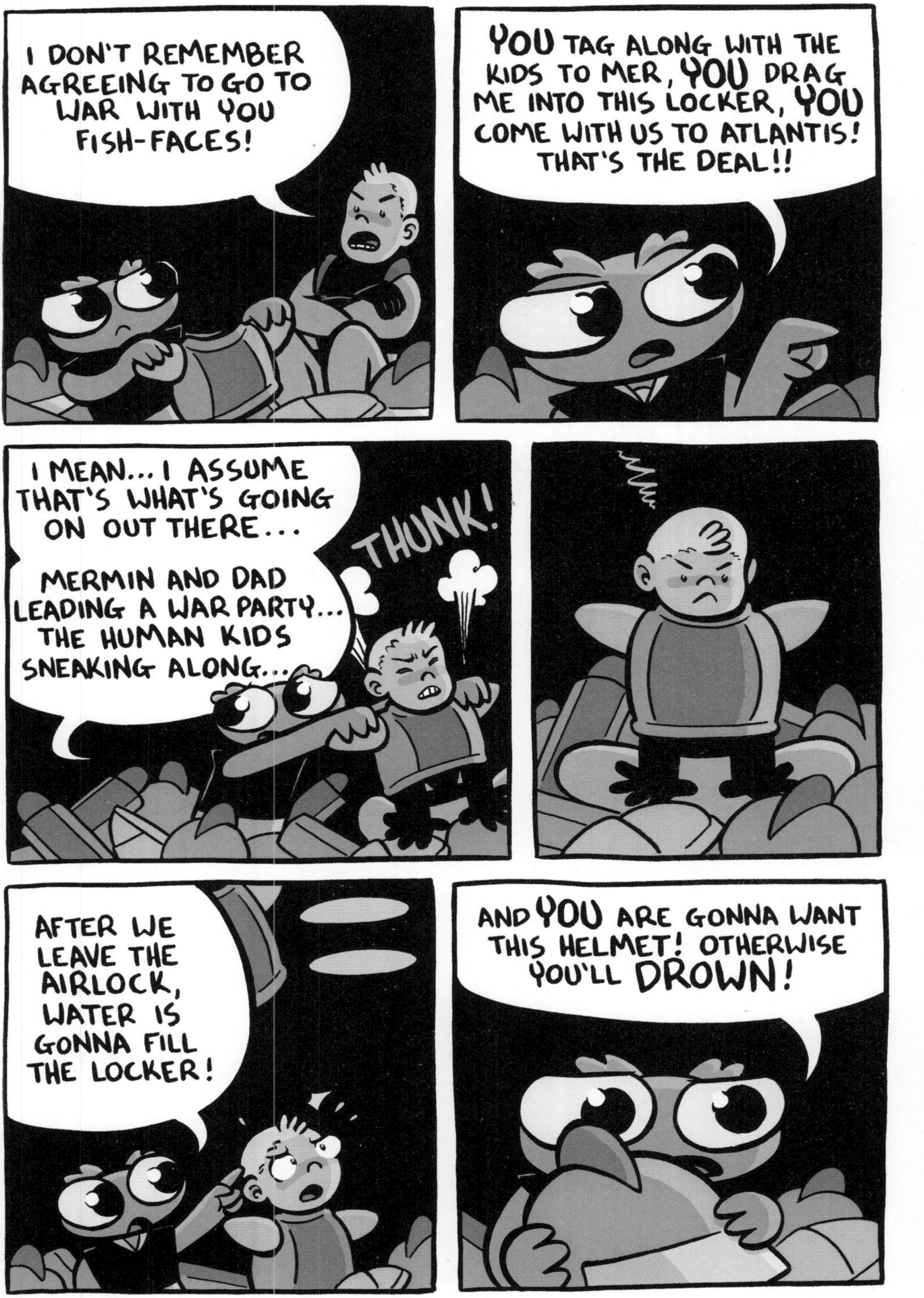
I DON'T REMEMBER AGREEING TO GO TO WAR WITH YOU FISH-FACES!
YOU TAG ALONG WITH THE KIDS TO MER, YOU DRAG ME INTO THIS LOCKER, YOU COME WITH US TO ATLANTIS! THAT'S THE DEAL!!
I MEAN... I ASSUME THAT'S WHAT'S GOING ON OUT THERE...
MERMIN AND DAD LEADING A WAR PARTY... THE HUMAN KIDS SNEAKING ALONG...
THUNK!
AFTER WE LEAVE THE AIRLOCK, WATER IS GONNA FILL THE LOCKER!
AND YOU ARE GONNA WANT THIS HELMET! OTHERWISE YOU'LL DROWN!

WHY WOULD THEY EVEN MAKE IT LIKE THAT?!

VENTILATION IS VERY IMPORTANT. IT PREVENTS MOLD.

NOW, PUT YOUR HELMET ON!

VRRRMMMMM

SSHHKK!

SOUNDS LIKE WE'RE IN THE AIRLOCK!

...oh no...

WHAT!?

I... I JUST REALIZED! HUMANS ALSO NEED AN AIR TANK TO BREATHE UNDERWATER!

WHAT!?!

ACK! HERE COMES THE WATER!

THAT'S IT! I'M OUTTA HERE!!

LET ME BACK IN!!!

HOLD ON! YOU HAVE SOME TIME BEFORE YOU RUN OUT OF AIR!

BANG! BANG!

uh...

THERE!!

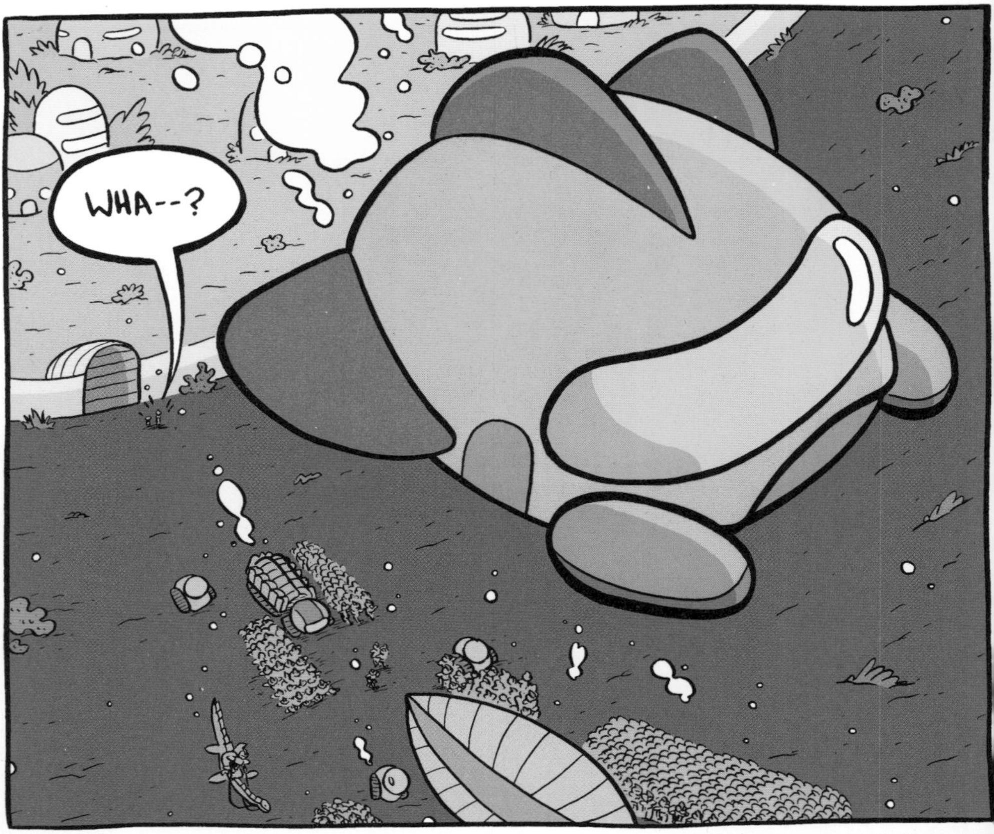
WHA--?

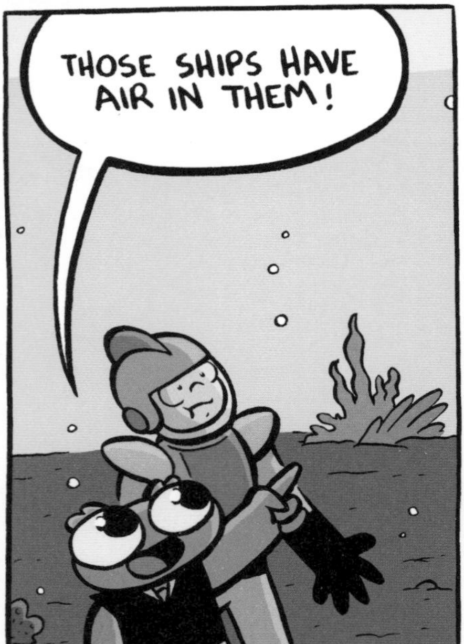
THOSE SHIPS HAVE AIR IN THEM!

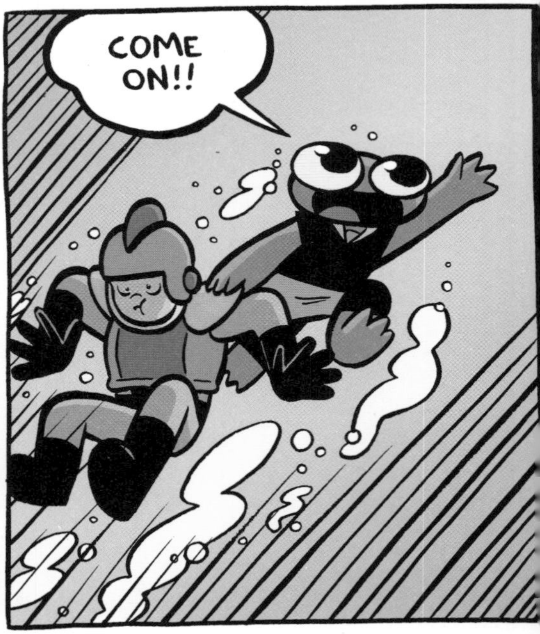
COME ON!!

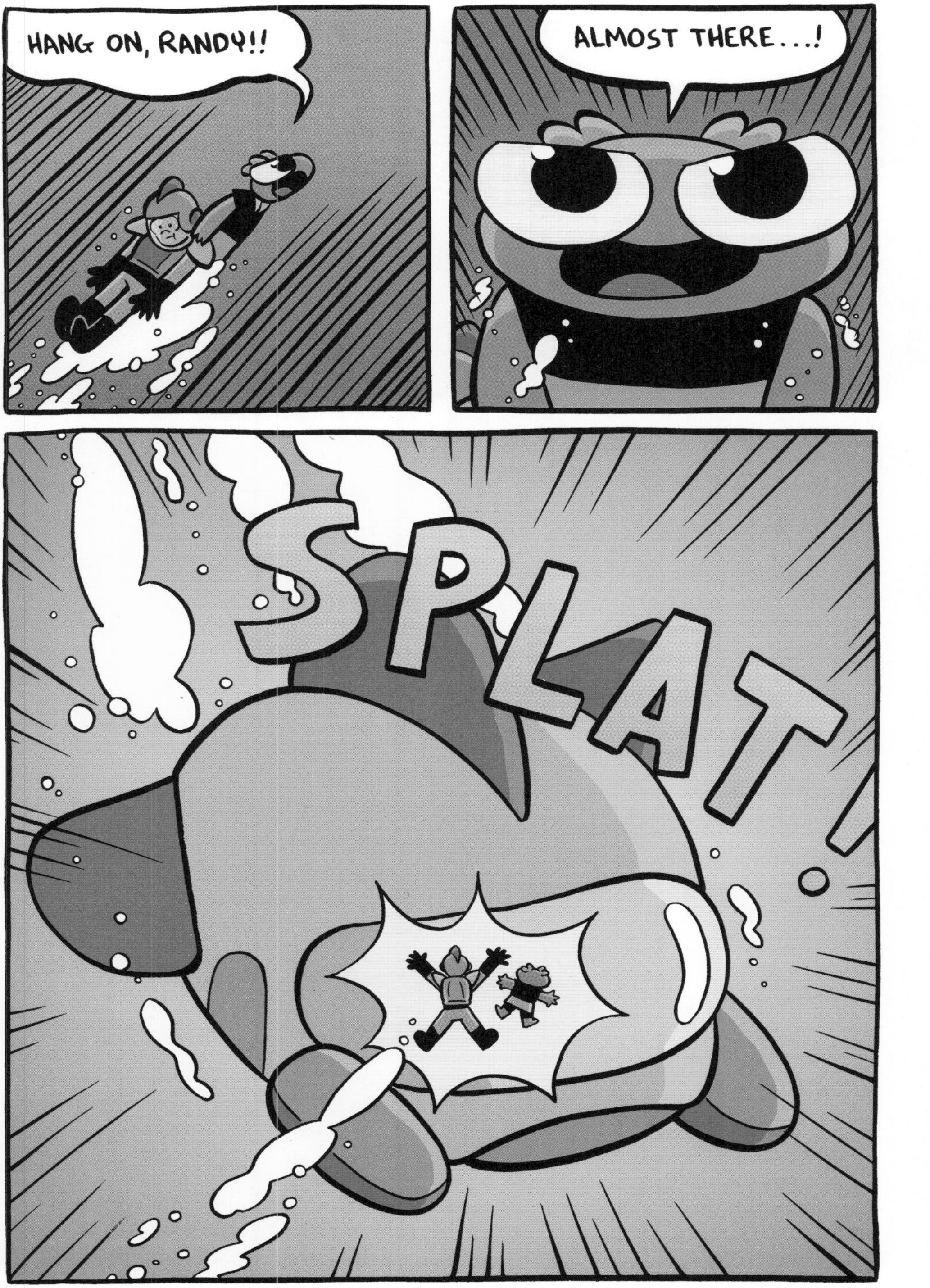
HANG ON, RANDY!!
ALMOST THERE...!
SPLAT!

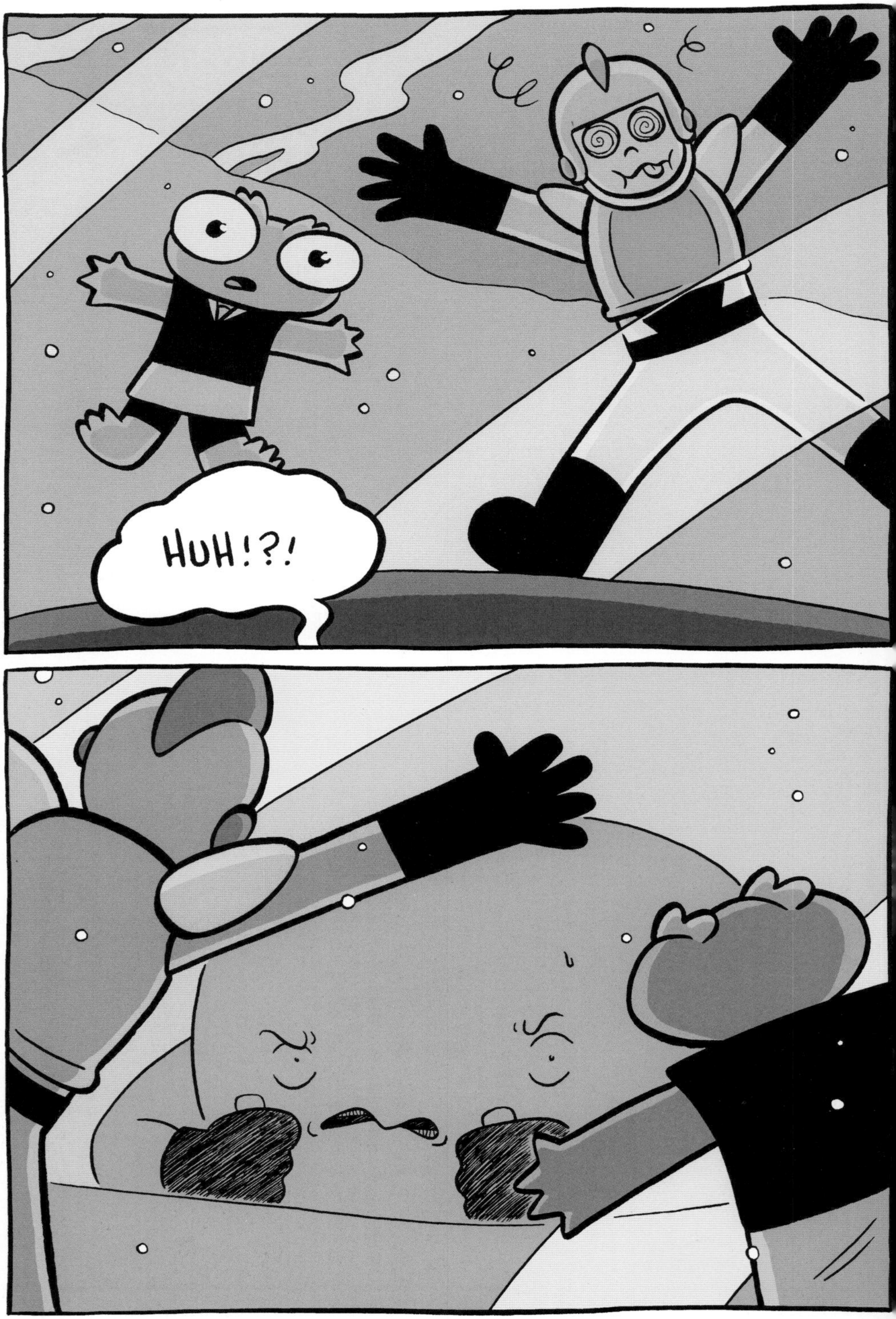
HUH!?!

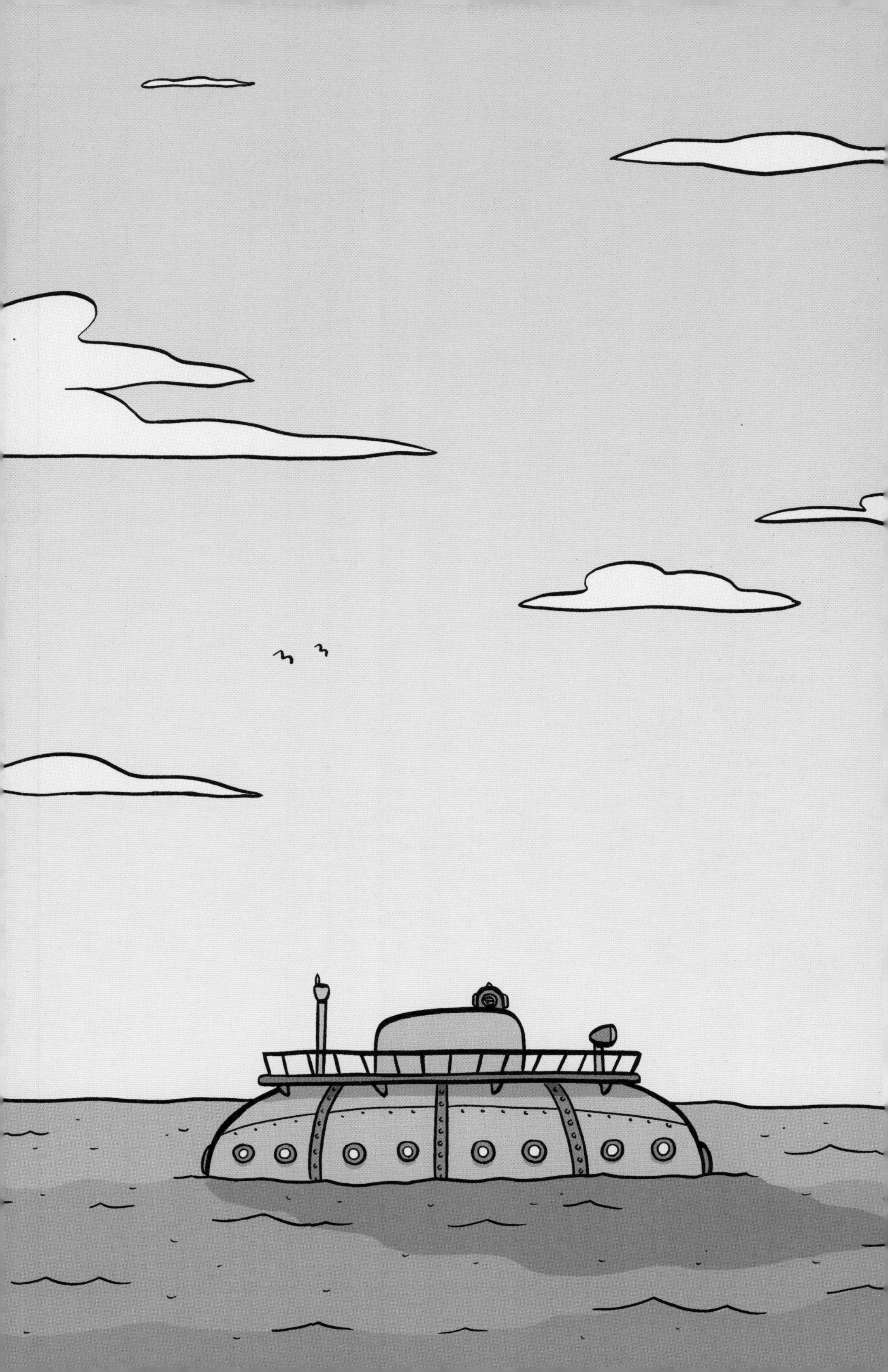

uh...IT'S SUPPOSED TO DO THAT.

Pop!

LISTEN... YOU'VE PAID FOR ME TO FIND YOUR CHILDREN...

...AND THAT'S WHAT I SHALL DO!

MY TEAM HAS BEEN RESEARCHING ODD SIGNALS FROM BELOW...

YES...

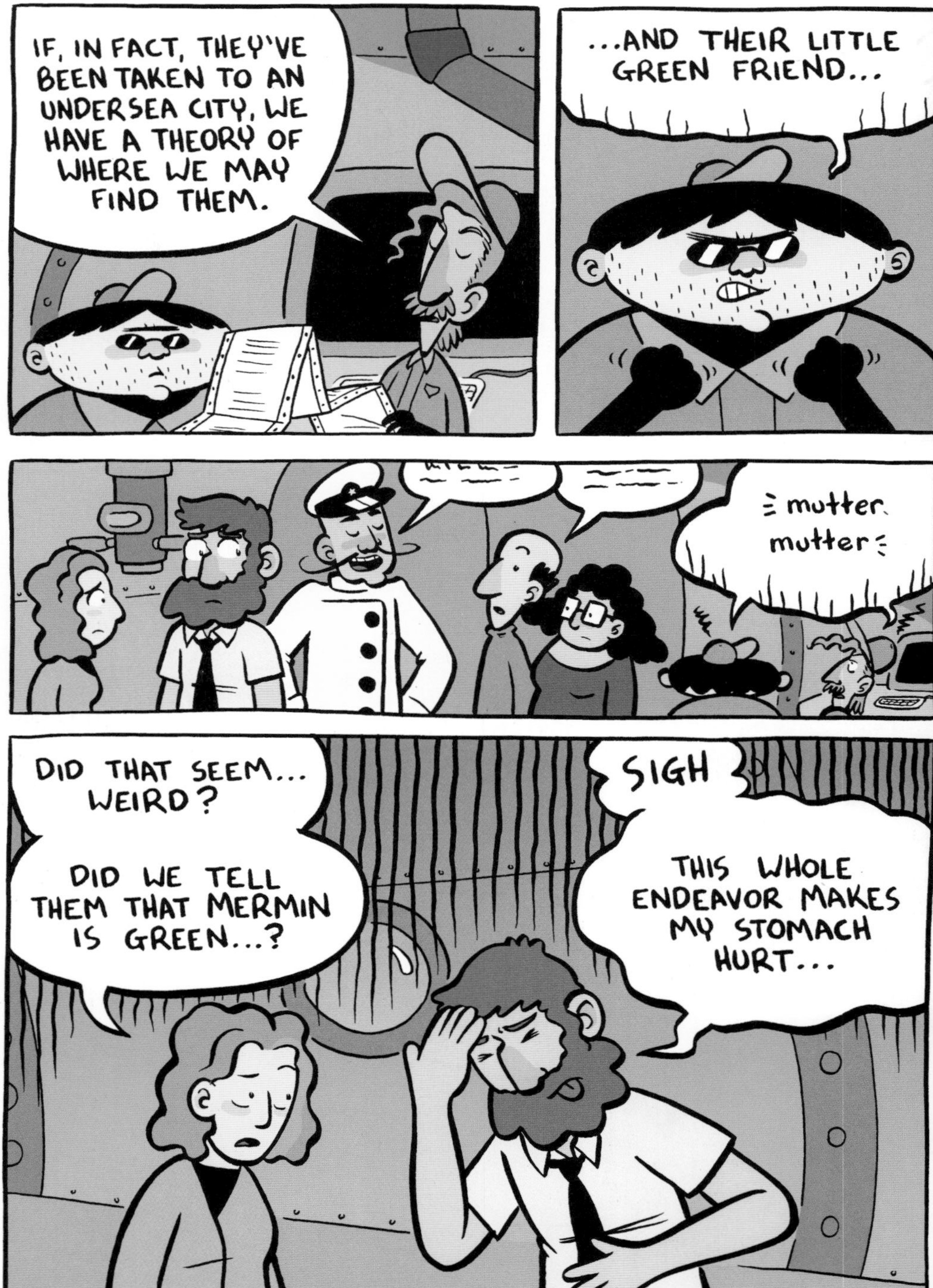
IF, IN FACT, THEY'VE BEEN TAKEN TO AN UNDERSEA CITY, WE HAVE A THEORY OF WHERE WE MAY FIND THEM.
...AND THEIR LITTLE GREEN FRIEND...
mutter mutter
DID THAT SEEM... WEIRD?
DID WE TELL THEM THAT MERMIN IS GREEN...?
SIGH
THIS WHOLE ENDEAVOR MAKES MY STOMACH HURT...

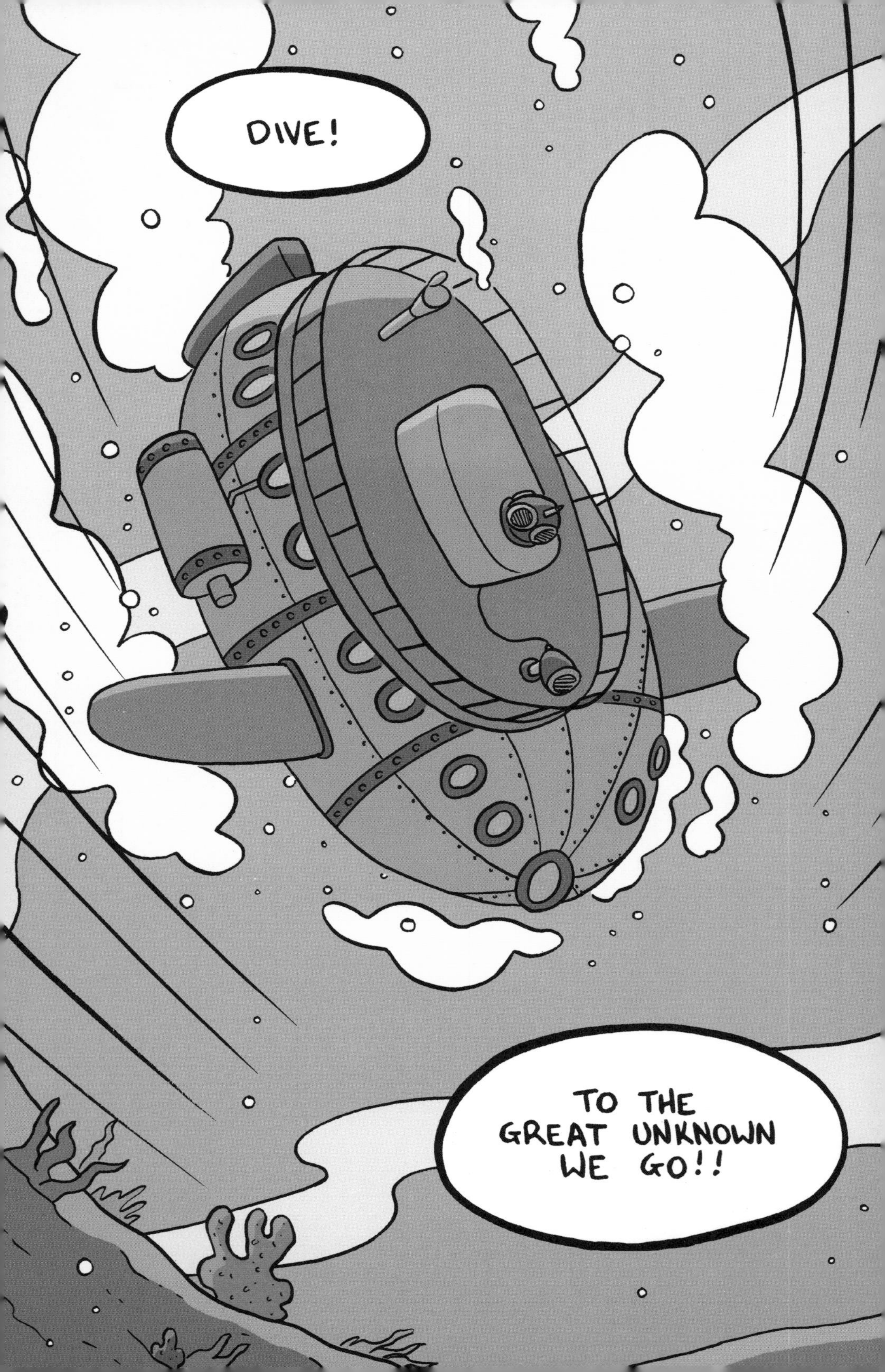
DIVE!
TO THE GREAT UNKNOWN WE GO!!

CHAPTER TWO

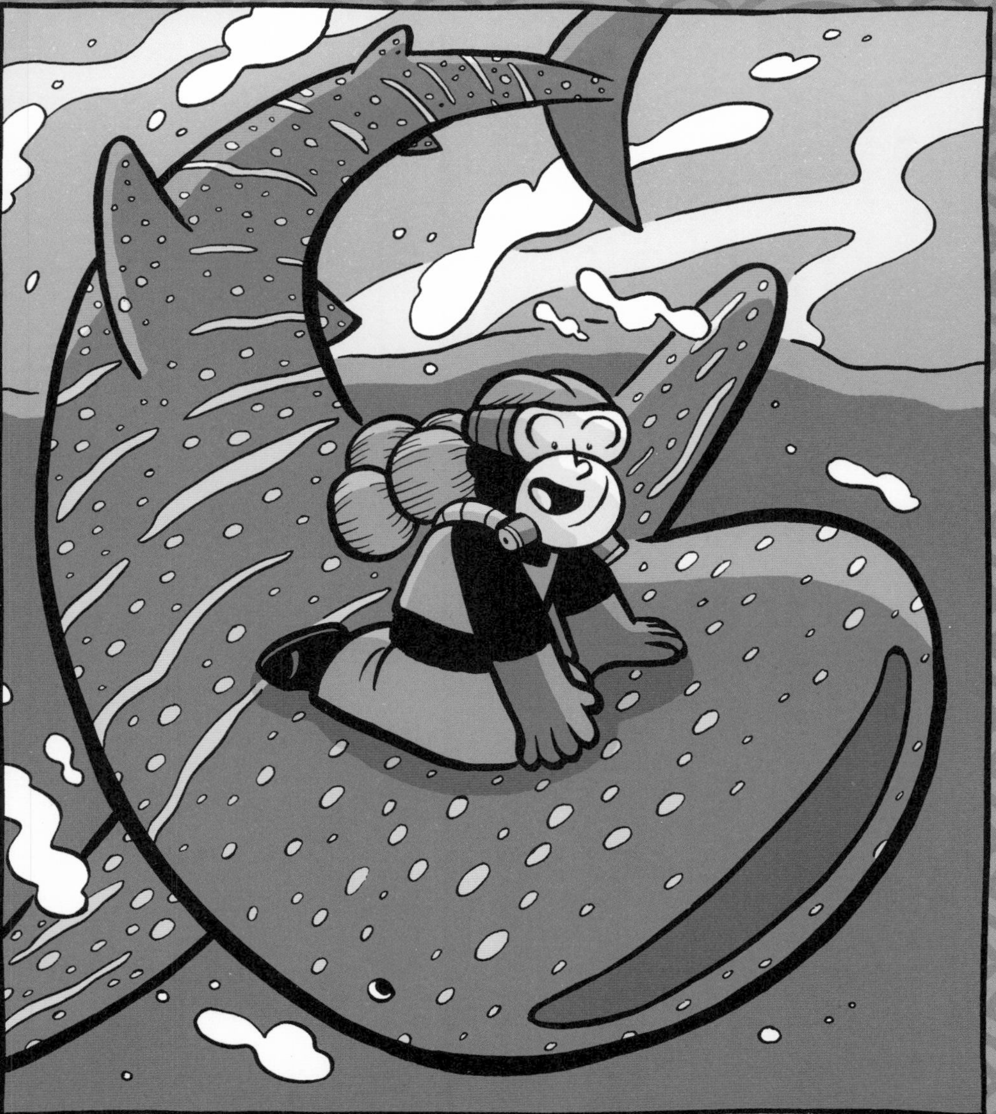

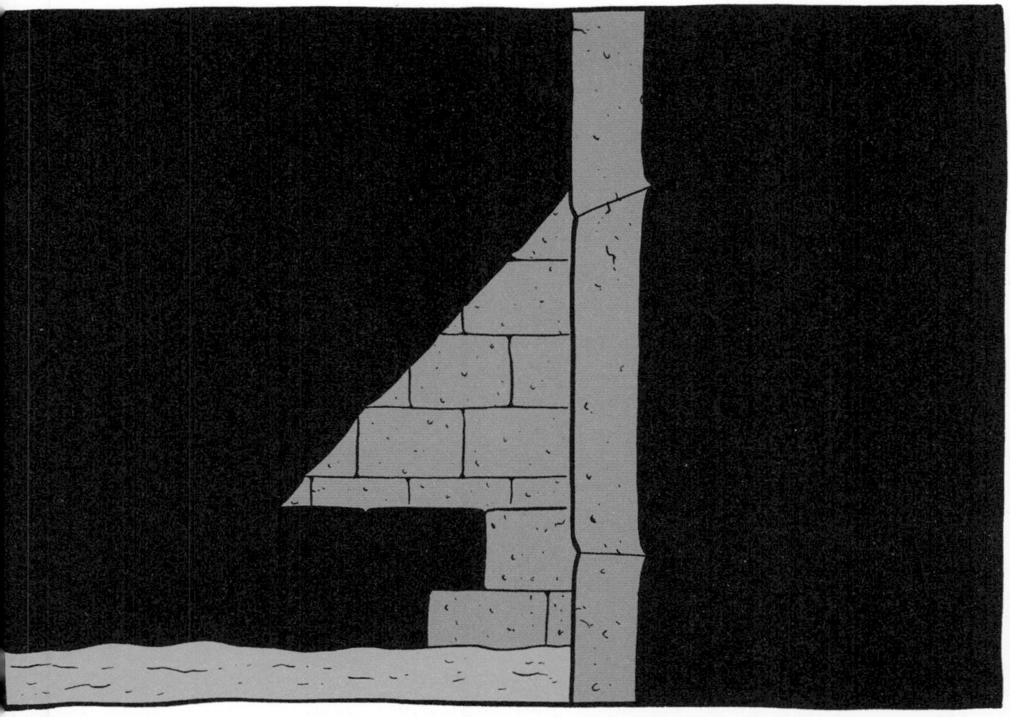

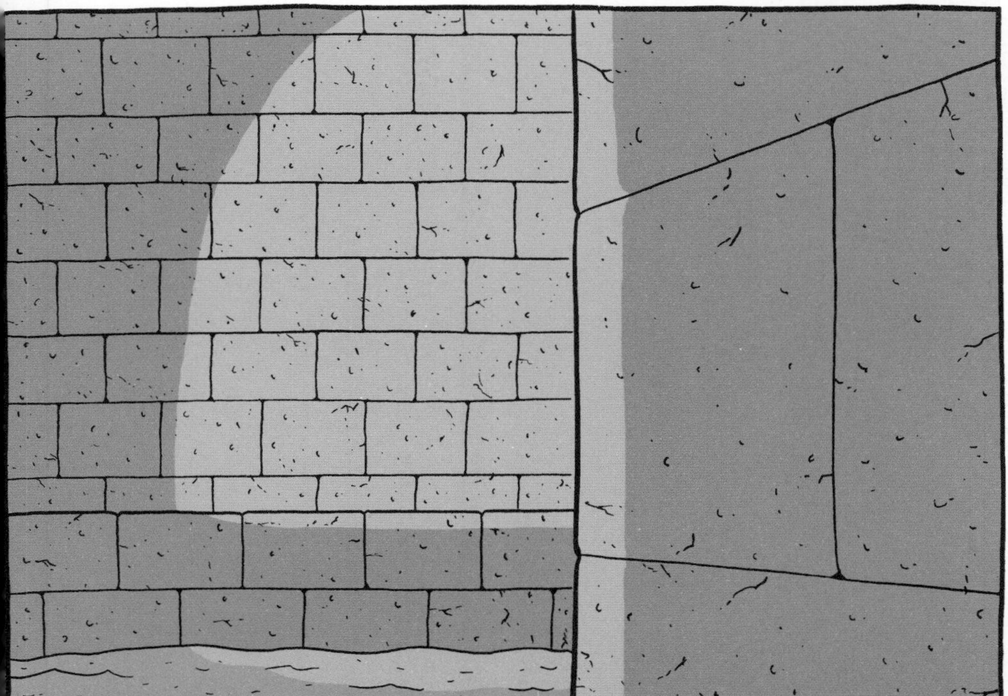

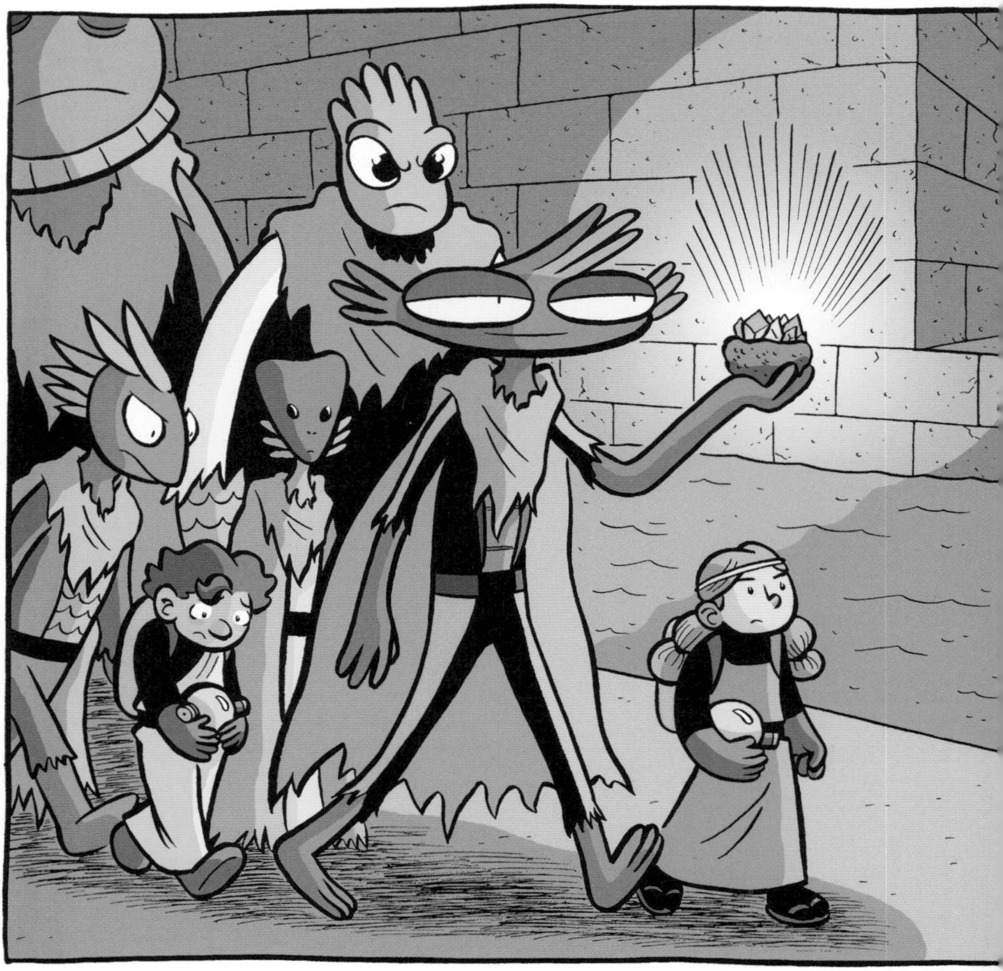

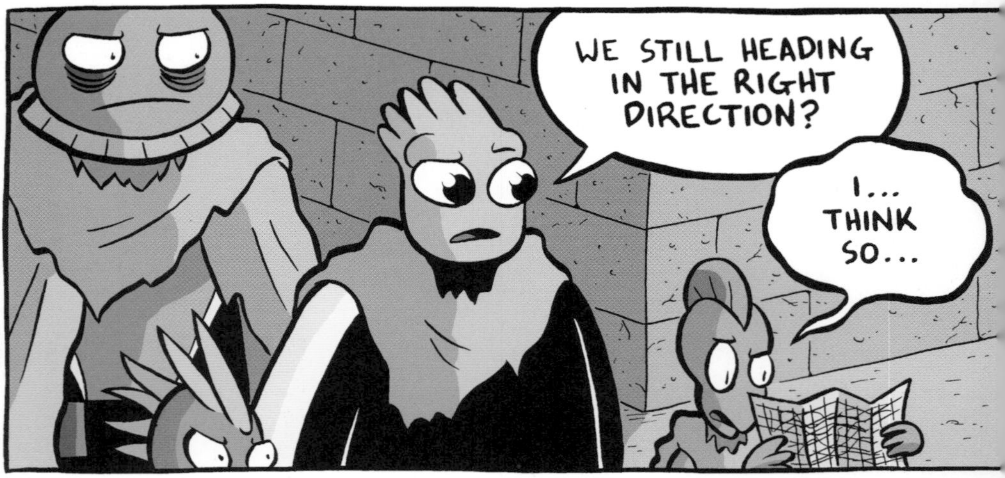
WE STILL HEADING IN THE RIGHT DIRECTION?
I... THINK SO...

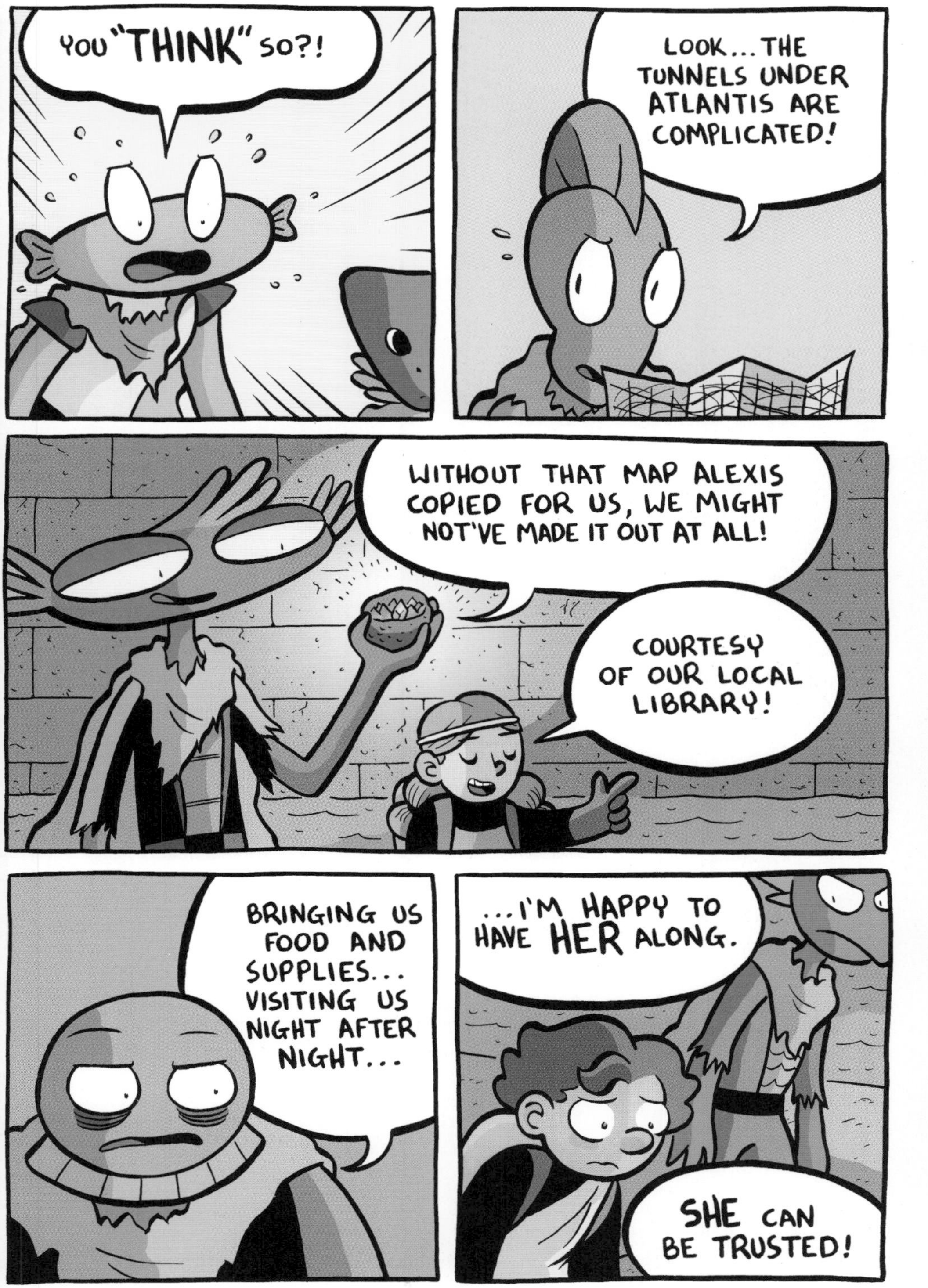
YOU "THINK" SO?!
LOOK... THE TUNNELS UNDER ATLANTIS ARE COMPLICATED!
WITHOUT THAT MAP ALEXIS COPIED FOR US, WE MIGHT NOT'VE MADE IT OUT AT ALL!
COURTESY OF OUR LOCAL LIBRARY!
BRINGING US FOOD AND SUPPLIES... VISITING US NIGHT AFTER NIGHT...
...I'M HAPPY TO HAVE HER ALONG.
SHE CAN BE TRUSTED!

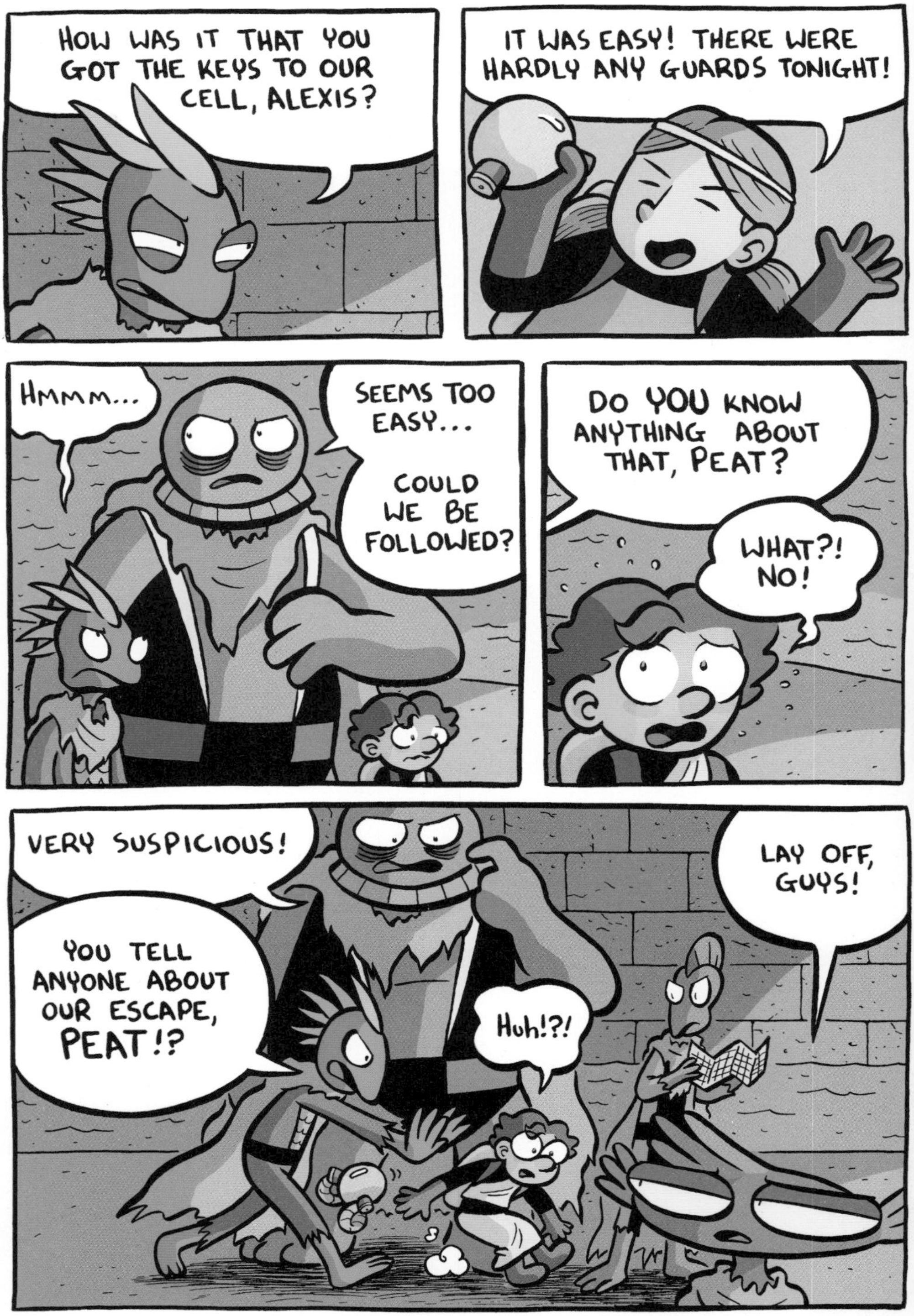
HOW WAS IT THAT YOU GOT THE KEYS TO OUR CELL, ALEXIS?
IT WAS EASY! THERE WERE HARDLY ANY GUARDS TONIGHT!
HMMM...
SEEMS TOO EASY...
COULD WE BE FOLLOWED?
DO YOU KNOW ANYTHING ABOUT THAT, PEAT?
WHAT?! NO!
VERY SUSPICIOUS!
YOU TELL ANYONE ABOUT OUR ESCAPE, PEAT!?
Huh!?!
LAY OFF, GUYS!

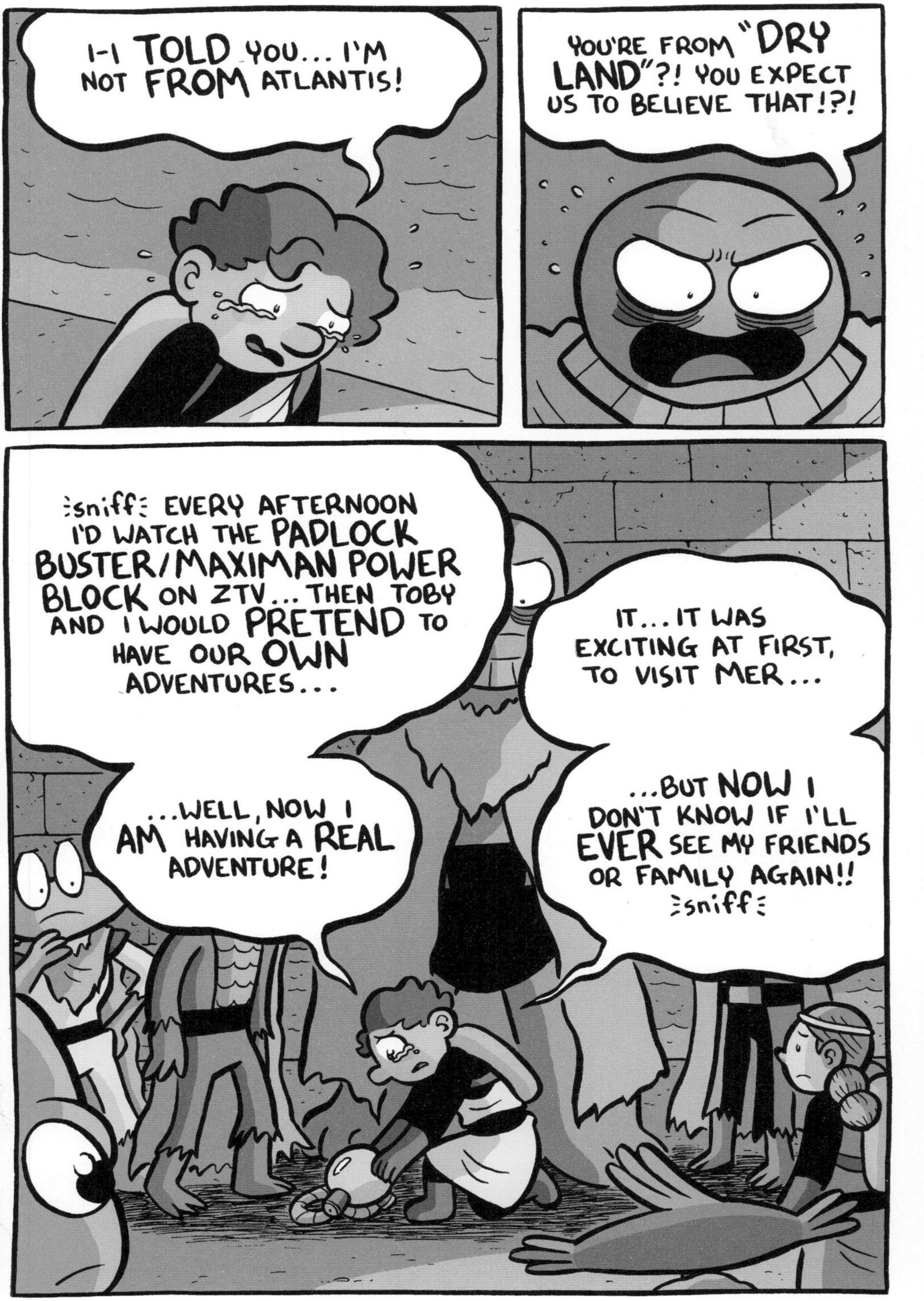
I-I TOLD YOU... I'M NOT FROM ATLANTIS!
YOU'RE FROM "DRY LAND"?! YOU EXPECT US TO BELIEVE THAT!?!
sniff EVERY AFTERNOON I'D WATCH THE PADLOCK BUSTER/MAXIMAN POWER BLOCK ON ZTV... THEN TOBY AND I WOULD PRETEND TO HAVE OUR OWN ADVENTURES...
...WELL, NOW I AM HAVING A REAL ADVENTURE!
IT... IT WAS EXCITING AT FIRST, TO VISIT MER...
...BUT NOW I DON'T KNOW IF I'LL EVER SEE MY FRIENDS OR FAMILY AGAIN!!
sniff

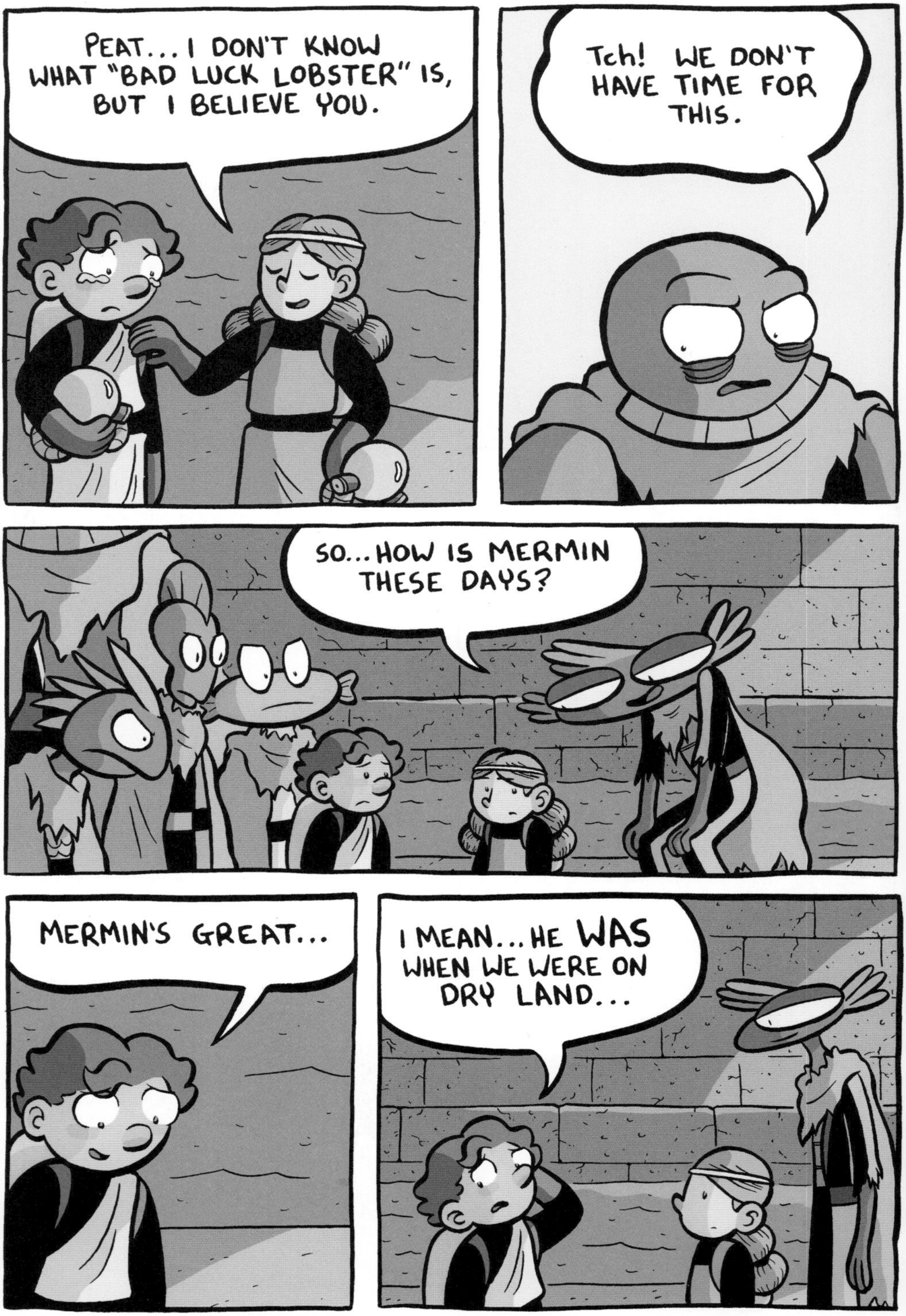
PEAT... I DON'T KNOW WHAT "BAD LUCK LOBSTER" IS, BUT I BELIEVE YOU.
Tch! WE DON'T HAVE TIME FOR THIS.
SO... HOW IS MERMIN THESE DAYS?
MERMIN'S GREAT...
I MEAN... HE WAS WHEN WE WERE ON DRY LAND...

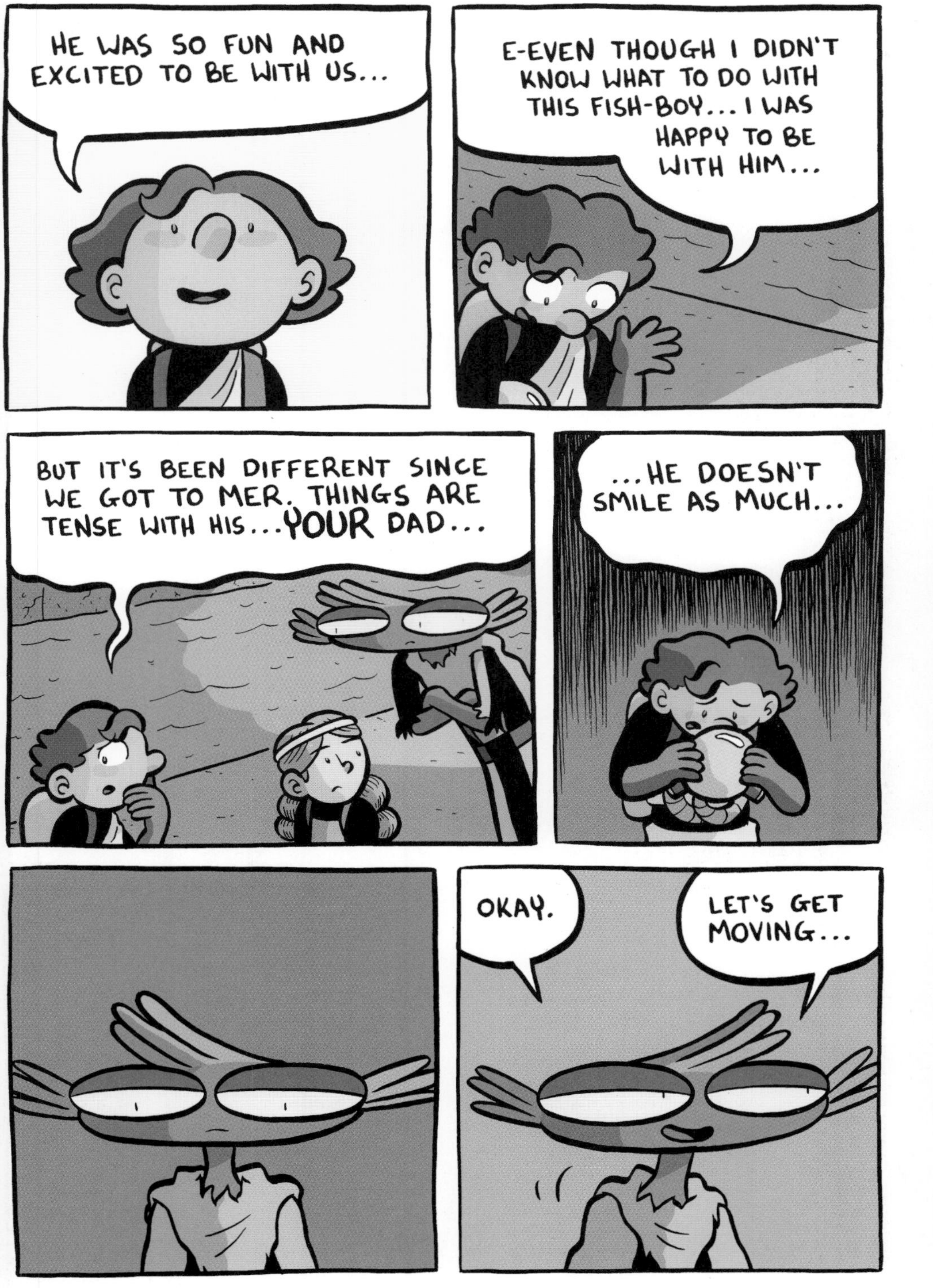
HE WAS SO FUN AND EXCITED TO BE WITH US...
E-EVEN THOUGH I DIDN'T KNOW WHAT TO DO WITH THIS FISH-BOY... I WAS HAPPY TO BE WITH HIM...
BUT IT'S BEEN DIFFERENT SINCE WE GOT TO MER. THINGS ARE TENSE WITH HIS... YOUR DAD...
...HE DOESN'T SMILE AS MUCH...
OKAY.
LET'S GET MOVING...

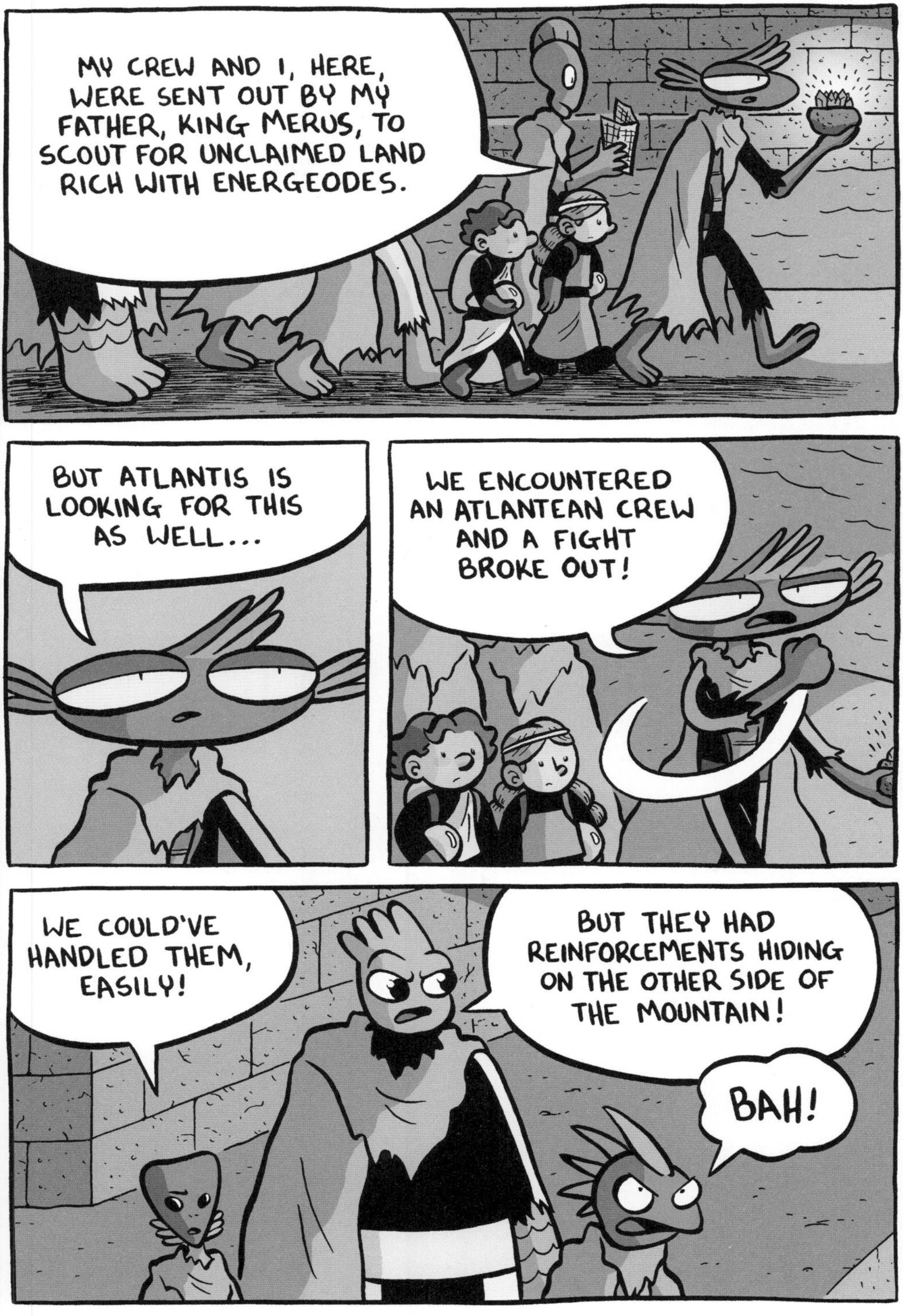
MY CREW AND I, HERE, WERE SENT OUT BY MY FATHER, KING MERUS, TO SCOUT FOR UNCLAIMED LAND RICH WITH ENERGEODES.
BUT ATLANTIS IS LOOKING FOR THIS AS WELL...
WE ENCOUNTERED AN ATLANTEAN CREW AND A FIGHT BROKE OUT!
WE COULD'VE HANDLED THEM, EASILY!
BUT THEY HAD REINFORCEMENTS HIDING ON THE OTHER SIDE OF THE MOUNTAIN!
BAH!

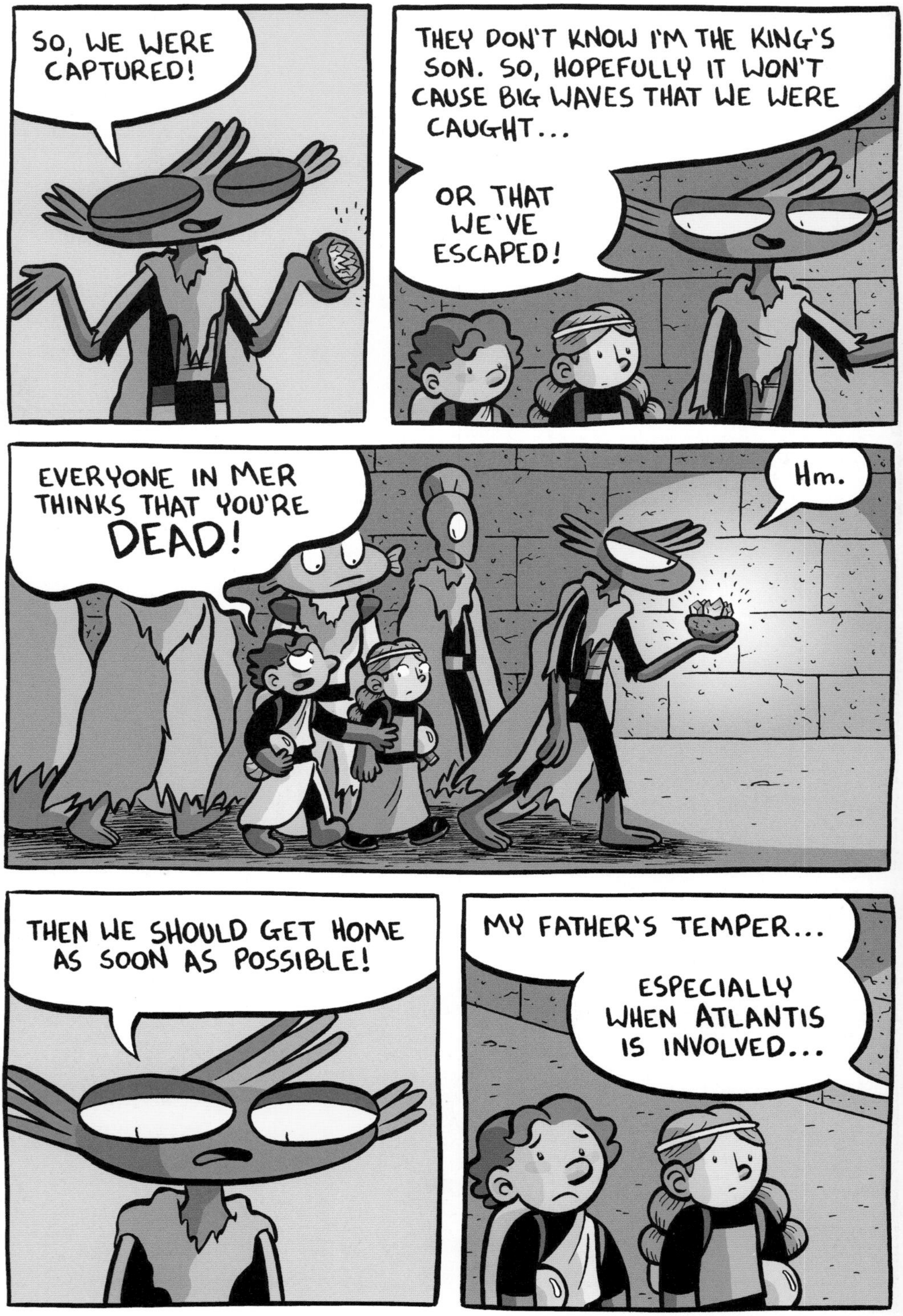
SO, WE WERE CAPTURED!
THEY DON'T KNOW I'M THE KING'S SON. SO, HOPEFULLY IT WON'T CAUSE BIG WAVES THAT WE WERE CAUGHT...
OR THAT WE'VE ESCAPED!
EVERYONE IN MER THINKS THAT YOU'RE DEAD!
Hm.
THEN WE SHOULD GET HOME AS SOON AS POSSIBLE!
MY FATHER'S TEMPER...
ESPECIALLY WHEN ATLANTIS IS INVOLVED...

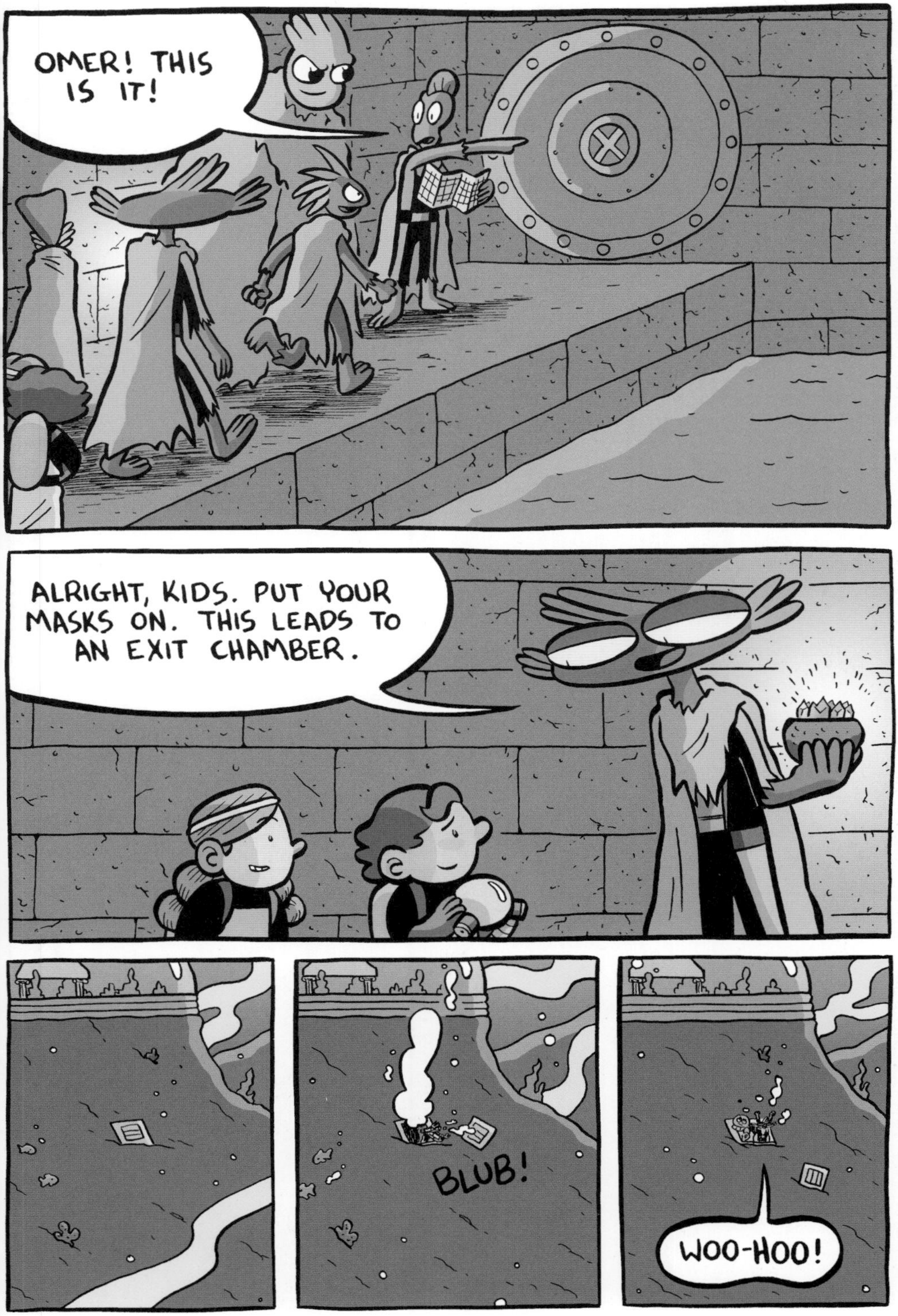
OMER! THIS IS IT!
ALRIGHT, KIDS. PUT YOUR MASKS ON. THIS LEADS TO AN EXIT CHAMBER.
BLUB!
WOO-HOO!

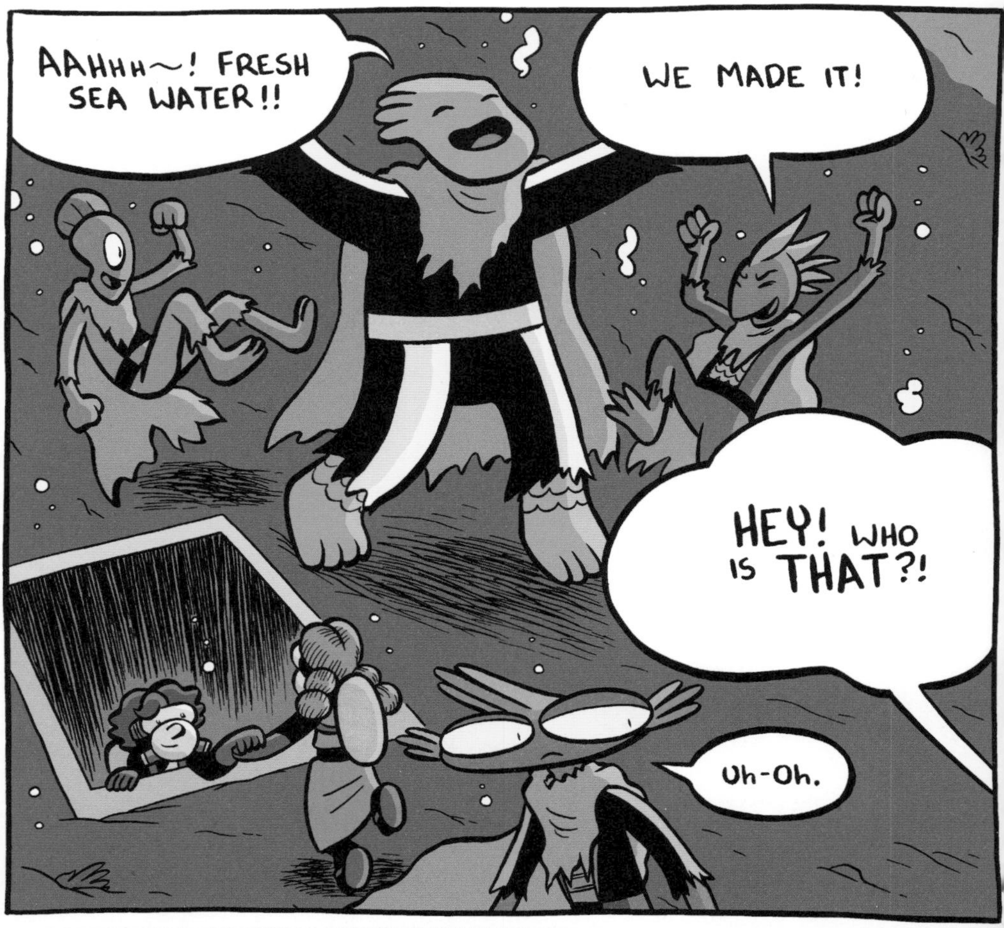
AAHHH~! FRESH SEA WATER!!
WE MADE IT!
HEY! WHO IS THAT?!
Uh-Oh.

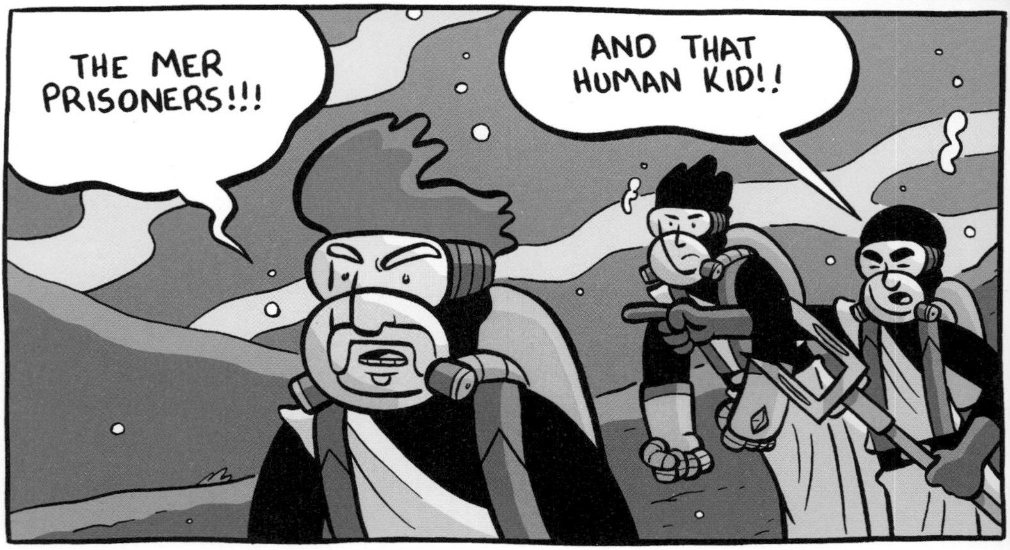
THE MER PRISONERS!!!
AND THAT HUMAN KID!!

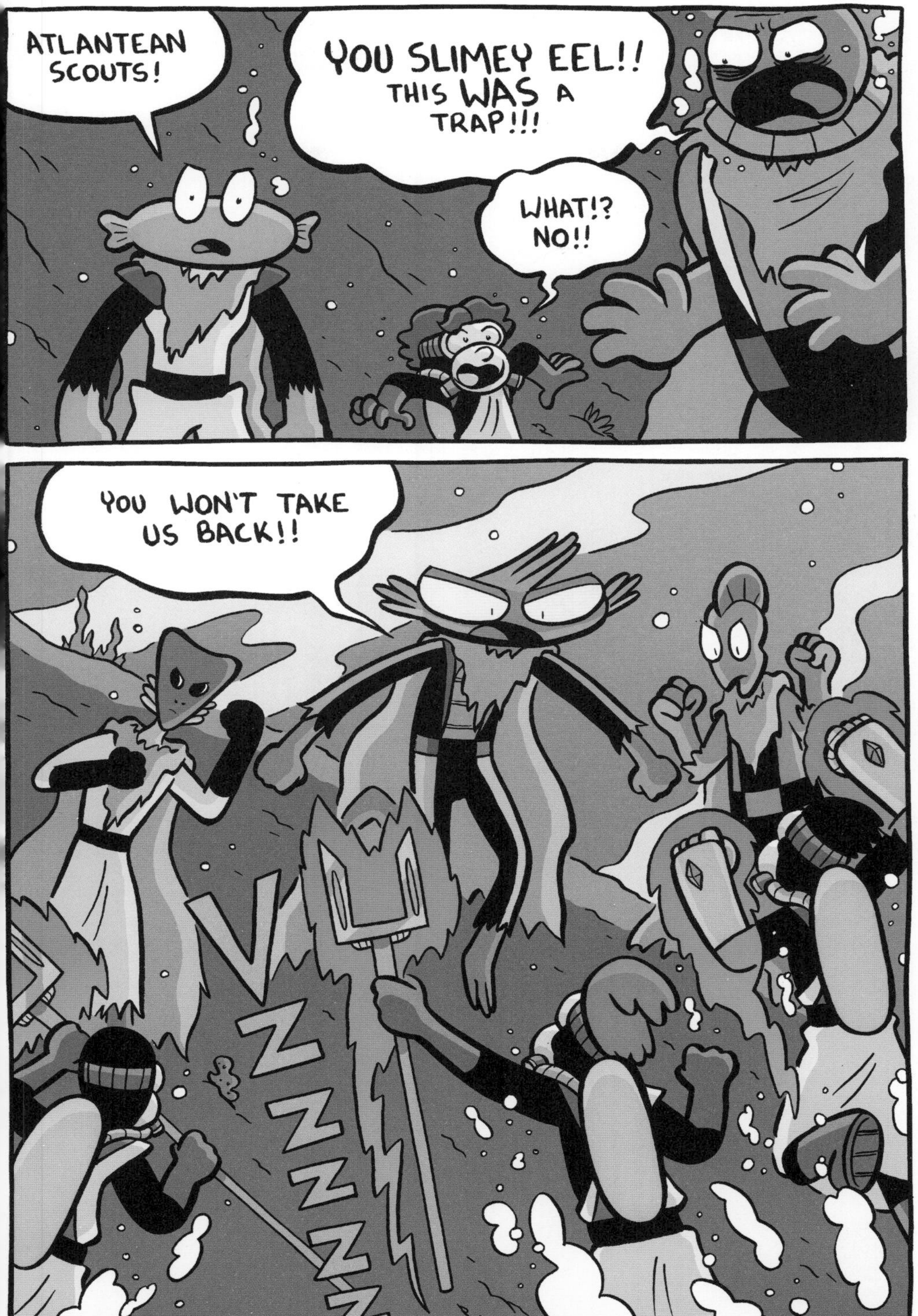
ATLANTEAN SCOUTS!
YOU SLIMEY EEL!! THIS WAS A TRAP!!!
WHAT!? NO!!
YOU WON'T TAKE US BACK!!
VZZZZZ

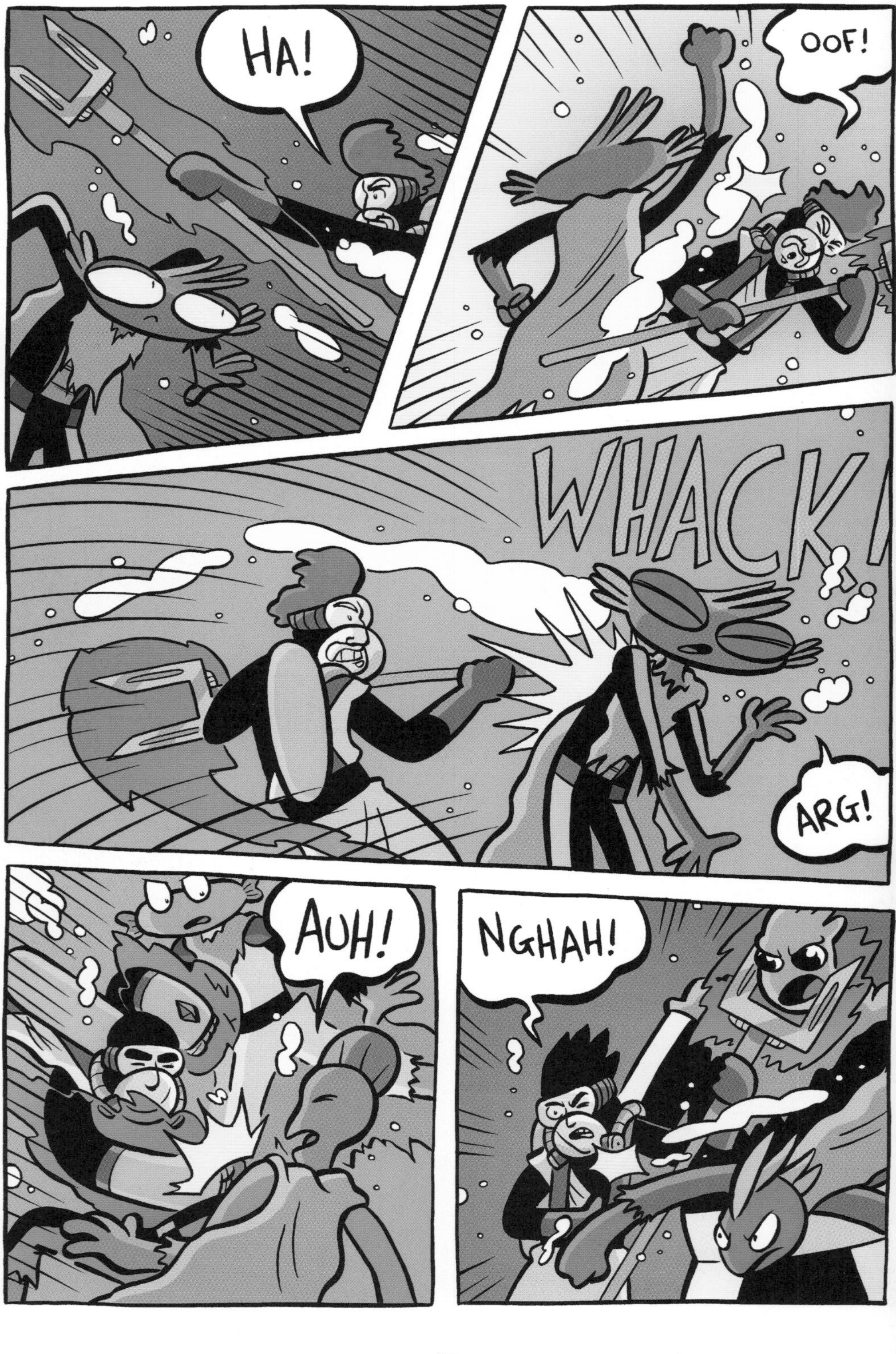
HA!
OOF!
WHACK!
ARG!
AUH!
NGHAH!

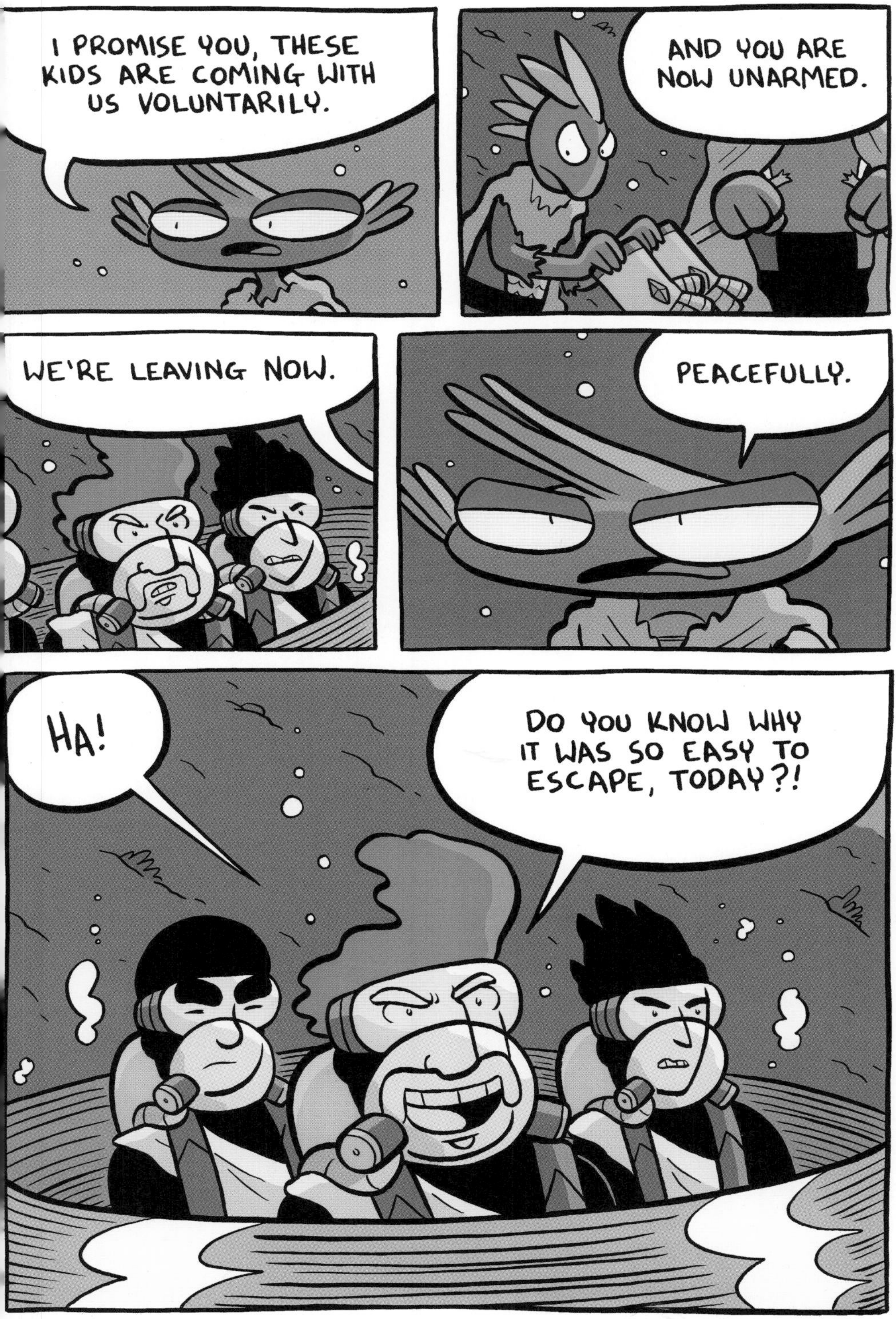
I PROMISE YOU, THESE KIDS ARE COMING WITH US VOLUNTARILY.
AND YOU ARE NOW UNARMED.
WE'RE LEAVING NOW.
PEACEFULLY.
HA!
DO YOU KNOW WHY IT WAS SO EASY TO ESCAPE, TODAY?!

CHAPTER THREE

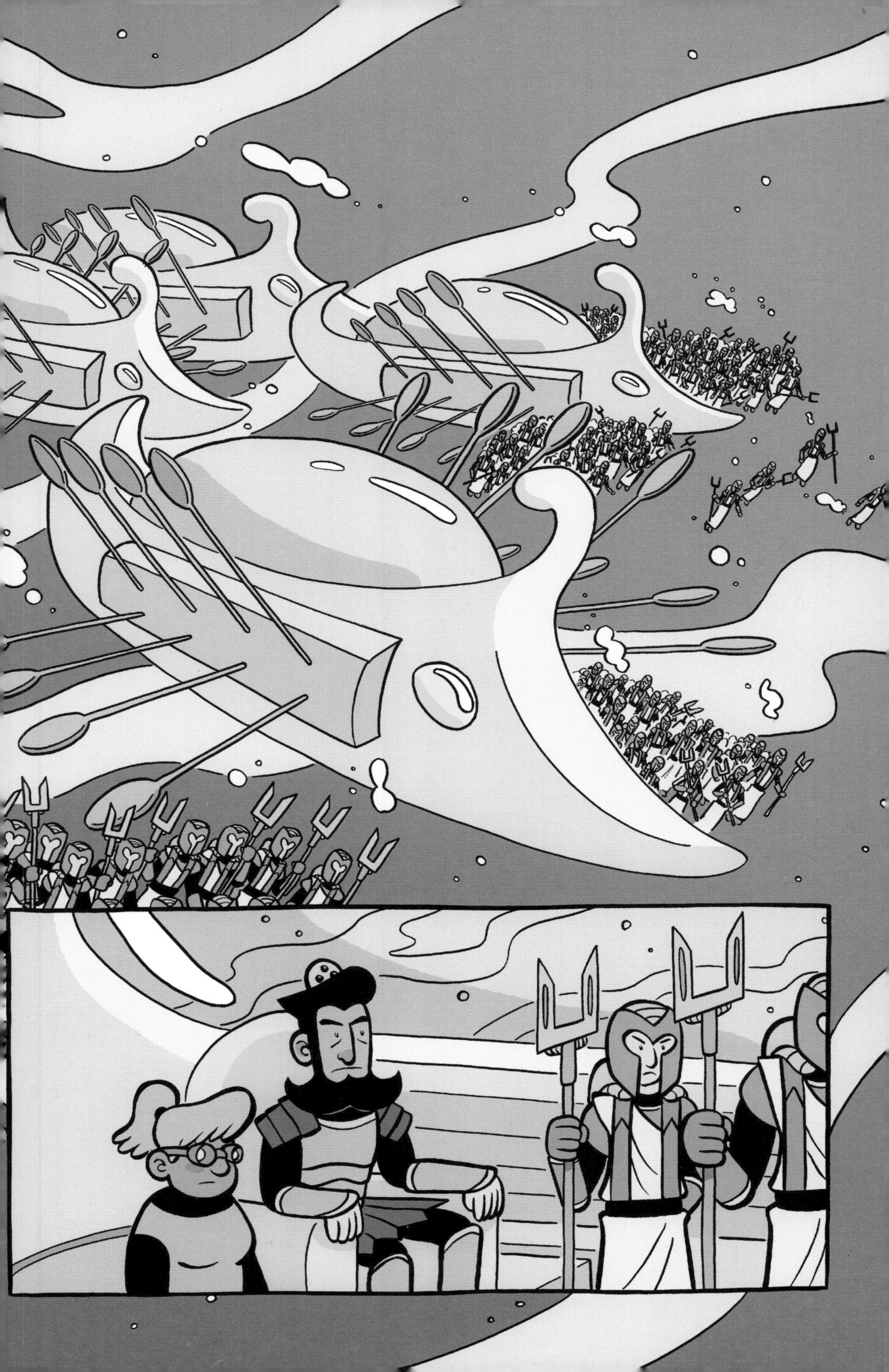

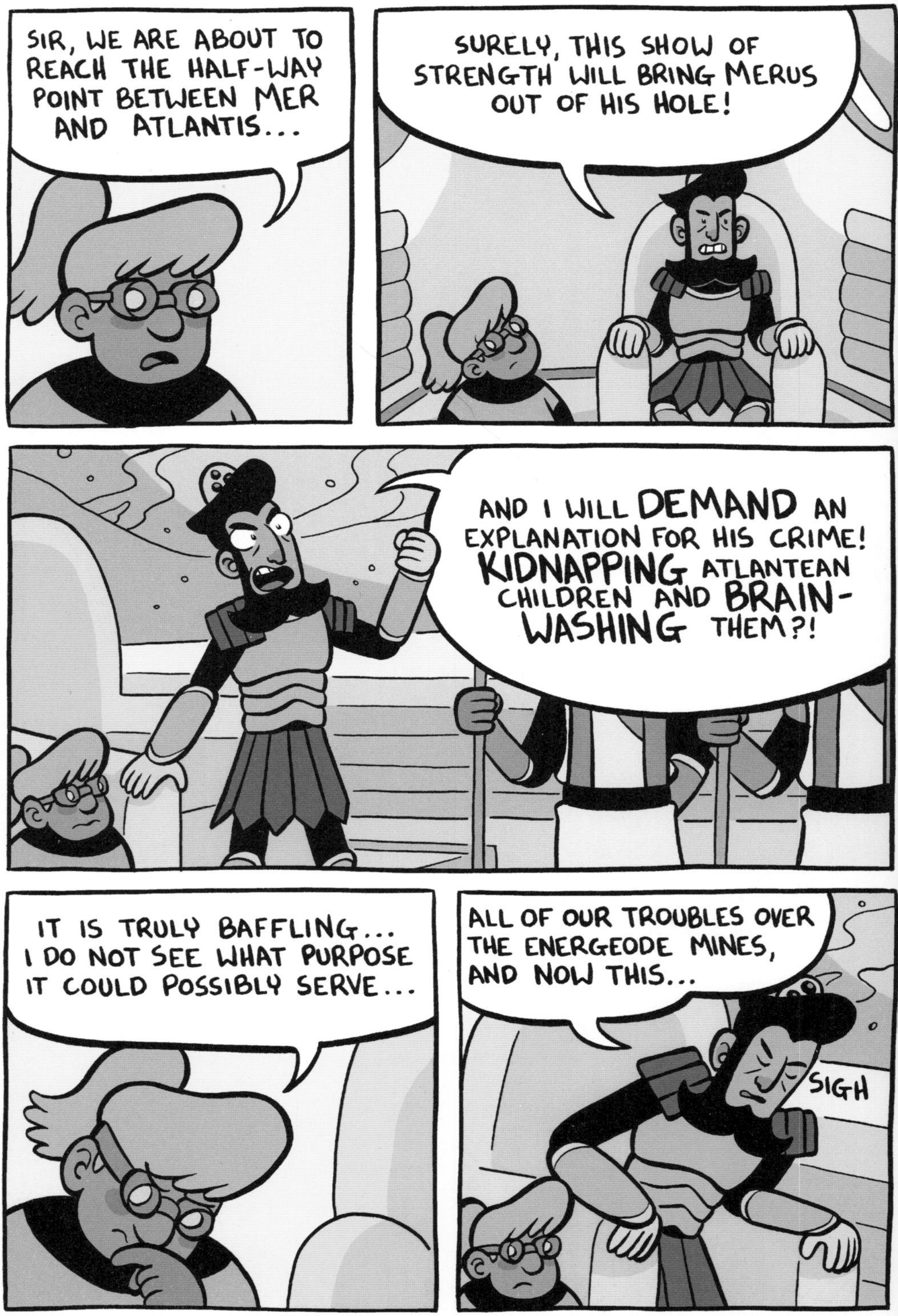
SIR, WE ARE ABOUT TO REACH THE HALF-WAY POINT BETWEEN MER AND ATLANTIS...
SURELY, THIS SHOW OF STRENGTH WILL BRING MERUS OUT OF HIS HOLE!
AND I WILL DEMAND AN EXPLANATION FOR HIS CRIME! KIDNAPPING ATLANTEAN CHILDREN AND BRAIN-WASHING THEM?!
IT IS TRULY BAFFLING... I DO NOT SEE WHAT PURPOSE IT COULD POSSIBLY SERVE...
ALL OF OUR TROUBLES OVER THE ENERGEODE MINES, AND NOW THIS...
SIGH

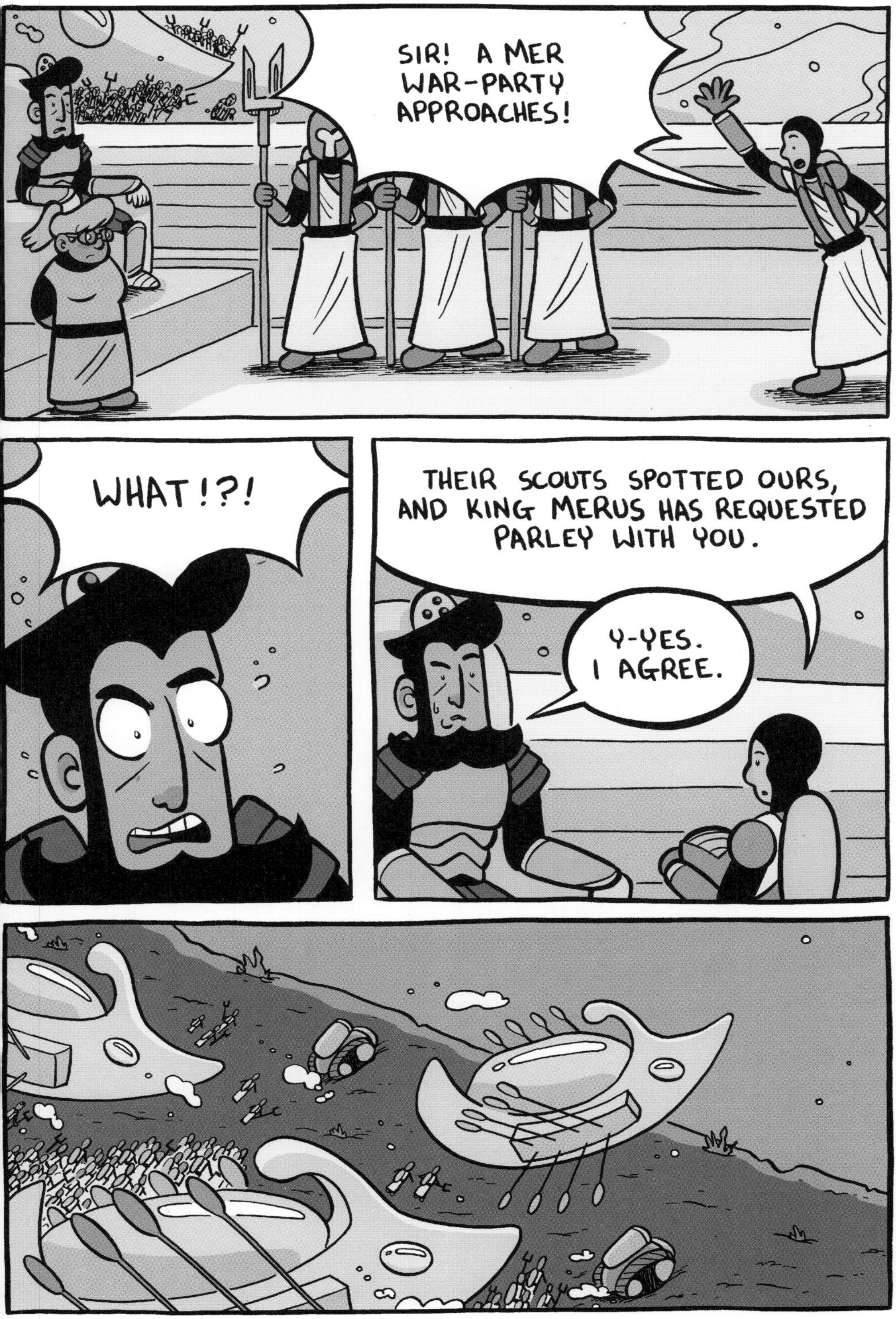
SIR! A MER WAR-PARTY APPROACHES!
WHAT!?!
THEIR SCOUTS SPOTTED OURS, AND KING MERUS HAS REQUESTED PARLEY WITH YOU.
Y-YES. I AGREE.

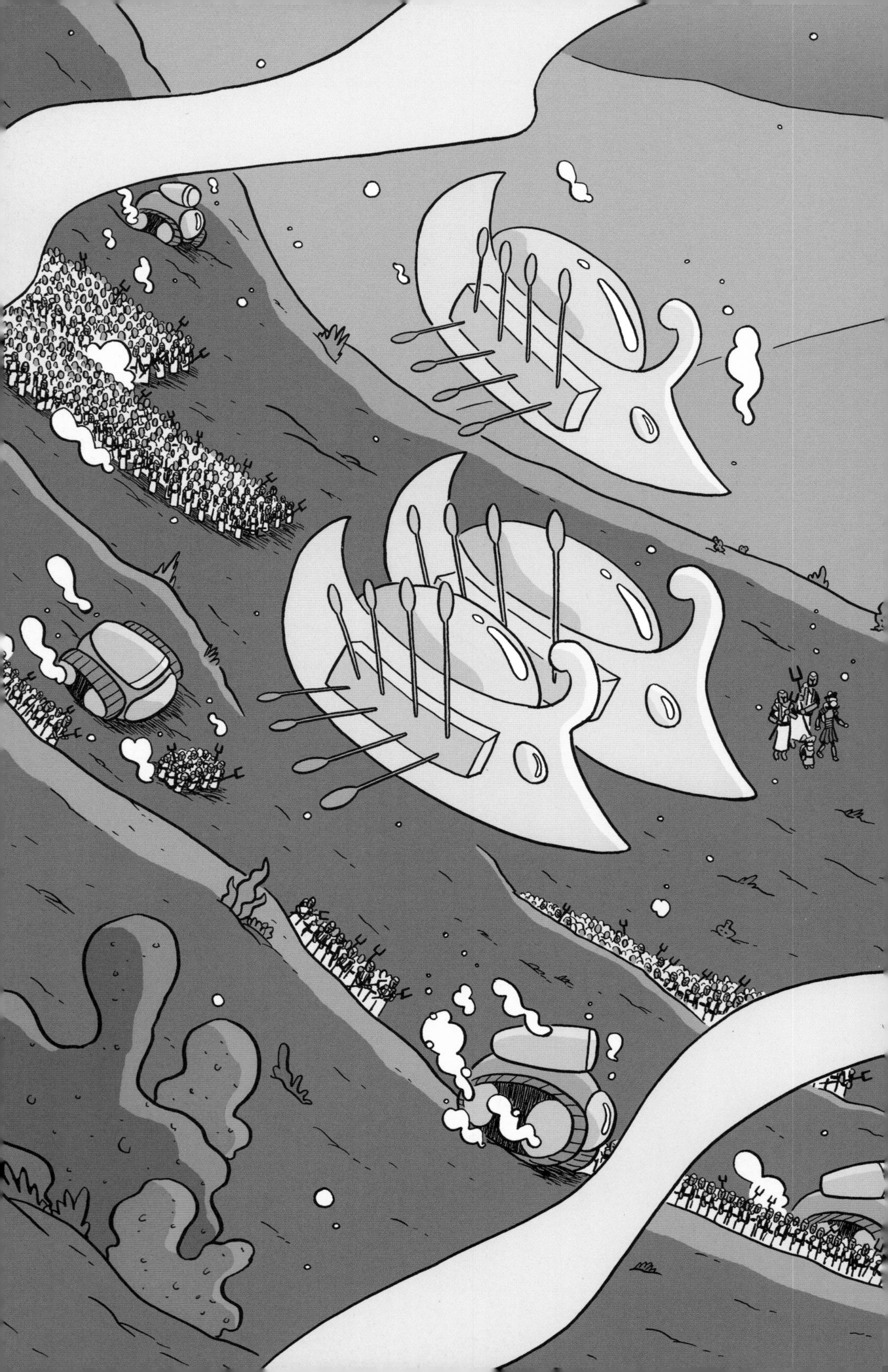

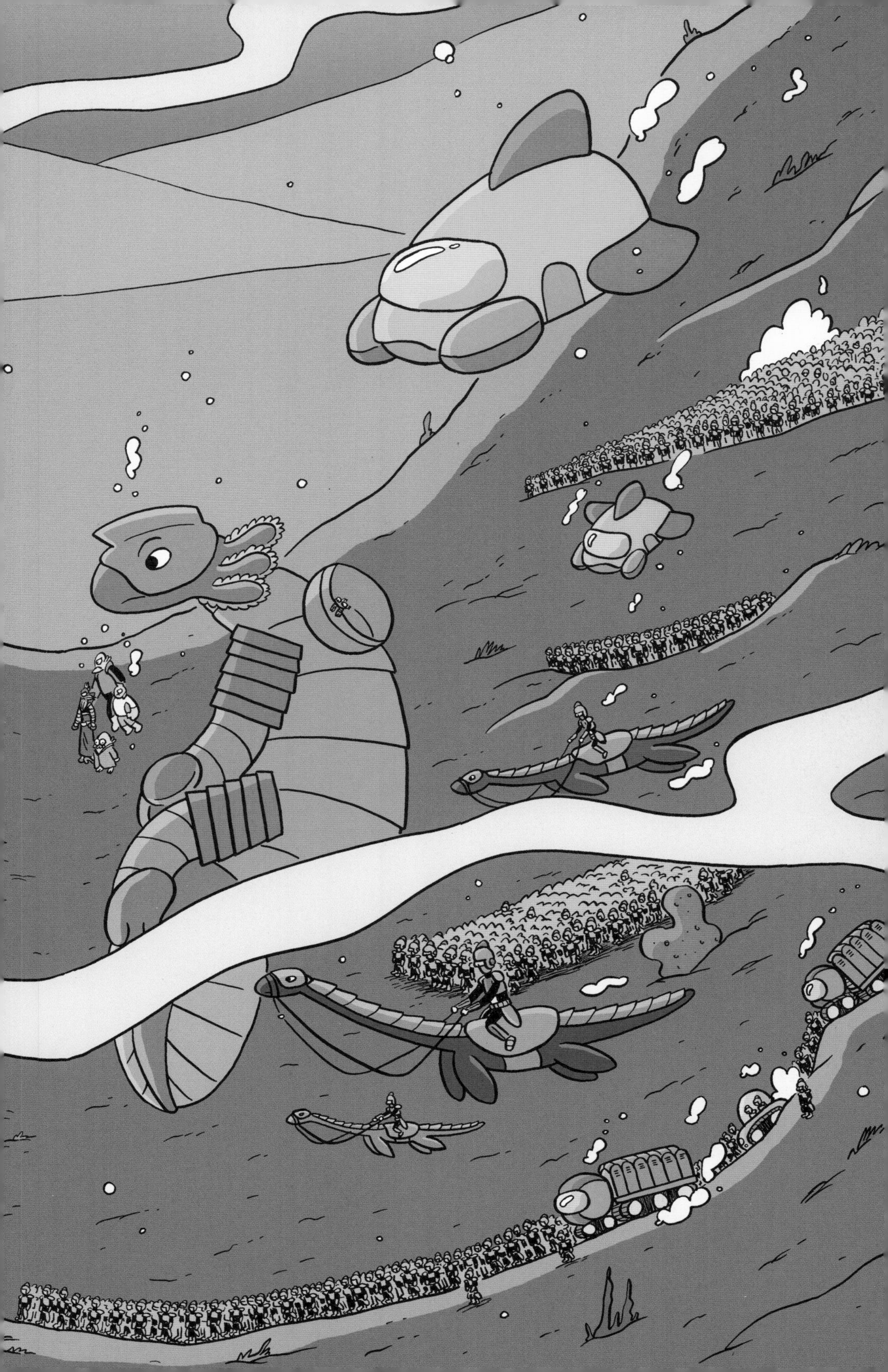

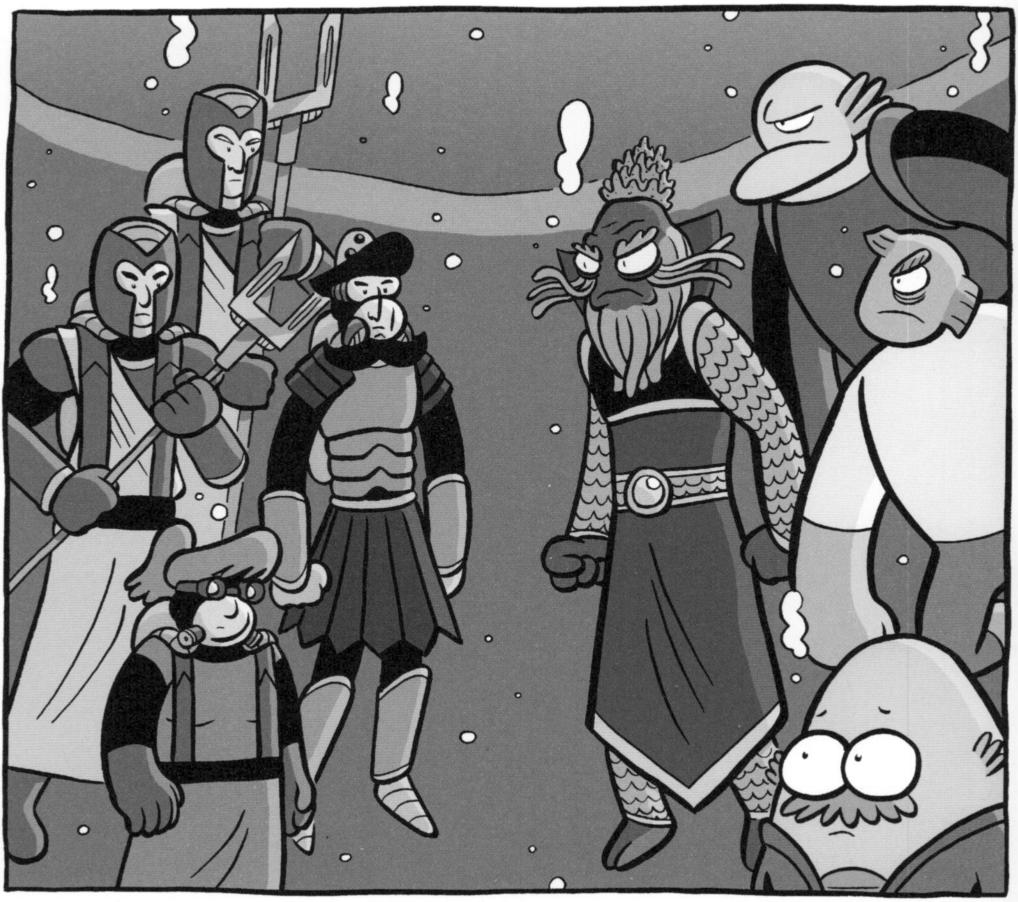

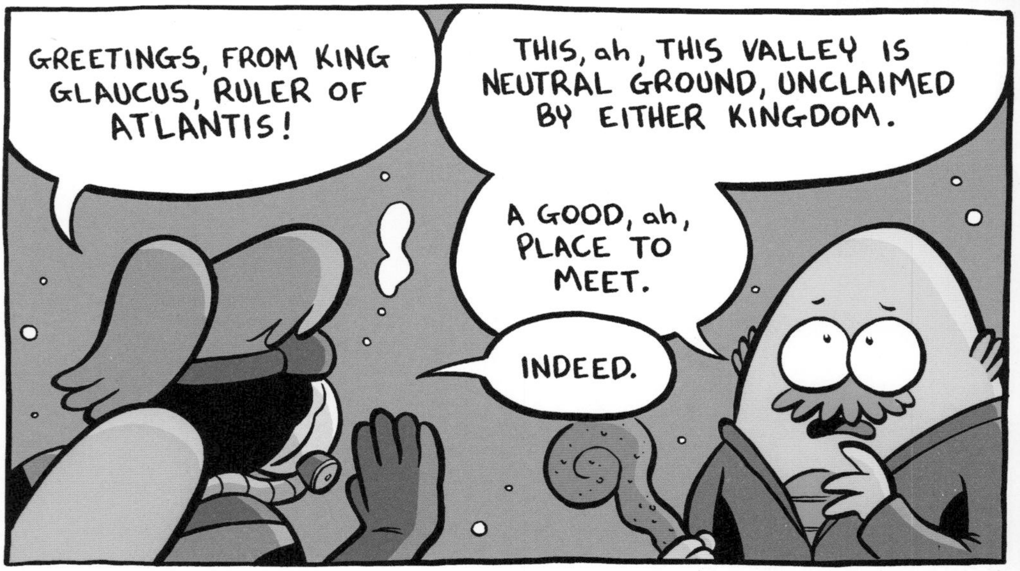
GREETINGS, FROM KING GLAUCUS, RULER OF ATLANTIS!
THIS, ah, THIS VALLEY IS NEUTRAL GROUND, UNCLAIMED BY EITHER KINGDOM.
A GOOD, ah, PLACE TO MEET.
INDEED.

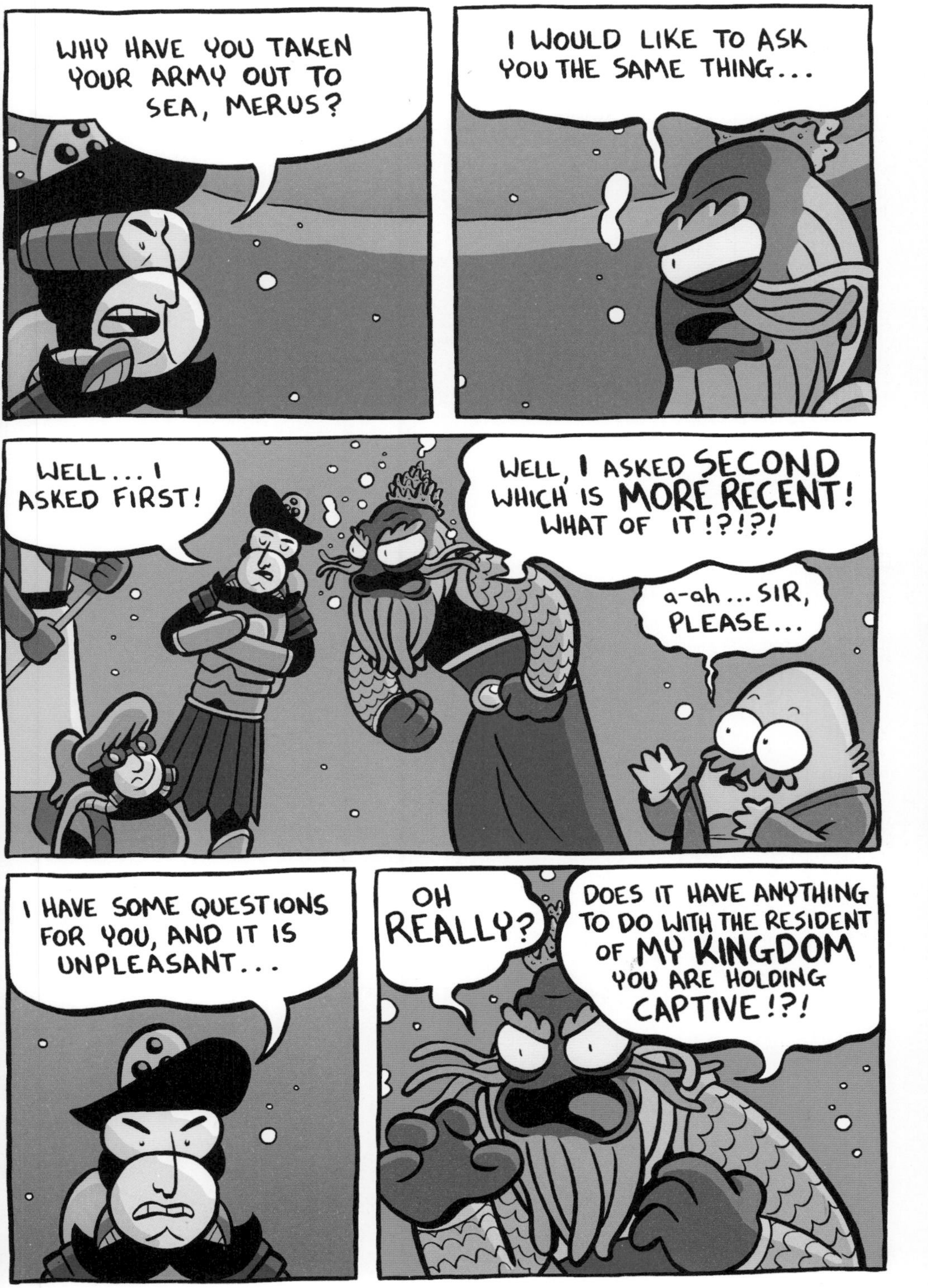
WHY HAVE YOU TAKEN YOUR ARMY OUT TO SEA, MERUS?
I WOULD LIKE TO ASK YOU THE SAME THING...
WELL... I ASKED FIRST!
WELL, I ASKED SECOND WHICH IS MORE RECENT! WHAT OF IT!?!?!
a-ah... SIR, PLEASE...
I HAVE SOME QUESTIONS FOR YOU, AND IT IS UNPLEASANT...
OH REALLY?
DOES IT HAVE ANYTHING TO DO WITH THE RESIDENT OF MY KINGDOM YOU ARE HOLDING CAPTIVE!?!

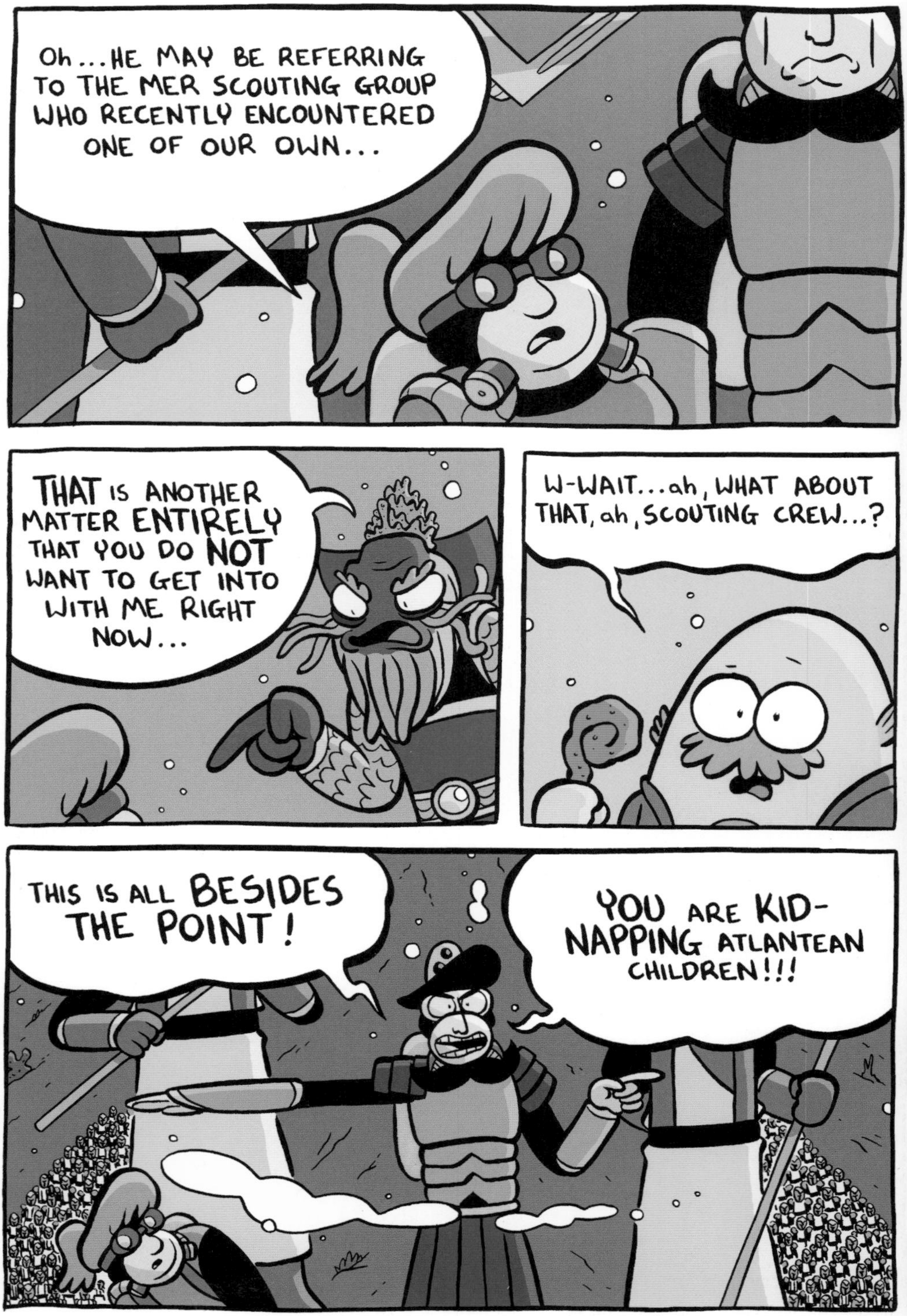
Oh...HE MAY BE REFERRING TO THE MER SCOUTING GROUP WHO RECENTLY ENCOUNTERED ONE OF OUR OWN...
THAT IS ANOTHER MATTER ENTIRELY THAT YOU DO NOT WANT TO GET INTO WITH ME RIGHT NOW...
W-WAIT...ah, WHAT ABOUT THAT, ah, SCOUTING CREW...?
THIS IS ALL BESIDES THE POINT!
YOU ARE KID-NAPPING ATLANTEAN CHILDREN!!!

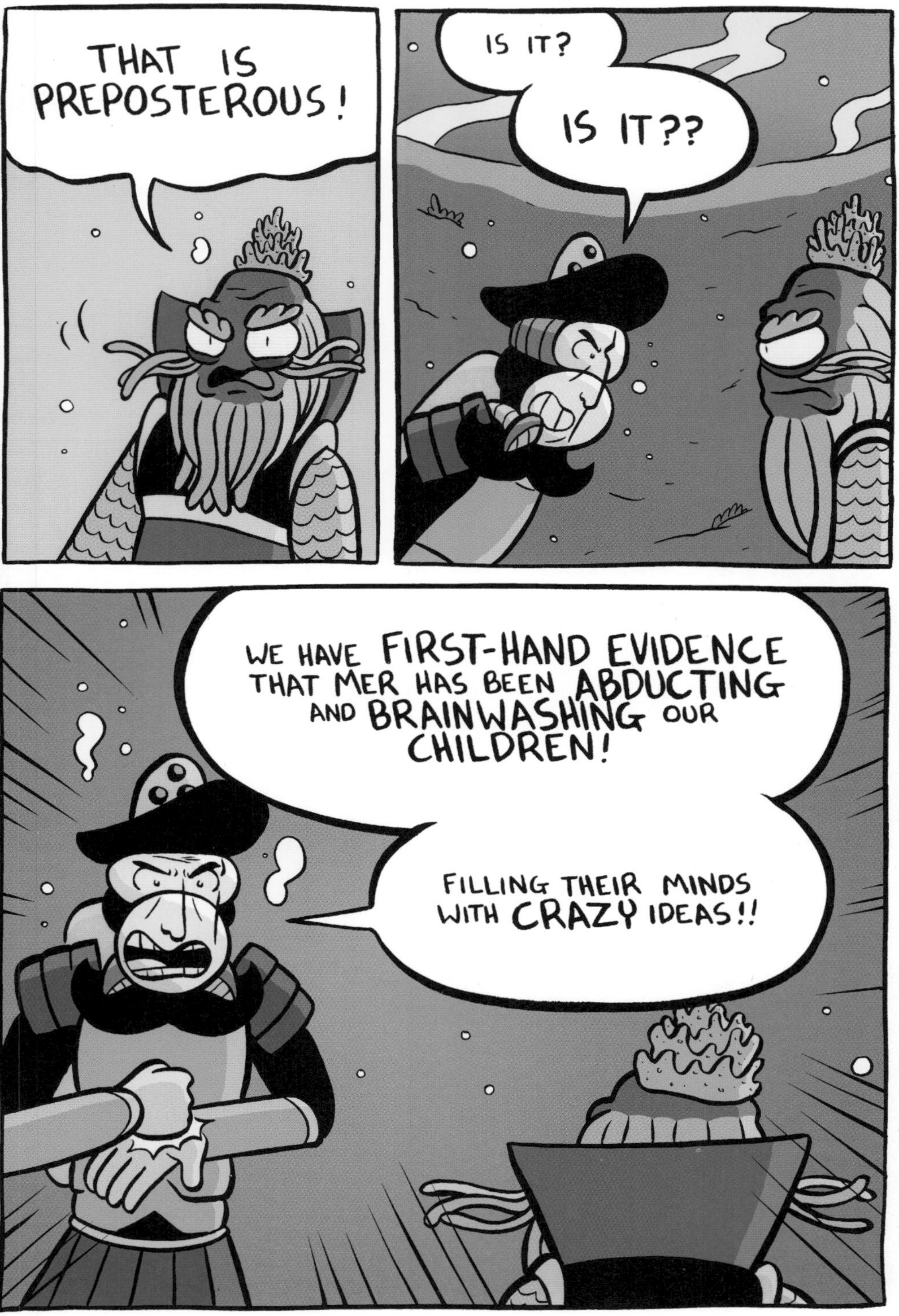
THAT IS PREPOSTEROUS!
IS IT?
IS IT??
WE HAVE FIRST-HAND EVIDENCE THAT MER HAS BEEN ABDUCTING AND BRAINWASHING OUR CHILDREN!
FILLING THEIR MINDS WITH CRAZY IDEAS!!

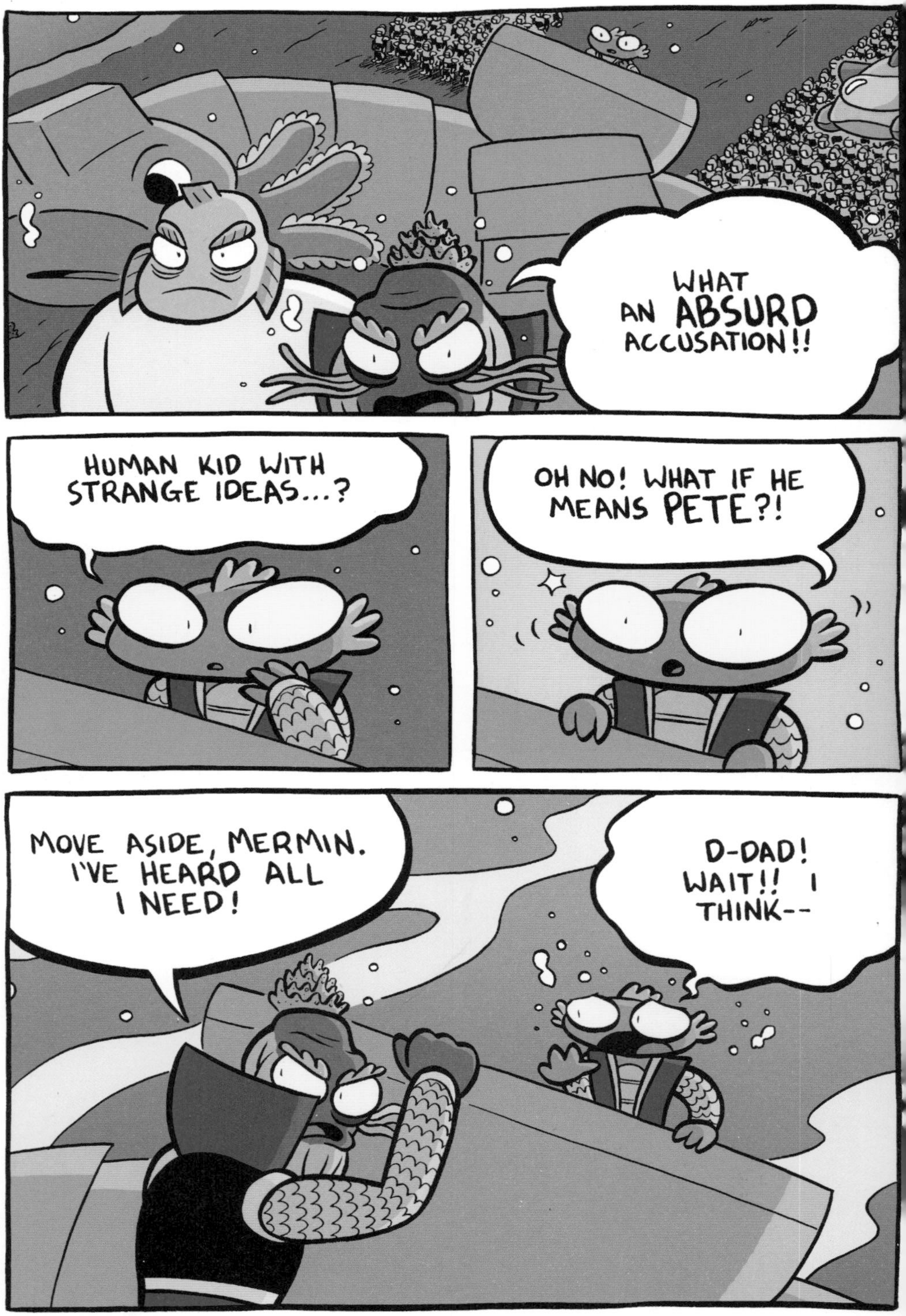
WHAT AN ABSURD ACCUSATION!!
HUMAN KID WITH STRANGE IDEAS...?
OH NO! WHAT IF HE MEANS PETE?!
MOVE ASIDE, MERMIN. I'VE HEARD ALL I NEED!
D-DAD! WAIT!! I THINK--

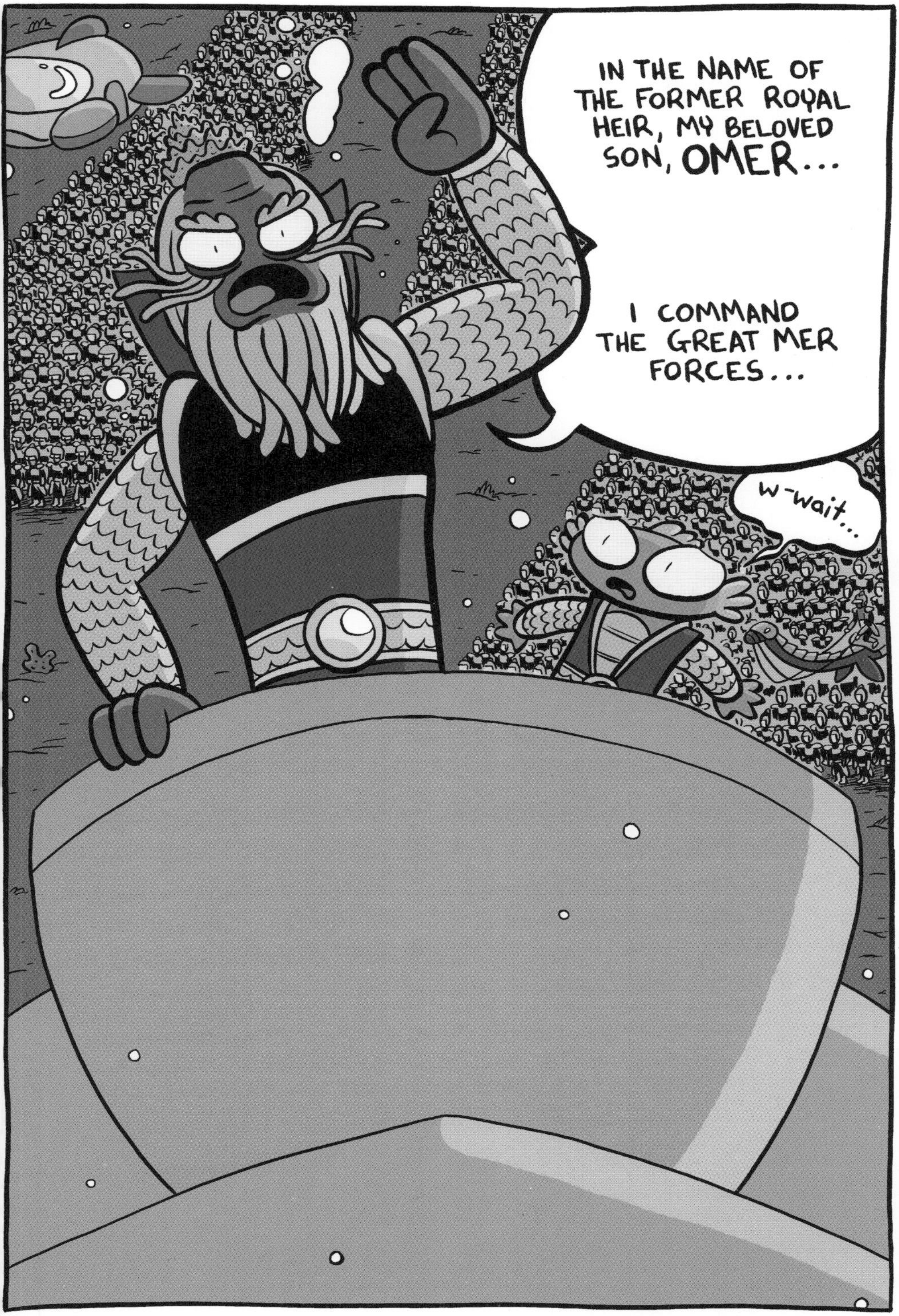
IN THE NAME OF THE FORMER ROYAL HEIR, MY BELOVED SON, OMER...
I COMMAND THE GREAT MER FORCES...
W-wait...

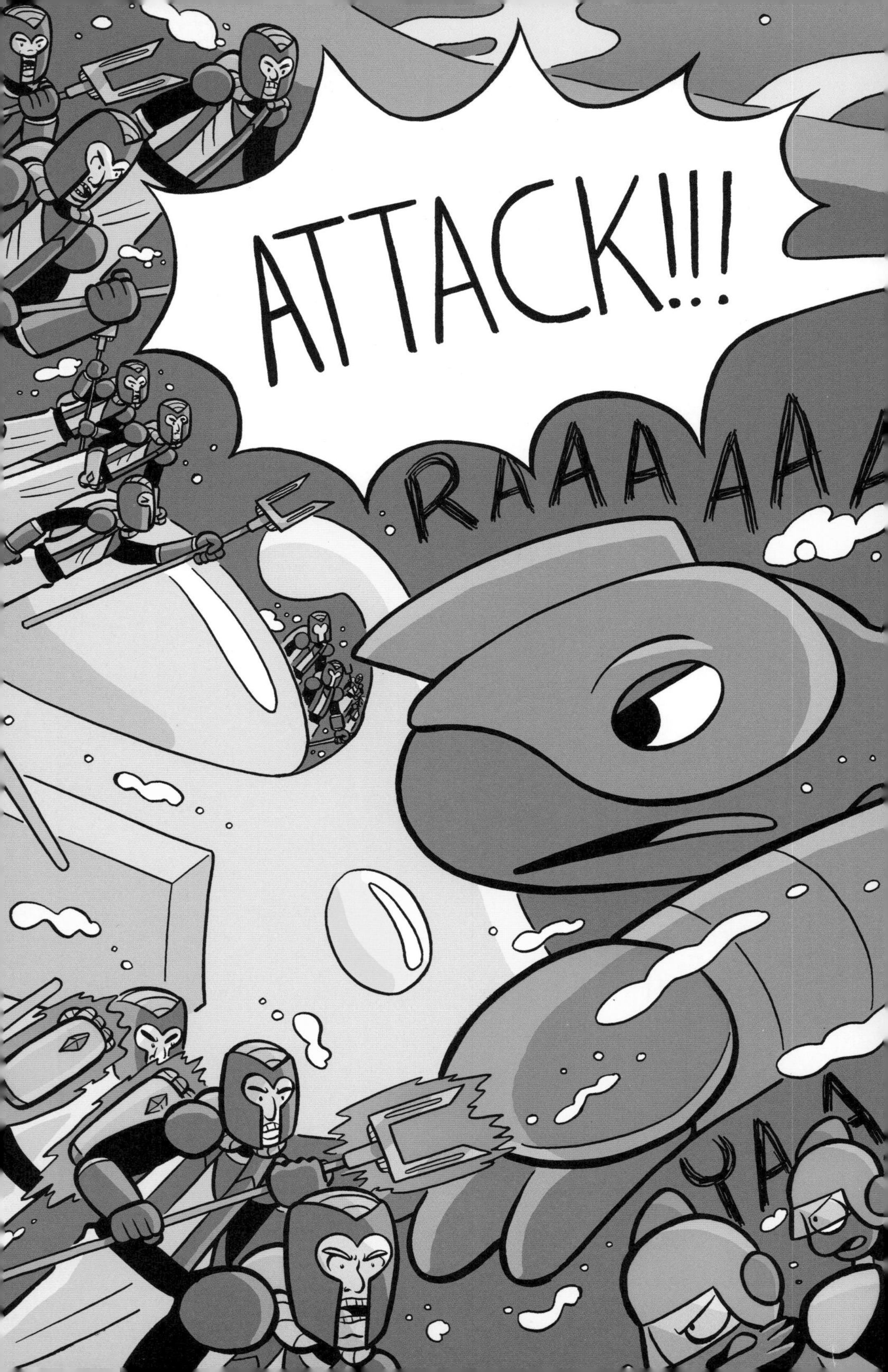
ATTACK!!!
RAAAAAA

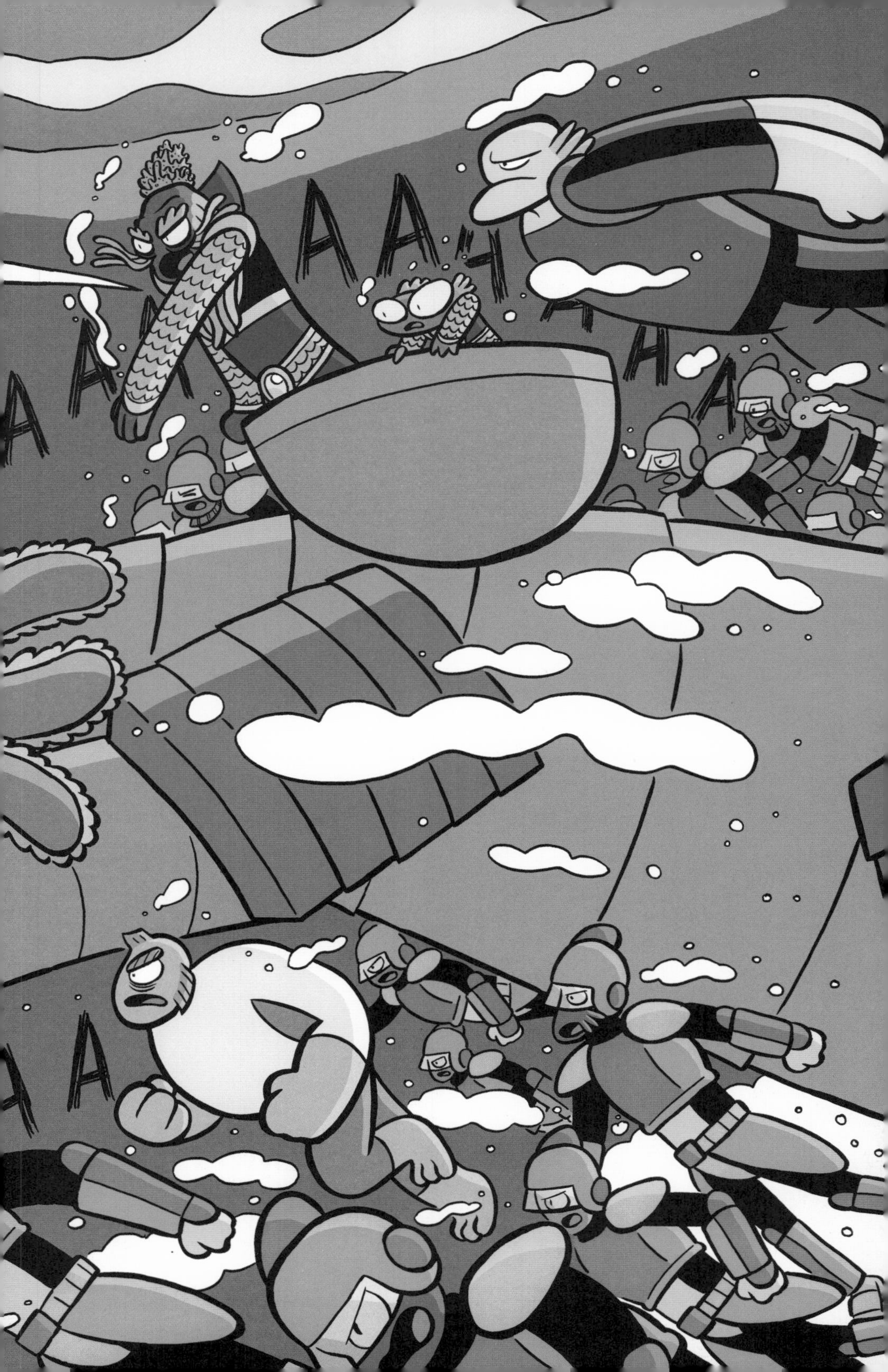

AAA
AAH
AAAH
AA

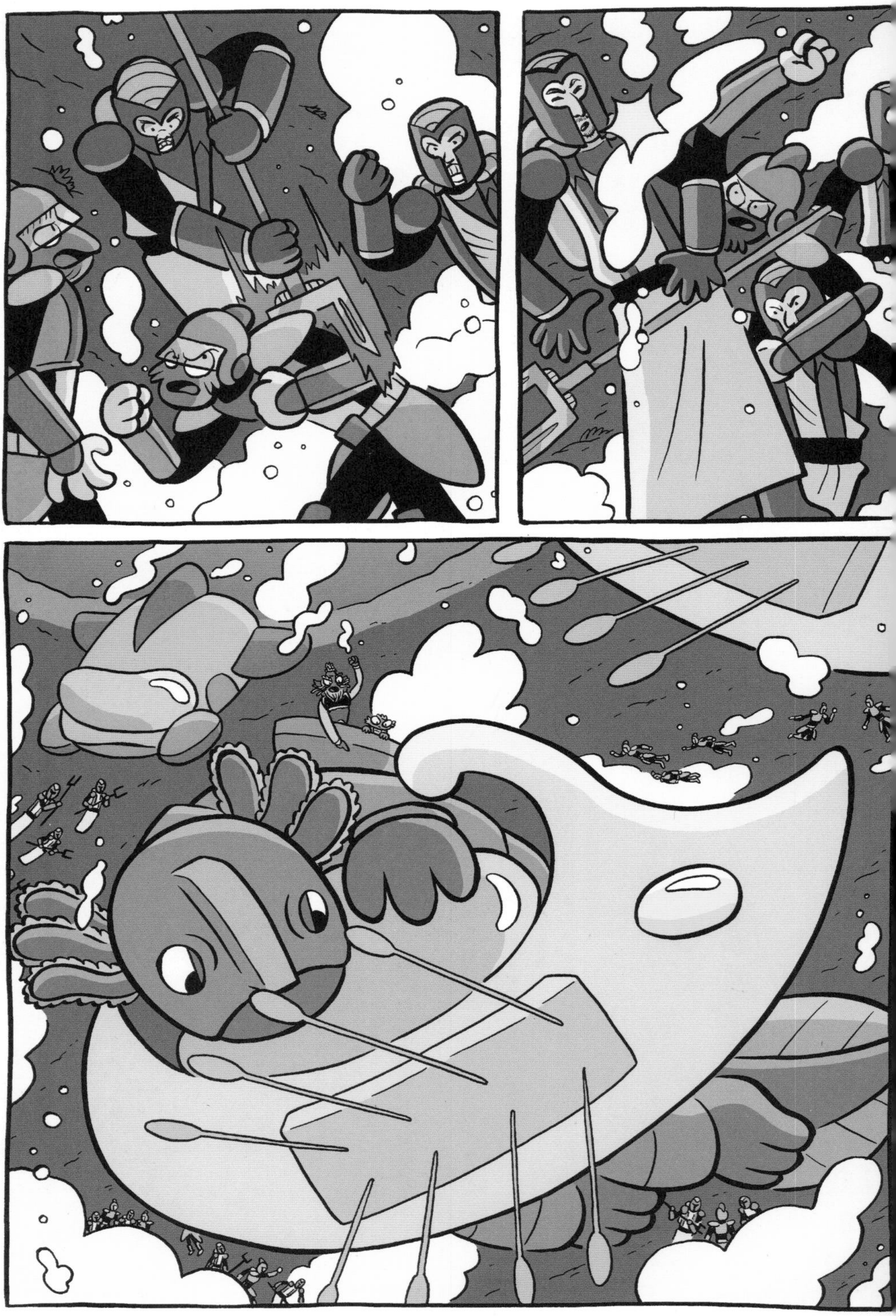

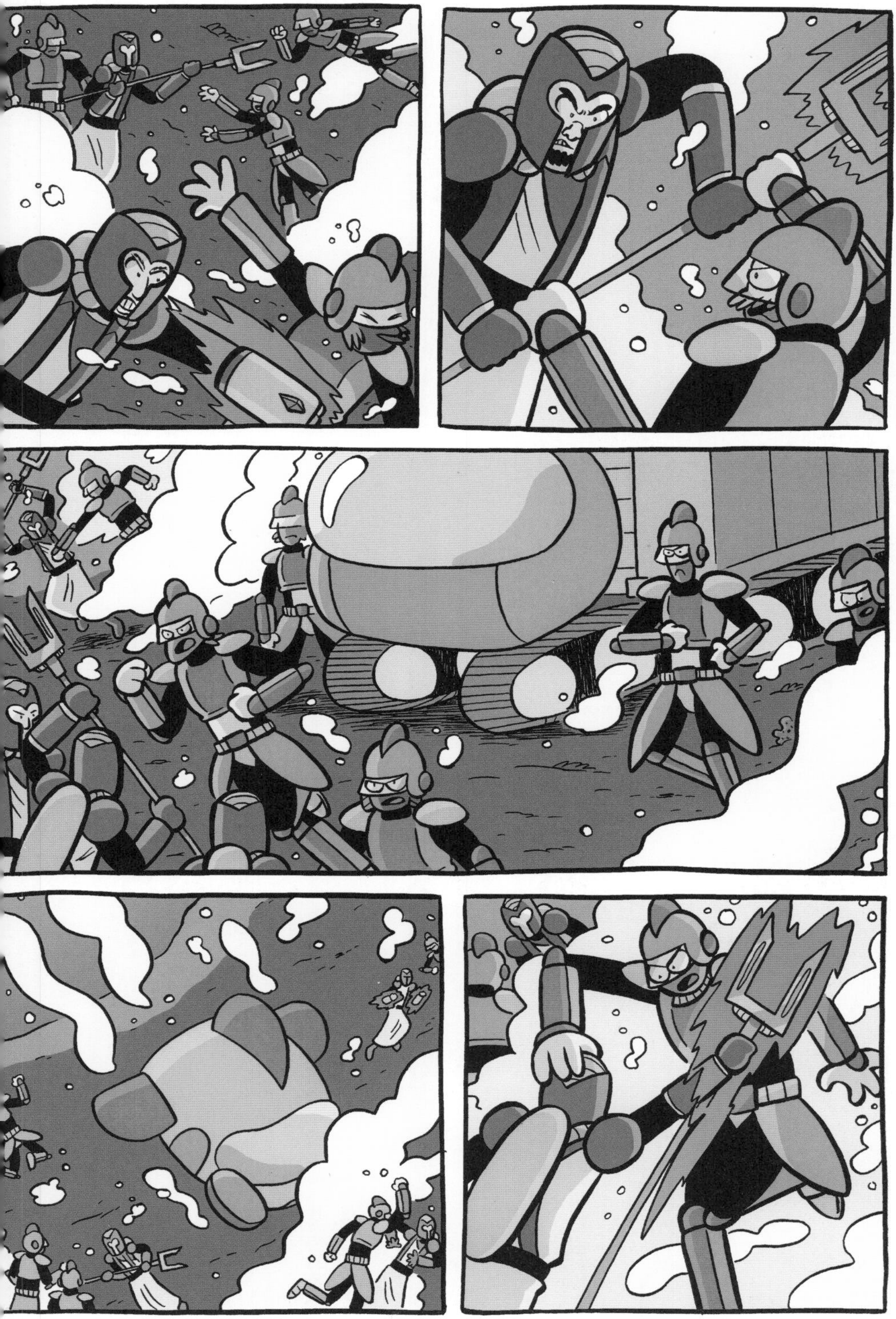

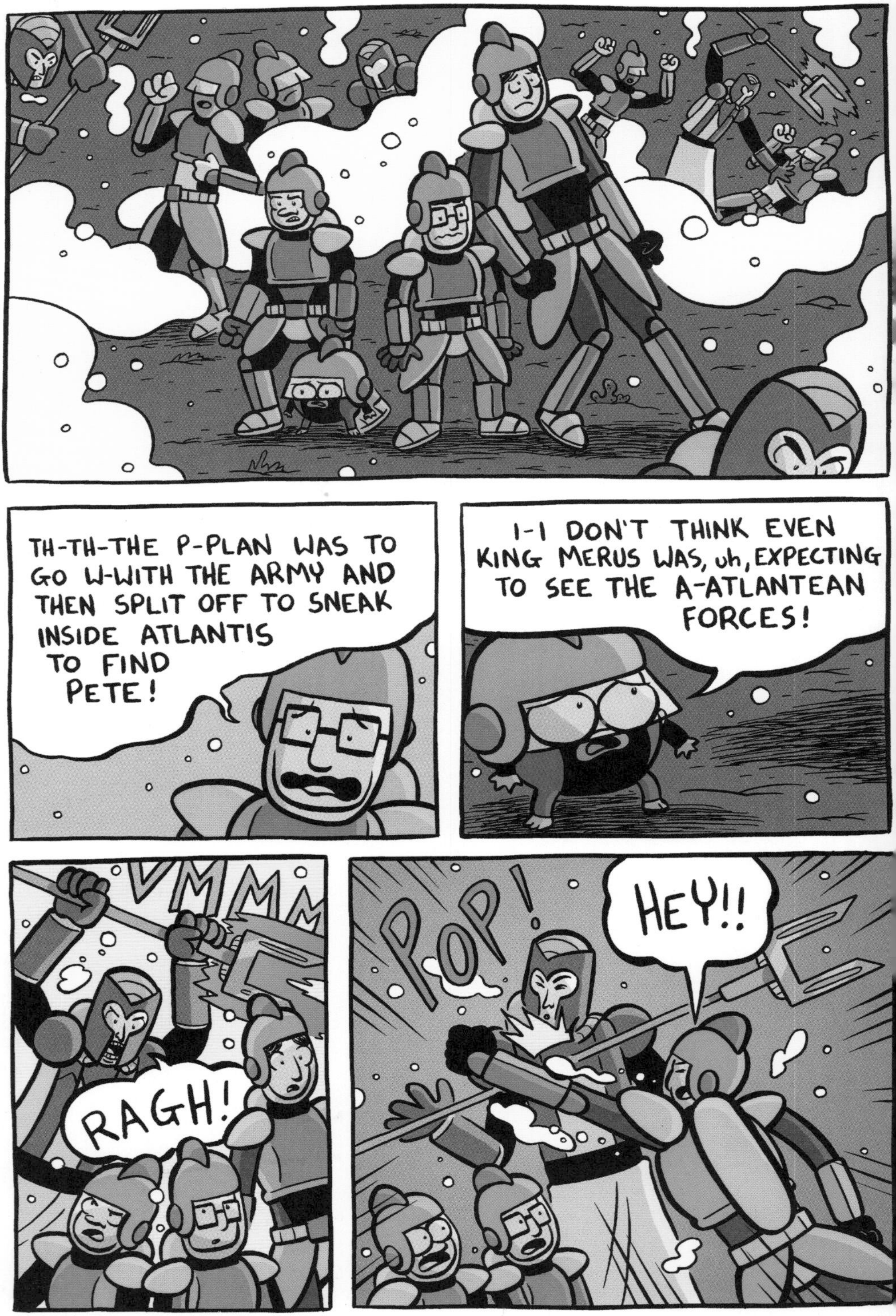
TH-TH-THE P-PLAN WAS TO GO W-WITH THE ARMY AND THEN SPLIT OFF TO SNEAK INSIDE ATLANTIS TO FIND PETE!
I-I DON'T THINK EVEN KING MERUS WAS, uh, EXPECTING TO SEE THE A-ATLANTEAN FORCES!
VMMM
RAGH!
POP!
HEY!!

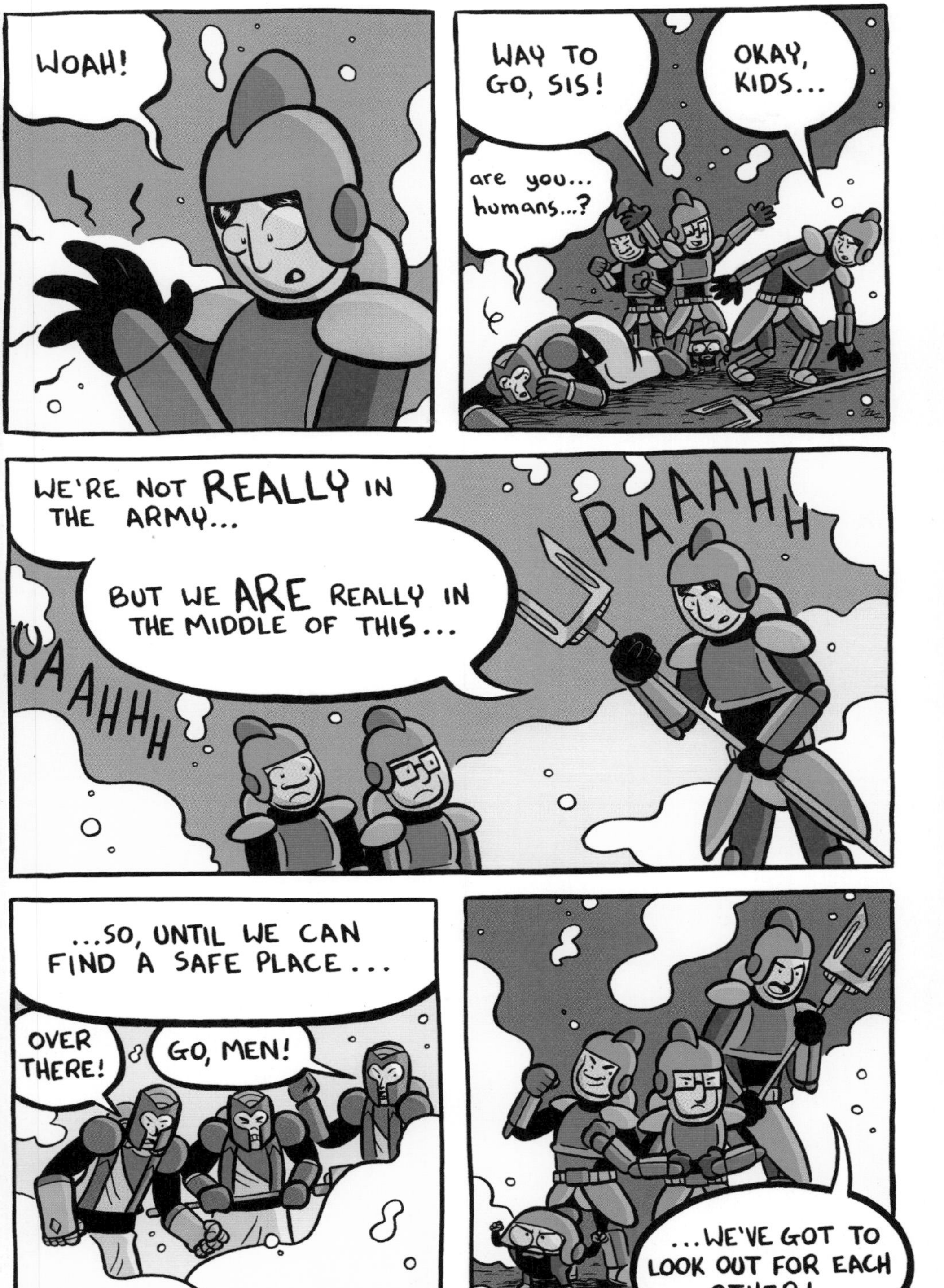
WOAH!
WAY TO GO, SIS!
OKAY, KIDS...
are you... humans...?
WE'RE NOT REALLY IN THE ARMY...
BUT WE ARE REALLY IN THE MIDDLE OF THIS...
RAAAHH
YAAHHH
...SO, UNTIL WE CAN FIND A SAFE PLACE...
OVER THERE!
GO, MEN!
...WE'VE GOT TO LOOK OUT FOR EACH OTHER!

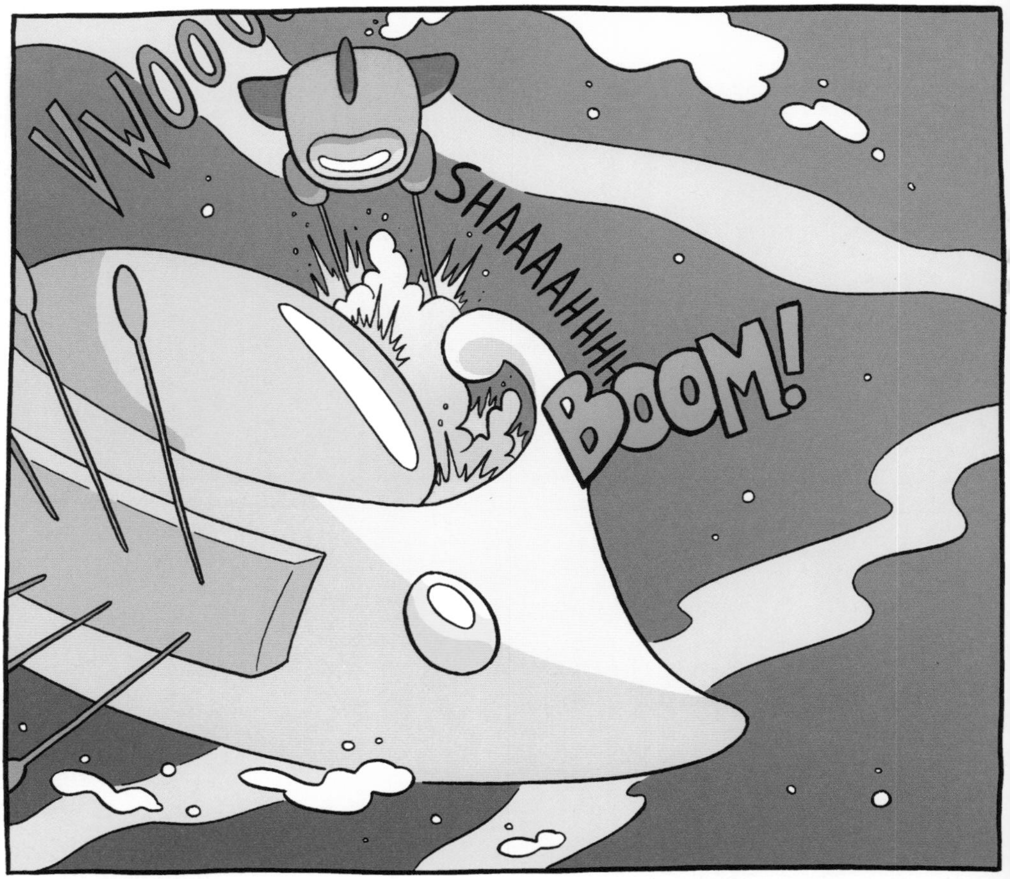
VWOOO
SHAAAAAHHHH
BOOM!

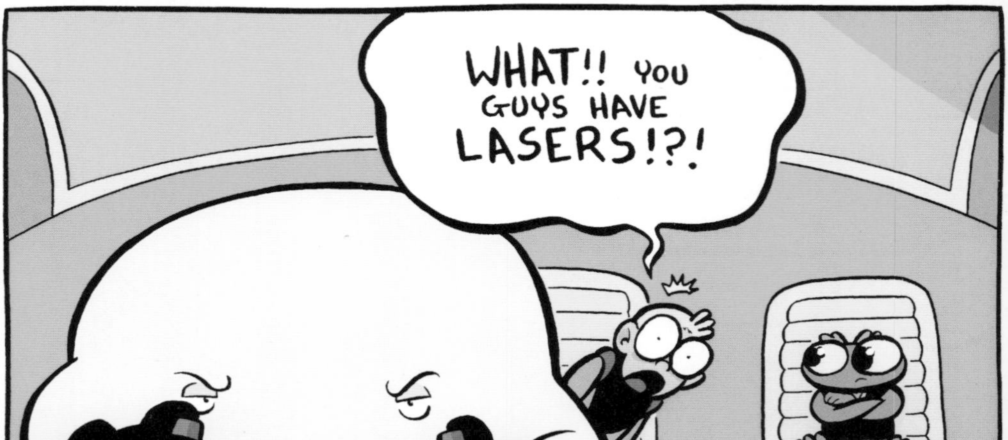
WHAT!! YOU GUYS HAVE LASERS!?!

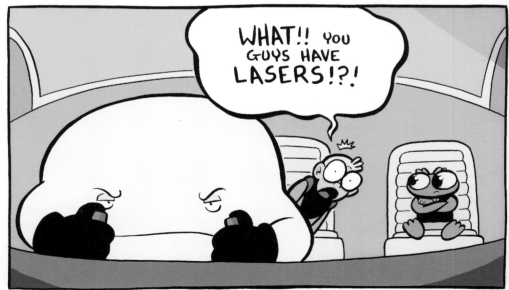

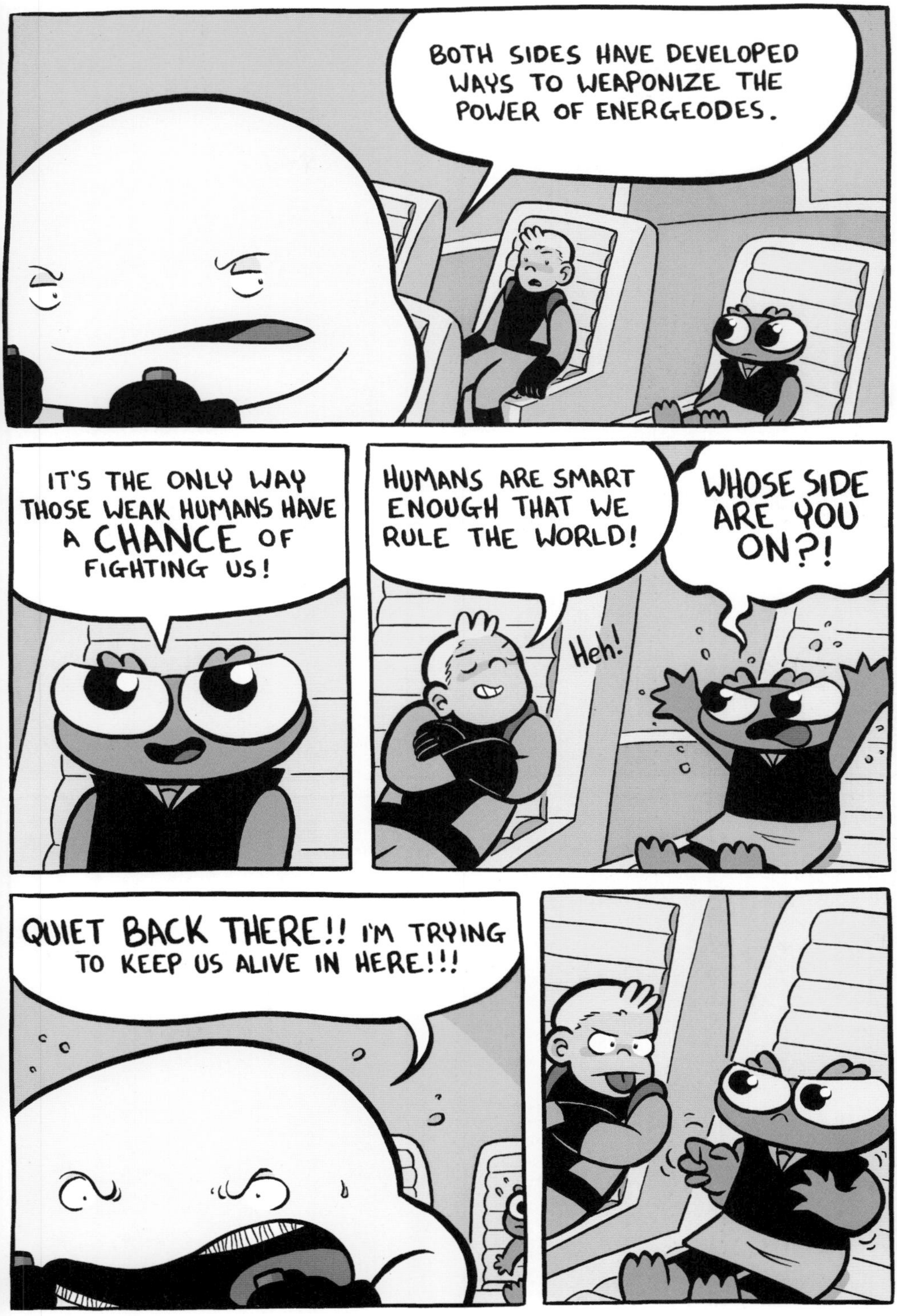
BOTH SIDES HAVE DEVELOPED WAYS TO WEAPONIZE THE POWER OF ENERGEODES.
IT'S THE ONLY WAY THOSE WEAK HUMANS HAVE A CHANCE OF FIGHTING US!
HUMANS ARE SMART ENOUGH THAT WE RULE THE WORLD!
Heh!
WHOSE SIDE ARE YOU ON?!
QUIET BACK THERE!! I'M TRYING TO KEEP US ALIVE IN HERE!!!

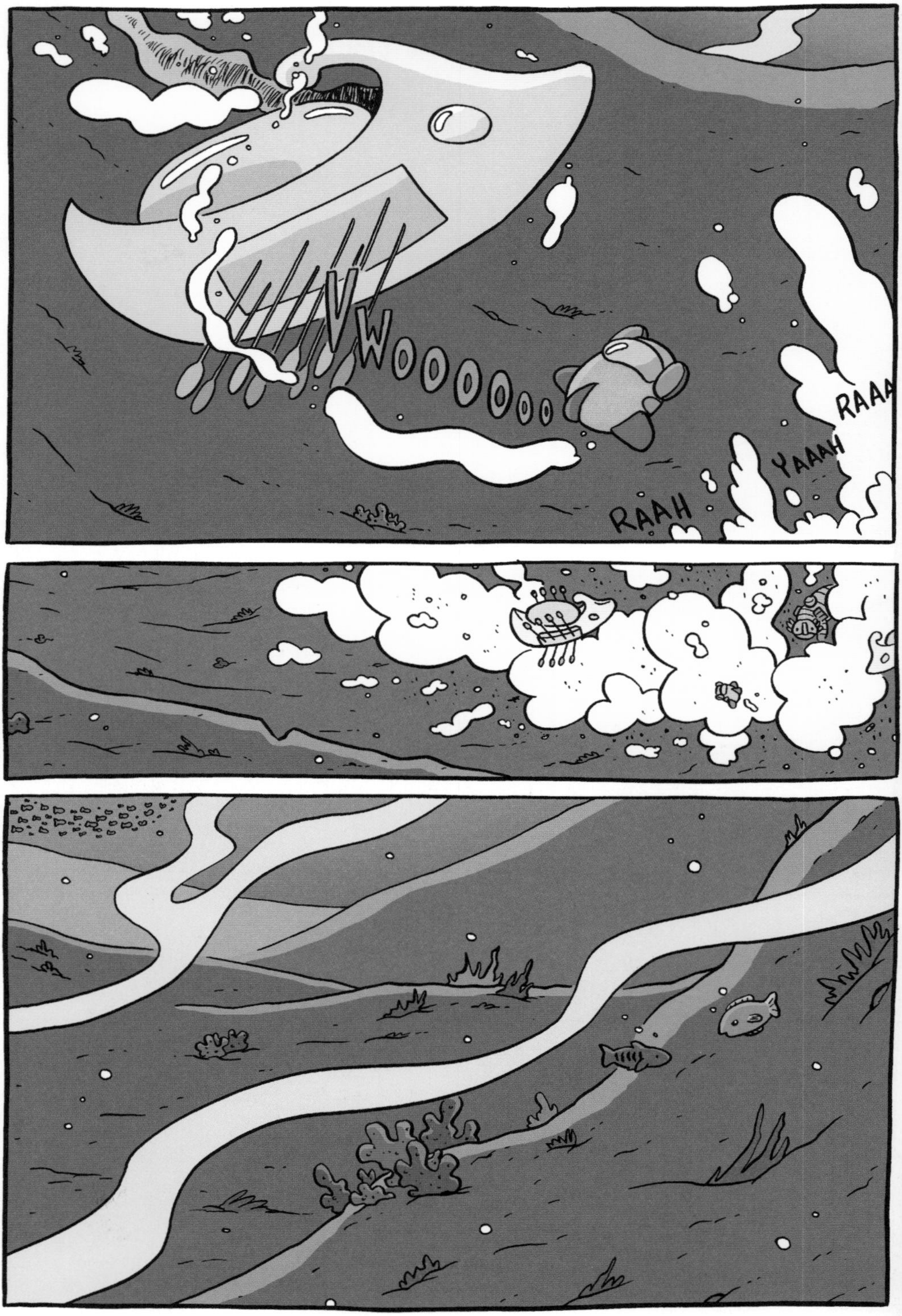
VWOOOOOoo
RAAA
YAAAH
RAAH

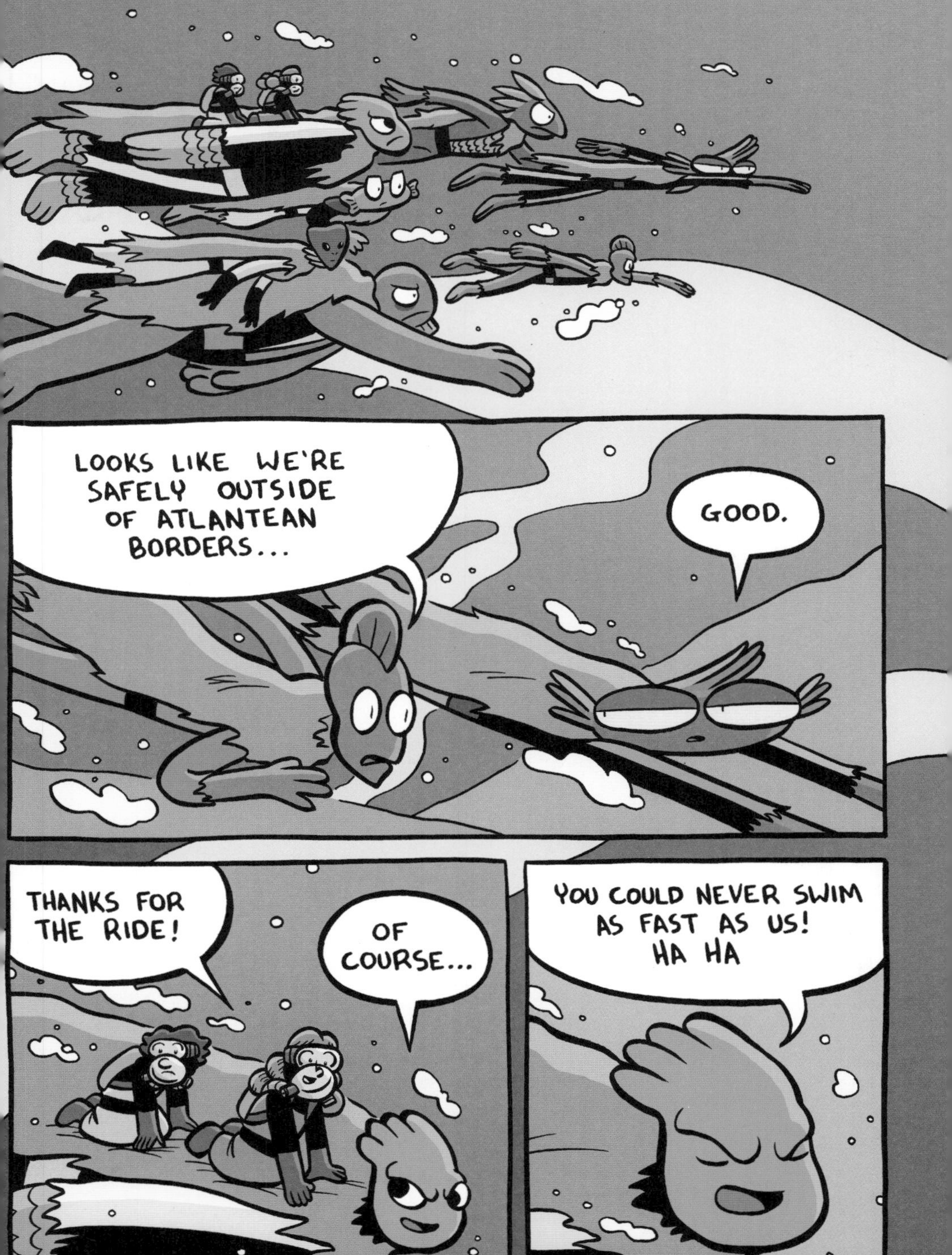
LOOKS LIKE WE'RE SAFELY OUTSIDE OF ATLANTEAN BORDERS...
GOOD.
THANKS FOR THE RIDE!
OF COURSE...
YOU COULD NEVER SWIM AS FAST AS US! HA HA

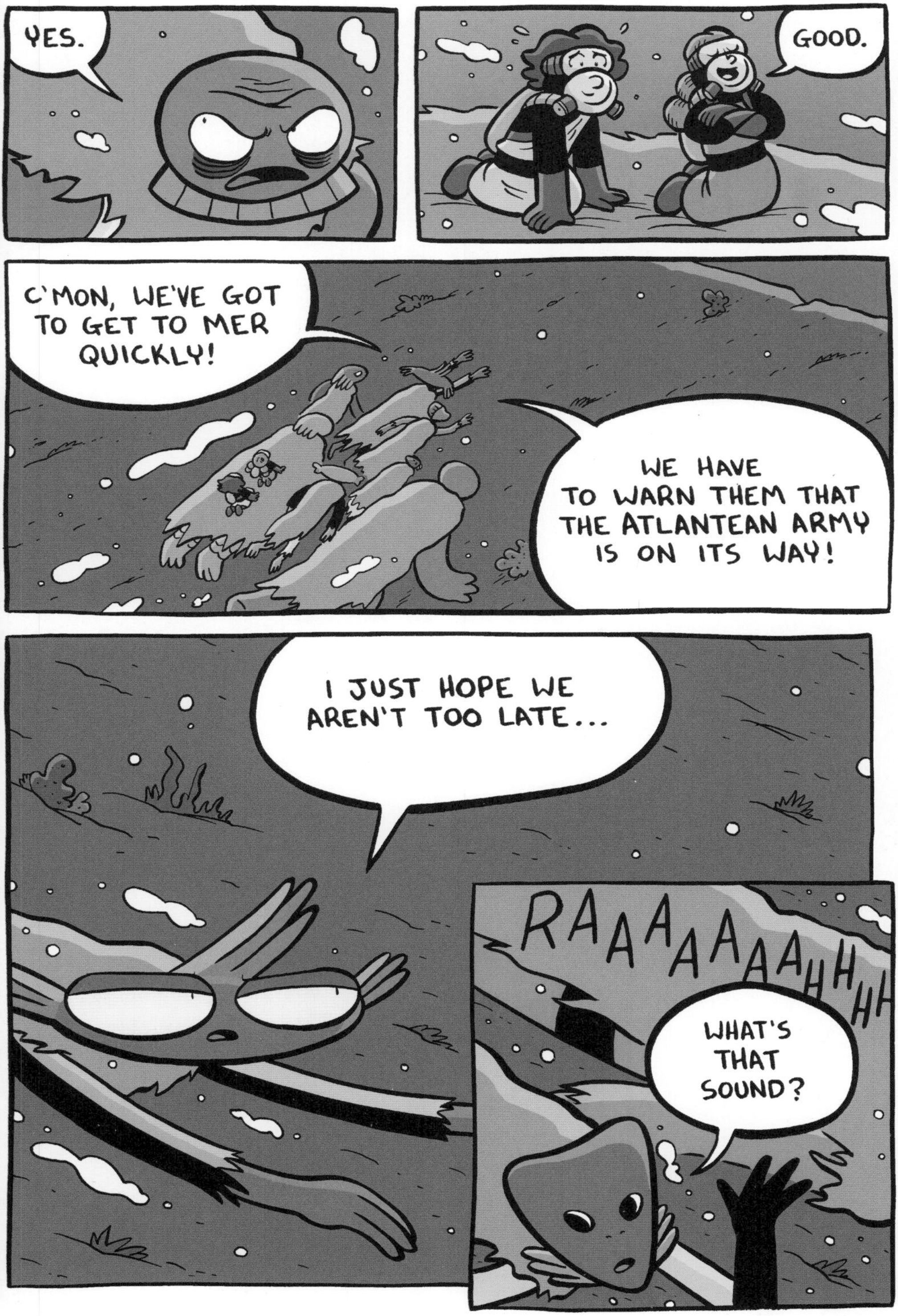
YES.
GOOD.
C'MON, WE'VE GOT TO GET TO MER QUICKLY!
WE HAVE TO WARN THEM THAT THE ATLANTEAN ARMY IS ON ITS WAY!
I JUST HOPE WE AREN'T TOO LATE...
RAAAAAAAAHHHH
WHAT'S THAT SOUND?

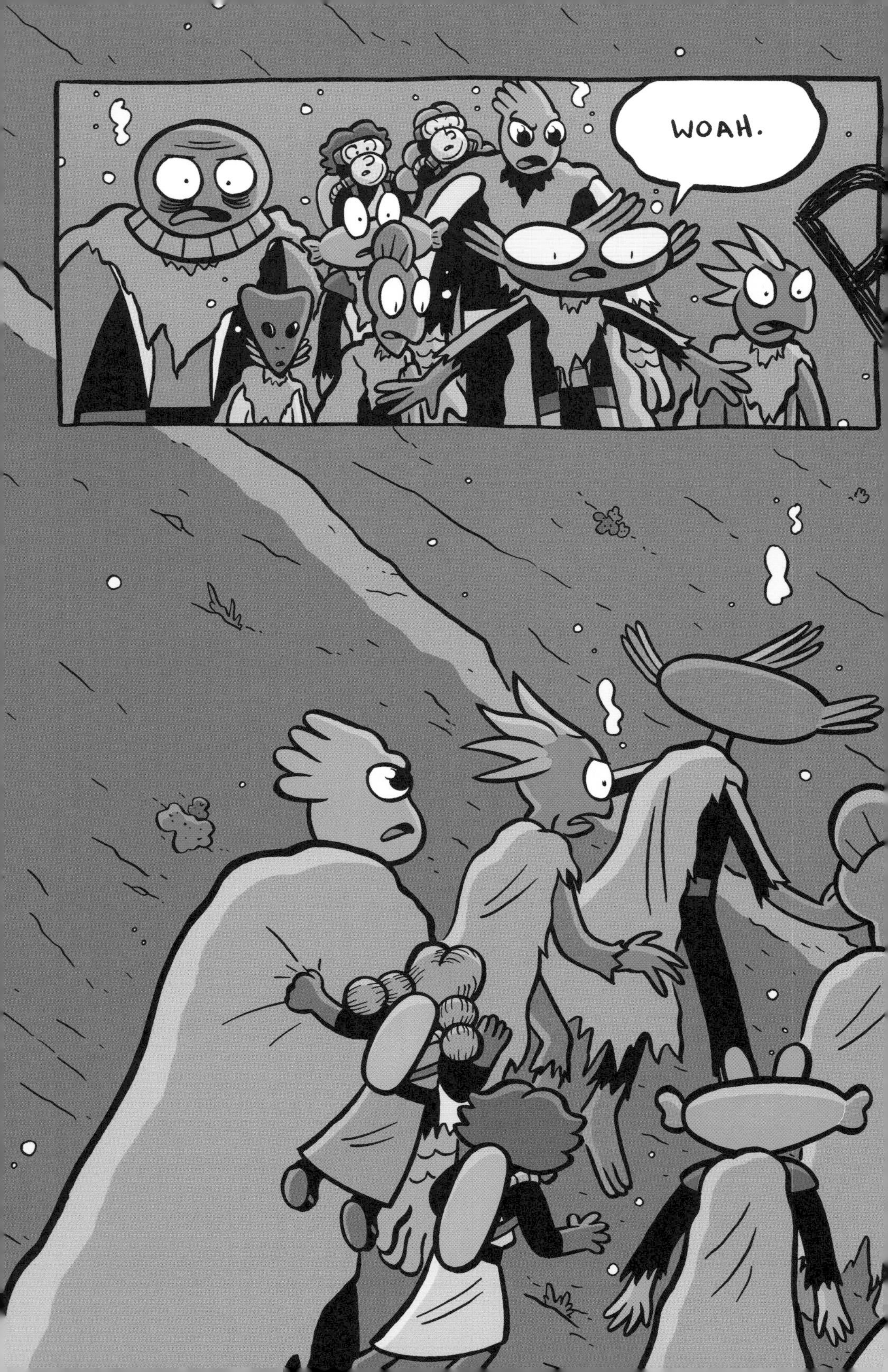
WOAH.

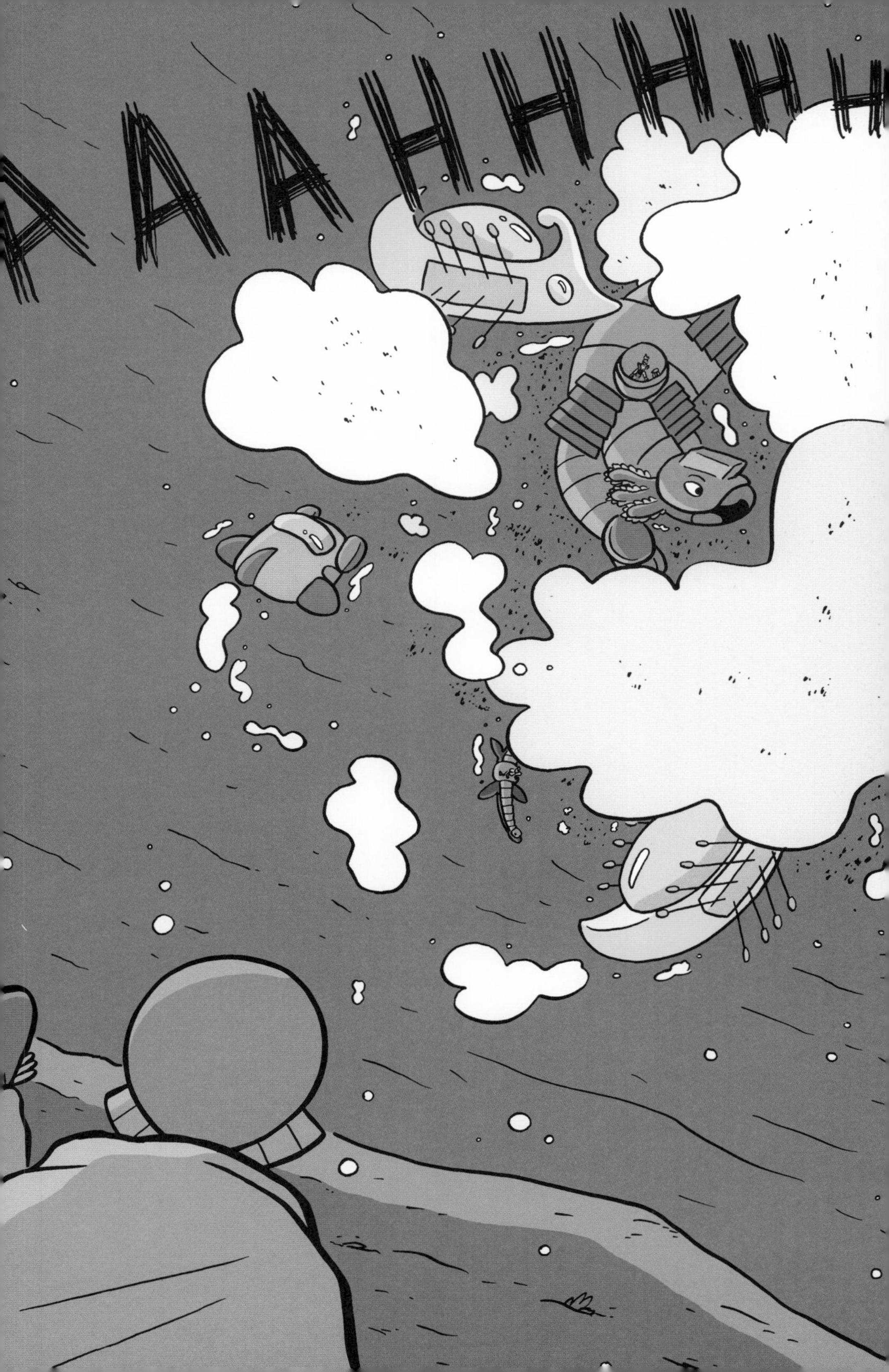
AAAHHHHH

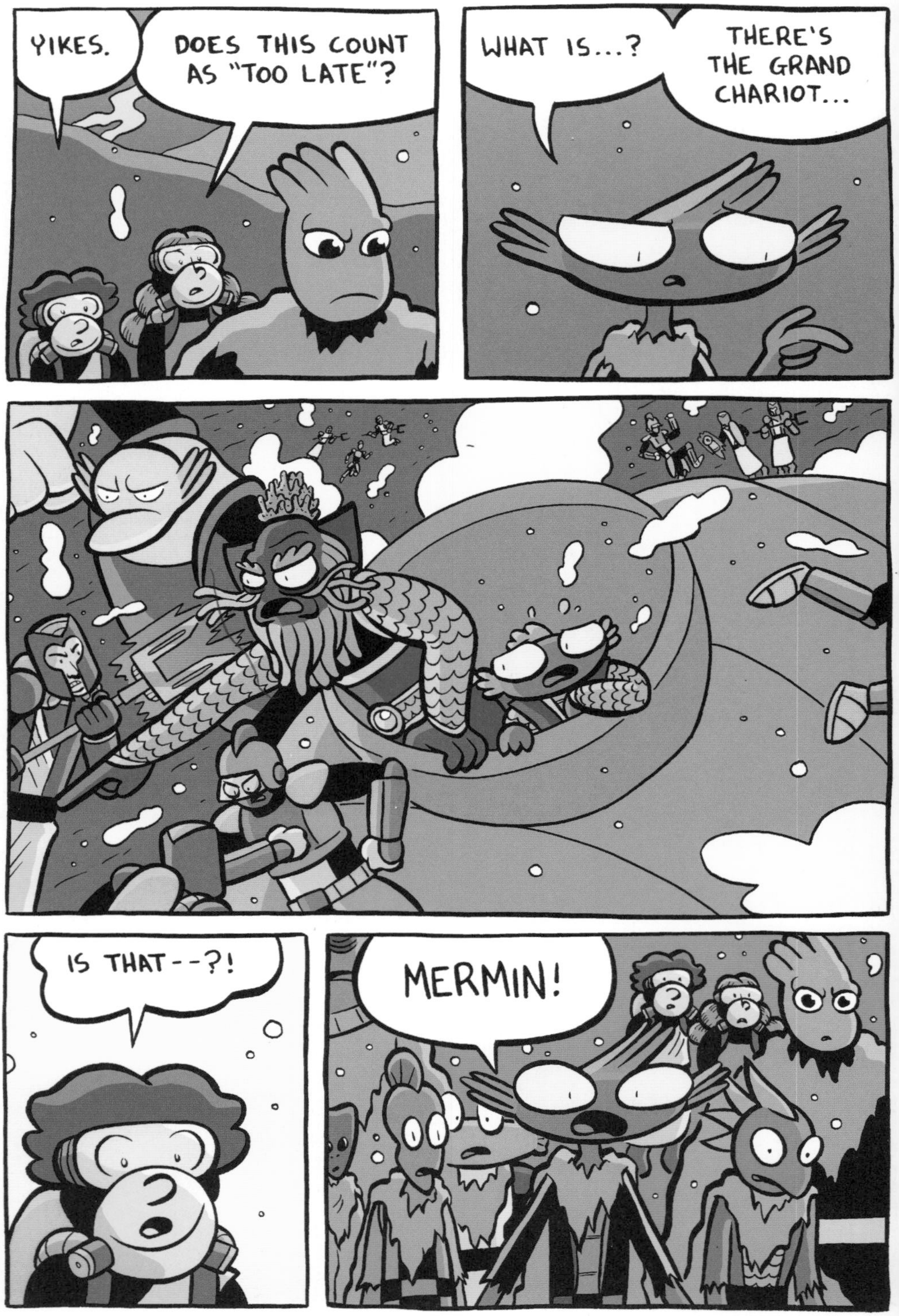
YIKES.
DOES THIS COUNT AS "TOO LATE"?
WHAT IS...?
THERE'S THE GRAND CHARIOT...
IS THAT--?!
MERMIN!

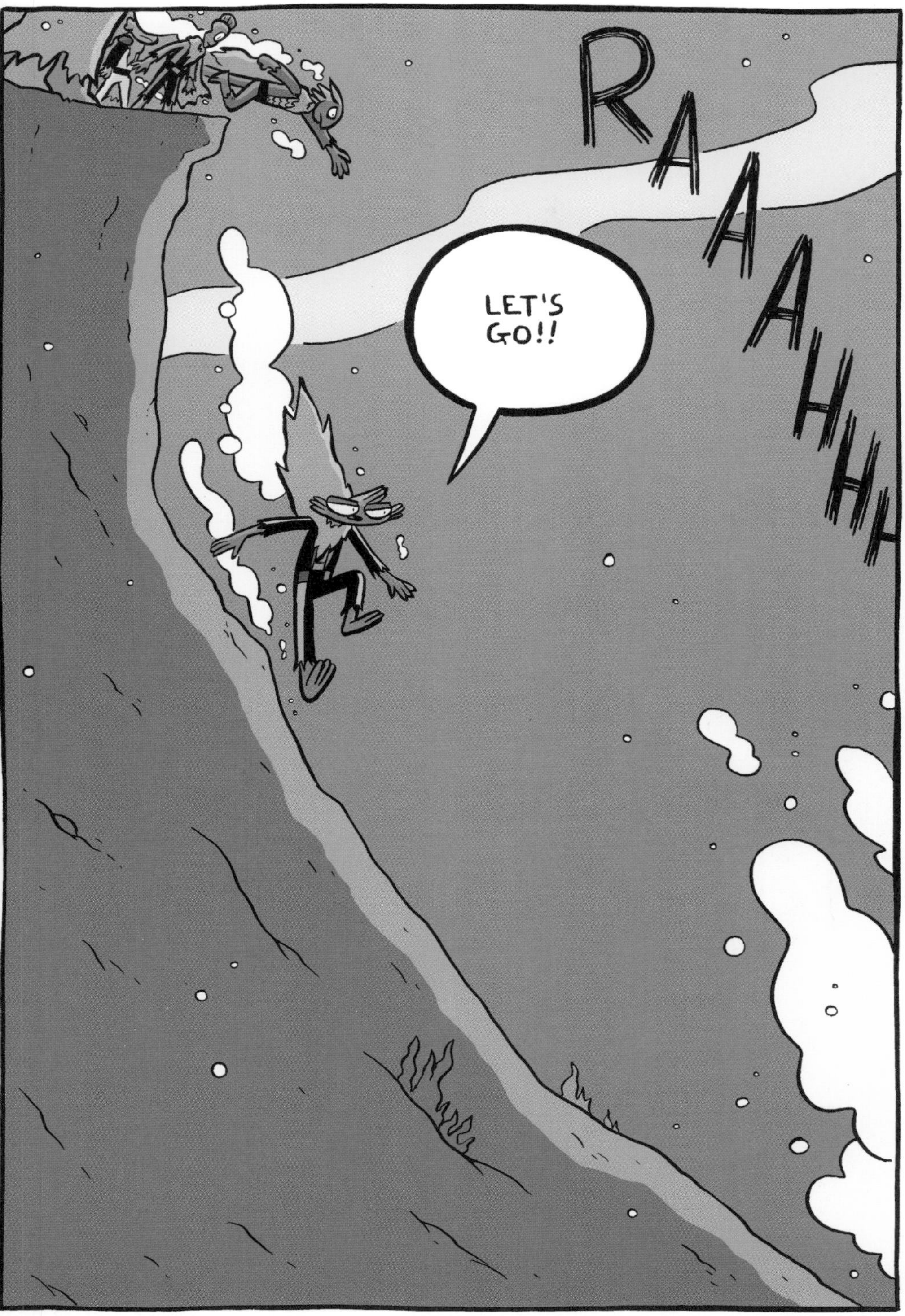
RAAAAHHH
LET'S GO!!

CHAPTER FOUR

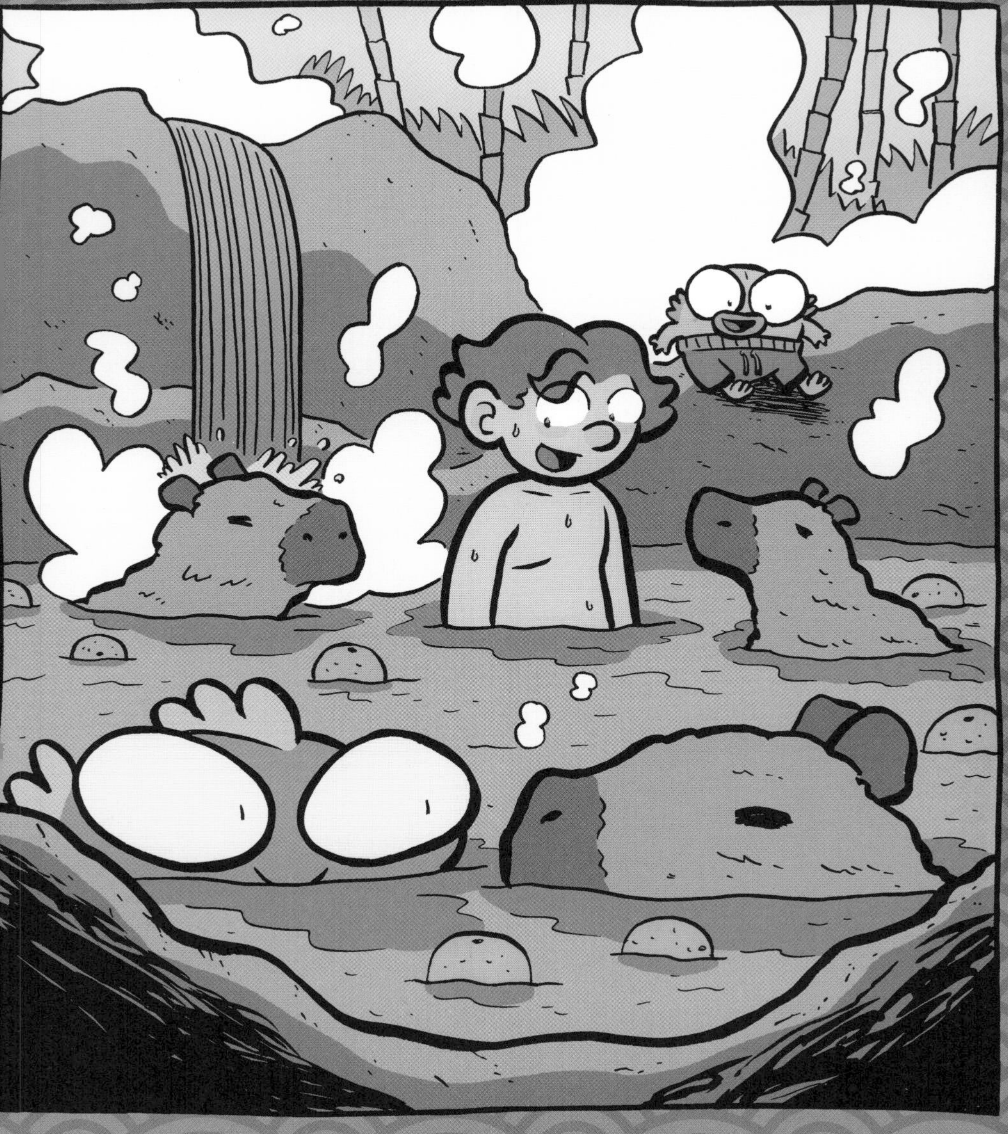

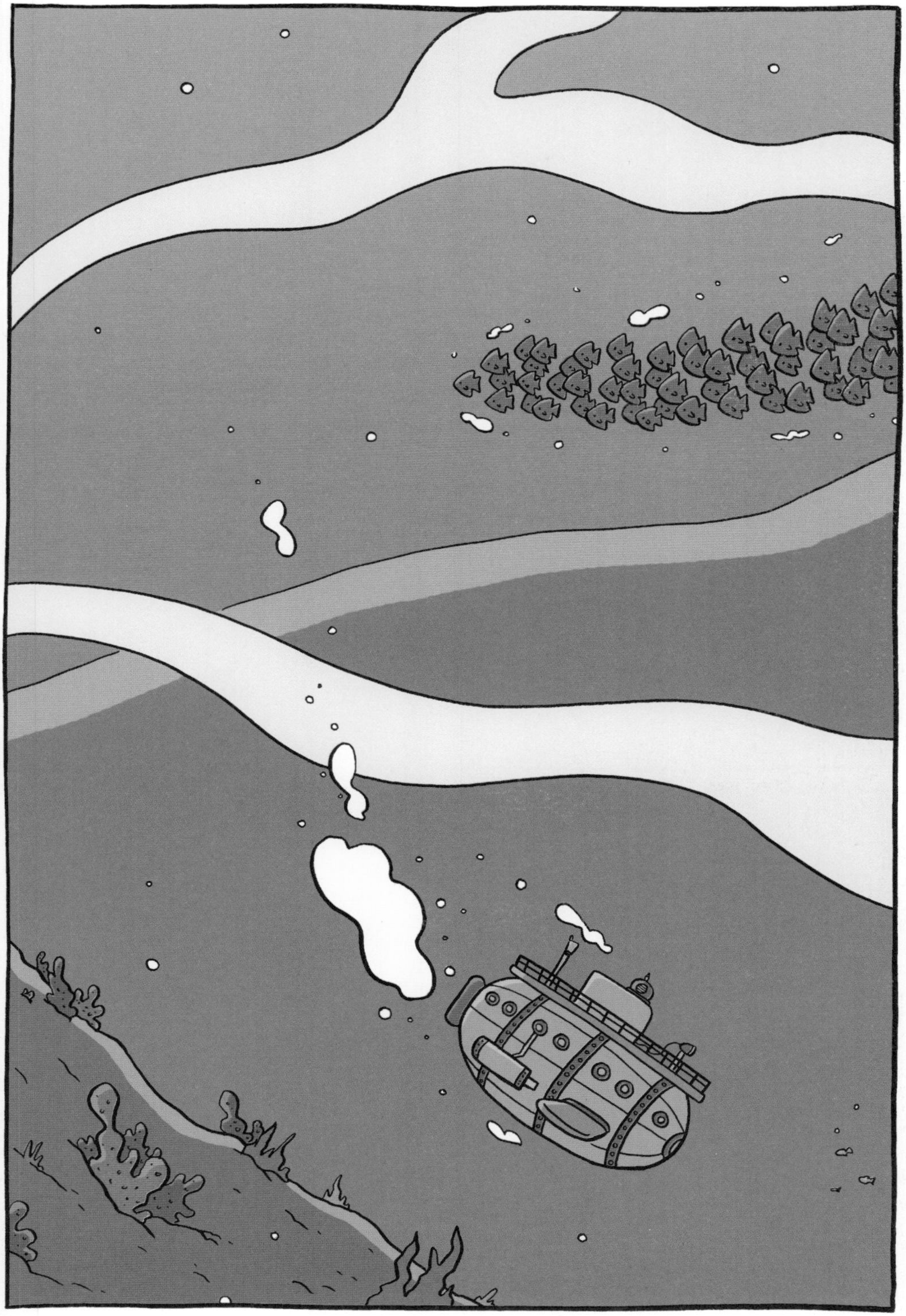

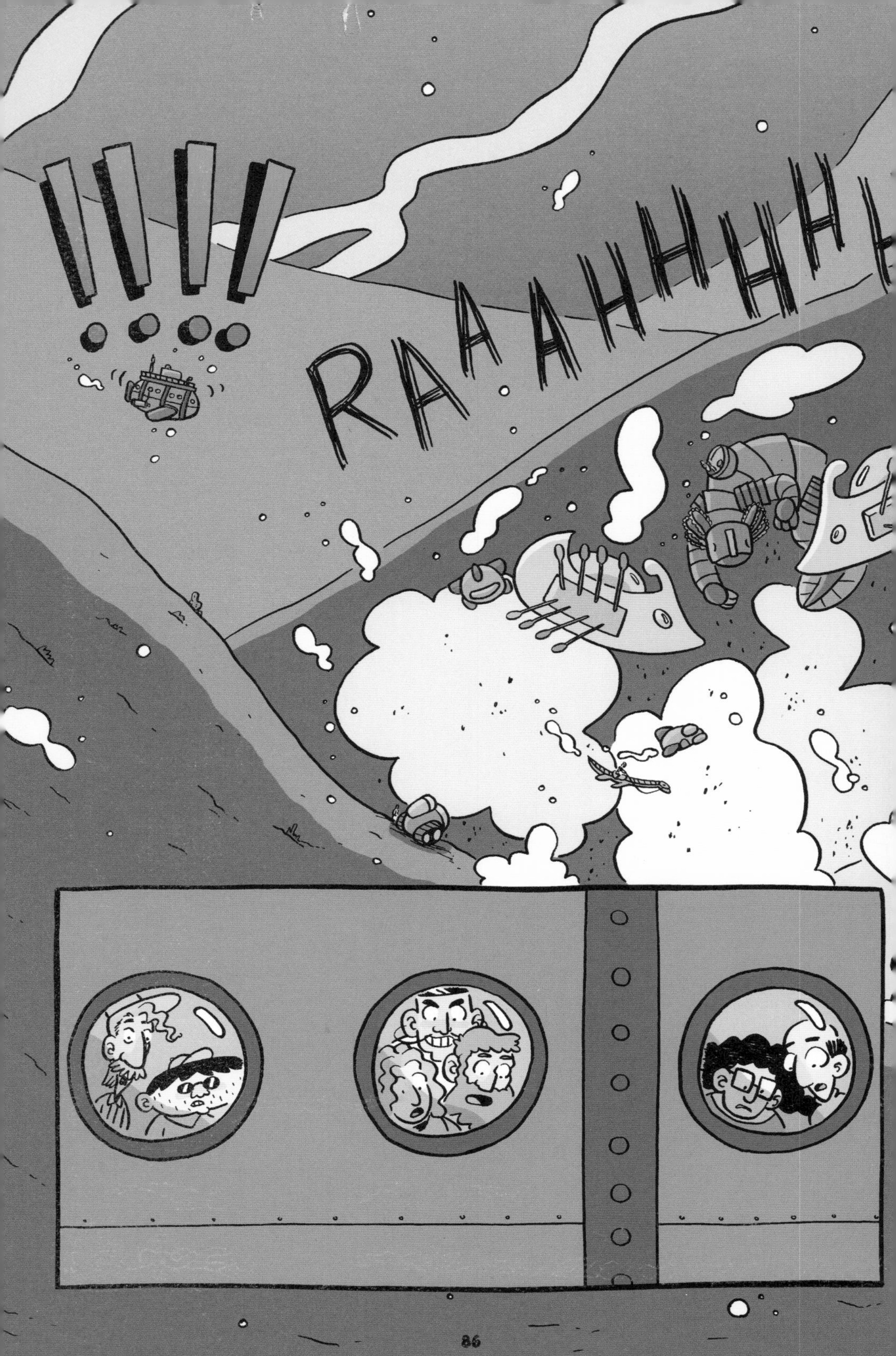
!!!!
RAAAHHHHHH

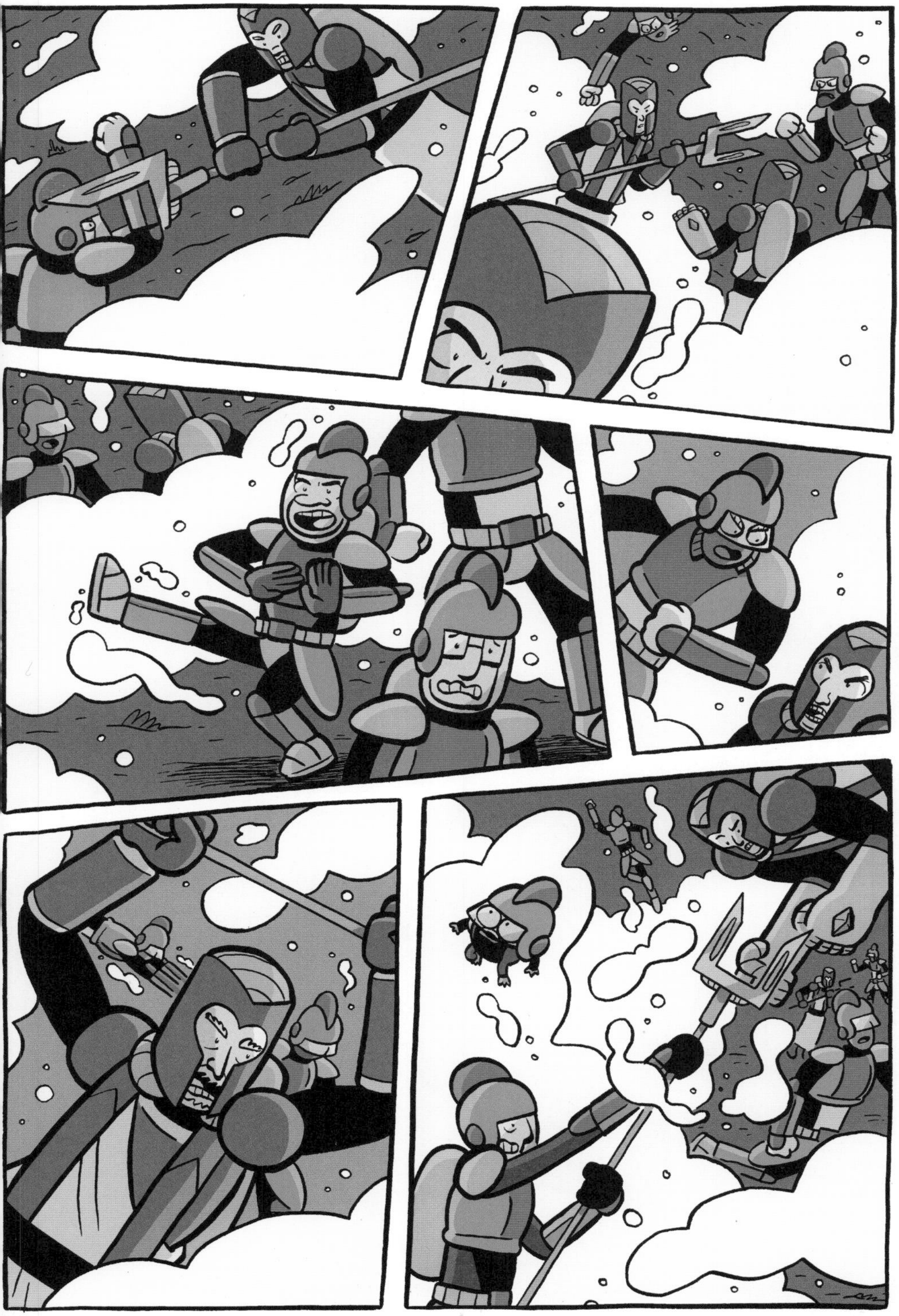

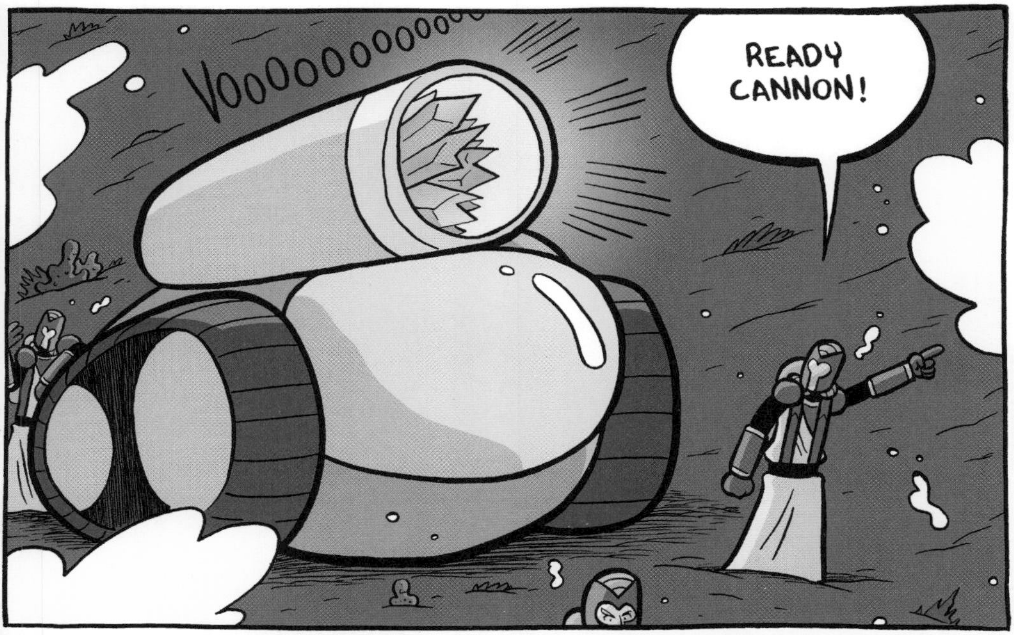
VOOOOOOOOOOO
READY CANNON!

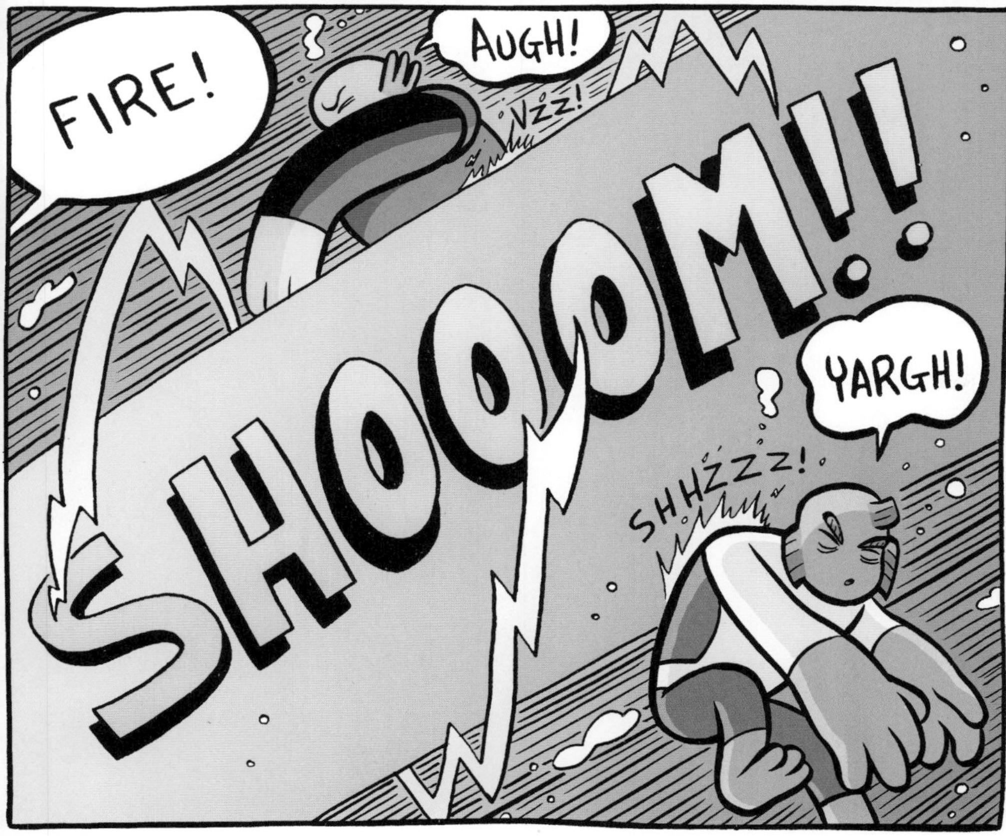
FIRE!
AUGH!
VZZ!
SHOOOOM!!!
YARGH!
SHHZZZ!

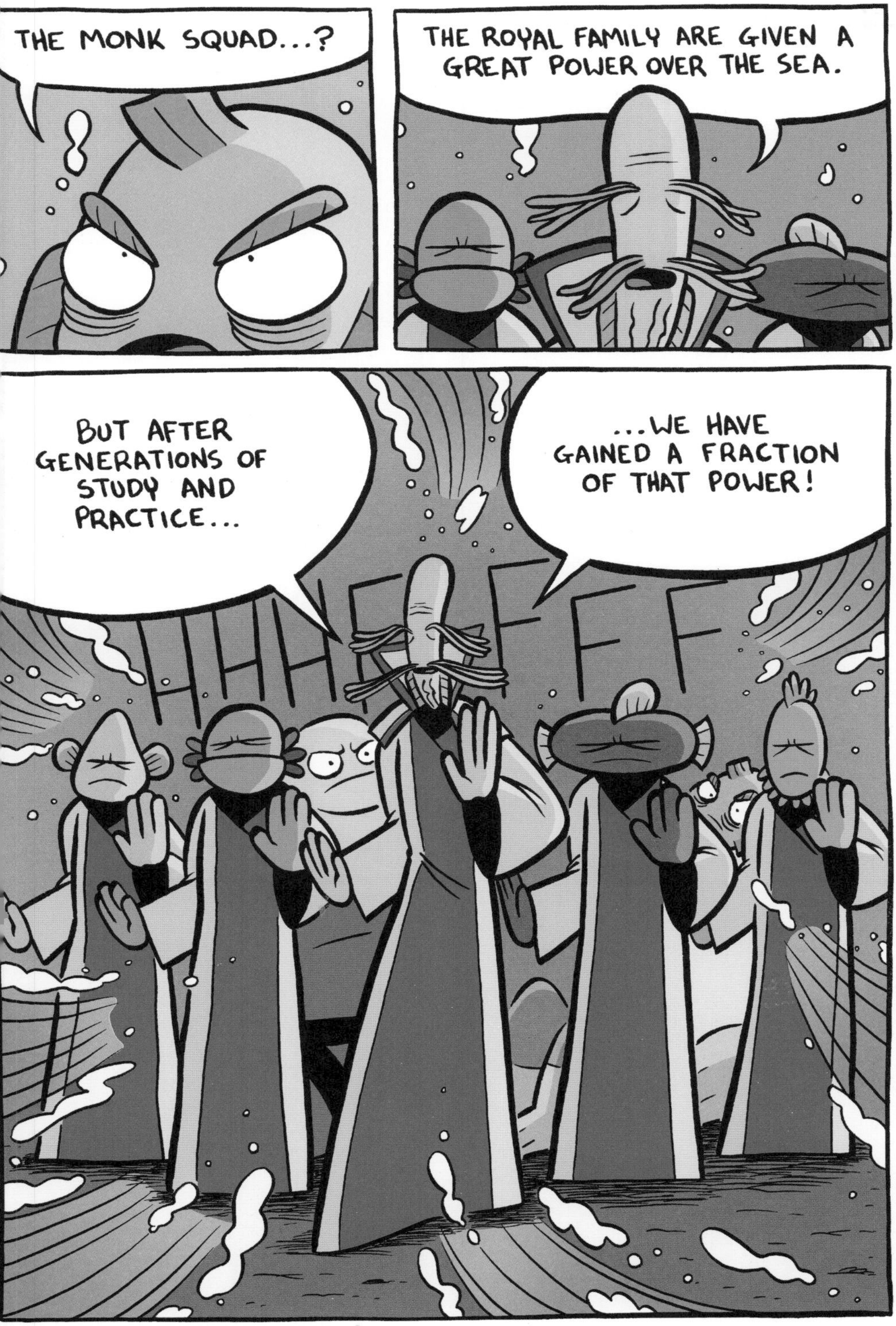
THE MONK SQUAD...?
THE ROYAL FAMILY ARE GIVEN A GREAT POWER OVER THE SEA.
BUT AFTER GENERATIONS OF STUDY AND PRACTICE...
...WE HAVE GAINED A FRACTION OF THAT POWER!
HHHFFFF

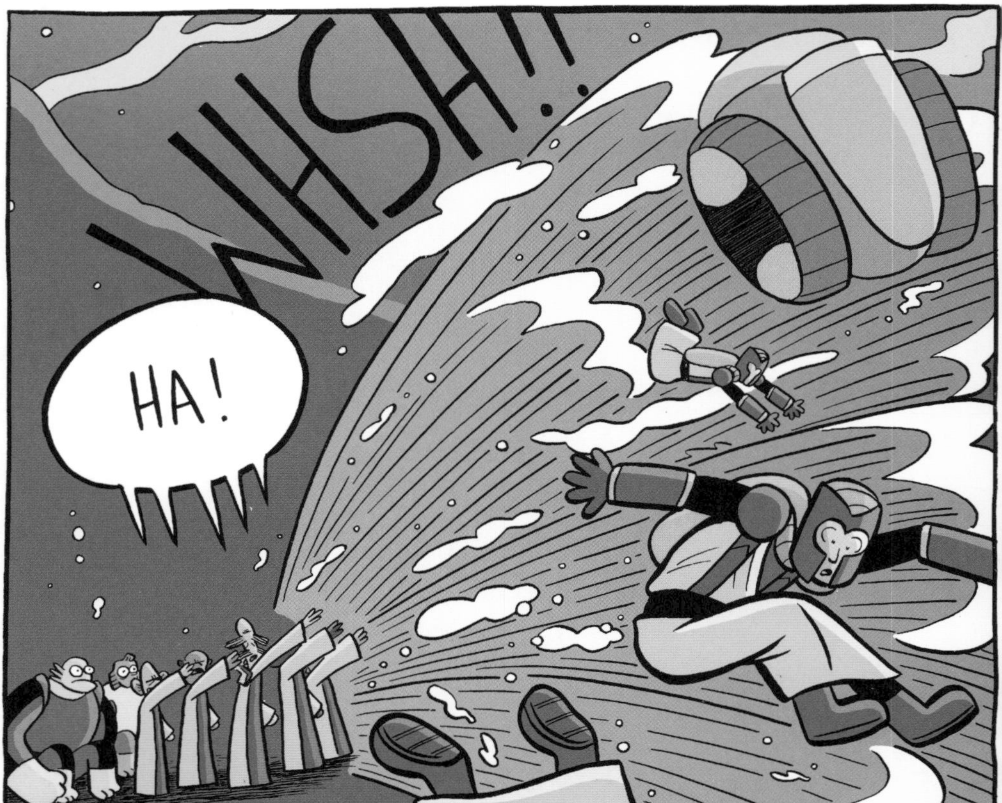
WHSH!!
HA!

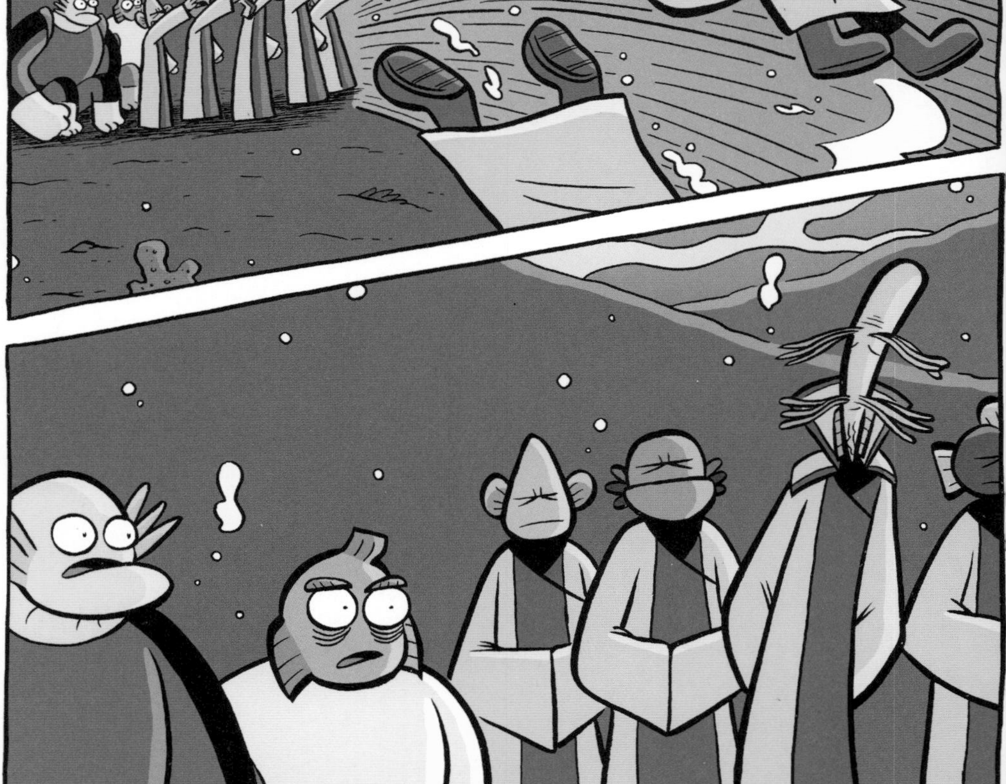

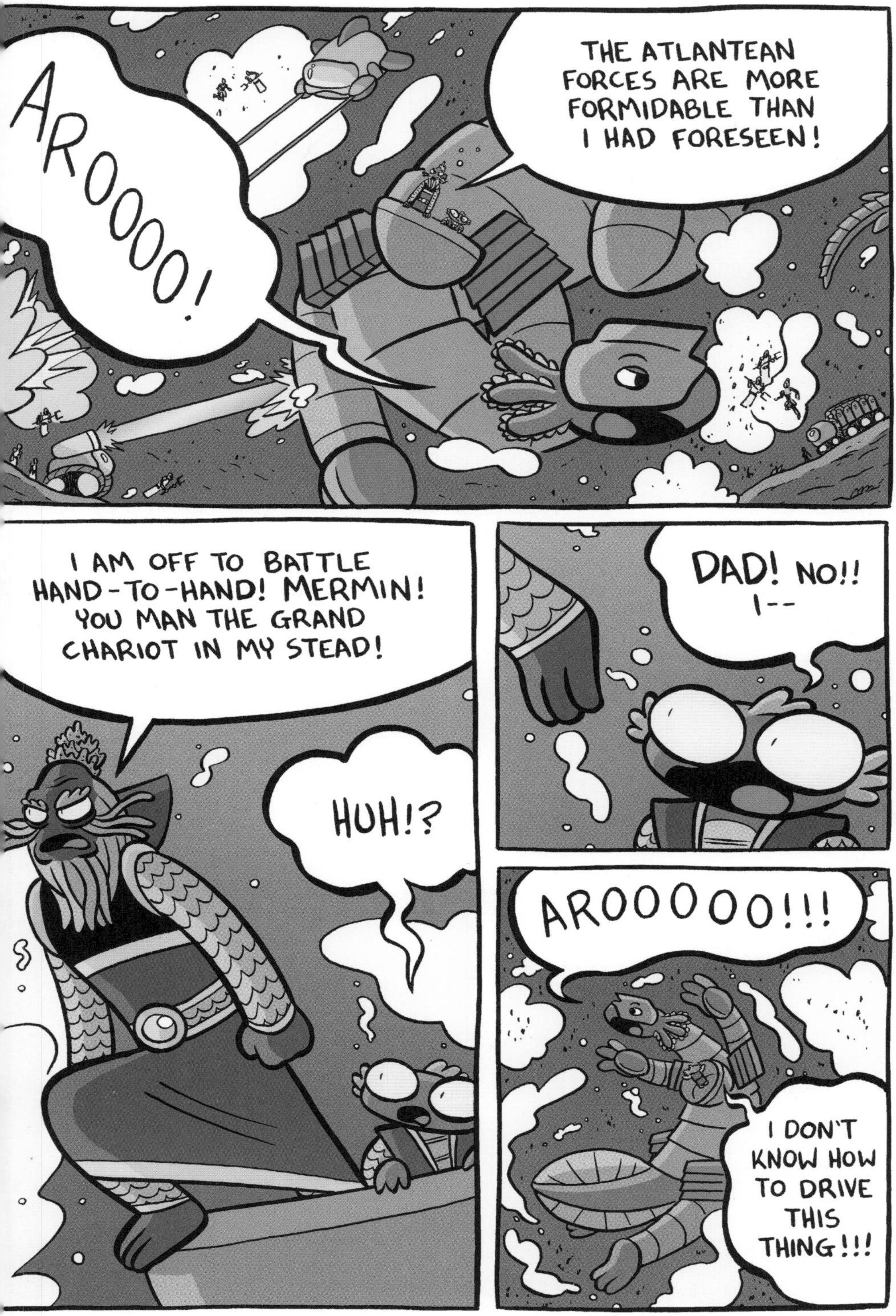
AROOOO!
THE ATLANTEAN FORCES ARE MORE FORMIDABLE THAN I HAD FORESEEN!
I AM OFF TO BATTLE HAND-TO-HAND! MERMIN! YOU MAN THE GRAND CHARIOT IN MY STEAD!
HUH!?
DAD! NO!! I--
AROOOOO!!!
I DON'T KNOW HOW TO DRIVE THIS THING!!!

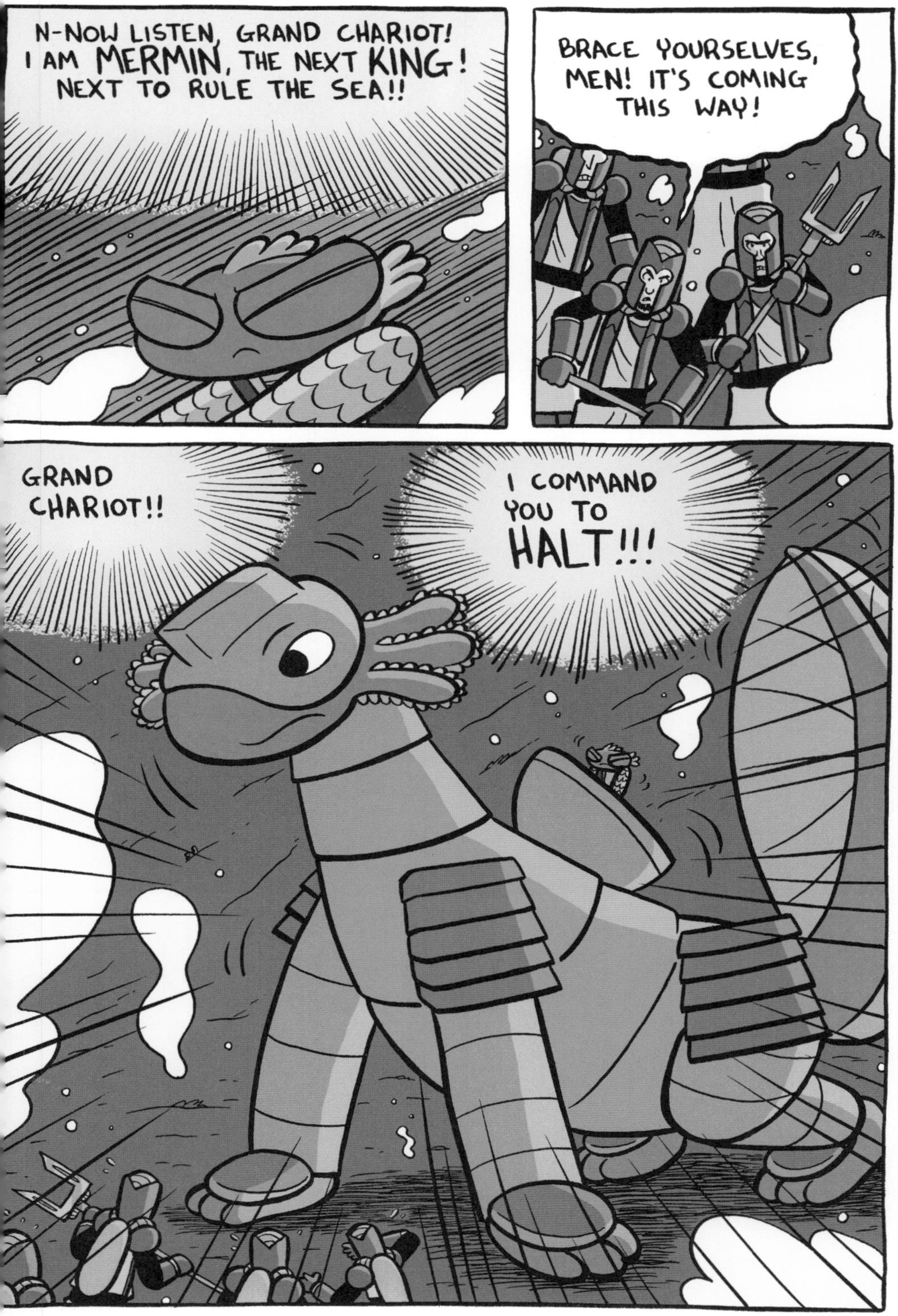
N-NOW LISTEN, GRAND CHARIOT! I AM MERMIN, THE NEXT KING! NEXT TO RULE THE SEA!!
BRACE YOURSELVES, MEN! IT'S COMING THIS WAY!
GRAND CHARIOT!!
I COMMAND YOU TO HALT!!!

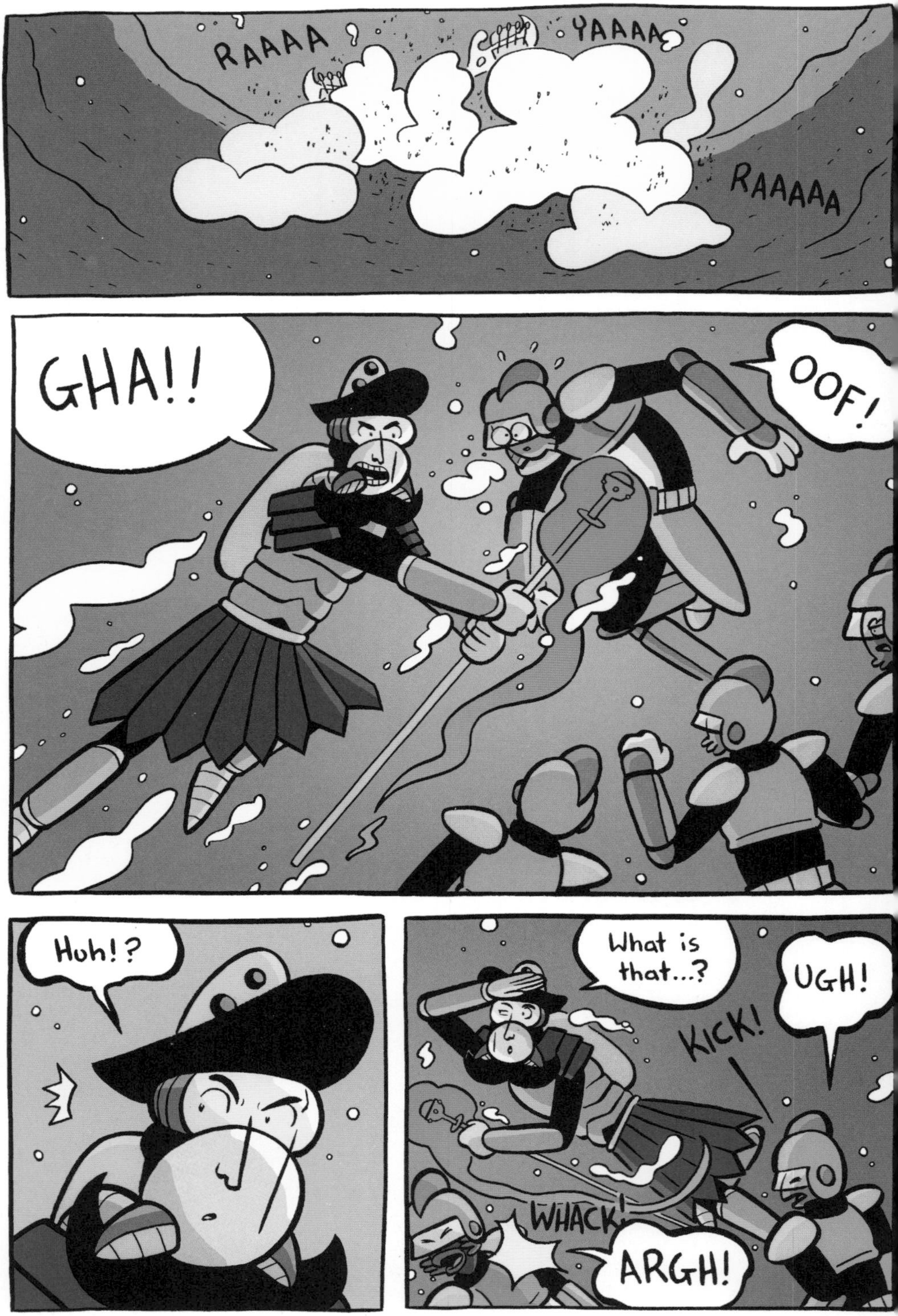
RAAAA
YAAAA
RAAAAA
GHA!!
OOF!
Huh!?
What is that...?
UGH!
KICK!
WHACK!
ARGH!

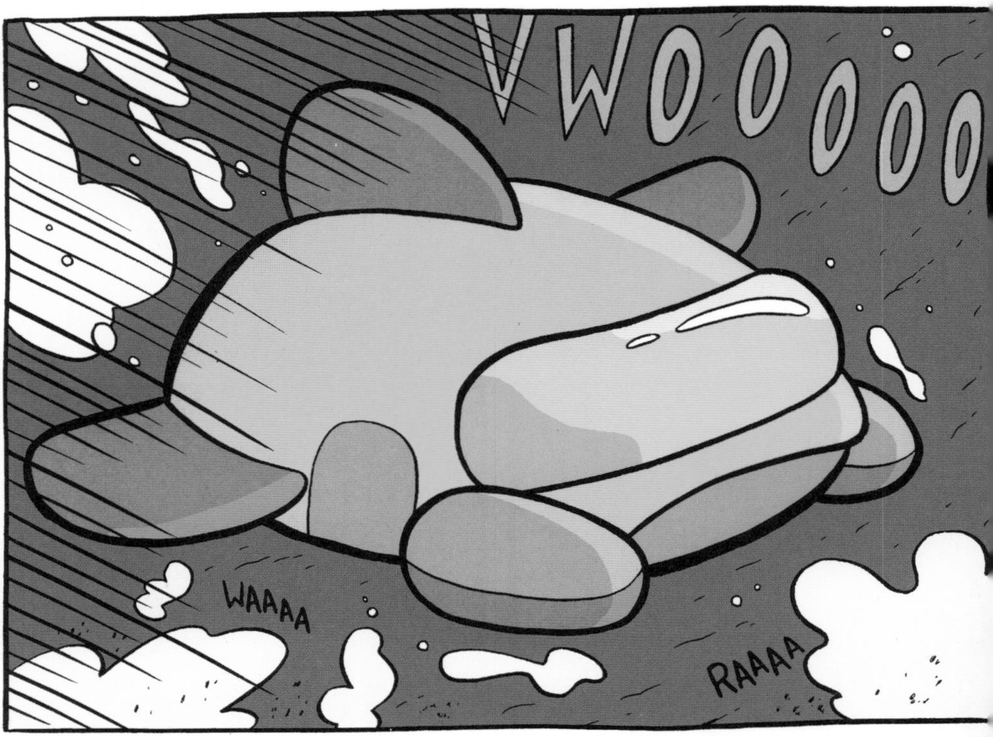
VWOOOOO
WAAAA
RAAAA

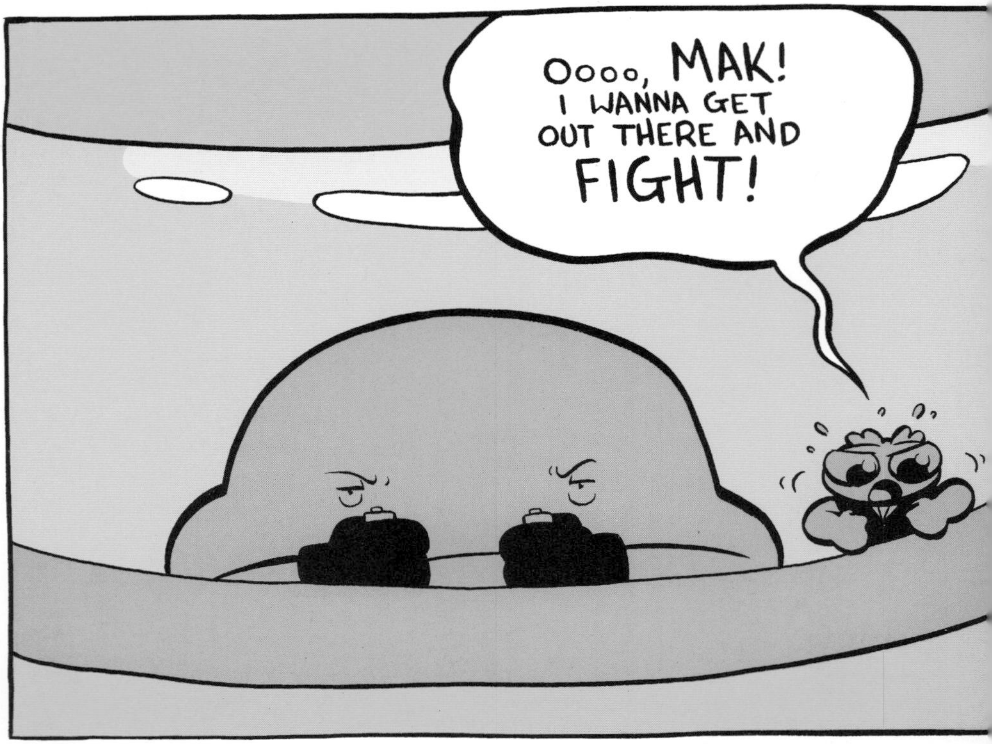
Oooo, MAK! I WANNA GET OUT THERE AND FIGHT!

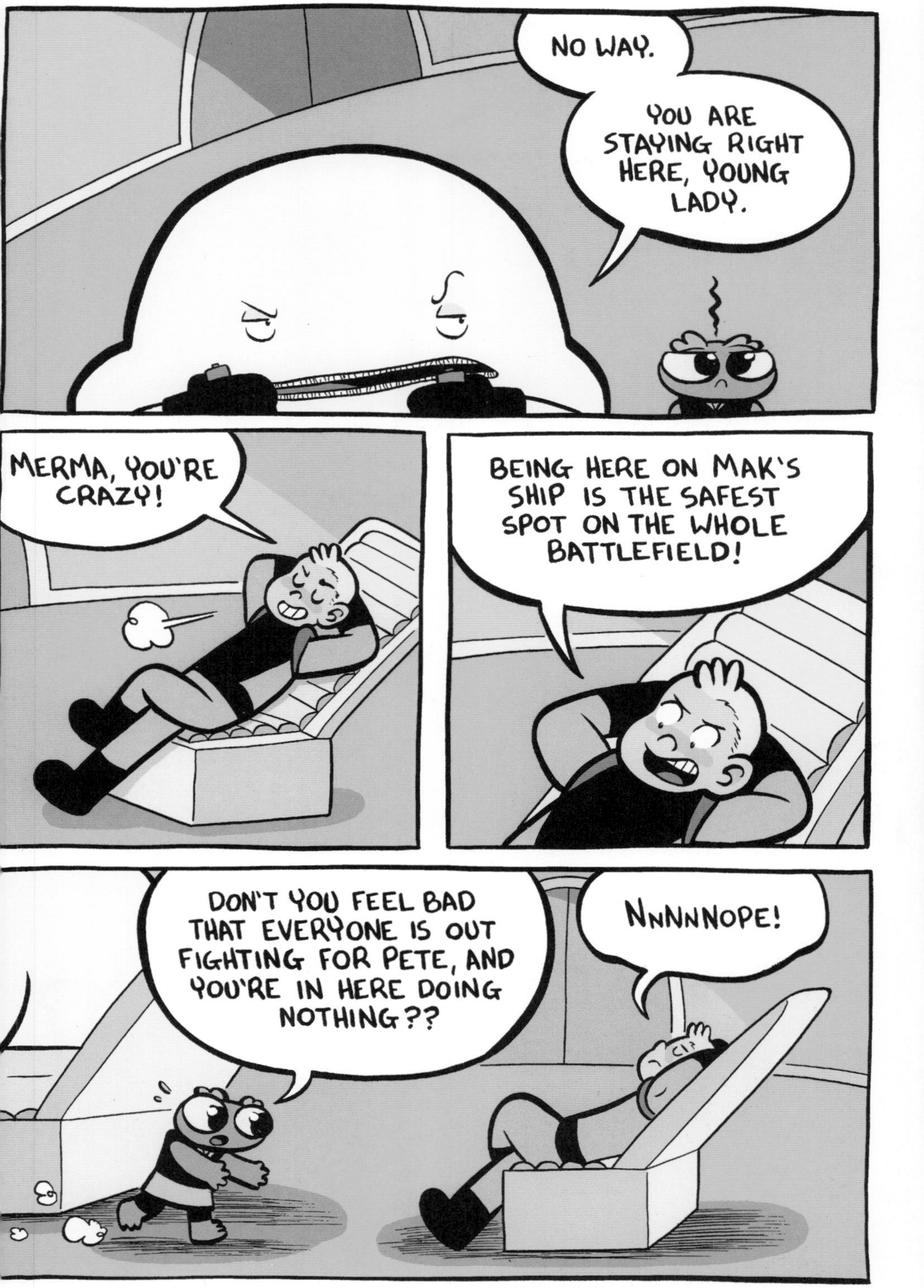

NO WAY.
YOU ARE STAYING RIGHT HERE, YOUNG LADY.
MERMA, YOU'RE CRAZY!
BEING HERE ON MAK'S SHIP IS THE SAFEST SPOT ON THE WHOLE BATTLEFIELD!
DON'T YOU FEEL BAD THAT EVERYONE IS OUT FIGHTING FOR PETE, AND YOU'RE IN HERE DOING NOTHING??
NNNNNOPE!

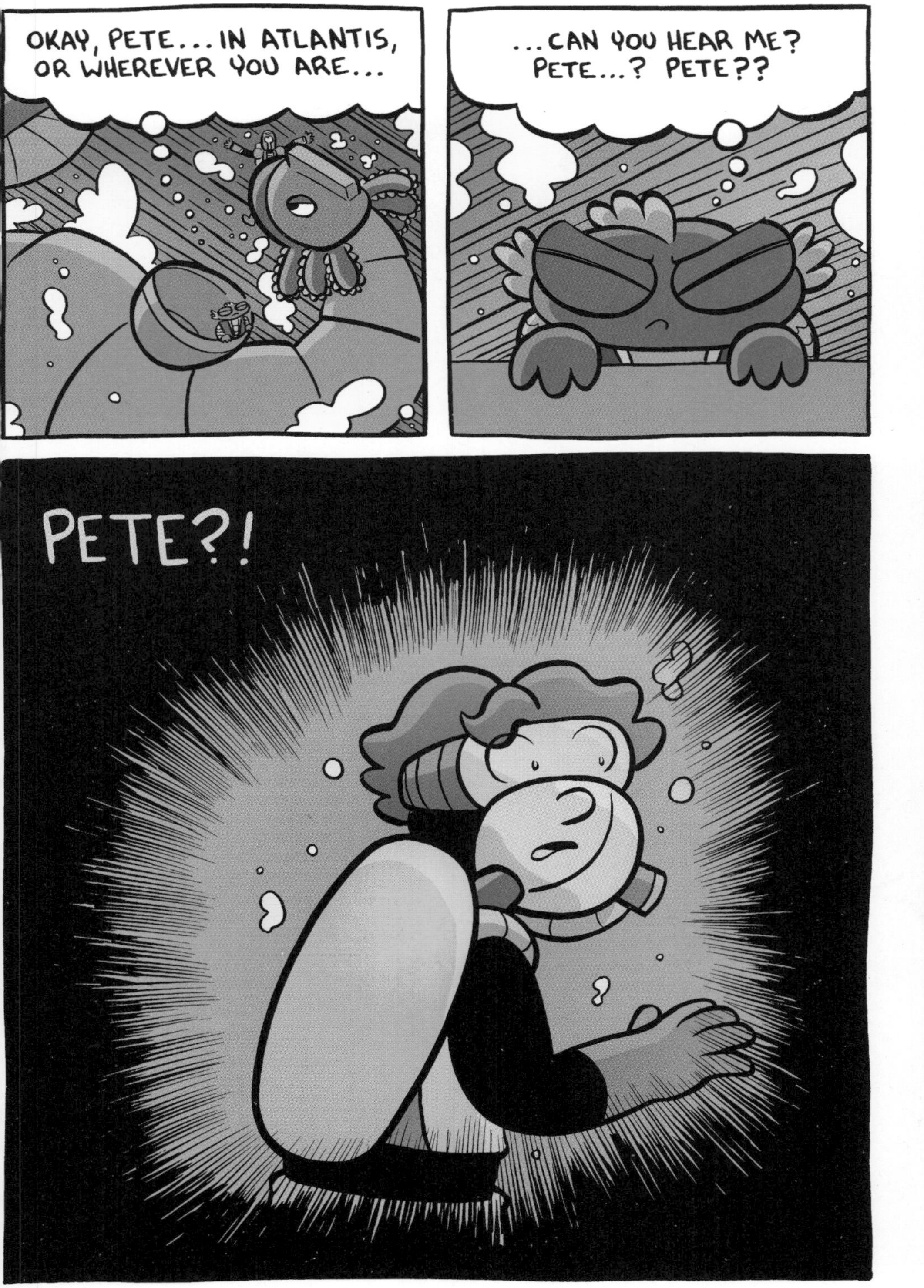
OKAY, PETE... IN ATLANTIS, OR WHEREVER YOU ARE...
...CAN YOU HEAR ME? PETE...? PETE??
PETE?!

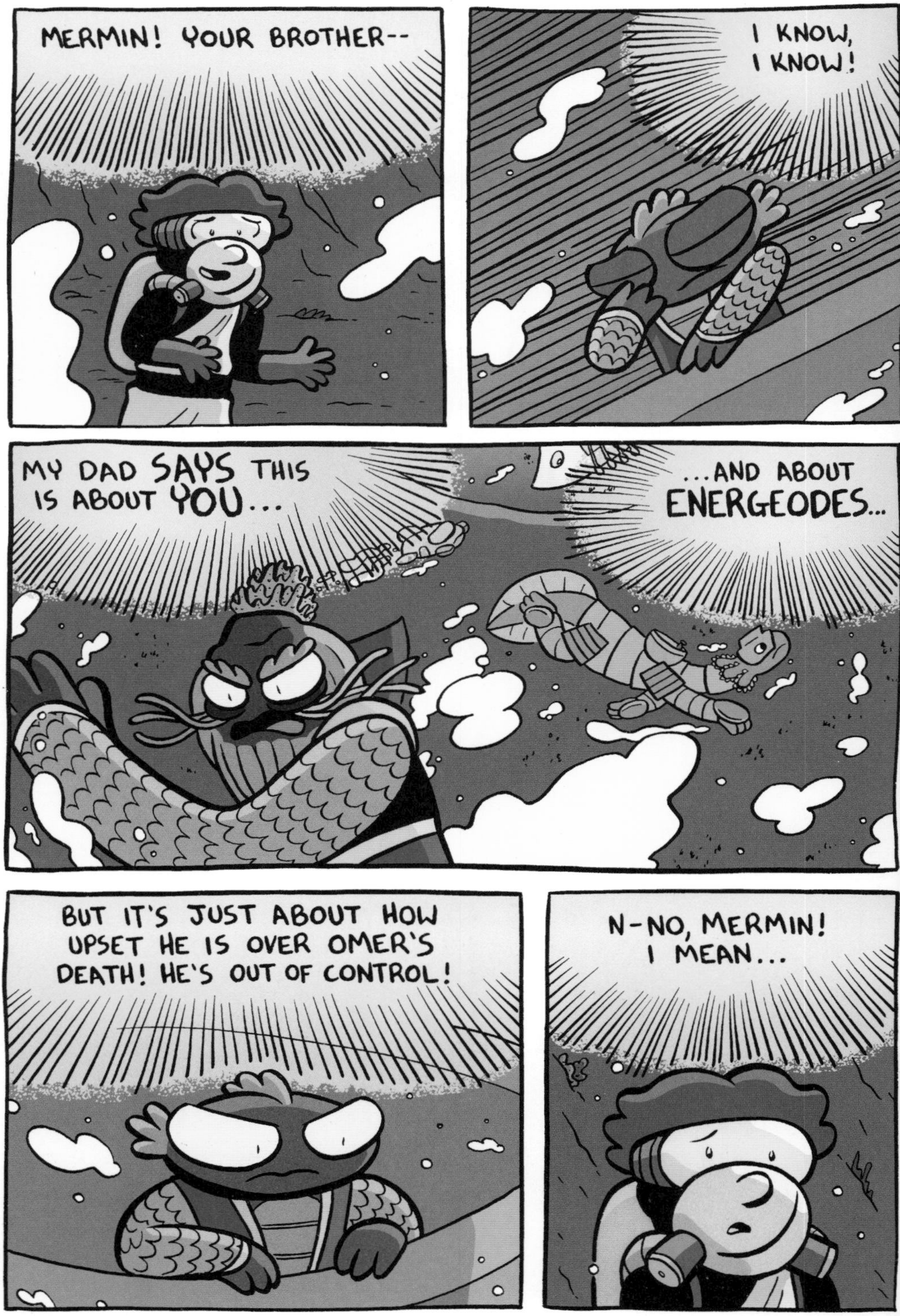
MERMIN! YOUR BROTHER--
I KNOW, I KNOW!
MY DAD SAYS THIS IS ABOUT YOU...
...AND ABOUT ENERGEODES...
BUT IT'S JUST ABOUT HOW UPSET HE IS OVER OMER'S DEATH! HE'S OUT OF CONTROL!
N-NO, MERMIN! I MEAN...

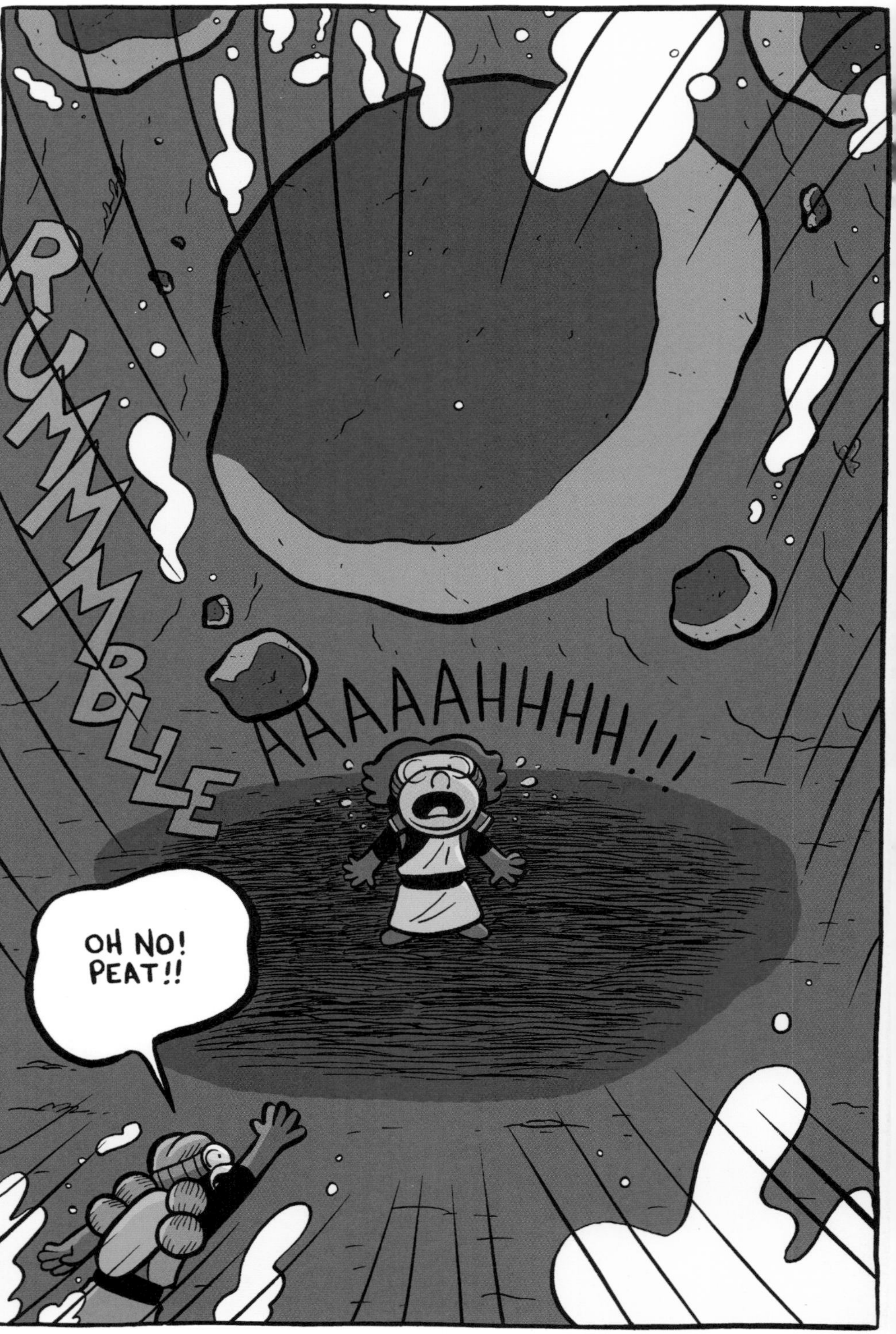
RUMMMMBLLE
AAAAAHHHHH!!!
OH NO! PEAT!!

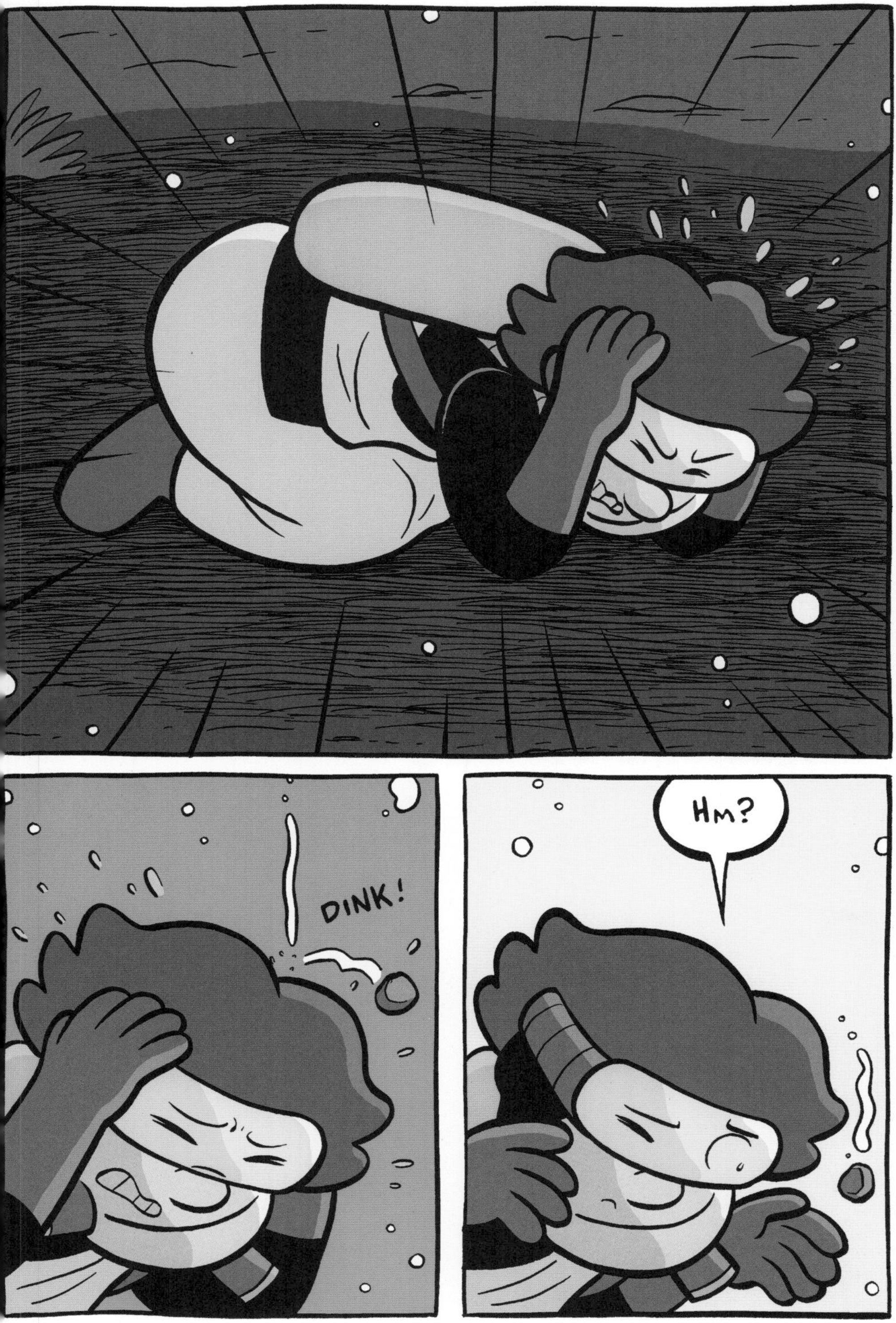
DINK!
HM?

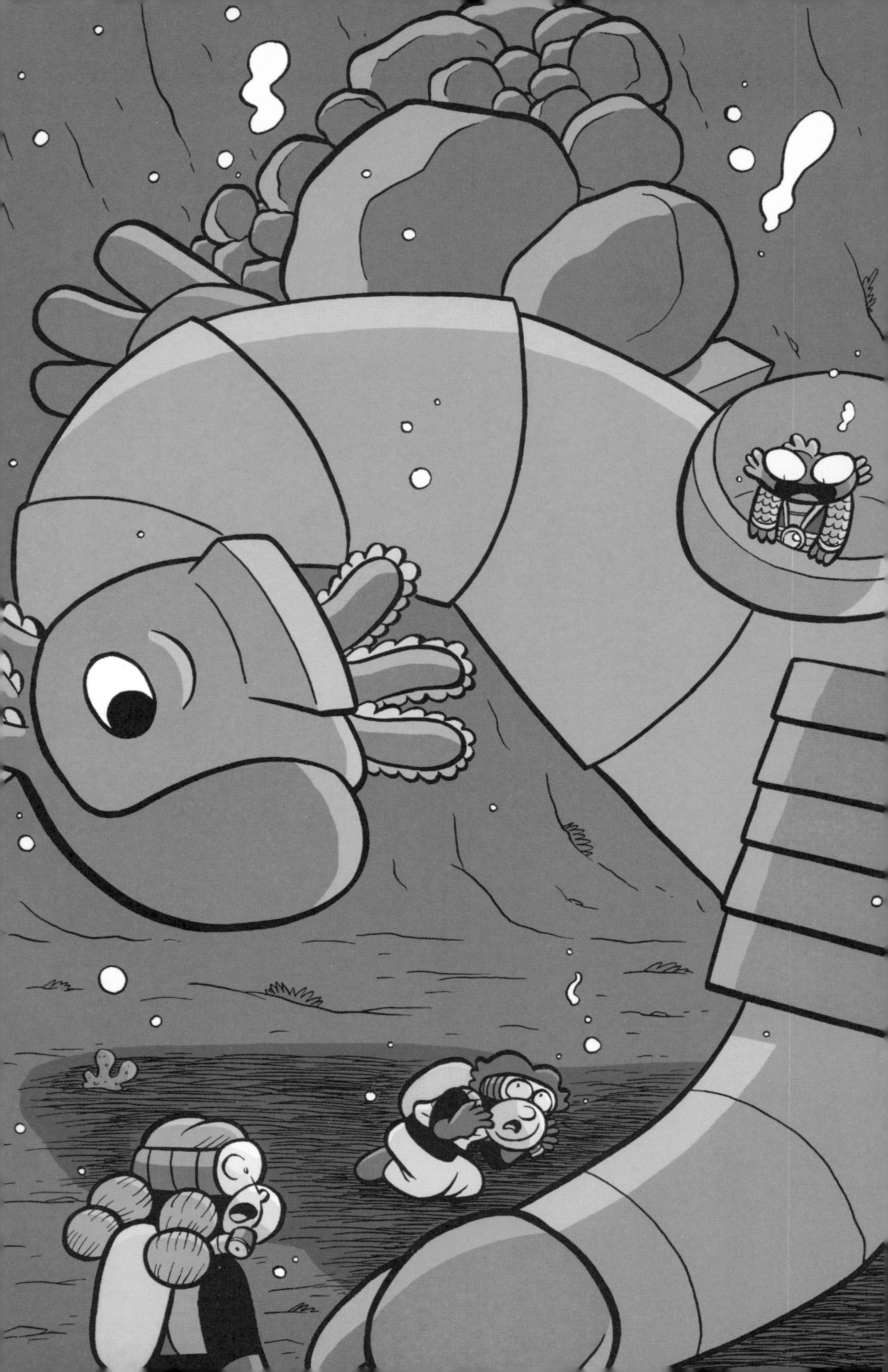

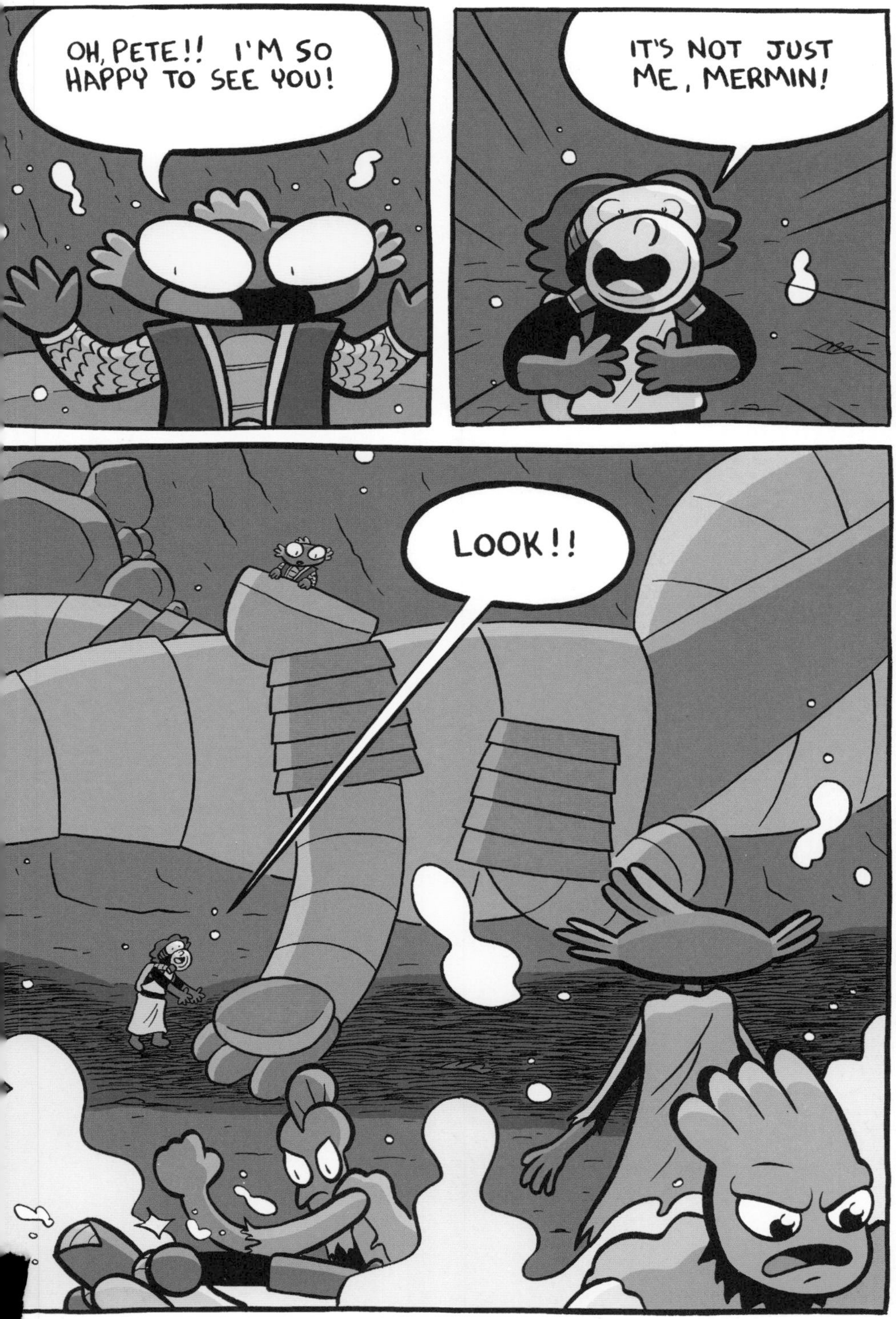
OH, PETE!! I'M SO HAPPY TO SEE YOU!
IT'S NOT JUST ME, MERMIN!
LOOK!!

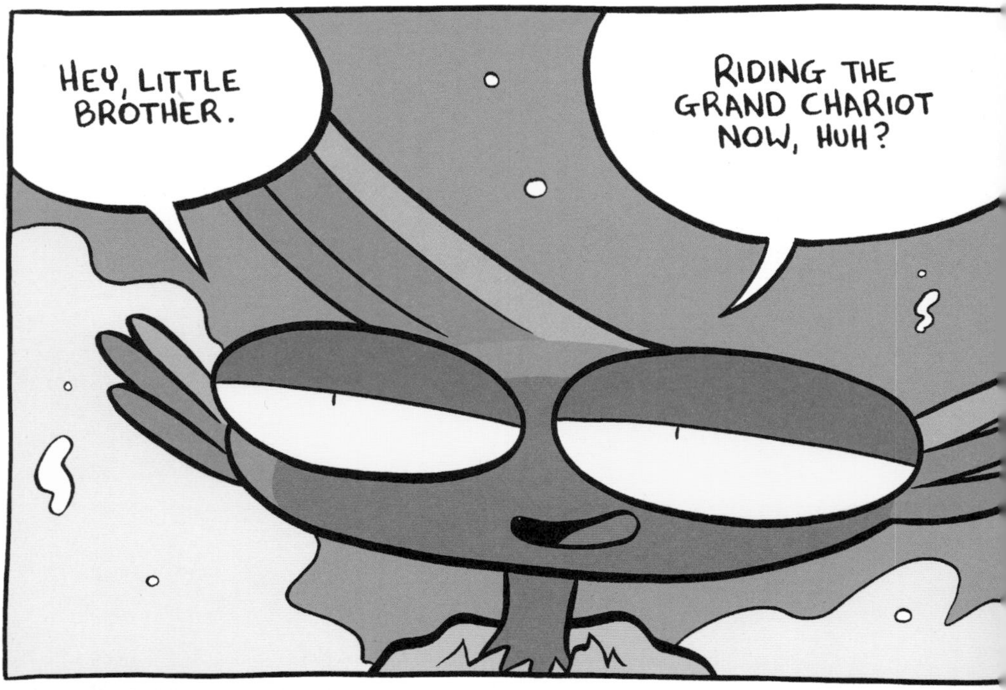
HEY, LITTLE BROTHER.
RIDING THE GRAND CHARIOT NOW, HUH?

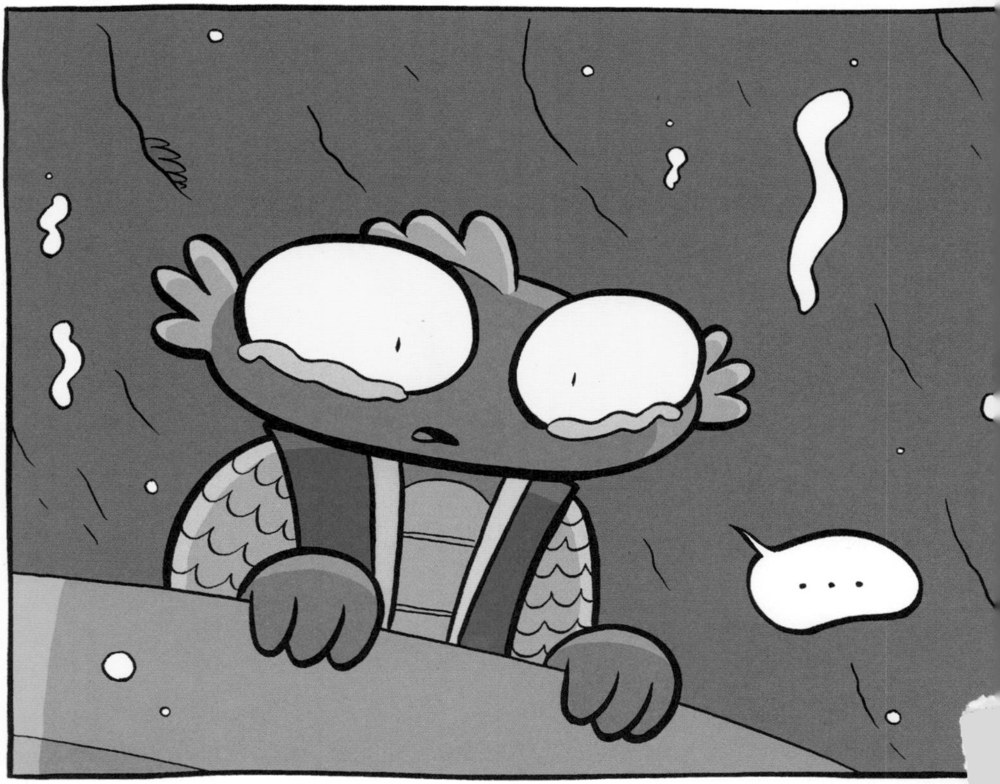
...

CHAPTER FIVE

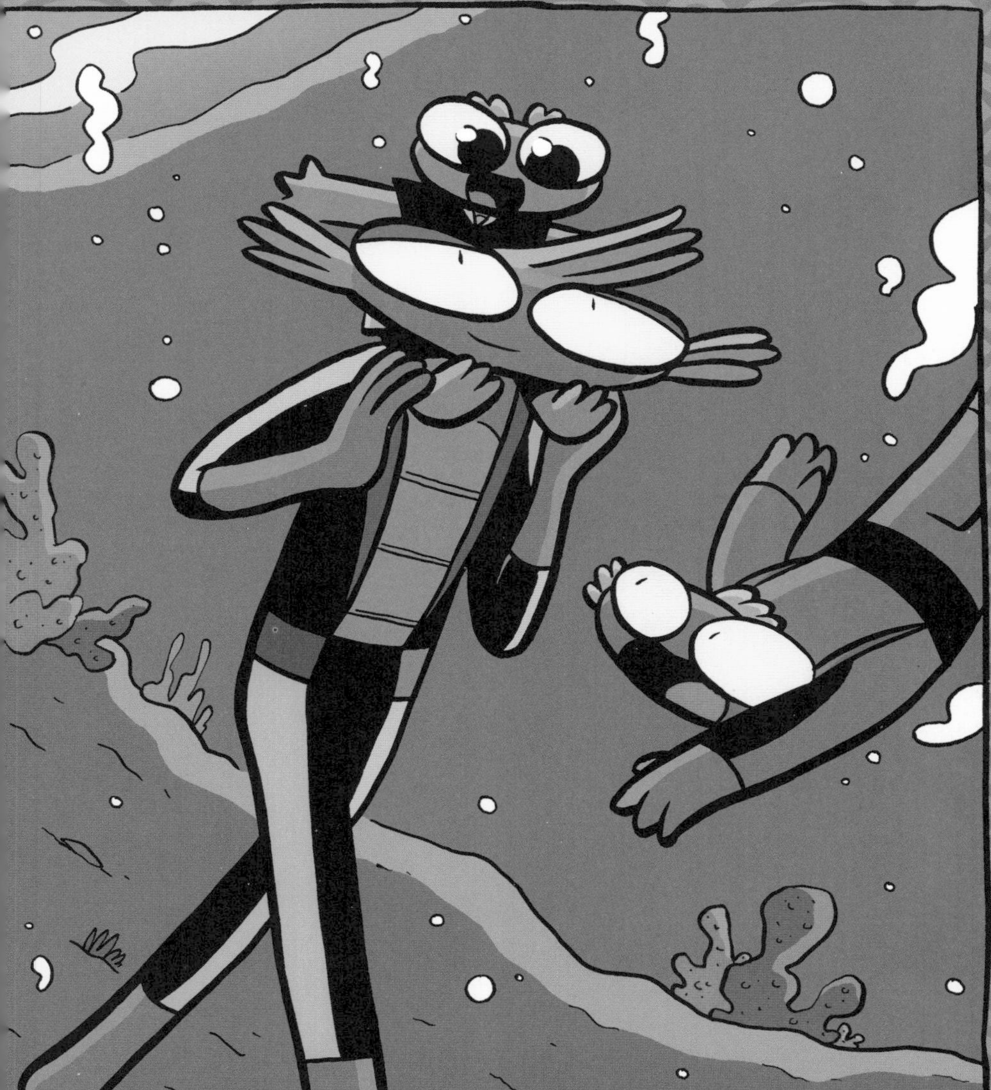

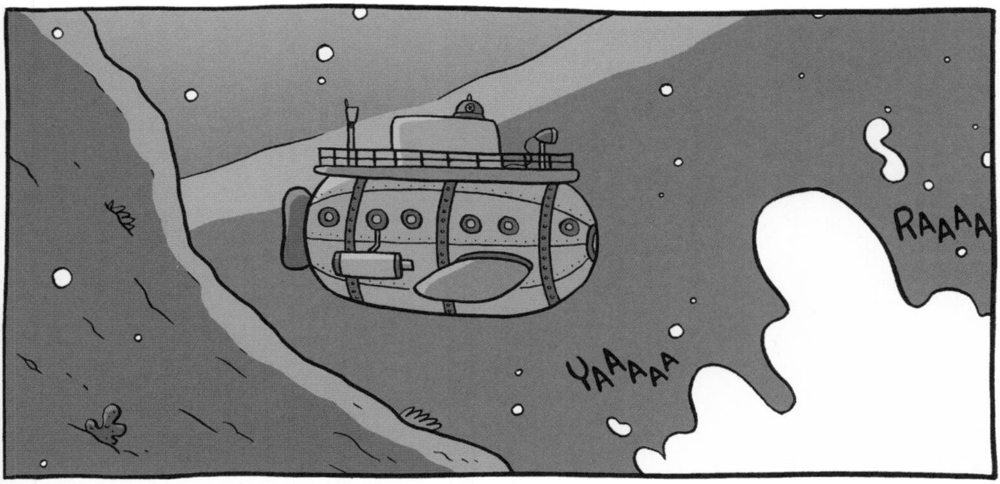
RAAAA
YAAAAA

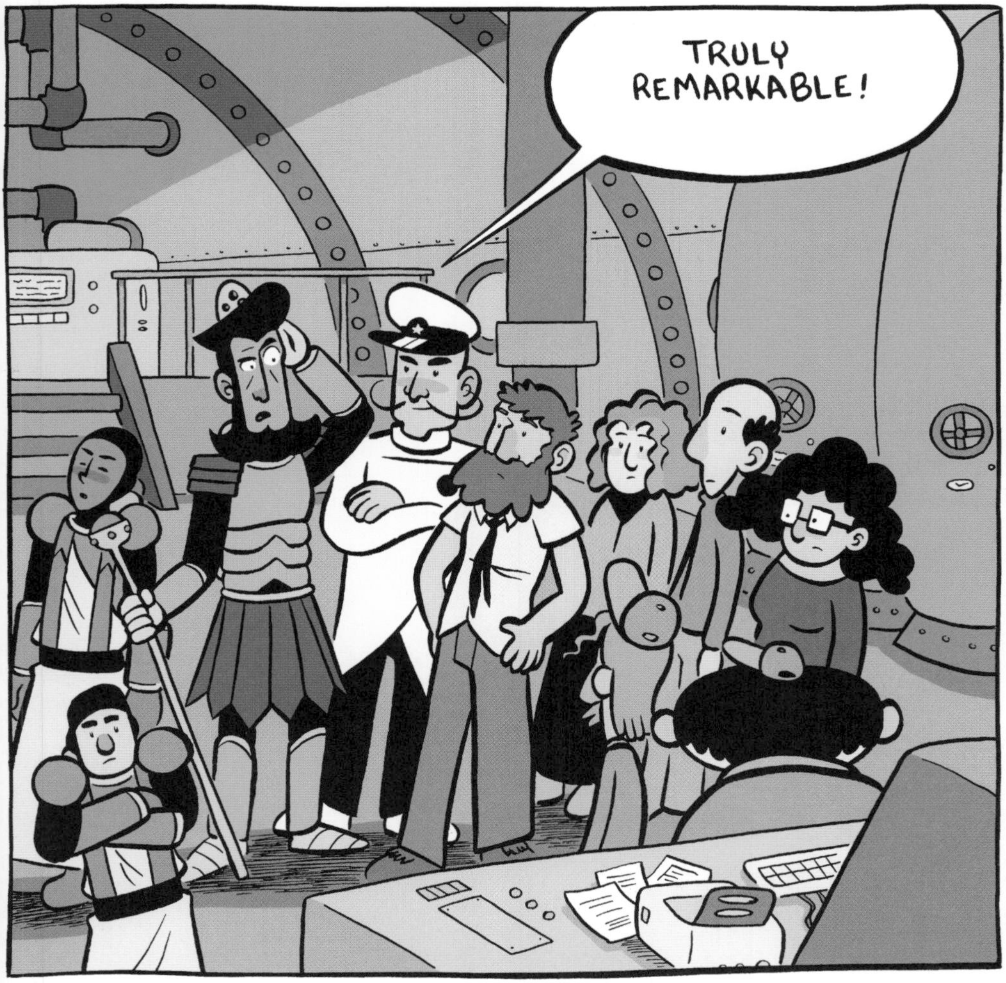
TRULY REMARKABLE!

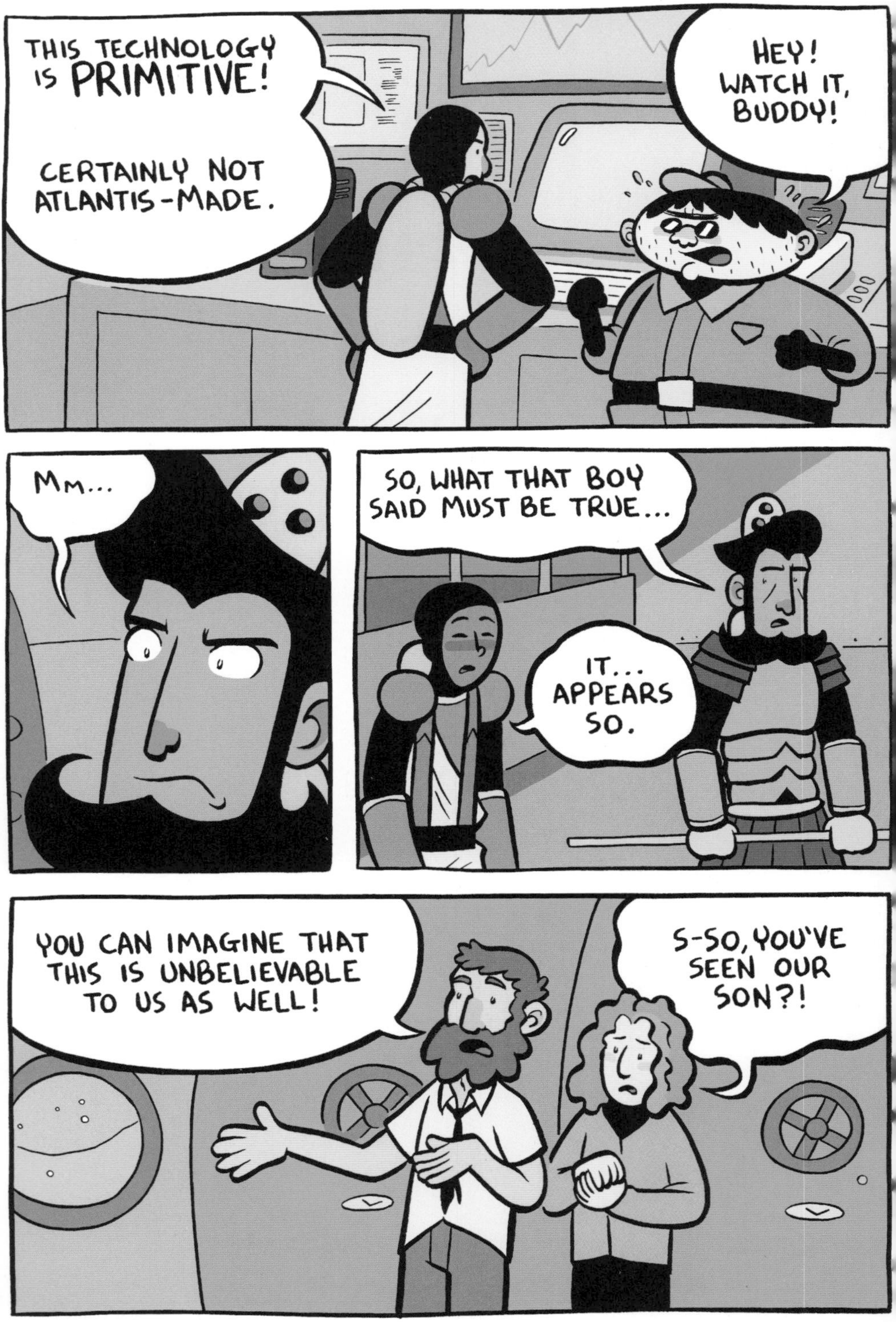
THIS TECHNOLOGY IS PRIMITIVE!
CERTAINLY NOT ATLANTIS-MADE.
HEY! WATCH IT, BUDDY!
Mm...
SO, WHAT THAT BOY SAID MUST BE TRUE...
IT... APPEARS SO.
YOU CAN IMAGINE THAT THIS IS UNBELIEVABLE TO US AS WELL!
S-SO, YOU'VE SEEN OUR SON?!

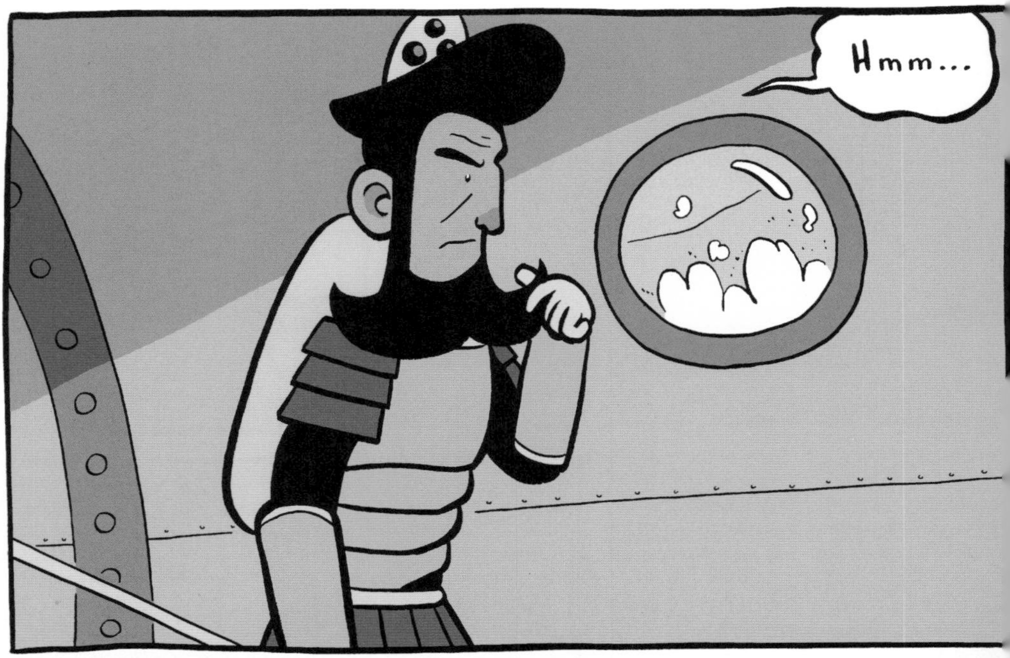
Hmm...

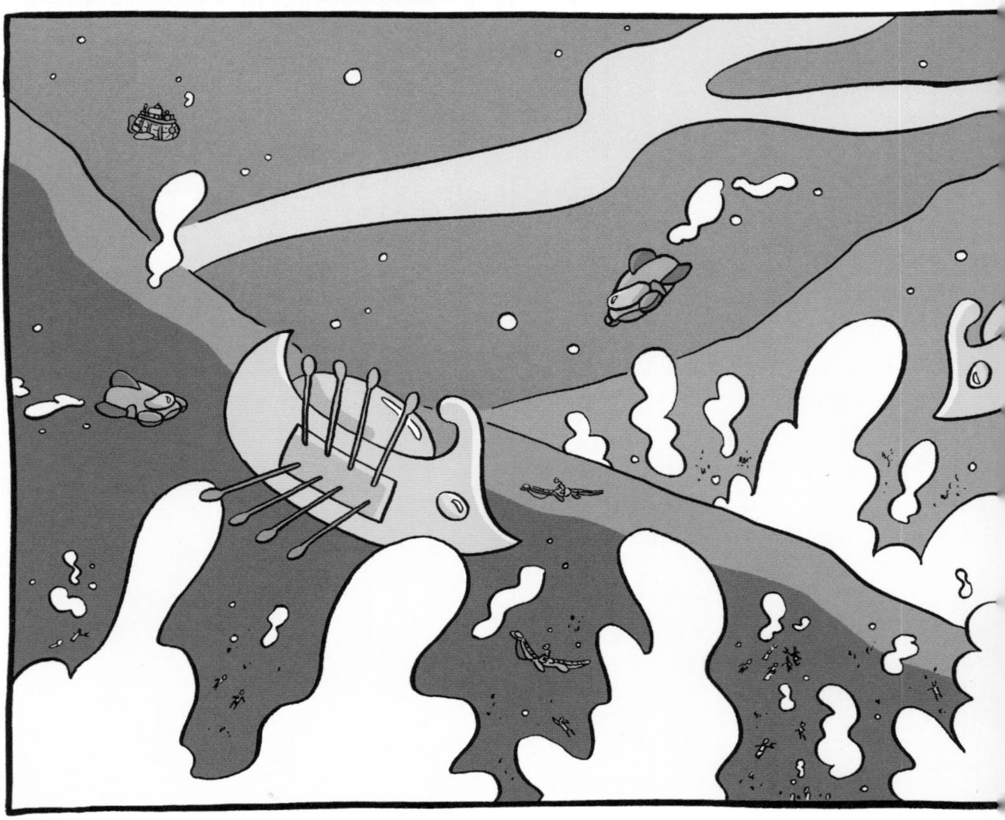

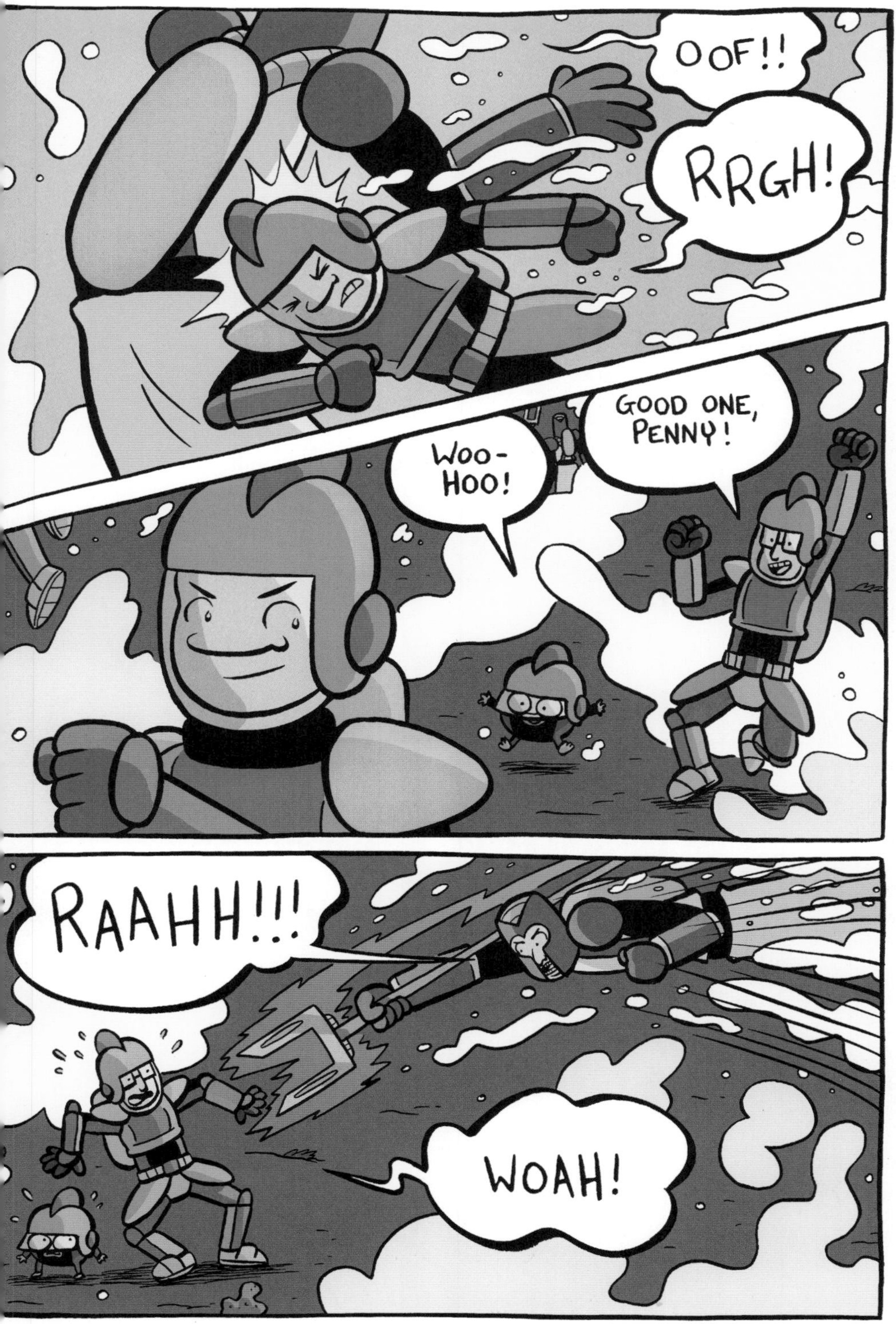
OOF!!
RRGH!
WOO-HOO!
GOOD ONE, PENNY!
RAAHH!!!
WOAH!

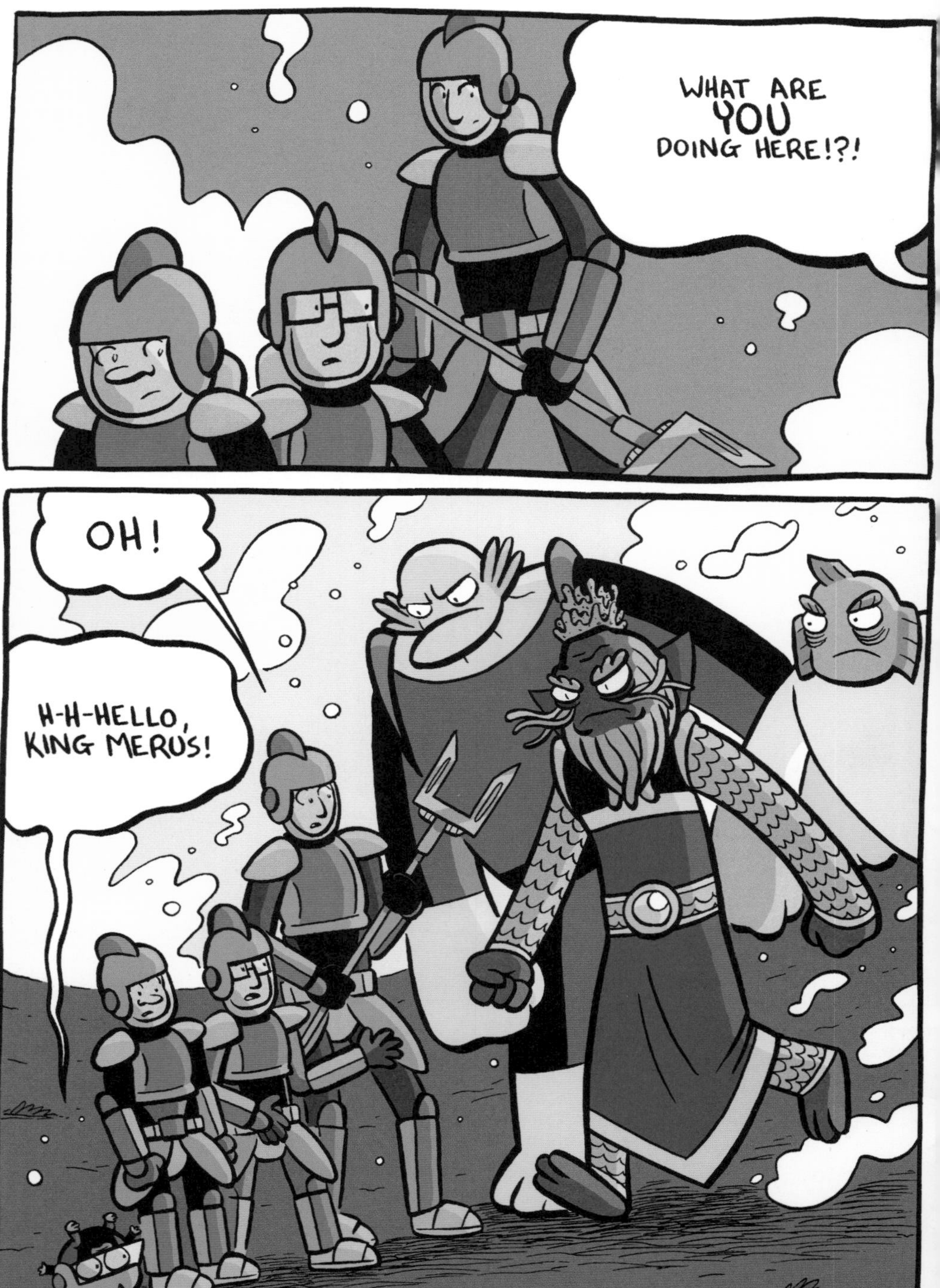
WHAT ARE YOU DOING HERE!?!
OH!
H-H-HELLO, KING MERUS!

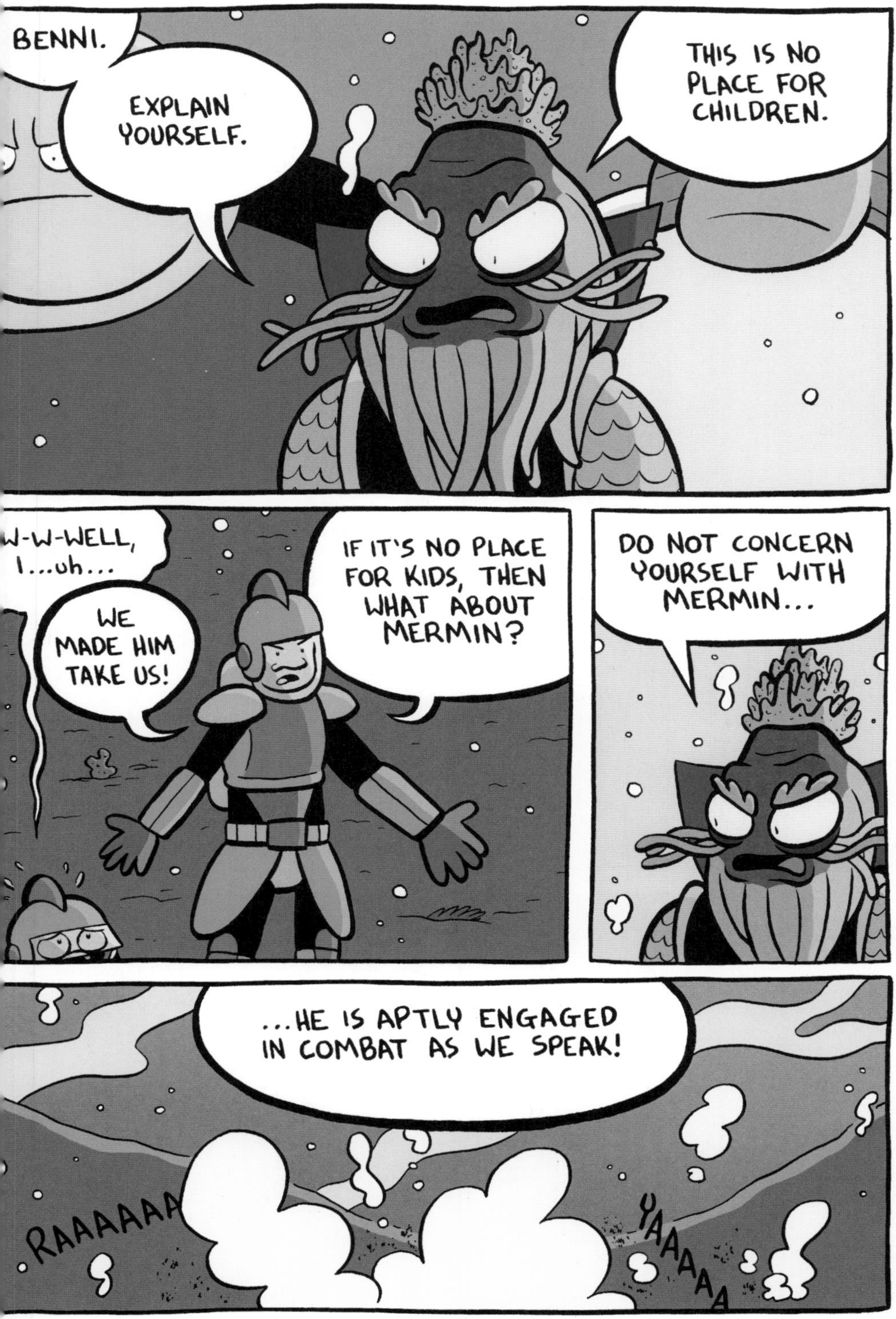
BENNI.
EXPLAIN YOURSELF.
THIS IS NO PLACE FOR CHILDREN.
W-W-WELL, I...uh...
WE MADE HIM TAKE US!
IF IT'S NO PLACE FOR KIDS, THEN WHAT ABOUT MERMIN?
DO NOT CONCERN YOURSELF WITH MERMIN...
...HE IS APTLY ENGAGED IN COMBAT AS WE SPEAK!
RAAAAAA
YAAAAAA

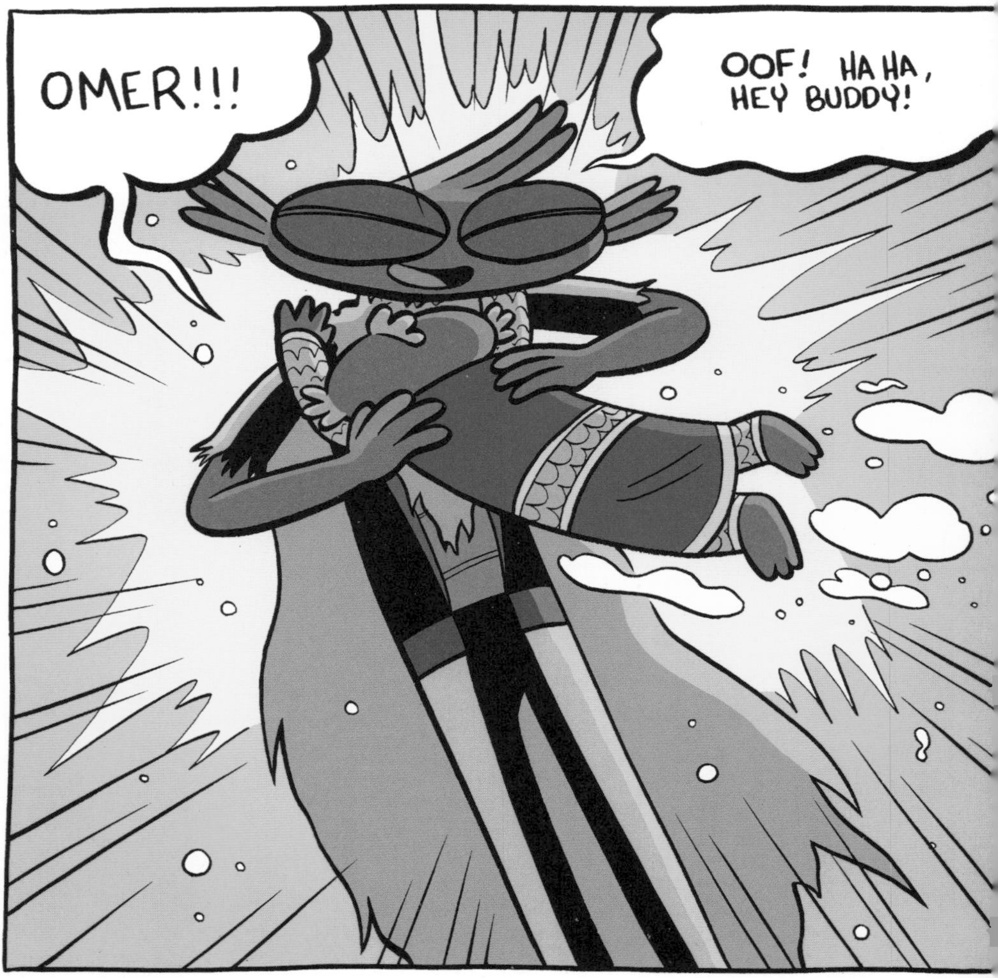
OMER!!!
OOF! HA HA, HEY BUDDY!

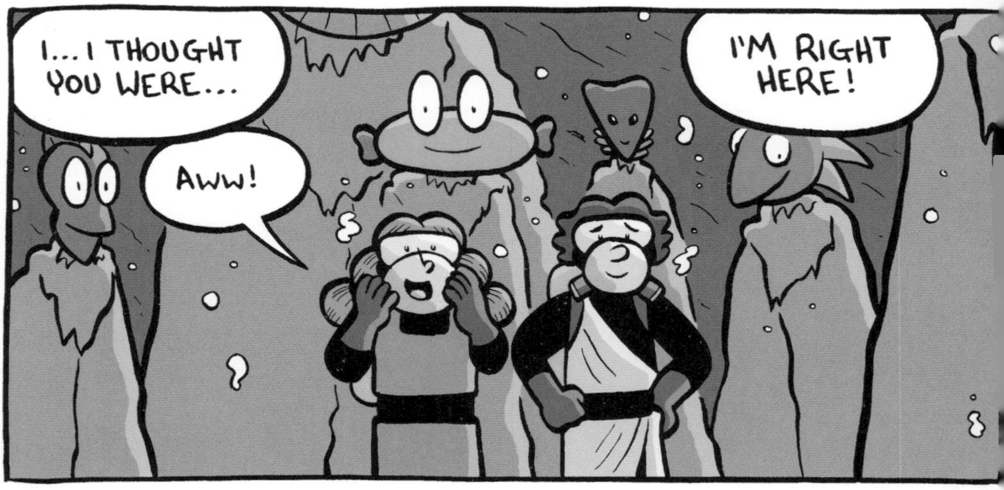
I... I THOUGHT YOU WERE...
AWW!
I'M RIGHT HERE!

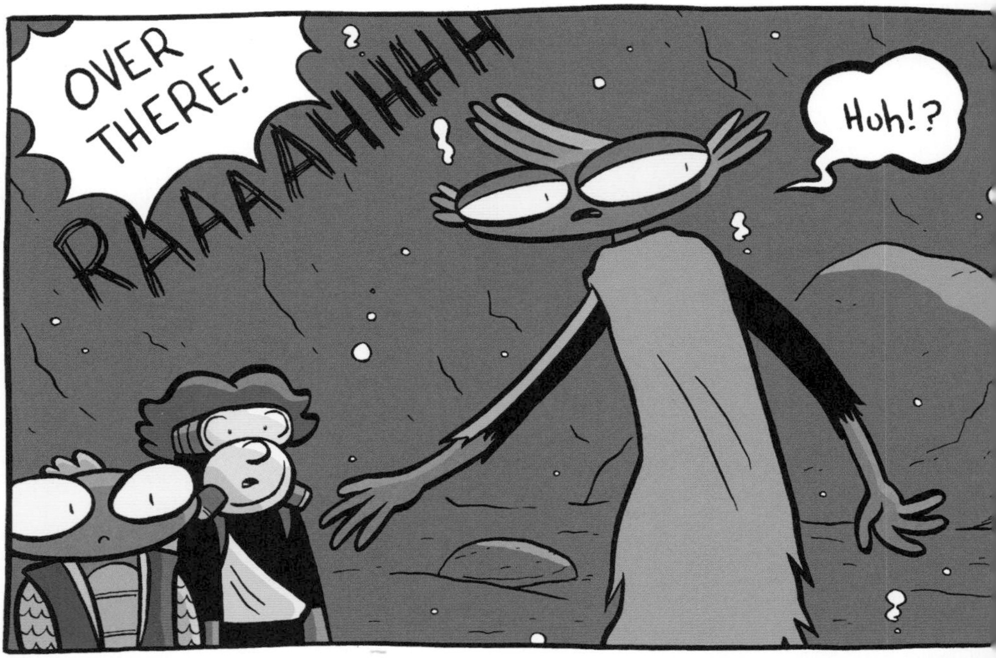
OVER THERE!
RAAAAAHHHHH
Huh!?

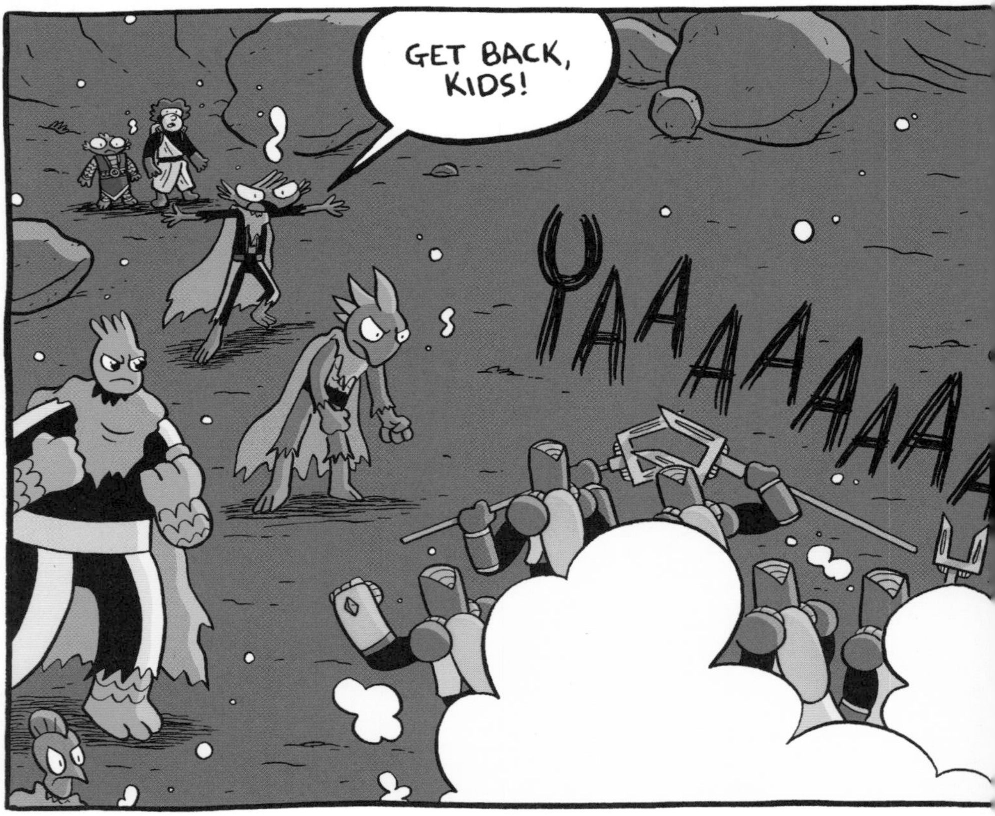
GET BACK, KIDS!
YAAAAAAAAA

YAAAAAHHH!
VWOO!
RAA
RAAA!
WAAA!
WHAT A MESS.

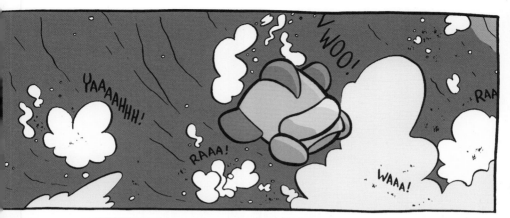

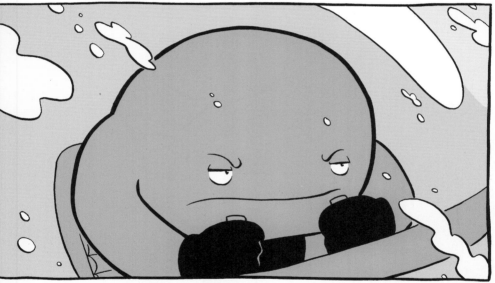

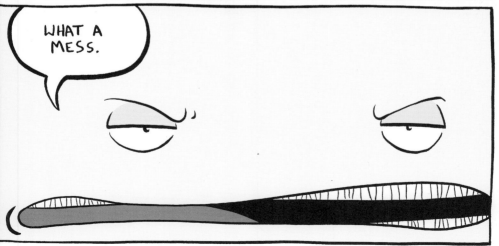

EVERYWHERE YOU LOOK, IT'S JUST CHAOS...

EVEN--huh?

WHAT IS **THAT**?

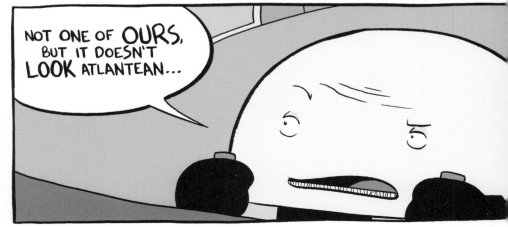

NOT ONE OF **OURS,** BUT IT DOESN'T **LOOK** ATLANTEAN...

YOU ARE STILL SO MUCH BETTER AT USING POWERS THAN ME!!

PUNCH!

ARGH!

YAAAA!

WHOOOOO

WAAAA!

SSHHH

Aw, C'MON BROTHER!

YOU'LL GET THERE WITH PRACTICE!

I GUESS SO...

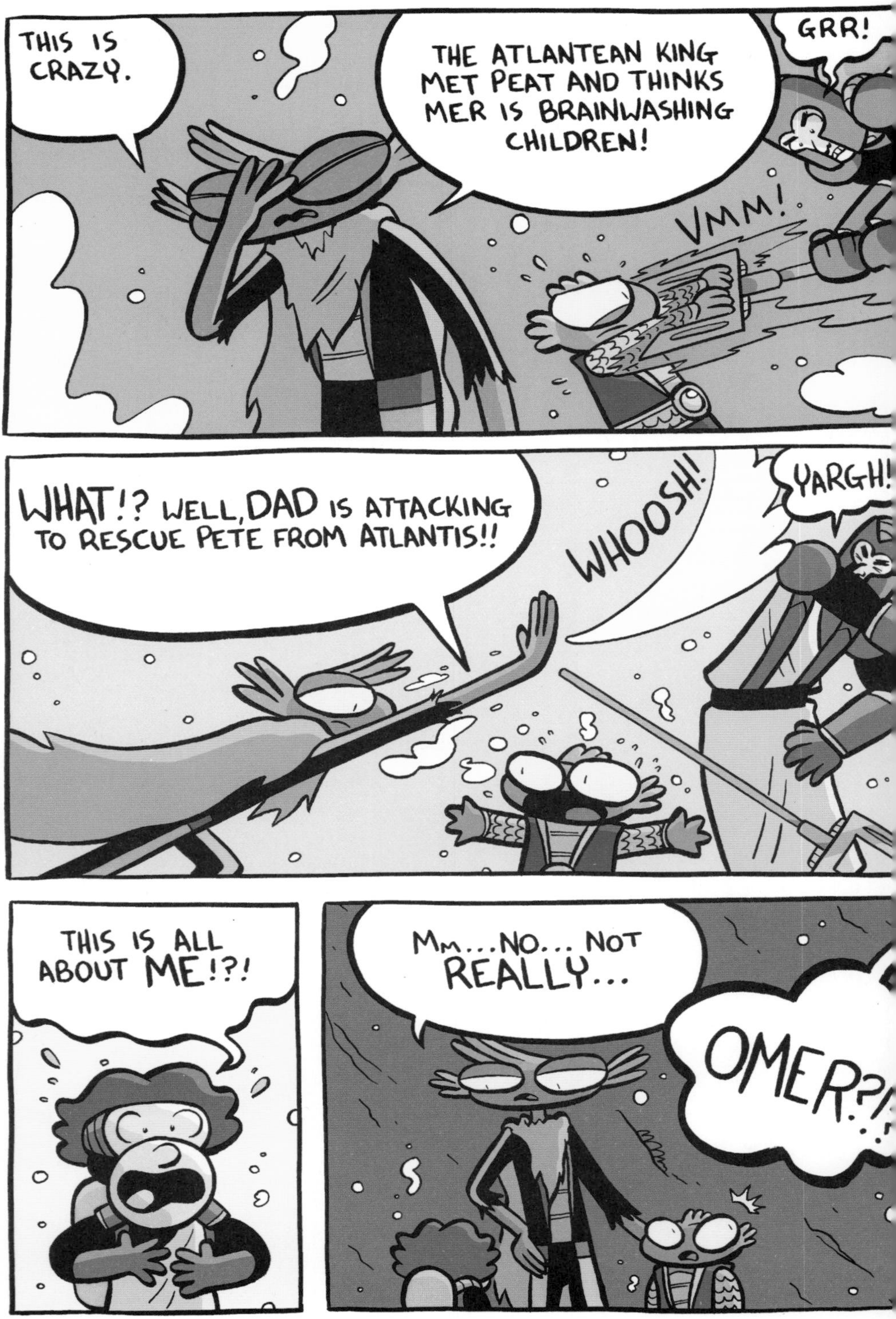
THIS IS CRAZY.
THE ATLANTEAN KING MET PEAT AND THINKS MER IS BRAINWASHING CHILDREN!
GRR!
VMM!
WHAT!? WELL, DAD IS ATTACKING TO RESCUE PETE FROM ATLANTIS!!
WHOOSH!
YARGH!
THIS IS ALL ABOUT ME!?!
MM...NO...NOT REALLY...
OMER?!

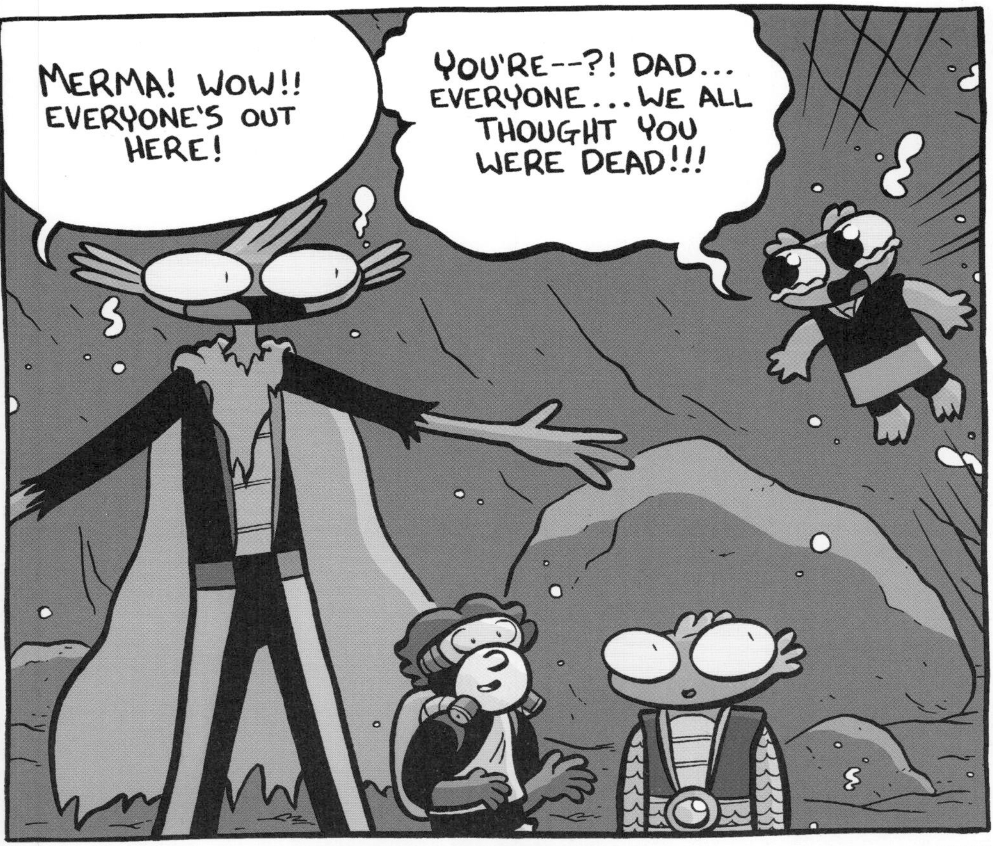
MERMA! WOW!! EVERYONE'S OUT HERE!
YOU'RE--?! DAD... EVERYONE...WE ALL THOUGHT YOU WERE DEAD!!!

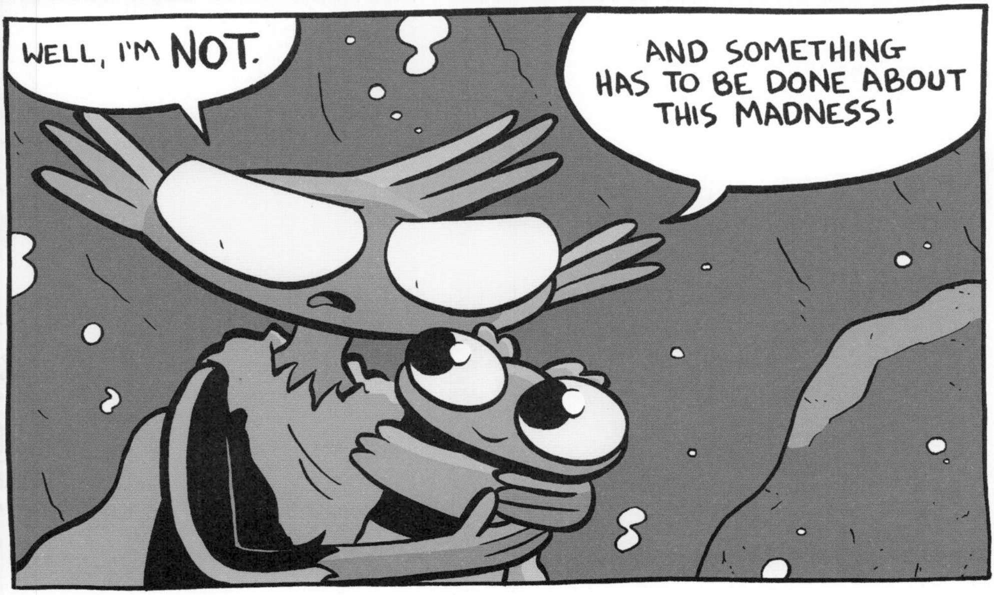
WELL, I'M NOT.
AND SOMETHING HAS TO BE DONE ABOUT THIS MADNESS!

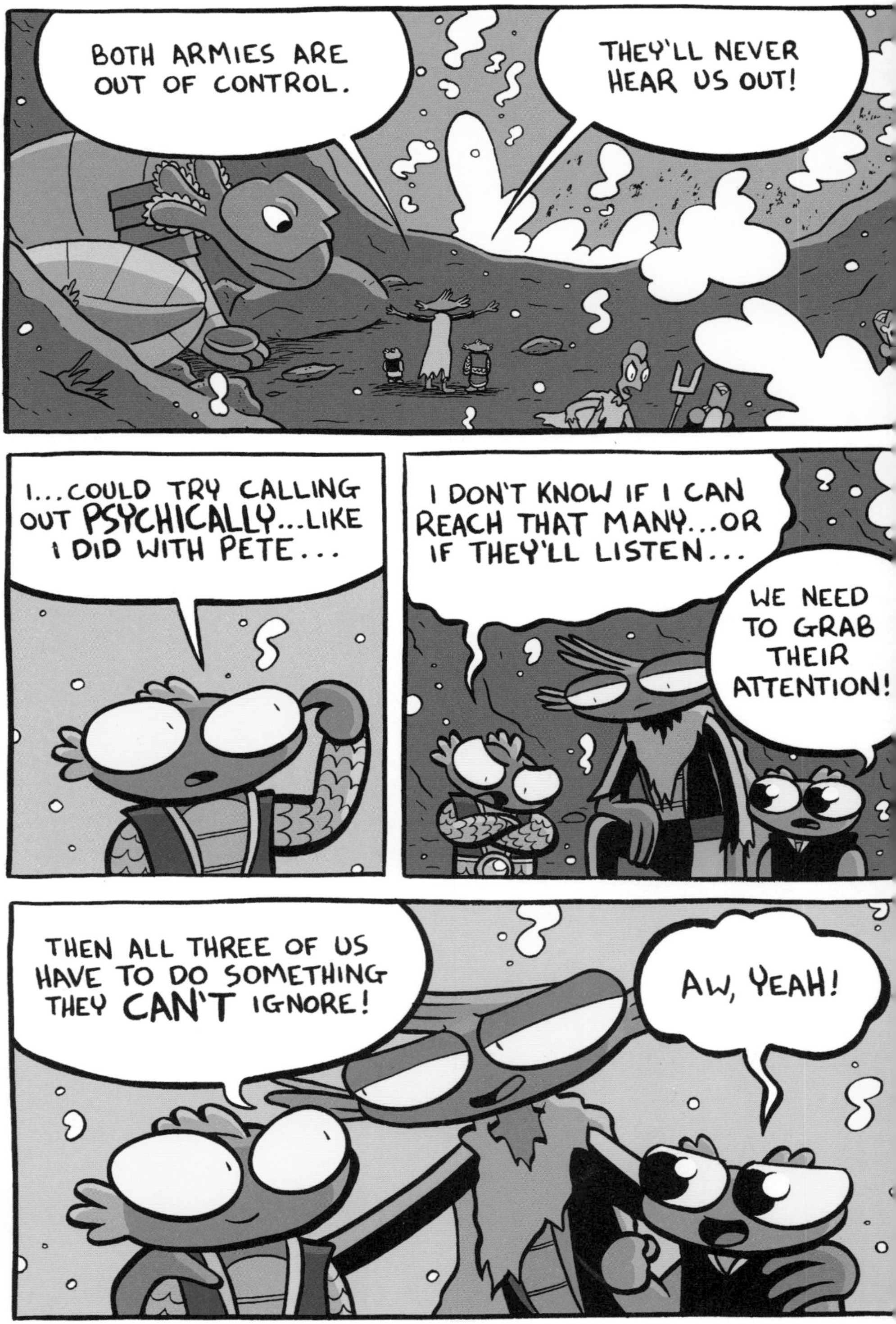
BOTH ARMIES ARE OUT OF CONTROL.
THEY'LL NEVER HEAR US OUT!
I...COULD TRY CALLING OUT PSYCHICALLY...LIKE I DID WITH PETE...
I DON'T KNOW IF I CAN REACH THAT MANY...OR IF THEY'LL LISTEN...
WE NEED TO GRAB THEIR ATTENTION!
THEN ALL THREE OF US HAVE TO DO SOMETHING THEY CAN'T IGNORE!
AW, YEAH!

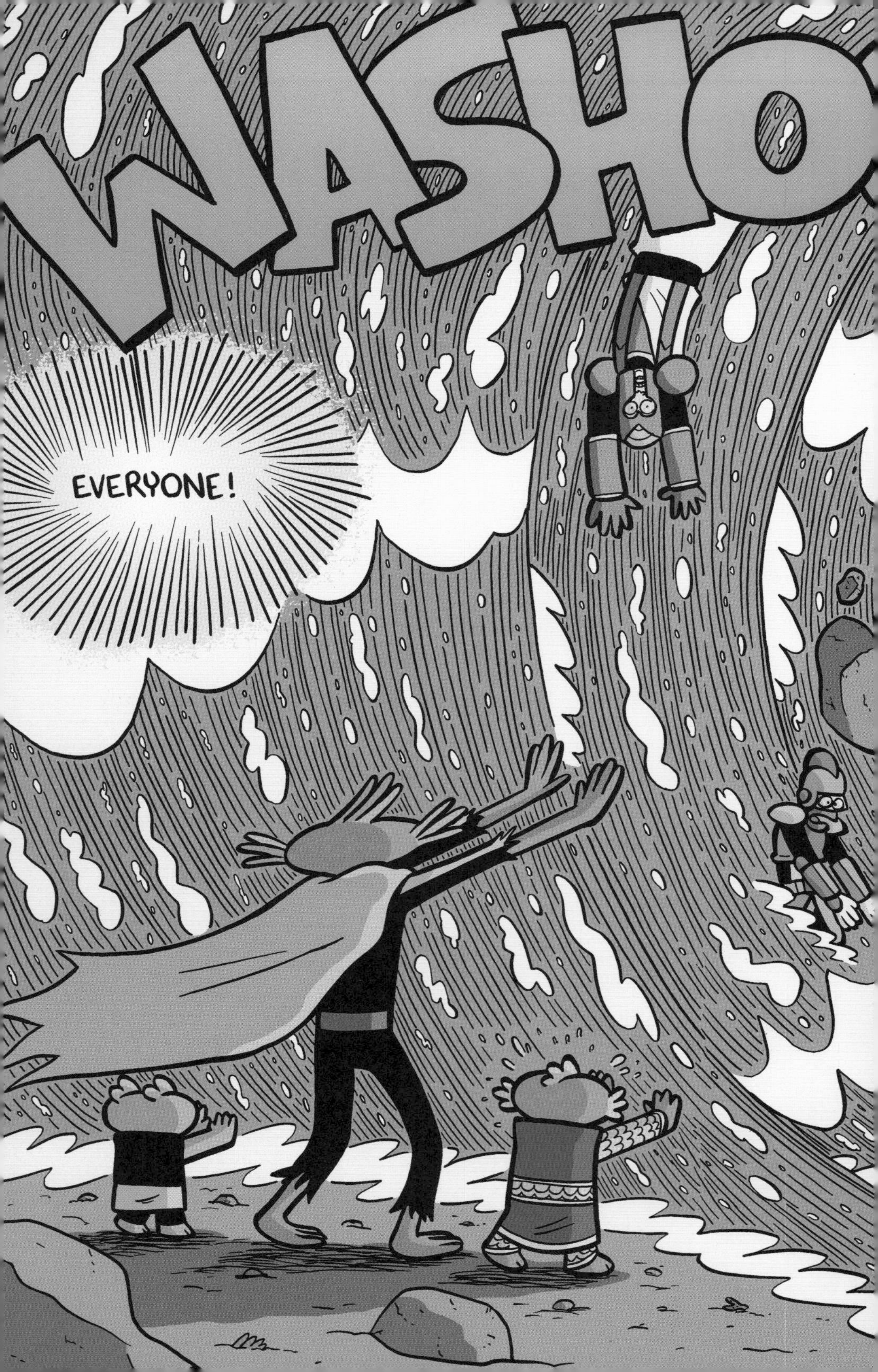
WASHO
EVERYONE!

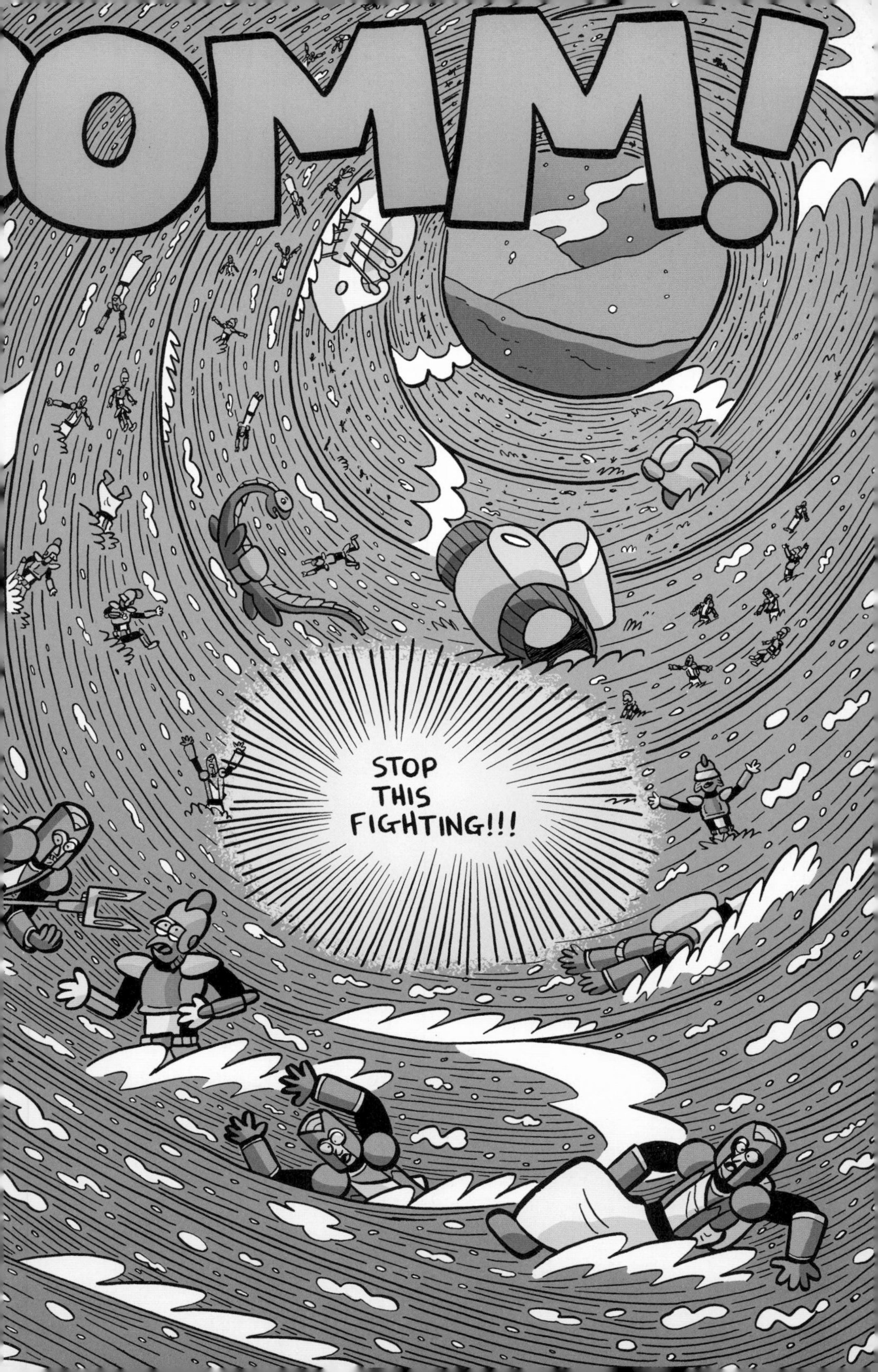
OMM!
STOP THIS FIGHTING!!!

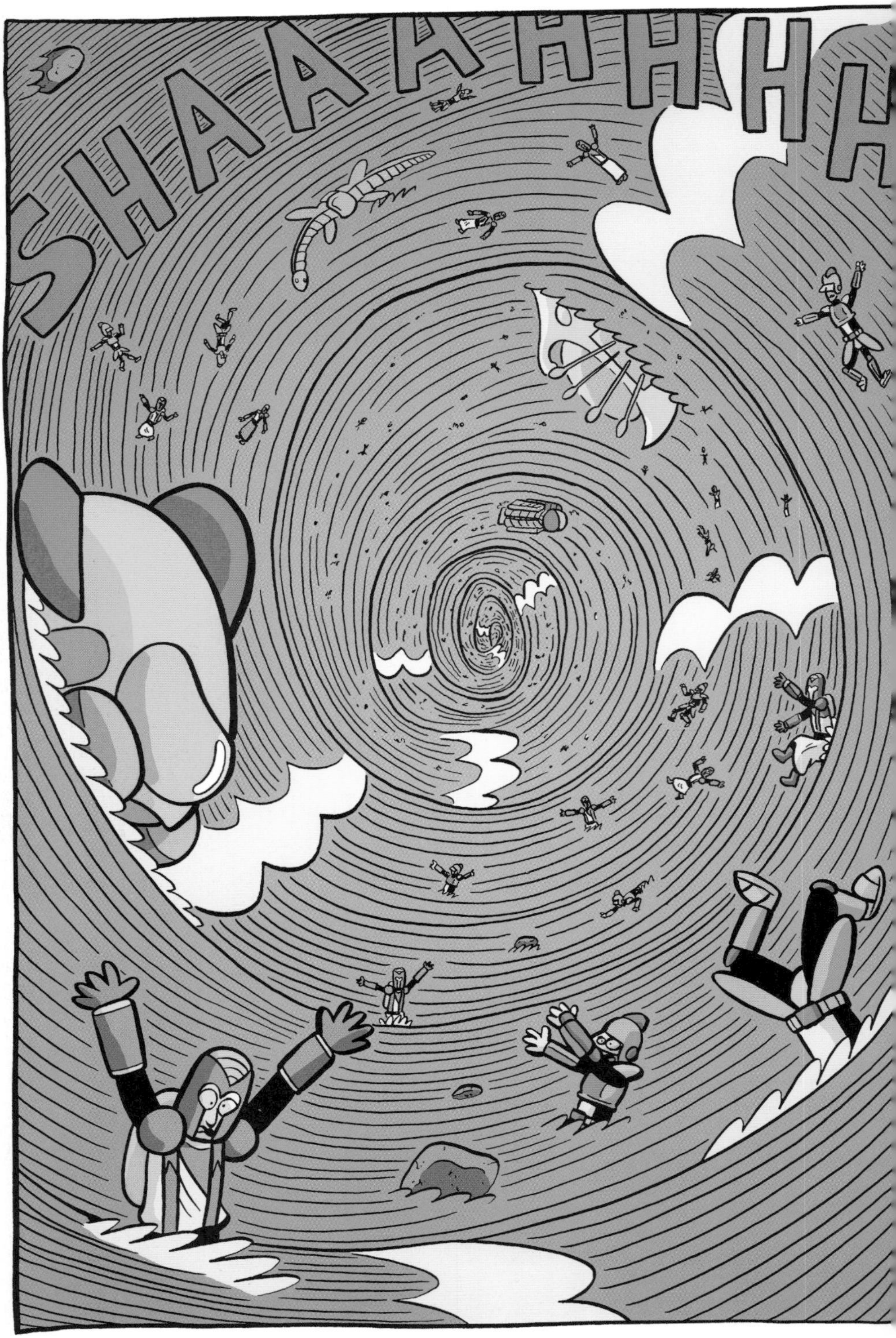
SHAAAHHHH

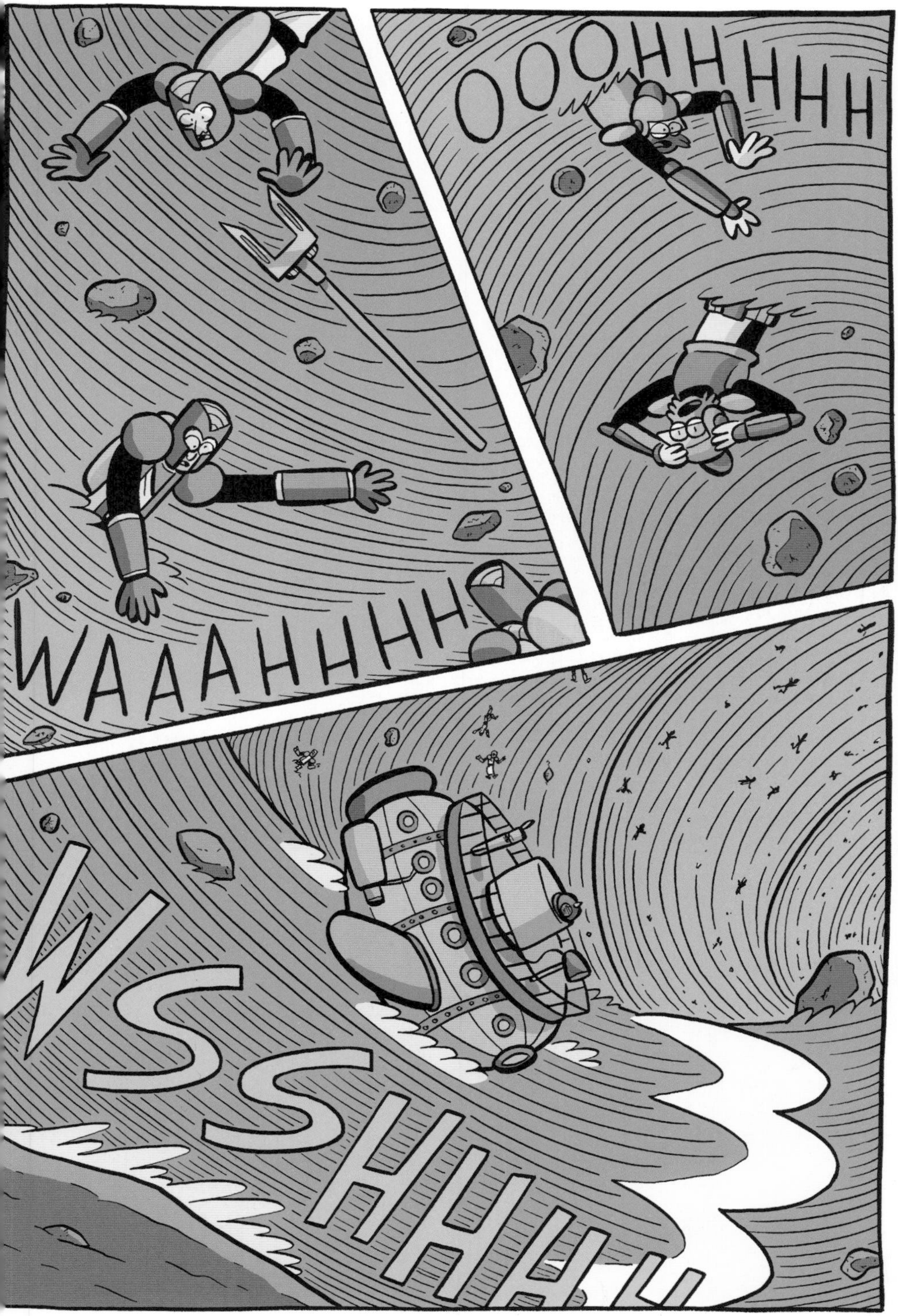
WAAAHHHH
OOOOHHHHHH
WSSHHHHH

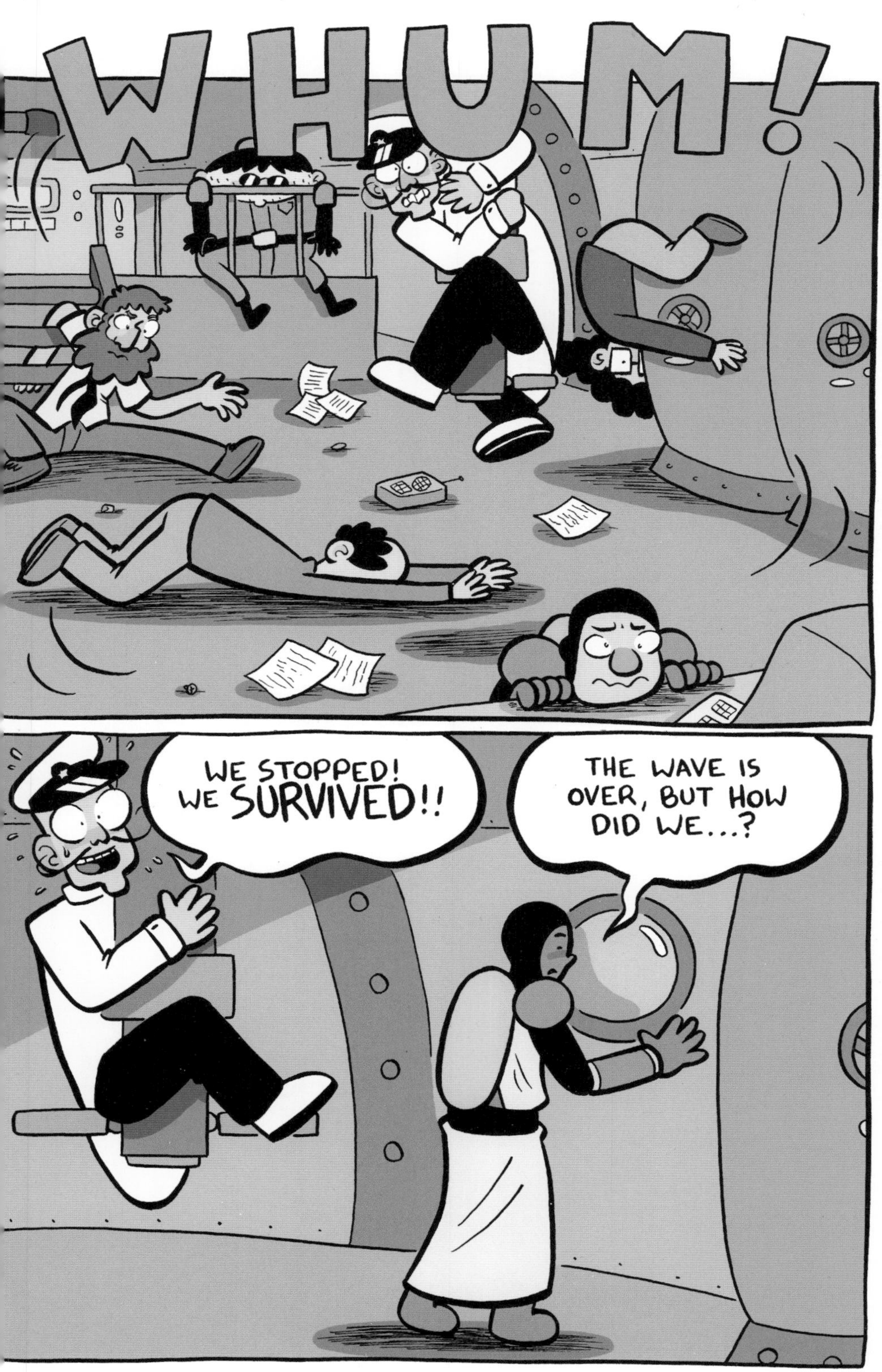
WHUM!
WE STOPPED! WE SURVIVED!!
THE WAVE IS OVER, BUT HOW DID WE...?

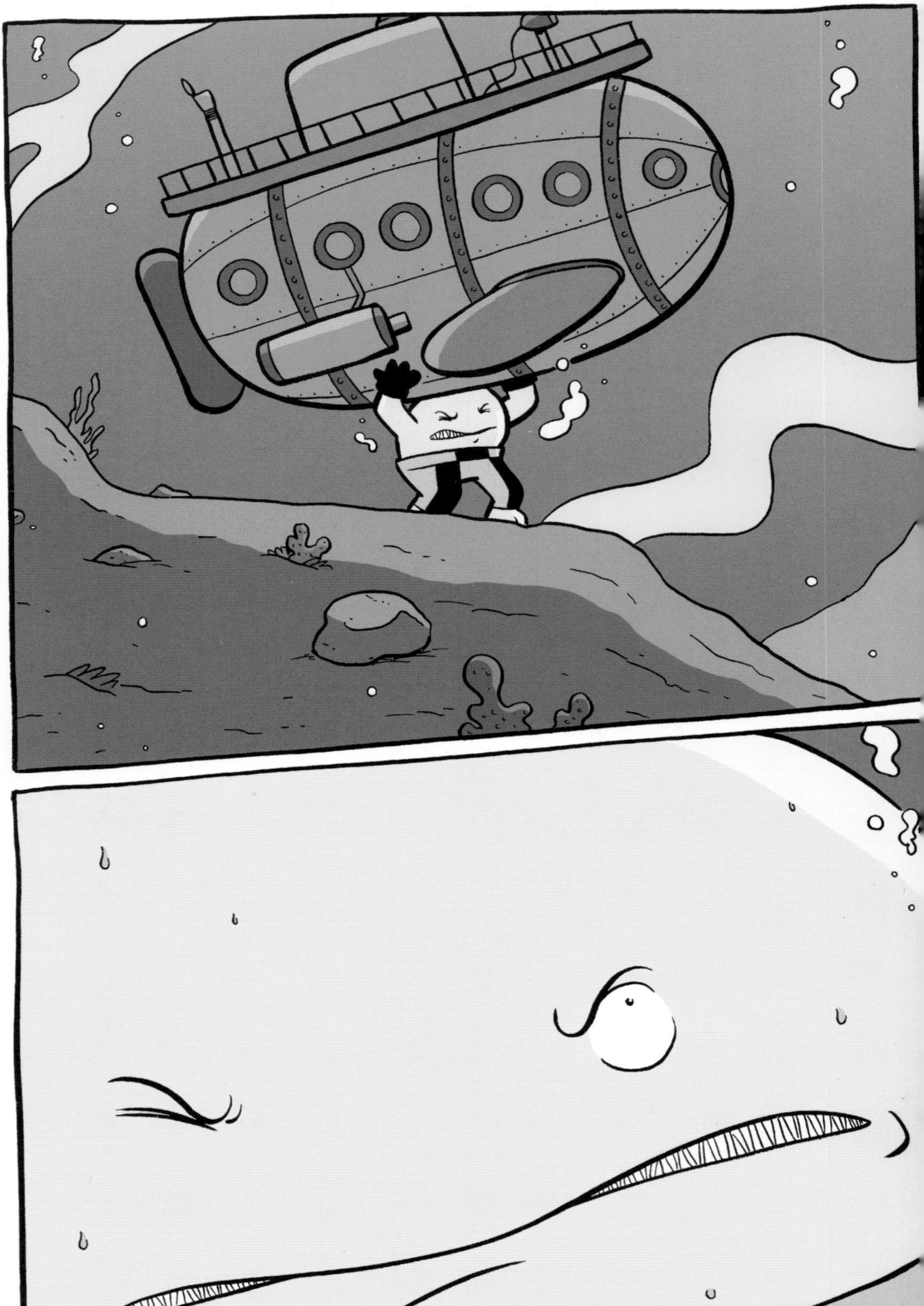

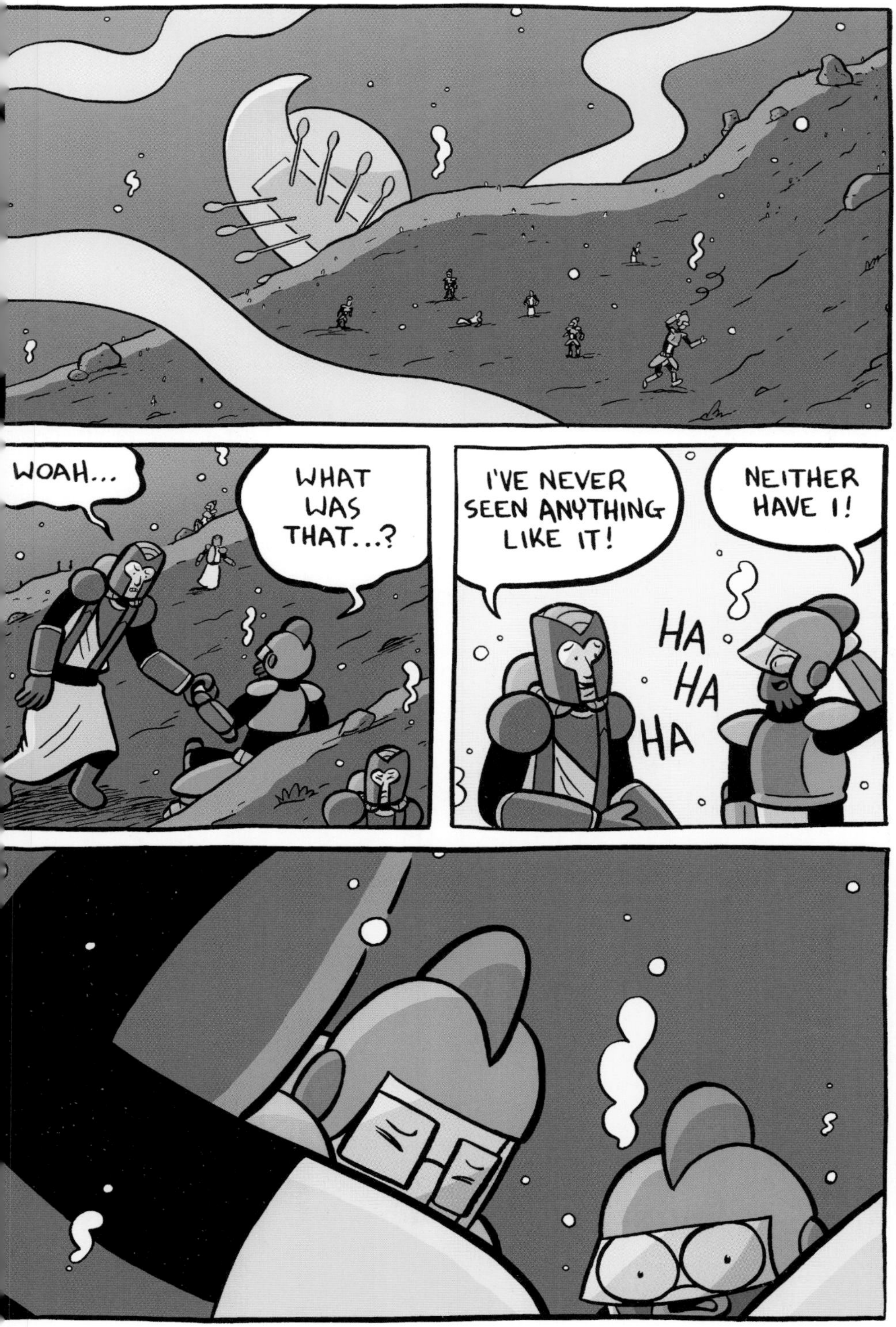
WOAH...
WHAT WAS THAT...?
I'VE NEVER SEEN ANYTHING LIKE IT!
NEITHER HAVE I!
HA HA HA

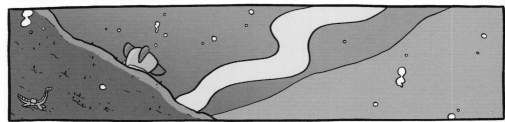

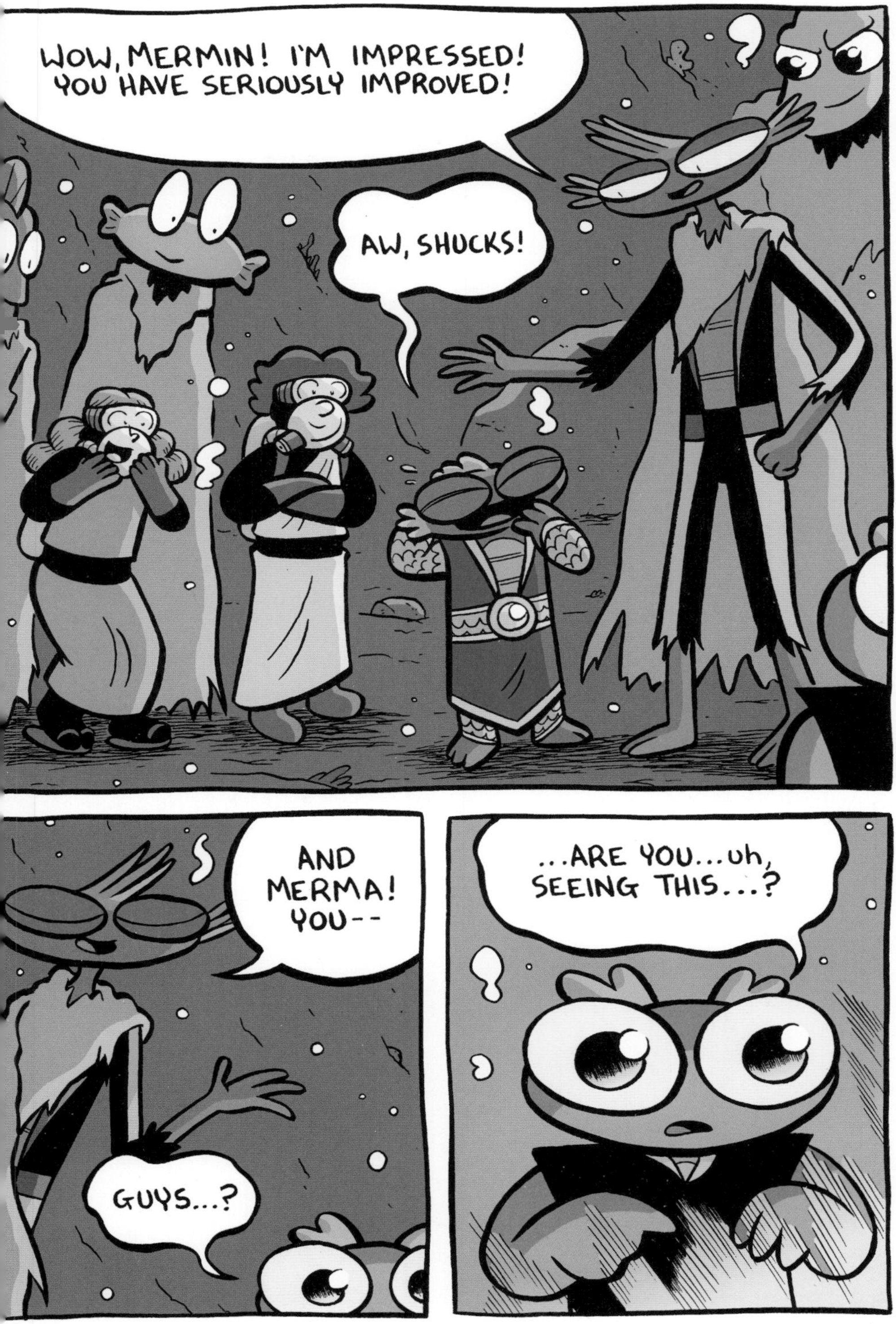
WOW, MERMIN! I'M IMPRESSED! YOU HAVE SERIOUSLY IMPROVED!
AW, SHUCKS!
AND MERMA! YOU--
GUYS...?
...ARE YOU...uh, SEEING THIS...?

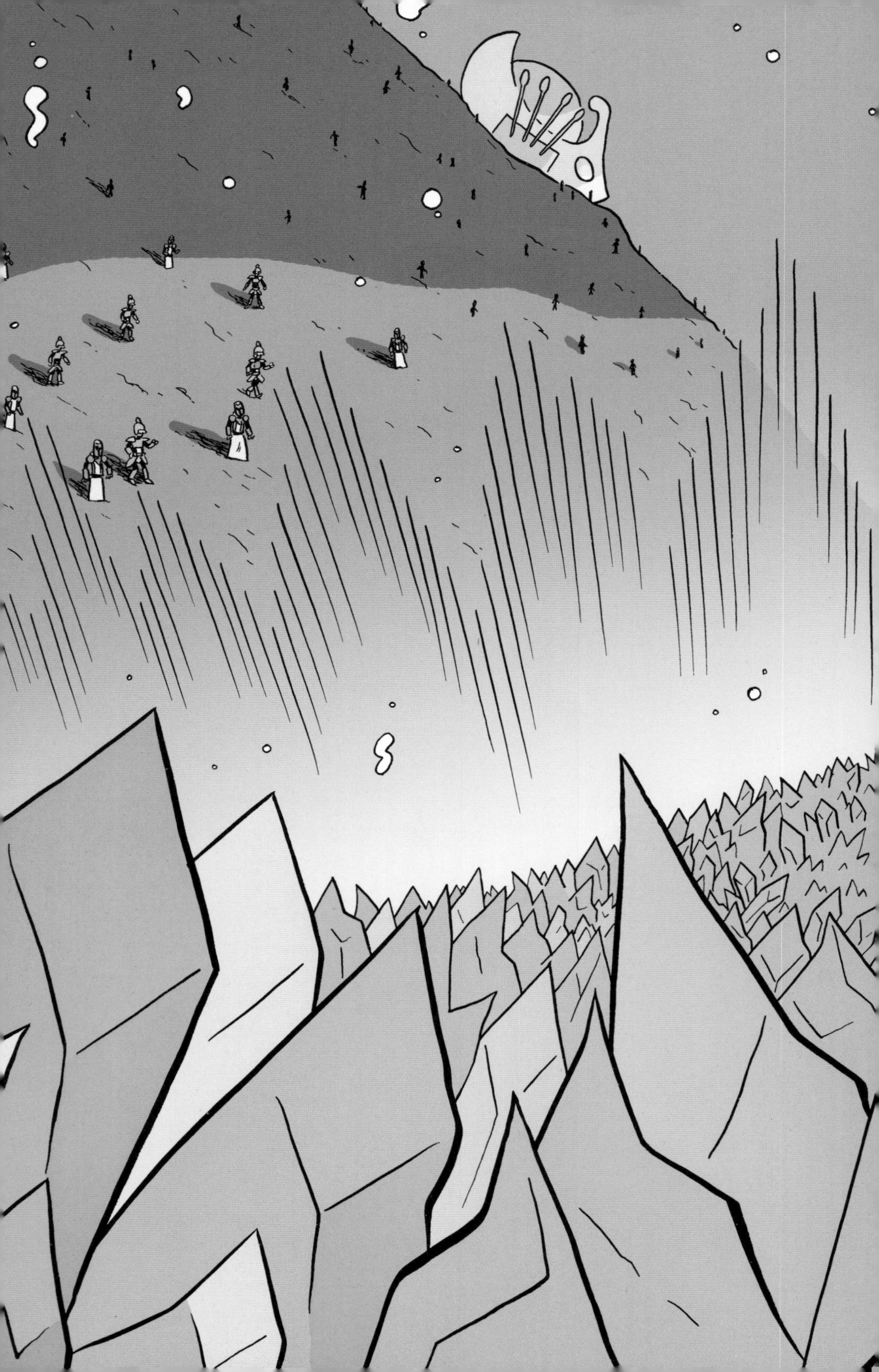

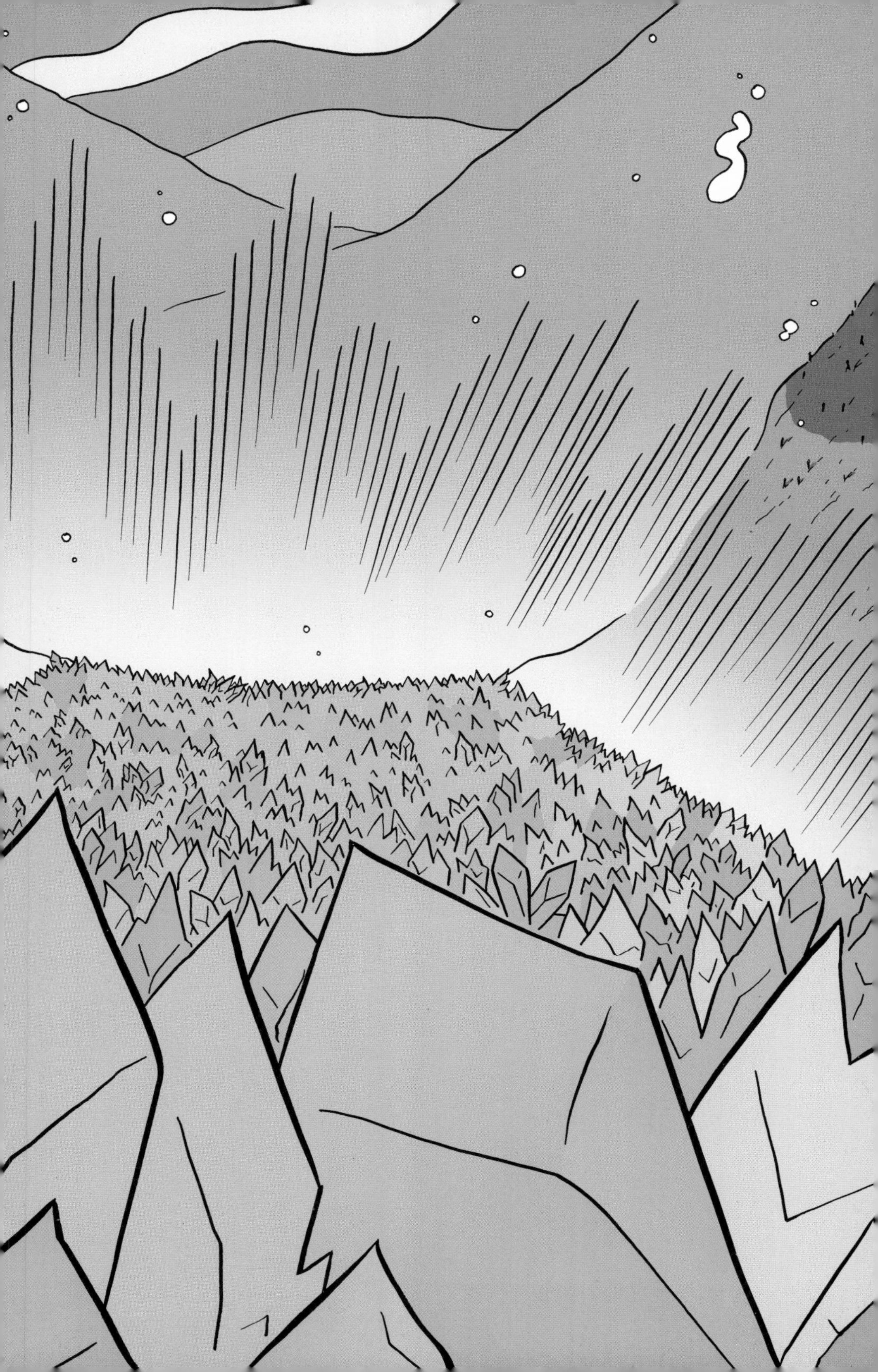

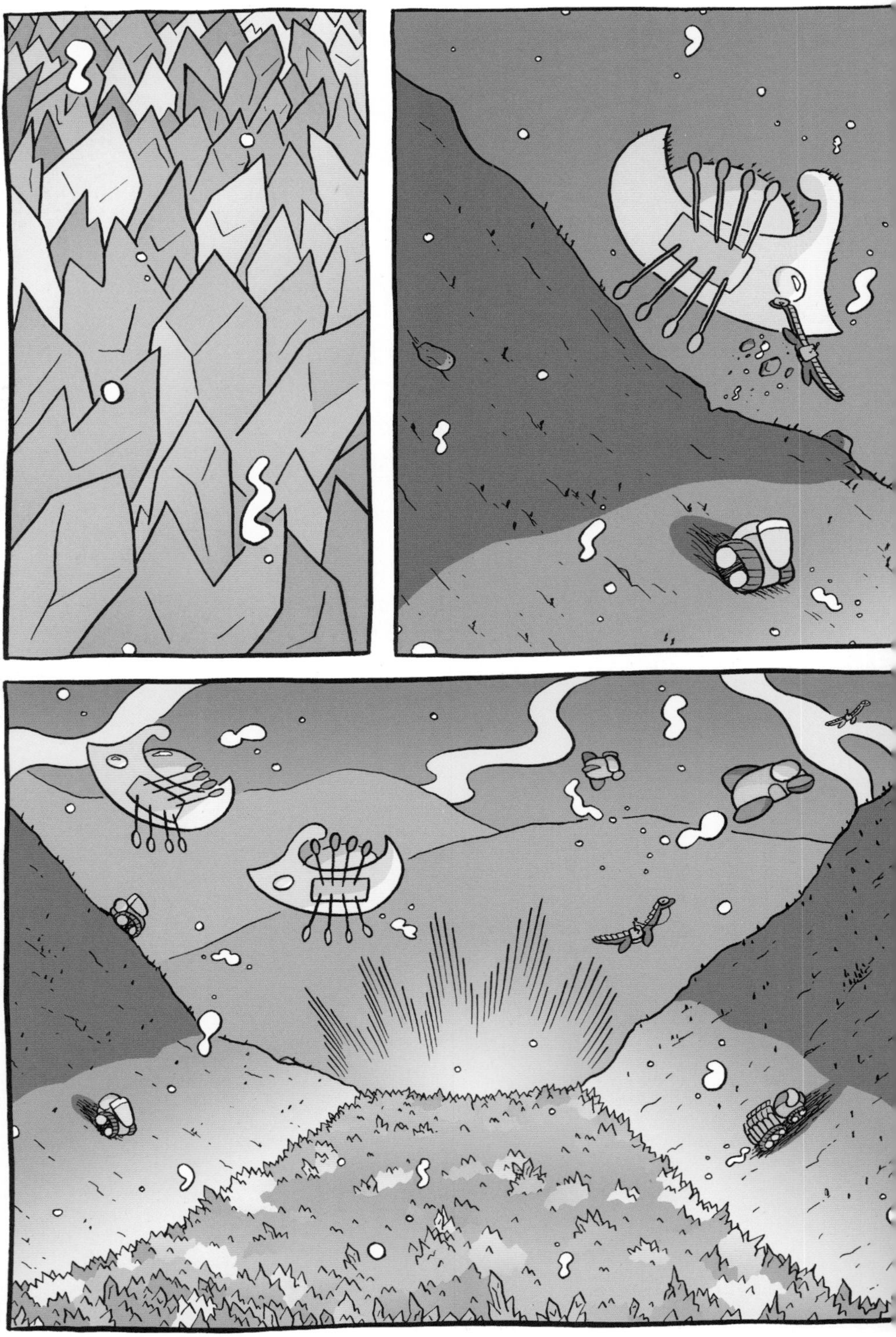

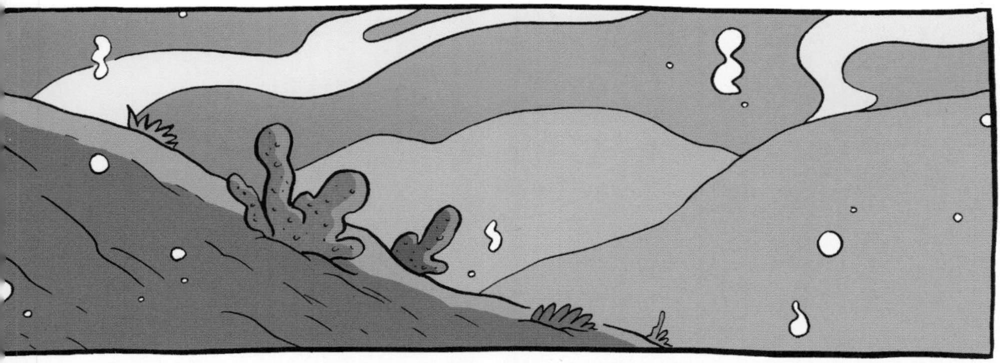

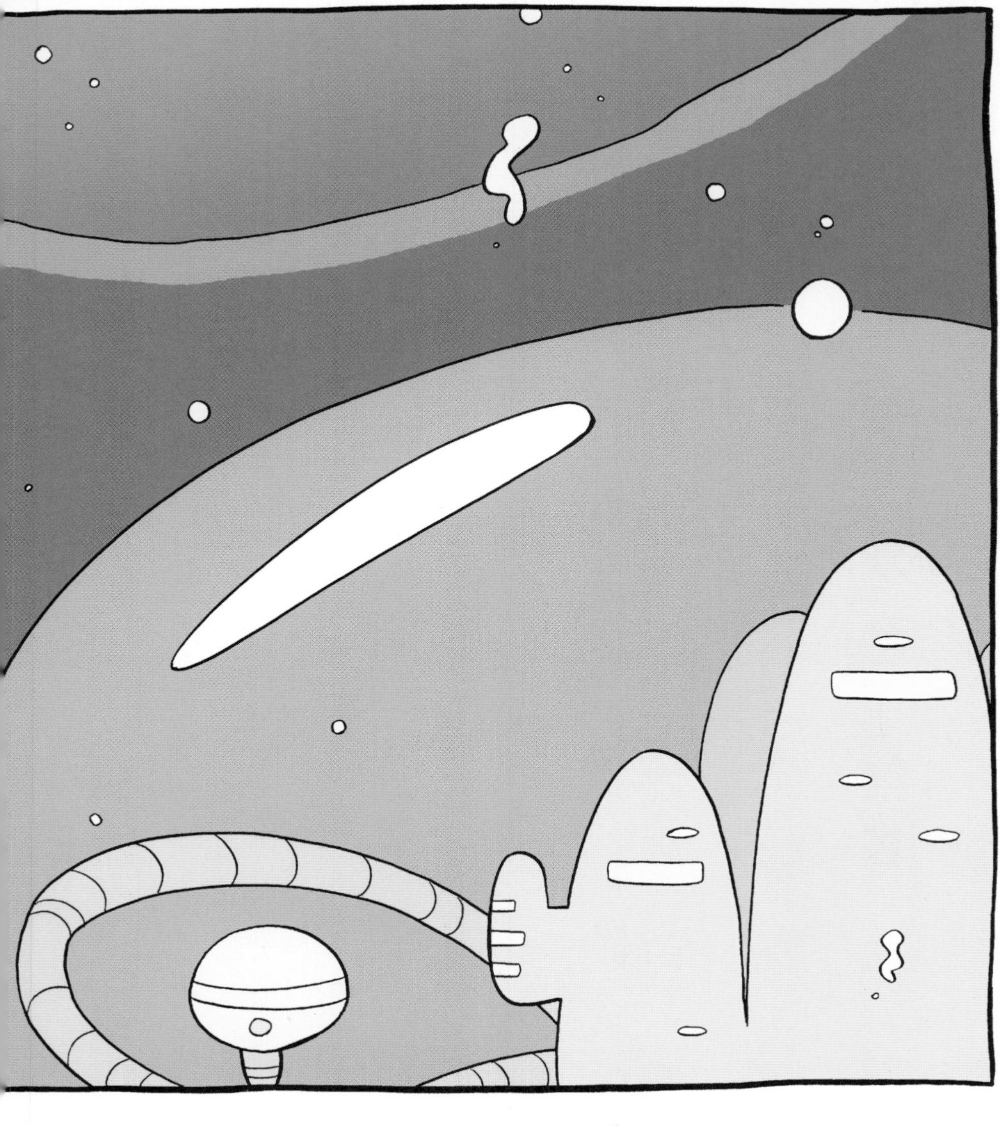

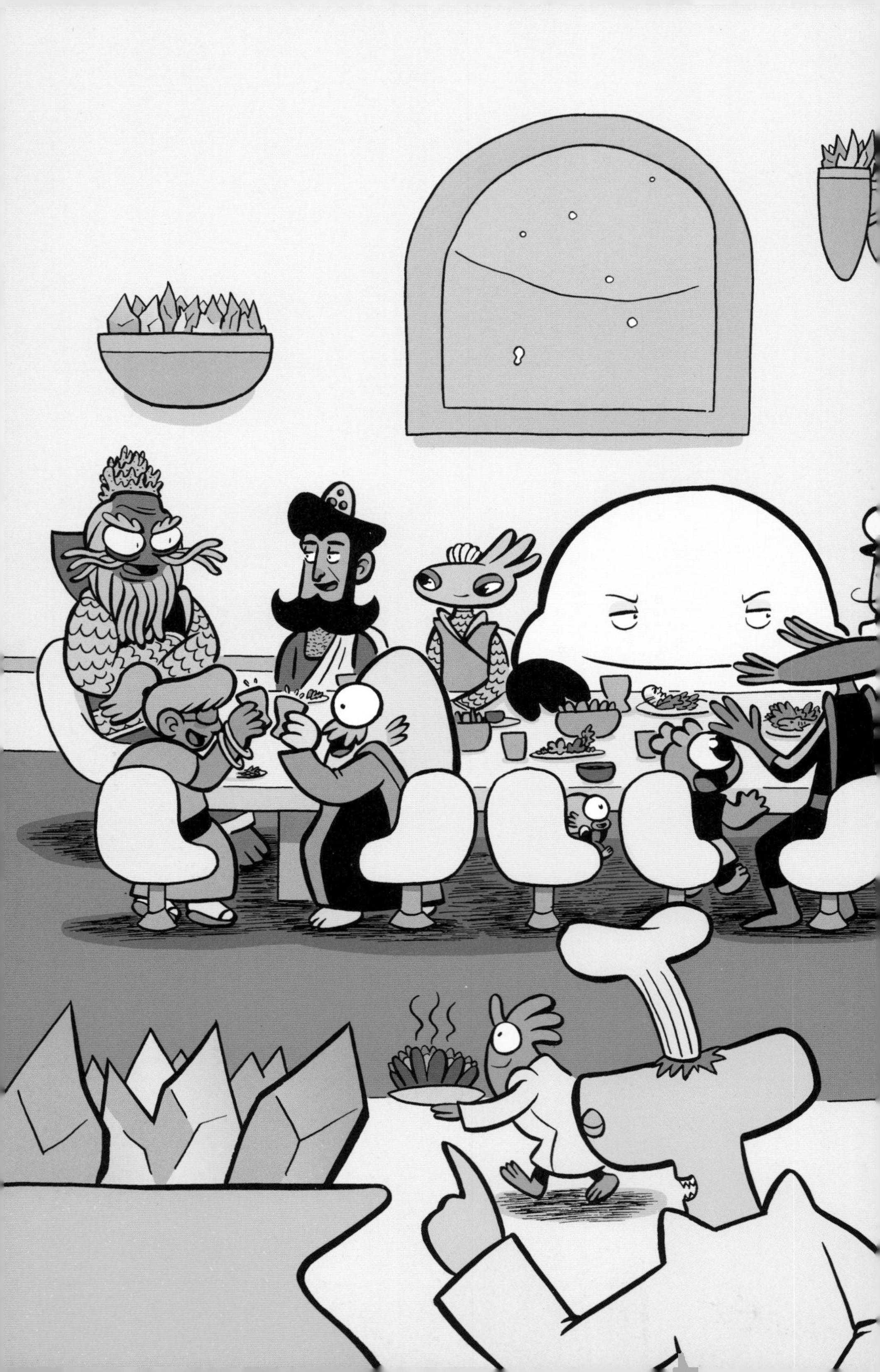

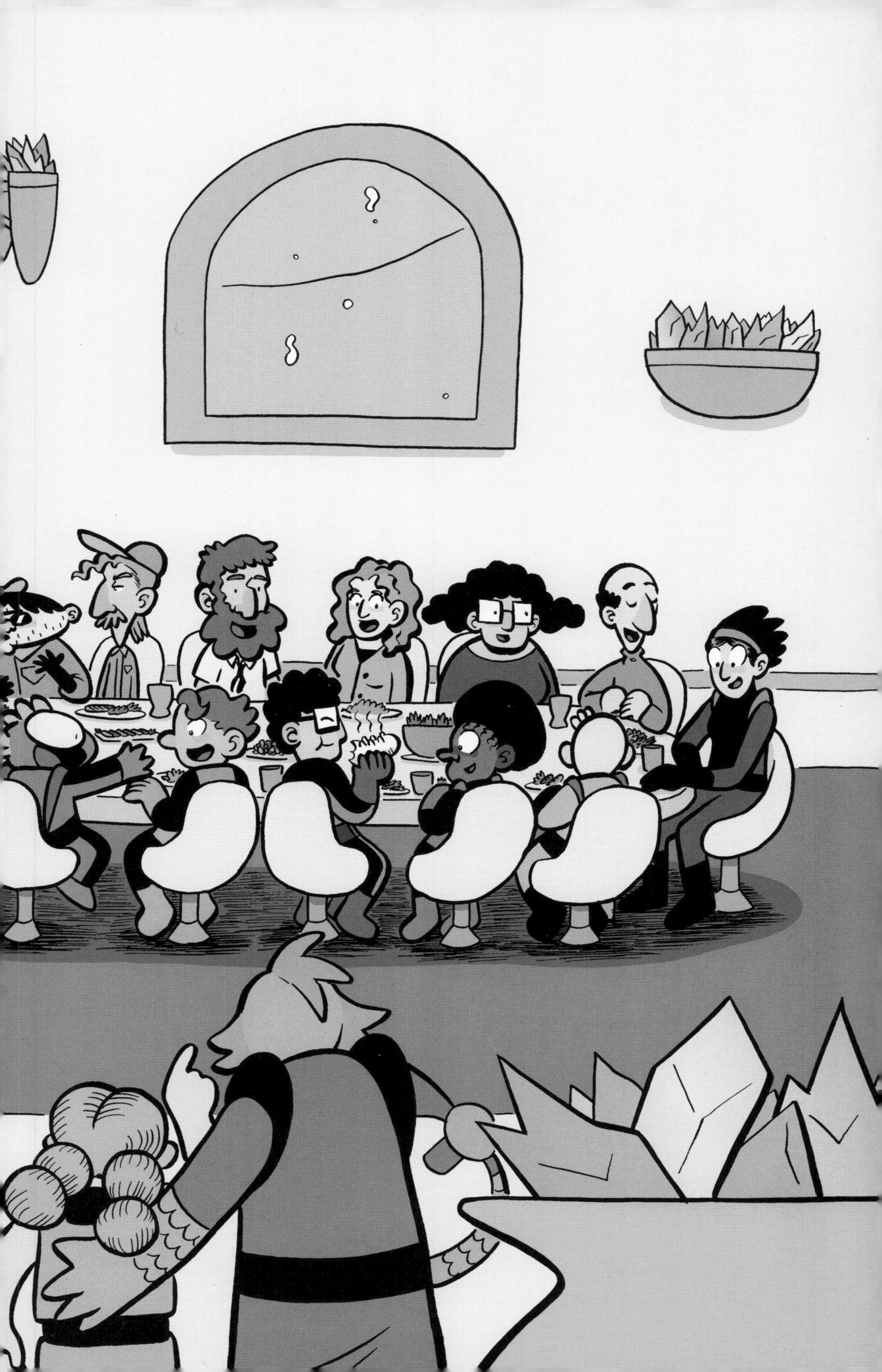

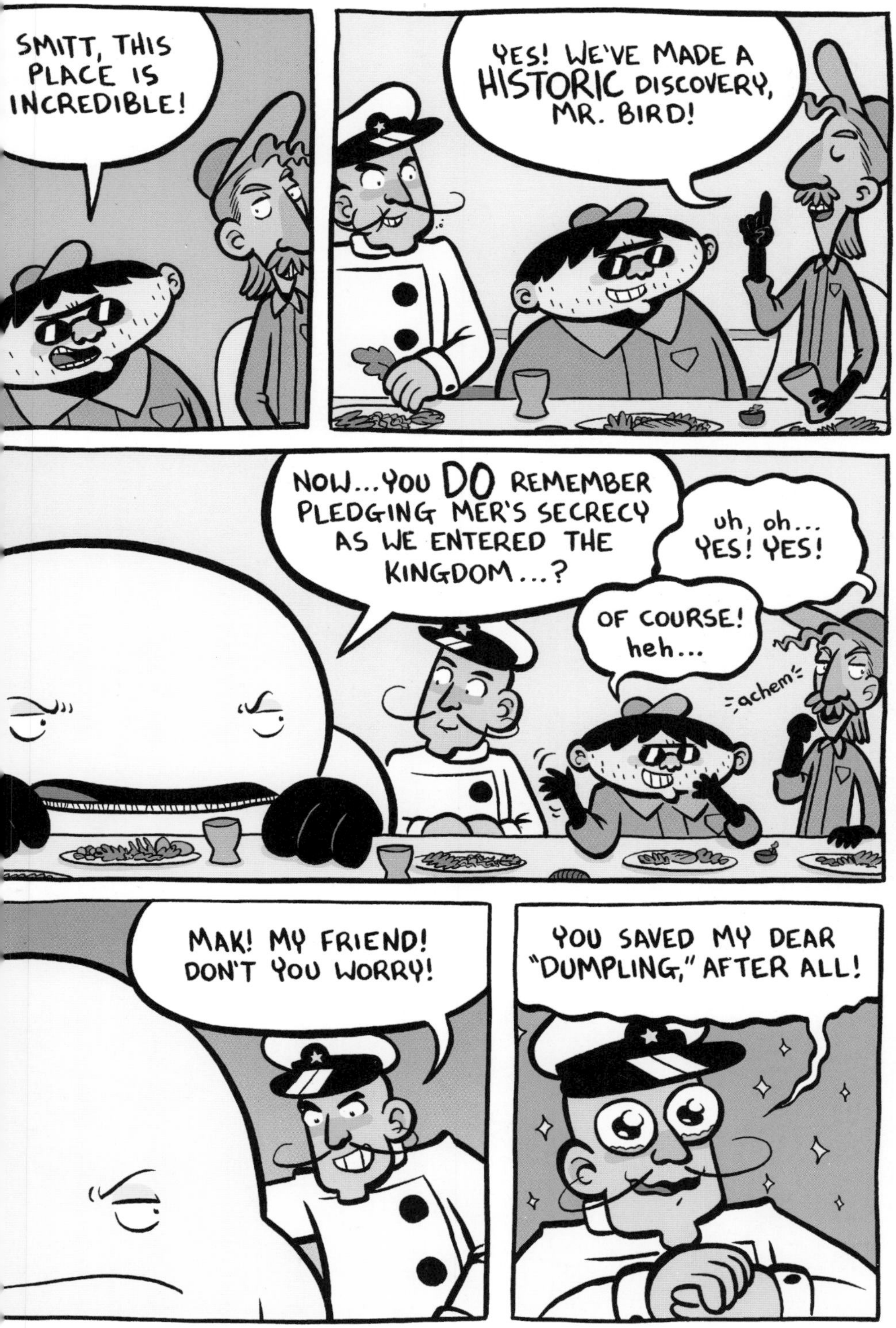

SMITT, THIS PLACE IS INCREDIBLE!
YES! WE'VE MADE A HISTORIC DISCOVERY, MR. BIRD!
NOW...YOU DO REMEMBER PLEDGING MER'S SECRECY AS WE ENTERED THE KINGDOM...?
uh, oh... YES! YES!
OF COURSE! heh...
achem
MAK! MY FRIEND! DON'T YOU WORRY!
YOU SAVED MY DEAR "DUMPLING," AFTER ALL!

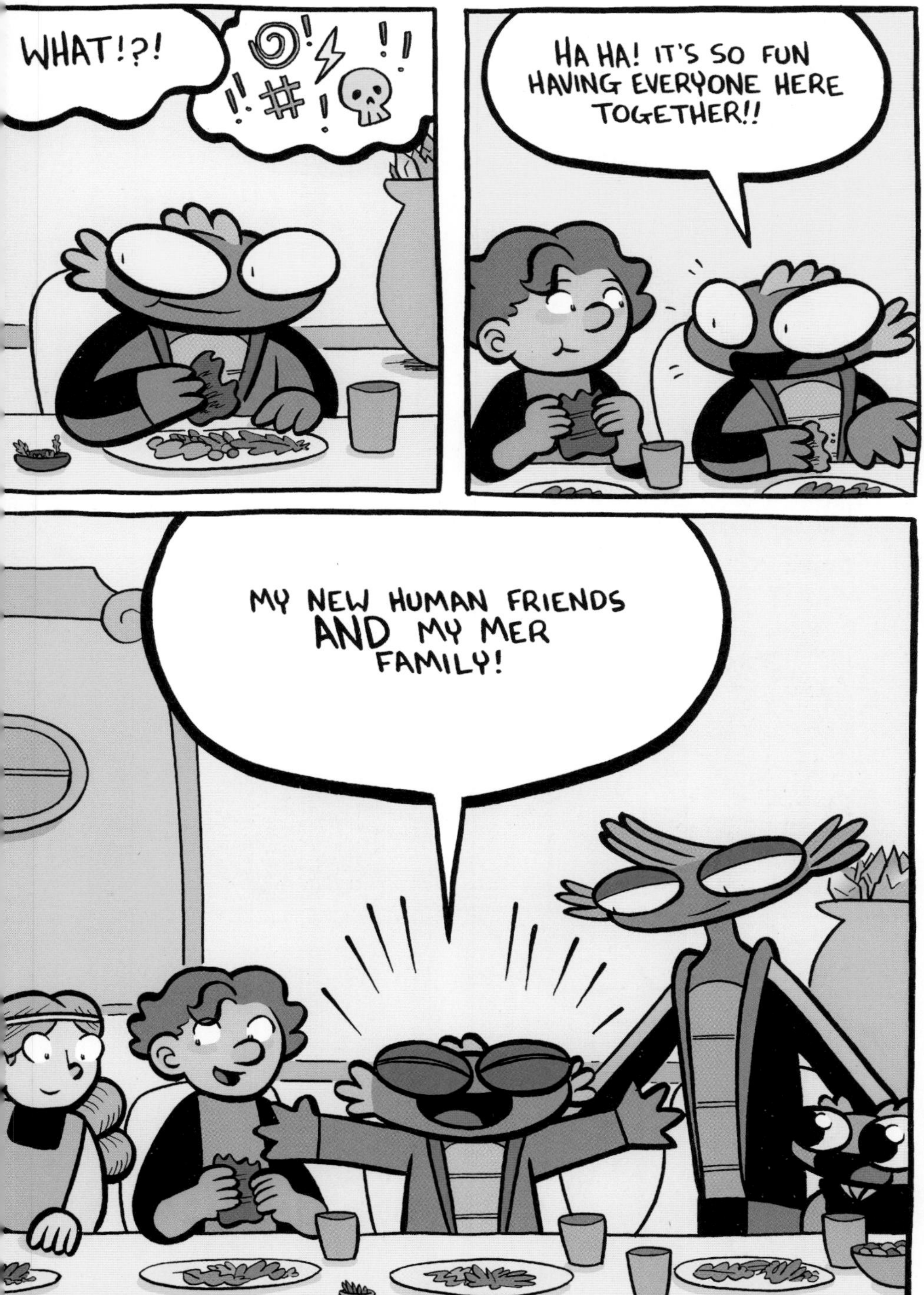
WHAT!?!
HA HA! IT'S SO FUN HAVING EVERYONE HERE TOGETHER!!
MY NEW HUMAN FRIENDS AND MY MER FAMILY!

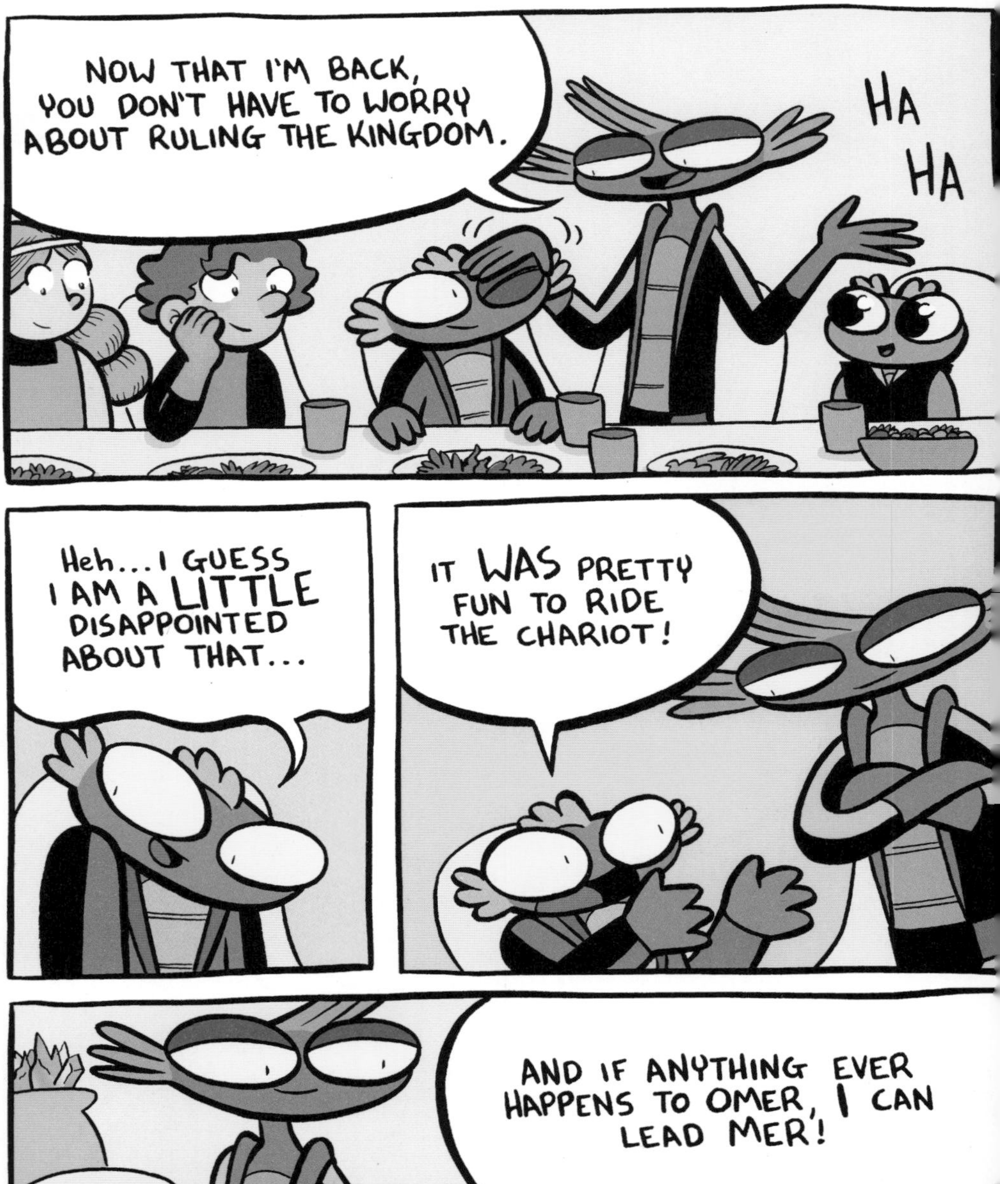
NOW THAT I'M BACK, YOU DON'T HAVE TO WORRY ABOUT RULING THE KINGDOM.
HA HA
Heh... I GUESS I AM A LITTLE DISAPPOINTED ABOUT THAT...
IT WAS PRETTY FUN TO RIDE THE CHARIOT!
AND IF ANYTHING EVER HAPPENS TO OMER, I CAN LEAD MER!

"QUEEN MERMA," HUH? PFFFFF!

HA HA HA

I LIKE IT!

WELL, YES...BUT LET'S HOPE OMER STAYS WELL...

MM-HM!

TRADITIONALLY, ah, THE **SONS** INHERIT THE THRONE, BUT, ah, I SUPPOSE...

≡achem!≡

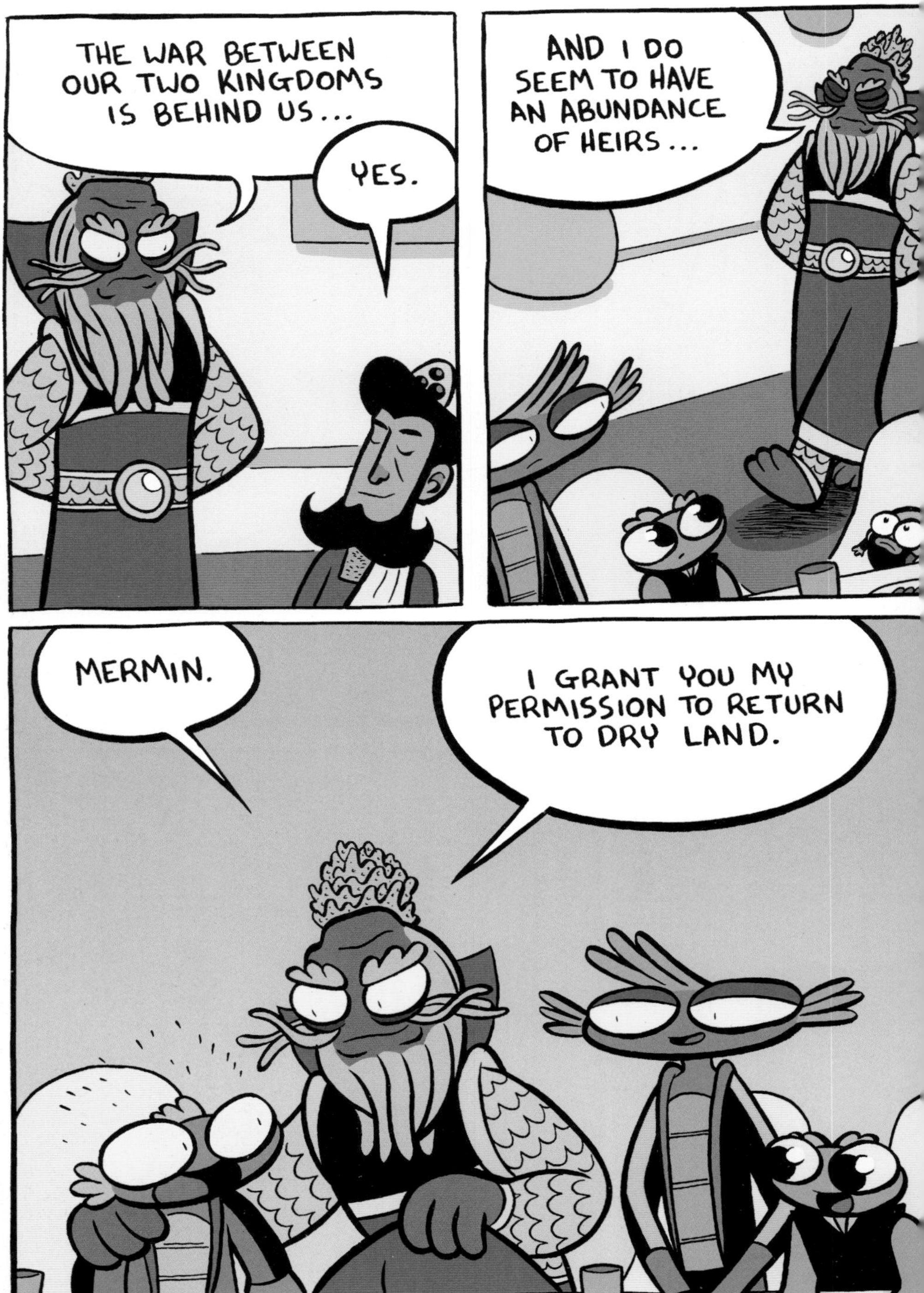
THE WAR BETWEEN OUR TWO KINGDOMS IS BEHIND US...
YES.
AND I DO SEEM TO HAVE AN ABUNDANCE OF HEIRS...
MERMIN.
I GRANT YOU MY PERMISSION TO RETURN TO DRY LAND.

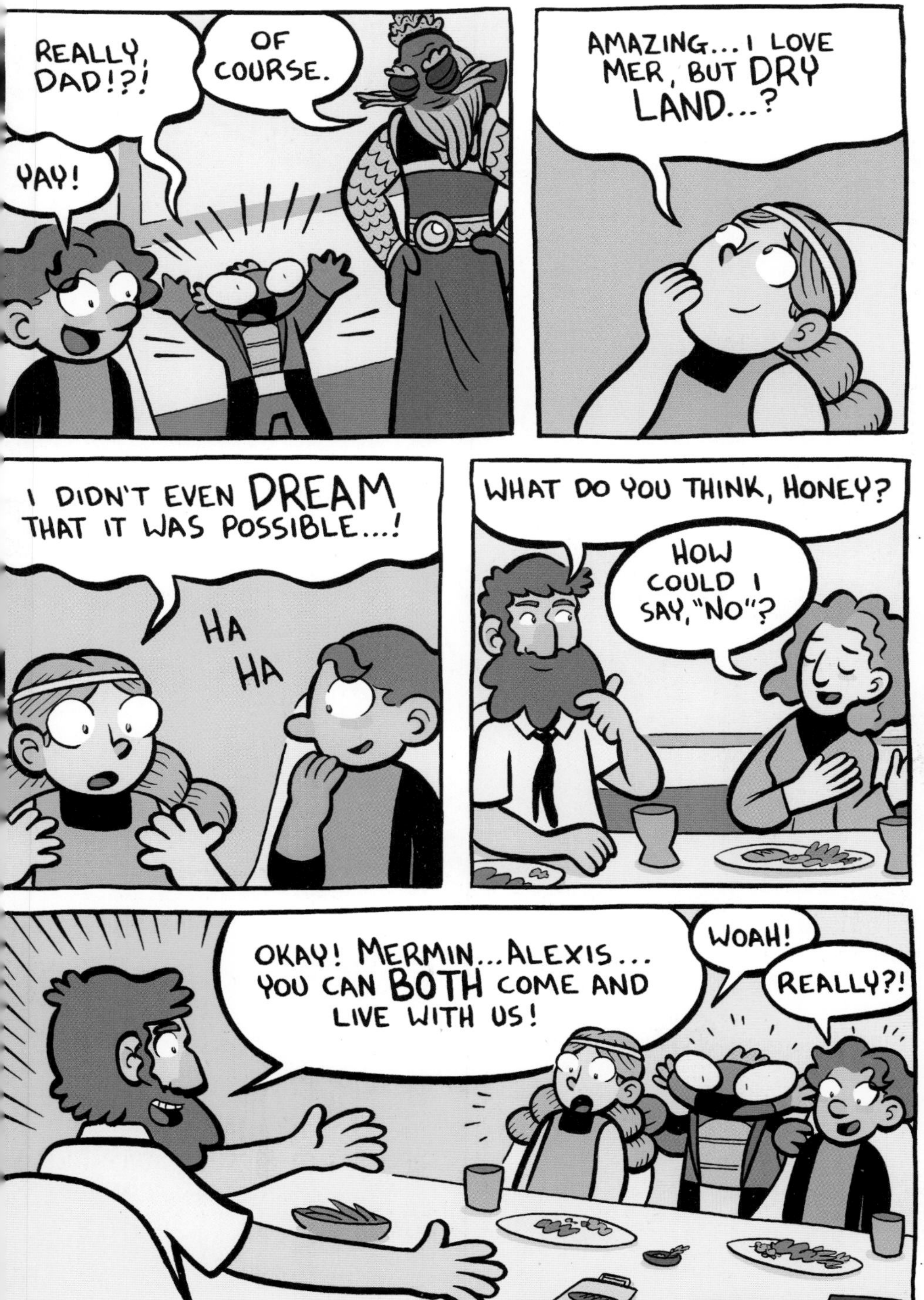
REALLY, DAD!?!
OF COURSE.
YAY!
AMAZING... I LOVE MER, BUT DRY LAND...?
I DIDN'T EVEN DREAM THAT IT WAS POSSIBLE...!
HA HA
WHAT DO YOU THINK, HONEY?
HOW COULD I SAY, "NO"?
OKAY! MERMIN...ALEXIS... YOU CAN BOTH COME AND LIVE WITH US!
WOAH!
REALLY?!

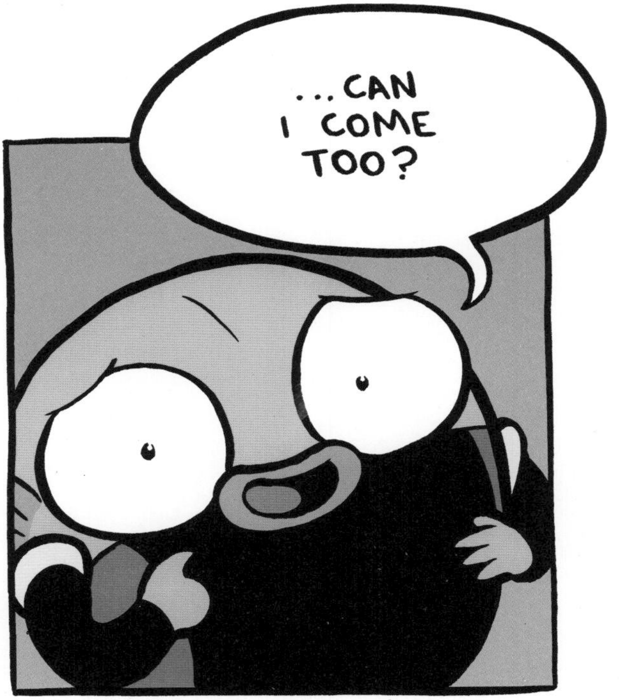
...CAN I COME TOO?

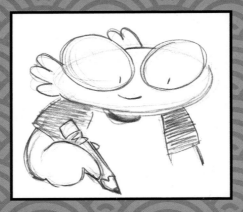

MERMIN is, without a doubt, the longest project I've ever worked on.
From humble beginnings as a mini-comic series in 2010 to the fifth graphic novel
publishing in 2017, this little fishboy has gone on quite a journey! Five books in seven
years certainly ain't bad, but I appreciate every moment that it took to get from there
to here. Even more so, I appreciate those who helped me along the way. I create art in
order to share it with others, and other people have aided in this being possible for me.

A big thanks to everyone at Oni Press, like Joe Nozemack and James Lucas Jones
for putting their faith in the series. It means a lot to me. The books are gorgeous, and
for that I am super grateful to Keith Wood and the Oni design team. Thank you so much
to my editor Robin Herrera! Robin, you've helped me shape *MERMIN* to the end.
And a mega, quadruple blue whale-sized thank you to Jill Beaton, *MERMIN*'s original
editor. Jill believed in the series from the beginning, and without her you would not be
holding this book in your hands. Love you, Jill!

Thank you to all of my family, friends, and fellow cartoonists in Athens and beyond
who have supported *MERMIN* over the years. I am surrounded by people who I can
come to for advice, comradery, and moral support at my highest and lowest moments.
Thank you so much to Michele Chidester for everything she's done for me since we met.

Finally, a tidal wave of 'thank you's to the readers and retailers who support
my work. Meeting enthusiastic readers is the greatest joy I feel as a cartoonist,
and I continue to meet great folks of all ages who love *MERMIN*. That love is felt
and reciprocated!

The little green fish-prince's adventure has concluded, but he and his friends are
still together and who knows what kind of situations they will find themselves in the
future. In the meantime, I've got new stories to tell, and I look forward to sharing them
with you. I also look forward to seeing what kinds of stories you will create, be it
through art, literature, or any sort of passion you follow! Let's keep making things to
share with each other!

JOEY WEISER
November 2016

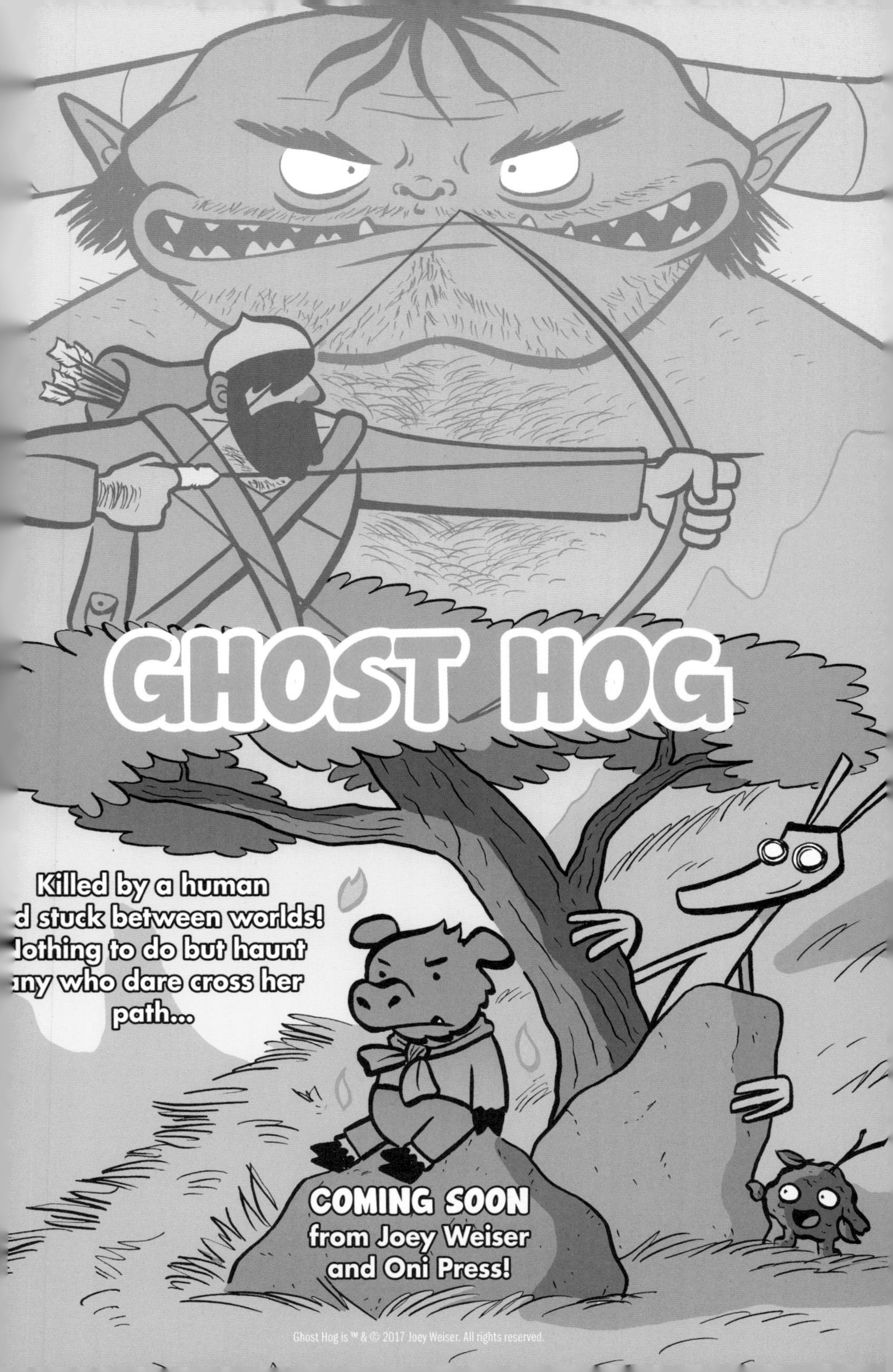
GHOST HOG
Killed by a human
d stuck between worlds!
lothing to do but haunt
ny who dare cross her
path...
COMING SOON
from Joey Weiser
and Oni Press!

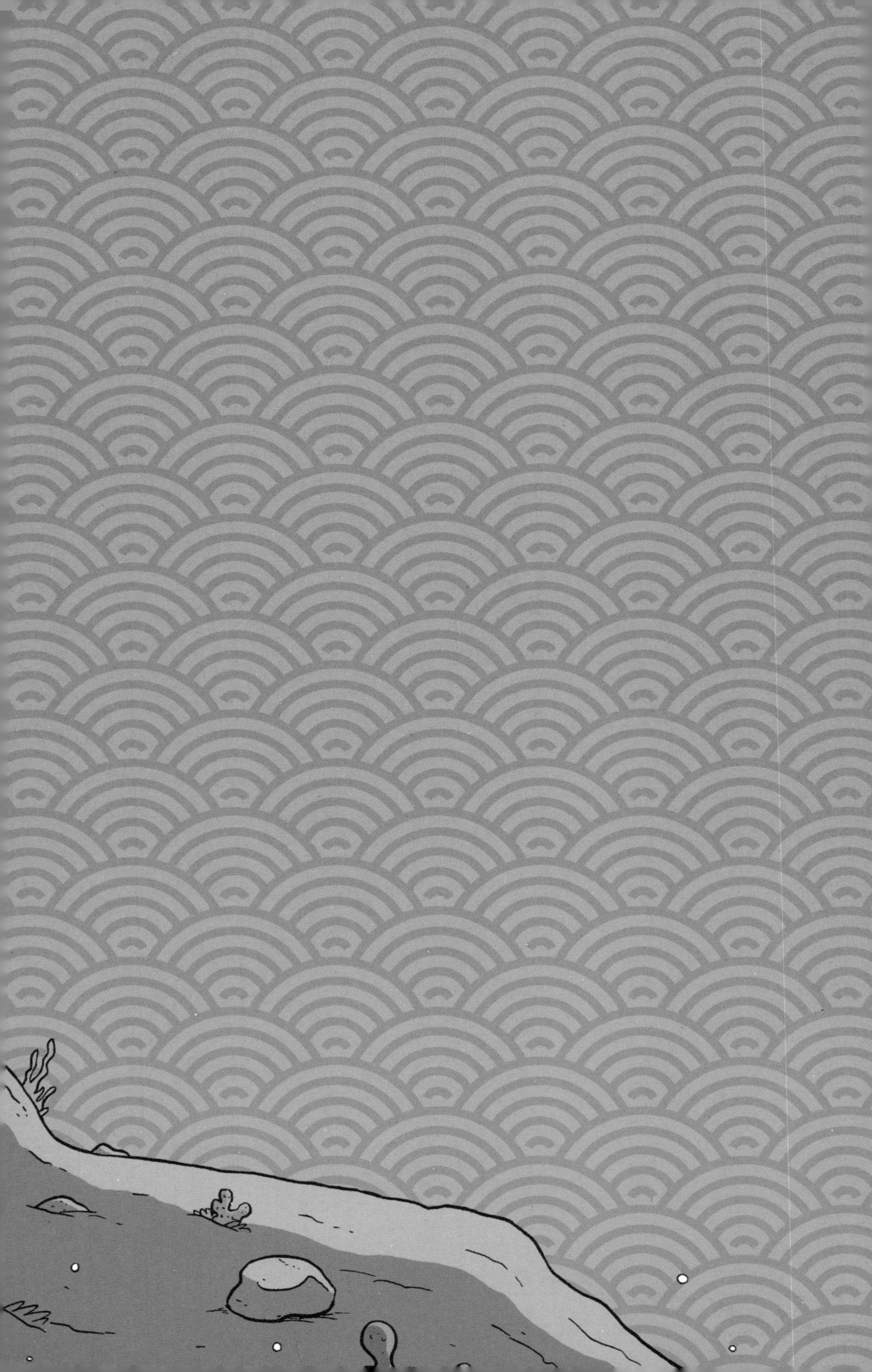

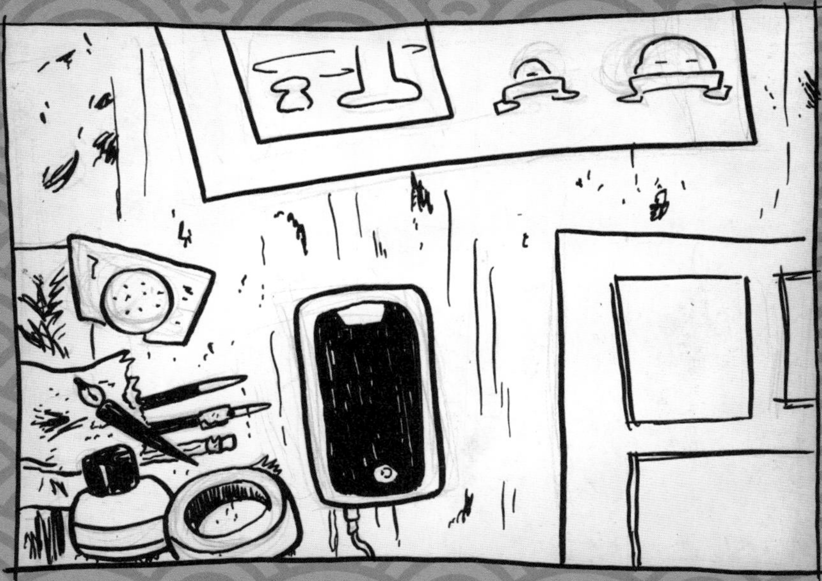

Joey Weiser's comics have appeared in several publications including *SpongeBob Comics* and the award-winning *Flight* series. His debut graphic novel, *The Ride Home,* was published in 2007 by AdHouse Books, and the first *Mermin* graphic novel was published in 2013 by Oni Press. He is a graduate of the Savannah College of Art & Design, and he currently lives in Athens, Georgia.

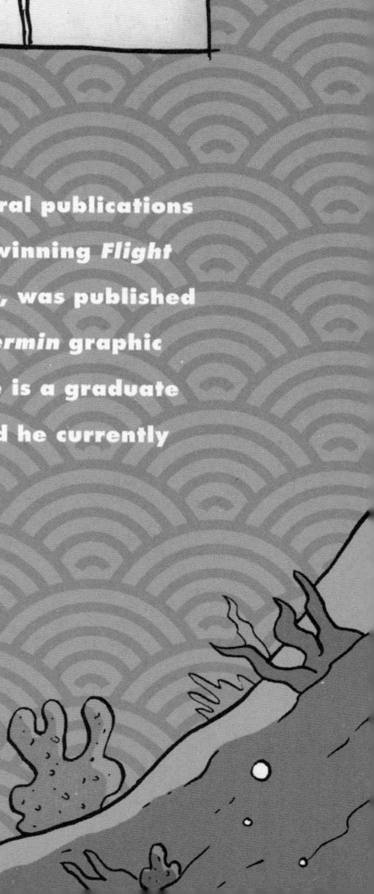

GET MORE MERMIN

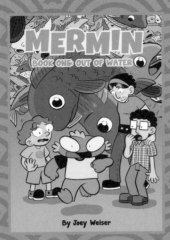

**MERMIN, BOOK 1:
OUT OF WATER**
By Joey Weiser

152 Pages, Hardcover, Color
ISBN 978-1-934964-98-9

**MERMIN, BOOK 2:
THE BIG CATCH**
By Joey Weiser

144 Pages, Hardcover, Color
ISBN 978-1-62010-101-8

**MERMIN, BOOK 3:
DEEP DIVE**
By Joey Weiser

160 pages, Hardcover, Color
ISBN 978-1-62010-174-2

**MERMIN, BOOK 4:
INTO ATLANTIS**
By Joey Weiser

154 pages, Hardcover, Color
ISBN 978-1-62010-258-9

**THE CROGAN ADVENTURES:
CATFOOT'S VENGEANCE**
By Chris Schweizer and Joey Weiser

200 pages, Softcover
ISBN 978-1-62010-203-9

**THE CROGAN ADVENTURES
LAST OF THE LEGION**
By Chris Schweizer and Joey Weis

224 pages, Softcover
ISBN 978-1-62010-243-5

www.onipress.com

**For more information on these and other fine Oni Press comic books and graphic nove
visit onipress.com. To find a comic specialty store in your area visit comicshops.us.**